BROOKE TAKES
QUEEN

What Reviewers Say About Alaina Erdell's Work

Flowers and Gemstones

"The writing flows effortlessly, drawing me in with its vivid descriptions and raw, authentic character dynamics. It's the kind of book that doesn't just tell a story—it makes you *feel* every moment. ...*Flowers and Gemstones* is one of those stories that sticks with you long after you've turned the last page. The unique storyline immediately pulled me in, and the way it's told—with rich details, well-developed characters, and beautifully crafted sentences—made it all the more powerful. The emotions in this book hit hard (in the best way), and the themes of love, resilience, and self-discovery add so much depth."—*The Lesbian Review*

"A beautiful, sensitive story of finding that special connection with someone when life has made you weary. ...Alaina Erdell proves, once again, that she is a unique voice within the sapphic genre. Flowers and Gemstones is beautifully written, treats sensitive objects with care and leaves a lingering imprint."—*Reading with Caz*

"Her writing is beautiful and she is quickly becoming one of my favorite authors. ...I will read anything she puts out there! Her stories are filled with heart and humor and complex, messy, flawed characters that will stick with you."—*Queer AFictionado*

Alaina Erdell has quickly become one of those authors whose releases I always keep an eye out for. ...Erdell's writing is smooth and well-rounded. There is an air of mystery surrounding the characters, with a storyline that is original and fresh. It's impossible not to connect with Hannah and Vanessa."—*Queer Aussie Reviews*

"Alaina Erdell's *Flowers and Gemstones* is a beautifully layered sapphic romance that blends grief, second chances, and self-discovery into a compelling, emotional read. With complex characters, unexpected connections, and a journey of healing, this book keeps you invested from start to finish. ...Erdell does a fantastic job balancing the heavier themes of grief, betrayal, and self-worth with moments of levity and warmth. And let's talk about the romance: swoon-worthy in all the right places, yet refreshingly realistic. ...Erdell crafts a love story that is complex, messy, and ultimately worth the journey."—*Sterling Sapphic Reads*

"A cute romance, with a lot of depth and emotion, things to unpack and analyse, and lots of takeaways and lessons to learn about forgiveness, being aware in relationships, and taking chances. I loved it and thought it had beautiful sentiments."—*LESBIreviewed*

"I've been a loyal reader since Erdell's debut. Each book has impressed me in its own way. Her latest, *Flowers and Gemstones*, marks a turn for Erdell. There's a growth and understanding for story crafting displayed inside these pages that's notable, making it a real standout. ...Story-worthy problems are the heartbeat of all fiction, and Erdell takes it to the next level with this novel, giving it a whopper of one. ...Poignant and uniquely original, *Flowers and Gemstones* is well-plotted and well-constructed. The characters are richly drawn, displaying raw and genuine emotions."—*Women Using Words*

All Things Beautiful

"There's so much to love about this story. The characters are vibrant and well-developed, the story beautifully crafted and multi-layered, and the backdrop of the art world depicted so skillfully it drew me into its beauty and depth. ...If you like a romance with depth that reflects how falling in love weaves into the fabric of our lives, this book is for you."—*Lesbian Review*

"Every time Leighton and Casey are on page together, magic happens."—*Jude in the Stars*

"[I] could not put this book down. ...With a plot that moves from educational and emotional to suspenseful and steamy, *All Things Beautiful* is a heartfelt journey of finding and following the path that truly makes you happy."—*Queer Aussie Reviews*

"The book's smartly-crafted prose and well-developed characters lend themselves to an enjoyable and captivating read, one that hooks readers from beginning to end. ...Filled with the complexities of life, the beauty of art, and the joy of finding true love, this heartwarming love story is an absorbing and enjoyable read"—*Women Using Words*

"From the art details to the MCs chemistry to the suspense, it was absolutely incredible."—*lesbereading*

"I was beyond invested in these characters and seeing how this story played out. ...Erdell has a way of truly pulling you into all elements of the story with her descriptive writing. I absolutely cannot wait to read more of Erdell's books!"—*Queer AFictionado*

"Erdell is amazing at writing books about what she knows, and it shows so well with her knowledge of painting and art. I know nothing about the art world, and Erdell made it easy to follow and I even learned some things."—*Jess Reads With Pride*

Two Women, Two Weddings *in* Hot Hires

"[Alaina Erdell] never misses with her work. One of the things that readers appreciate about Erdell is the way she weaves her unique passions into her storytelling. She has a real knack for captivating readers with the details. ...Erdell demonstrates that she knows how to create believable tension while keeping the romance fun. Her vivid descriptions and fluid prose add so much life to the storytelling. Erdell may have just recently cut her teeth in this business, but she's proven she's quite comfortable on the page. Whether it's a full-length novel or a short story, she always provides a pleasurable read."—*Women Using Words*

"All the stories were fantastic and I enjoyed them thoroughly. They took me through a range of emotions, and have left me hoping these wonderful characters are going to turn up in future stories."—*LesBIreviewed*

"This was my first taste of Erdell's writing & will undoubtedly come back for more. With family expectations & drama, this novella gave me everything I didn't know I was craving."—*Station12reads*

"Alaina writes such wonderful chemistry between the characters in her books and this read was no different!"—*BlossomBookish*

"It is a delightful read, and I particularly appreciated the portrayal of the Indian wedding ceremony. The vivid descriptions painted a beautiful picture in my mind."—*Lez.be.readin.ya*

Off the Menu

"In terms of the actual writing, Erdell has an easy-to-read writing style. She excels at creating chemistry between the main characters and she is not afraid to have the characters do things that are not necessarily in line with expectations around romance novels. ...I like the way Erdell writes chemistry. I loved the restaurant setting and how awesome it was to have such a realistic feel for it. ...Erdell's books explore genuine character flaws rather than romanticised ones and I am here for it."—*Lesbian Review*

"The frying pan isn't the only thing sizzling in the kitchen—the heat between Taylor and Erin is palpable in this contemporary romance, brimming with drama and effervescent characters. ...One of the best books I've read in some time—five gleaming stars!"—*Reader Views*

"Erdell's writing style is engaging and thought-provoking, leaving the readers with a lasting impression of the power of understanding and collaboration in both the kitchen and in relationships."
—*Literary Titan*

Fire, Water, and Rock

"Erdell's love for the desert flowed out of the story like a love poem. One of my highlights of the book was getting to discover the setting through the author's words."—*Lesbian Review*

"When I read a book with themes that I know next to nothing about and the narrative makes me want to go investigate. ...Well, credit must go to that writer. This is Erdell's first published novel and one can easily see the passion she has for storytelling. Using colorful language and vivid detail, she immerses her readers in an impressive story world. Erdell's debut is a compelling and read-worthy tale; it's definitely a sign of exciting things to come."
—*Women Loving Words*

By the Author

Fire, Water, and Rock

Off the Menu

All Things Beautiful

Flowers and Gemstones

Brooke Takes Queen

Novella:

Two Women, Two Weddings in Hot Hires

BROOKE TAKES QUEEN

by

Alaina Erdell

2026

BROOKE TAKES QUEEN

ISBN 13: 978-1-63679-886-8

This Trade Paperback Original Is Published By
Bold Strokes Books, Inc.
P.O. Box 249
Valley Falls, NY 12185

First Edition: January 2026

CREDITS
EDITOR: CINDY CRESAP
PRODUCTION DESIGN: SUSAN RAMUNDO
COVER DESIGN BY INKSPIRAL DESIGN

Acknowledgments

My eternal gratitude goes out to Bold Strokes Books, who gave me the opportunity to publish six books and taught me so many things along the way. Rad, Sandy, Cindy, Ruth, and the rest of the team, I thank you with all my heart.

Inkspiral Design, thank you pulling various components together to make a cover that captured the essence of the story.

To my writing group and author friends, thank you for keeping me sane, on task, and making sure my outlook resembles Brooke's rather than Elizabeth's. To my friend J, I bow down to your genius, creative mind for coming up with the title. When you suggested it with the caveat I'd have to change one of my main character's names, I did it so quickly I can't even recall what Brooke used to be called.

I thank my son for providing the inspiration for Rory. I'd know far less without you in the world. I cherish your brilliant mind, huge heart, love of nature, and joy in sharing what you've learned.

To my family, I appreciate your support and your willingness to skip past the scenes where they braid one another's hair. It's time to move Auntie's books to the top shelf of the bookcases as my smart little nephews begin to read.

I couldn't do this without my girlfriend, whose continual support and pride I hold close to my heart. *Your* writing is an inspiration and has been for many years now.

To my readers, I thank each of you who has picked up one of my books. Your emails, messages, and in-person exuberance after reading one of my stories warms my heart. People like you are the reason I do what I do. Thank you for sharing your experiences. I've enjoyed meeting and getting to know many of you, and I'm proud to be a part of this wonderful community.

Dedication

For the children, especially my son, whose did-you-know questions brighten our days and educate the rest of us.

CHAPTER ONE

Elizabeth crossed her legs and glanced at the framed degrees from Yale and Stanford on the wall behind Ayumi Nakamura, the latter being where the attorney had studied law, and the reason Elizabeth needed her now. She'd received the shock of Margaret's death two weeks ago and hadn't known what to do next.

"Ms. Underwood's lawyer sent these over on Tuesday." Ayumi pushed a stack of papers toward her to the only section of the mahogany desk not covered with files. "I'll need a few signatures, but it's straightforward. You're now the owner of a resort in Napa Valley."

"I still don't understand." Elizabeth stared at the built-in bookshelves filled with tan and maroon legal journals, appreciating how the hues, along with the sage-green upholstered visitors' chairs, one of which she sat in, nicely accented the sand color scheme of the office. "Why me?"

"That's not explained anywhere, but it's been in place for quite a while. He said his records indicated Ms. Underwood asked him to alter her will right after she'd instructed him to make the final payment on your college education. That's the last time she changed it."

Elizabeth would've been only twenty-two. Who did that? She tugged the hem of her skirt down. And for someone who wasn't even blood. Margaret, who'd only known her for eight measly years back then, had left everything to her, including her business and property. In Calistoga, of all places, where Elizabeth hadn't set foot since she'd graduated high school. She ignored the twist of anxiety in her stomach at the thought of returning. Why hadn't Margaret said anything about it in the twenty years since?

As Ayumi searched for a pen, Elizabeth tried to recall the last time she'd seen Margaret. It had to be about two years ago. Why hadn't she gone to see her sometimes instead of always making her drive to San Jose? She should've, especially when Margaret had gotten older. Sure, being in her hometown would've been difficult, and she would've needed to get in and out without dredging up too many painful memories, but if she'd made the effort, maybe she would've known Margaret had cancer. Maybe she could've said thank you. Maybe she could've said good-bye.

Margaret had stated in her will that she wanted no funeral, service, or any kind of fanfare, so Elizabeth wouldn't even have that opportunity to pay her respects. She bit the tip of her tongue to keep her eyes from welling with tears. Elizabeth Bettancourt didn't cry in front of someone she'd hired. She didn't cry in front of *anyone*. She straightened, gathered her composure, and signed her name. No use dwelling on what could've been. "Is it open and operating? Who's running it? What do you know?" She pushed the papers back to Ayumi.

"Apparently, Ms. Underwood has been using a property management company for hotels and resorts. J & C something." Ayumi leafed through her notes. "J & C Hospitality Specialists. The general manager employed by them will continue to oversee things until you arrive."

"Are there any legal reasons I can't sell Harvest Springs right away?" Elizabeth remained perched on the edge of her seat, eager to be done with this mess. She'd thought Margaret was her last tie to Calistoga, but now there was the resort. Ever since she'd heard about it, it weighed on her like an albatross around her neck, perhaps a punishment for accepting wisdom, protection, and independence Margaret had offered, then neglecting her in her final years. Elizabeth swallowed hard against the self-recrimination. She hadn't known. The sooner she could get rid of it, the better. Then *nothing* would tie her to Calistoga anymore.

"No, nothing *legal*." Ayumi tucked her sleek black hair behind her ears. "But I highly urge you not to be hasty. Spend some time assessing the property." She sat back in her chair. "See what's there. Monitor how it's being run. Ask around and see what the market's like. If it's profitable, perhaps you should hold on to it. If you really want to wash your hands of it, simple improvements could increase the price you get. But who knows? Maybe you'll like it so much you'll decide to keep it."

Elizabeth gathered her purse and stood. "Not likely." Best to dispose of it quickly, then return to her comfortable life in Silicon Valley and her job she excelled at and forget all about Calistoga for good.

That said, she was nothing if not a numbers person. They'd always made sense to her, even when the rest of the world didn't. With her extensive background in finance and payroll, whether Harvest Springs Resort was profitable or struggling somewhat intrigued her.

Ayumi opened a drawer. "A friend of mine is a real estate agent up there. I have her card here somewhere." She dug around for a moment, then shut it. "You know what? If you decide you want to talk to her, call me, and I'll put you two in touch." She rose and handed her a manila envelope. "Your copies of everything are in here."

As Elizabeth stepped onto the sidewalk in front of the stately building that housed Ayumi's firm, she tipped her face to the cloudless azure sky and warmth of the sunshine that often graced the South Bay. It was one reason she'd stayed after college. That, and getting her foot in the door at a prestigious software company. And Margaret was the one who'd made the latter possible.

And yet, Elizabeth hadn't visited her once. No, she'd made Margaret make the two-hour trip. Margaret had never complained, always crushing her in a hug and smiling the first hour of every stay.

Elizabeth should've gone to Calistoga.

But what was done was done. She hadn't made time for Margaret, so she'd have to live with her choices—and regrets—*when* she wasn't trying to figure out what to do with a wine-country resort she didn't want.

As she pulled from her parking space, her thoughts turned to the next few weeks. She'd need to ask for time off. Of course, she had plenty banked. Vacations had been few, mostly because she didn't enjoy traveling alone. Some quick math told her the week she'd spent in Hawaii with Janice had been almost seven years ago. *Seven years?* Could that be right? And what ever happened to Janice? And what did Elizabeth have to show for her life since then? Nothing really. Oh, yeah—except an *extremely* successful career. She smiled to herself.

She wasn't a workaholic, but she liked her job, and the joy she received from it helped fill the void left by her nonexistent social calendar. She tried to limit her schedule to only fifty hours a week, and with her skills, that wasn't difficult. Plus, she'd fine-tuned her department, and her team was top-notch, starting with Geoff, whom she'd brought with her from her past two companies. He'd have no problem covering things while she was gone.

Seeing the resort again intrigued her. Would it look the same? Margaret had mentioned no large-scale renovations. Still, it made sense if it had undergone a remodel or two in the decades since Elizabeth had seen it. Did vineyards still surround it? They'd been one of her favorite places to walk. Had anyone repaired the wine cellar door that always stuck? Did the giant geothermal spring still exist, and did it still smell of sulfur?

Despite her curiosity, fear coiled in her stomach like a venomous snake preparing to defend itself. How would she manage being in Calistoga, especially that long? Would everything remind her of her childhood, or would she even recognize it? Would anyone know who she was? Would her painful memories resurface, and if they did, could she get in and out of that wretched little town without having to discuss what happened?

That was the real question. And if she had to, could she? She hadn't talked about it since she'd turned thirty and quit therapy. Now, at forty-two, she wondered if everything she'd learned in those many years of sessions had fully prepared her for what she was about to do. She certainly hoped so.

When she strode into the anteroom where Geoff sat at his computer, the clock on the wall told her she'd been gone less than two hours.

"Are those more changes?" he asked, holding out his hand for the envelope.

"No." Elizabeth walked past him toward her office. "Follow me." She dropped it onto her desk as she sank into her executive chair. "Close the door." She carefully stowed her sunglasses in their case, the case in her purse, and the purse in her lower left drawer, just like she did every morning.

Geoff slid into the seat directly opposite her and crossed one skinny jean-clad leg over the other, giving Elizabeth a view of the dirty sole of his white Vans.

His attire mirrored that of most of the employees, with casual taking on an entirely new meaning in Silicon Valley, where even CEOs wore shorts and flip-flops and played games of Ping-Pong between meetings. She didn't hold it against him though. His mind and work ethic more than made up for his dubious choices in clothing. Her? She'd keep her black and gray suits and skirts, thank you. And *they* could keep their taco Tuesdays and kegs downstairs, where employees only needed to scan their ID card for a pint of beer at any time of day. In her opinion, those things were best left to social functions. Not that she attended those either. She kept meaning to work on that.

With her fingertip, she aligned the manila envelope from Ayumi with the corner of her desk. Outside her window, the fountain in the middle of the small lake in the courtyard three floors down sprayed unnaturally turquoise water, but at least she'd earned one of the coveted offices with a view. "I have something I need to discuss with you," she said as she slipped off her heel beneath the desk. The early stage of a blister formed on the back of her ankle. "I need to take some time off."

Geoff frowned. "Are you all right?"

She lifted her chin. "Of course. Why do you ask?"

"Well, most people take leave when something is wrong." He shrugged. "Sickness, a loved one falling ill, perhaps a difficult pregnancy." He raised his eyebrows.

"Mr. Vasquez, when I want speculation, I will ask for it." She shot him a feigned glare. "I simply have something I need to take care of."

He planted both feet on the floor and leaned forward, his elbows on his knees. "How long are you thinking?"

"Likely a few weeks. A month at the longest. Can you handle that?" Could *she*?

He nodded. "Sure. As you know, I'm not going anywhere until Labor Day."

"Yes, that's right." She'd forgotten, but since she signed off on all her processors' vacation requests, she should've remembered. What they did with their personal lives rarely interested her. Geoff was different though, and if she'd given it more thought, she would've recalled it was the weekend he always went to the Yucatán Peninsula. He and his friends were going to Playa del Carmen this year. Elizabeth mentally patted herself on the back for unearthing that detail.

"You sure you're okay?" He'd already dropped the formality he typically used with her at work with the *difficult pregnancy* quip. This was her friend asking.

She gave a little laugh. "Believe it or not, I've inherited a resort up in Napa."

His mouth fell open. "From whom? And when can I come visit?" He scooted toward her and rested his forearms on her desk.

"A woman."

He whistled. "That must've been some fling."

She only let one corner of her lip curve upward before returning her gaze to the fountain. "It was no such thing. I used to work for her. She gave me my first job, and we kept in touch over the years." She omitted how much more Margaret had done to make sure she'd gotten an education and hadn't been left behind.

Left behind. Poor choice of words. A chill ran through her, and Elizabeth tugged the lapels of her blazer together. "Anyway, I plan on selling it, but I need to see what I have first. I'll be going there to look over their books, their tax records, the state of the property, and to assess the personnel. It'll take some time."

"Have you mentioned it to Leo yet?" Geoff scrunched up his face at the mention of Elizabeth's boss. "He won't like that."

"He'll have to get over it. You'll do a fine job running things. It'll be an excellent experience for you, and I'll only be a phone or Zoom call away if something unusual arises. If he makes it an issue, he can try to replace both of us." She gave Geoff a wicked grin. They all knew that'd be no easy task. There were very few other financial professionals with her knowledge and experience in US and global payroll, and the three or four other Bay Area companies who required someone as qualified as her all offered great packages, stock options, or a potential IPO. And she *would* take Geoff with her.

He leaned back. "Fill me in on how it goes."

"I plan to speak to him later today."

As she headed home to pack that evening, a mix of emotions washed over her. Leo must've had a late afternoon tee time occupying his mind because he hardly gave her request a second thought. She highly doubted she'd be staying in Calistoga more than a couple of weeks, but even that much time in a place that had caused her so much agony seemed like a life sentence.

The state of the resort piqued her curiosity, but was she ready to face everything that'd undoubtedly come up for her there without Margaret? Without her hugs or the way she'd throw her arm over Elizabeth's shoulder, whether Elizabeth was fourteen or forty, and ask, "You got this?"

"I got this," Elizabeth whispered into the confines of her car.

And she hoped to God it was true.

CHAPTER TWO

B rooke stepped off the elevator, still huffing from her race back to the resort, then swiped her keycard to let herself into her apartment. Now that Rory was on the bus—*with* her backpack today, score a point for them—she could finish readying herself for the meeting she wasn't looking forward to in the least.

As she snatched her half-full coffee mug from the table in the kitchenette, she bumped the edge of the chessboard holding the game she and Rory had begun the night before, toppling the pieces. Brooke gritted her teeth, catching the queen before it rolled onto the floor. She didn't have time for this. Plus, now she'd have to come up with a way to tell Rory they'd have to start over that wouldn't trigger her ASD. She took a minute to smile, though, as she remembered how excited Rory had been when Brooke first taught her to play, and how by the time Rory entered kindergarten, she was regularly besting Brooke and even teaching her a few things.

After a quick cleanup, Brooke headed to the bathroom where she pushed aside Rory's many hair ties, headbands, and butterfly hair clips to make room for her makeup. She rarely wore it, but she needed at least foundation and mascara today to look her best. Maybe a touch of lipstick, too.

It still felt strange not having Margaret around, laughing and joking, addressing everyone by name, even the valets, whose turnover seemed unusually high. She'd died just over two weeks ago, and while everything appeared normal on the surface, it wasn't.

An invisible cloud seemed to hang over the resort, but with daffodils blooming in the flowerbeds and the incredible weather of late, tourist season had gotten a head start, so they'd relegated grieving to the sidelines. Rory still didn't understand. In her seven young years, people who went to the hospital always came home with a cast, a bandage, or a new baby.

Not this time, darling. Brooke wiped away a tear, smearing the mascara she'd just applied. She reached for a tissue. At least Margaret wasn't suffering any longer. That provided *some* consolation.

Now though, additional worries hovered with ominous intent. She'd wondered what would happen to the resort when Margaret died since she had no children, but it hadn't been her place to ask. They'd known one another just short of a year. And she couldn't have predicted Margaret's passing would come so soon, given she hadn't once mentioned having cancer until the very end. But with the new owner arriving this morning and the possibility she'd want to sell, not only would Brooke be out of a job, but she'd also lose the on-site apartment where Margaret had let her and Rory reside since the separation.

Nothing major. Nope. She could handle this. With a pasted-on smile and some forced cheerfulness, she'd show this woman what a fantastic property this was and how well she ran it, all cool and composed. Yes, that's what she'd do. She couldn't uproot Rory again so soon. This was their home now, and Brooke would see it remained that way.

After shedding her loungewear for a professional look, she pinned her name tag to her blouse and gave her reflection in the mirror a smile. It wasn't the natural one that reached her eyes, but the new owner didn't know her to recognize the difference. This would have to do. Showtime.

Downstairs, she stopped at the front desk. "Good morning, Francine."

"Morning," Francine muttered as she held up one finger but continued to type.

Brooke glanced around the lobby as she waited. From the first time she'd seen it a year ago, she'd loved how the light modern minimalist decor complemented the beauty of the original 1880s stucco. It still took her breath away.

Seated beside Francine, Kinsey ran through the checkout process with a young man in an expensive suit who insisted he'd incurred no expenses from the minibar in his room, and at the far end of the counter, Nik gave an older couple dressed far too warmly for the weather suggestions on the prime places to go hiking. Everything seemed to be running smoothly. Brooke relaxed a little.

Francine finally turned on her stool and gave Brooke a once-over. "You look a sight better than the harried version of yourself that ran through here twenty minutes ago in yoga pants and a BottleRock T-shirt."

Brooke patted her chest and inhaled. "Thank you. And yes, we almost missed the bus again. You'd think by now I'd have it down. I've even started waking her fifteen minutes earlier."

Francine combed her manicured nails through the highlighted brown hair at her temples. "Go easy on yourself. Raising kids isn't a picnic. This job's a staycation compared to when I was bringing up my boys."

Her smart cut, designer tortoise shell frames, and impeccable dress made her appear much younger than her years. Francine had reached retirement age, but she adored her job and wasn't ready to leave it. Brooke had found that many of the employees viewed their coworkers as a pseudo-family, even if they had a lovely one at home. She understood completely. When she'd first started working here, a sense of belonging had settled over her in a matter of weeks.

"Missing the bus isn't the end of the world, dear." Francine held up a finger and answered the phone.

Brooke frowned. Maybe not, but having to drive Rory to school would've made Brooke late for her meeting with the new owner, and that wasn't the first impression she wanted to make. She needed to be professional, capable, dependable. An efficient multitasker. In charge. She was all those things and more, and she needed the new owner to see what she'd brought to the resort since Margaret had signed the contract with her family's business. Her stint here needed to be nothing short of stellar to prove her cleverness and value when managing and making vital improvements on-site. With Aunt Chris being her boss, Brooke had no room for missteps. She needed to rationalize why, as an asset of J & C Hospitality Specialists, she should remain right where she was.

"No, like I said before, sir, we'll only know if we can give you a late checkout if you call in the morning." Francine made a get-on-with-it motion with her hand. She turned and pointed toward the doorway behind her.

Brooke raised an eyebrow.

"Yes, sir. The staff tomorrow can assist you." Francine waved her toward it and mouthed, "Go."

Brooke walked around the long counter and into her office, then stopped short.

A statuesque woman, made even taller by three-inch heels that also showcased her toned and shapely calves, leaned over an open drawer of the filing cabinet, riffling through its contents. Her shoulder-length straight black hair—no, not quite black, a warm sable—fell forward to obscure her face. A purse and coffee sat atop Brooke's desk, and folders that hadn't been there yesterday covered Margaret's. The glass holding wildflowers Rory had picked for Brooke the previous afternoon had been moved to the far windowsill.

"Hello?" Brooke took another step inside.

The woman looked up, straightening to her full height and smoothing her jacket over her skirt. "You'll have to ask the people at the front desk for assistance. I don't work here."

Brooke bit back her first response and relaxed her jaw. She dug deep for what she hoped appeared to be a genuine smile and held out her hand. "I'm Brooke Staley. I worked with Margaret."

"Oh." The woman's expression remained impassive. "Elizabeth Bettancourt." The handshake could've made the Guinness Book of World Records for briefest and chilliest touches. "I'm the new owner." She looked around. "I'm going to need someone to help me with all this stuff. I'll be using Margaret's office while I'm here. As her assistant, I assume you'll have ample free time now."

Brooke's shoulders seized with tension. She'd battled this belittling assumption in every position she'd held. The consensus seemed to be that only middle-aged men were suitable for management—not younger women. "Oh, no. I wasn't—"

"Perhaps you can help me figure out some of this mess. I'll also need to know where I can find the general manager. We're supposed to meet at nine." Elizabeth pointed at the window. "And please dispose of those weeds. I have no idea why they're in here."

Brooke bristled, then used the length of an inhalation to regroup. She offered another smile, this one forced, her cheek muscles as taut as a piano wire. "Let's start over." She once again offered her hand. "I'm Brooke Staley, the general manager. Welcome to the office I used to share with Margaret. My condolences." Brooke paused a moment to give Margaret her rightful due.

Something drifted through Elizabeth's blue-gray eyes—embarrassment, shame, or maybe sadness over Margaret's passing? It was hard to tell. But her features remained stoic. This time the handshake was a bit less robotic.

Brooke broke contact to motion to the makeshift vase. "My daughter picked those for me yesterday on the edges of the vineyard."

Elizabeth glanced around the room, her keen gaze landing anywhere but on Brooke before she spoke. "Apologies." She picked up a folder, then dropped it onto the desk again. "I'll still need help with all of this. I'm afraid I don't understand half of it." She met Brooke's gaze. "Numbers, I get. The rest though…"

Suddenly, she didn't seem to take up as much space in the room, the admission softening some of her hard edges, revealing a flash of vulnerability. Only for a split second, though. Then it was gone.

"So, I'll need someone dedicated to helping me assess the state of the resort over the next few weeks."

To sell it. It didn't need to be said. Well, not if Brooke had anything to do with it.

"They'll need to be well-versed in how things operate. Perhaps a person with some longevity. If we need to hire someone temporarily to fill their position during that time, so be it."

Brooke wet her lips. "That won't be necessary. I'll be happy to teach you everything you need to know about the resort in that regard, and shadowing me is the best way for you to learn." She rested her hip on the front of her desk. "Unfortunately, Margaret took care of the financial side of things, so it's good that you're versed in that area. I have nothing more than a superficial knowledge of that side of the business, but I'll put you in touch with her accountant."

Elizabeth nodded. "Fine."

A knock sounded on the open door, and Francine leaned into the room with her cane. "Excuse me. Brooke, the school called and asked you to contact them. They couldn't get through to your cell."

Brooke pulled out her phone. A missed call. And a text announcing that, because of a broken water line in the building where the after-school program was held, children needed to be picked up at the end of classes. *Fuck.* "Thanks, Francine." She'd have to leave work now and figure out what to do with Rory this afternoon. "Did you two meet?"

"We did."

Francine's curt response and quick exit told Brooke exactly how it'd gone. She pushed aside her lingering annoyance and moved the purse and what turned out to be an empty coffee cup to Margaret's desk. "Let's set you up here. I'll get you signed into Margaret's laptop. Since you're early, I can let you familiarize yourself with things until nine, or we can get started now."

Elizabeth tossed the paper cup into the garbage. "Let's begin. I'd like to minimize my time here. I have a life to get back to in San Jose. And get rid of those, please." She jabbed a finger at the flowers. "I don't care for the smell."

Brooke dug her nails into her palms. Rory had lovingly chosen them for her, only picking pink and yellow ones, her favorite colors. She wasn't throwing them away.

"Hey, Brooke." Kinsey burst into the room, a ball of energy wearing bright blue eyeshadow. "Oh, sorry."

"What do you need?"

"The up escalator in the conference wing isn't working again, and the convention people are complaining."

Brooke held back a sigh at the second breakdown in as many weeks. "Call engineering, please. Tell Antonio to make it a priority."

"Got it." She darted out, her long braids swinging.

Could anything else go wrong? Maybe bad things really did come in threes. Did Elizabeth count as a fourth, or had she just hit a nerve with Brooke? She picked up her bouquet. "I'll take these upstairs to my place, and then we can dive in when I return."

Elizabeth's eyebrows shot up. "You live here?"

Brooke tensed, tightening her grasp around the glass holding the small blooms. She'd known it would come up at some point. Better sooner than later. Get it all out in the open and move forward with a smile and cheerfulness she now *knew* she'd need to dig deep for. "Yes. I'll tell you all about it in a few minutes." She walked to the alcove that housed the private elevator on the far side of the office that led to her and Margaret's apartments. She wanted away from this woman, but she needed her. Elizabeth Bettancourt held Brooke's future—and therefore Rory's—in her icy hands. Shit. Brooke relaxed her grip and turned. "Why don't you come along? I can show you where you'll be staying. You'll be right across the hall from me."

Elizabeth nodded. "Fine." She retrieved the suitcase Brooke hadn't noticed tucked between the filing cabinet and the wall and followed.

Brooke sighed inwardly. Nothing that'd transpired seemed remotely fine. They'd had a rocky start, and Brooke wasn't sure how to turn things around. She'd tread lightly, be her usually delightful self, and hope for the best. She was general manager for a reason. And letting Elizabeth sell the resort wasn't an option.

She lowered her nose into the flowers Rory had picked and given her with love and inhaled. The sweet scent calmed her. She could do this. She had to.

CHAPTER THREE

As Elizabeth waited for Brooke to open the door to Margaret's old apartment where Elizabeth had spent countless hours in her teens, memories stirred and pushed against the barriers they'd lived behind in her mind for so long. To deter them, she looked at Brooke, really *looked* at her for the first time. How her flaxen hair shined and curled toward the ends, and how the feminine cut of her shirt flattered her shapely curves. Shorter than Elizabeth, Brooke only came to Elizabeth's nose as they stood now, but she wore sensible flats where Elizabeth had on her usual pumps. Her skin was fair and smooth, and a pleasant scent, something subtly floral, wafted from her. A remnant of that primitive bouquet?

Elizabeth hoped Brooke had reached her maximum level of chipper. One notch higher, and Elizabeth wasn't sure she could stomach it. At any moment, she half expected unicorns and rainbows to parade along behind her. Did her cheeks ache from flashing so many smiles?

Luckily, Elizabeth had no desire to return them. She didn't care what Brooke thought of her. As soon as she wrapped up her assessment of the property, she'd be on the road.

She'd caught Brooke bristle slightly when she mentioned the weeds, but Brooke had covered her offense well, and she'd taken the ragged things upstairs to...*her* place. What had Margaret been thinking? Whatever Brooke paid for rent couldn't come close to what the suite would bring in from nightly guests.

Brooke moved aside and gestured for Elizabeth to enter.

Elizabeth's steps faltered. It was like going back in time. The same small dining table where she'd studied and Margaret had helped her fill out college and scholarship applications. The same vineyard prints decorating the walls, looking dated now. The rainbow of brightly colored mugs hanging from hooks in the kitchenette. And the fragrance, purely Margaret, somewhat overpowered by an evident recent cleaning, but still redolent. The number of framed photos on the bookshelf had multiplied though, drawing Elizabeth closer.

She barely scanned the vibrant hues of the recent ones and zeroed in on the older, faded pictures. There she was, her hair too big and makeup too garish, standing beside Margaret. Elizabeth grinned at the camera with her gap-toothed smile. Getting it fixed had been one of her top priorities when she'd landed her first career job.

"Is everything okay?" Brooke asked, moving beside her.

"I'm surprised she still has this," Elizabeth said, touching the frame. She remembered that day, the scent of the late fall crush in the air, the picnic for the employees behind the resort with the vineyard as a backdrop. It'd been a milestone birthday for Margaret. Sixty? Elizabeth appeared happy in the photo. Those years held such few bright spots. Being at Harvest Springs working for Margaret were some of the few pleasant memories she had of Calistoga.

"I'm not. She always spoke fondly of you." Brooke picked it up. "You obviously meant a great deal to her." She replaced it where it'd been.

"She mentioned me?" Elizabeth eased away, needing to put some distance between them. Sharing intimate details of her life with a stranger made her squirm. She didn't want Brooke in her personal space on top of it. Only a few feet separated the living and dining area of the apartment. It'd seemed bigger back then.

"Often." Brooke tilted her head and grinned. "If the employees had to hear the story of how you worked almost every job during your tenure here one more time, they might quit. Is the lore true?"

"Except for landscaping and the spa. Those were separate." Elizabeth ran her hand along Margaret's small wooden kitchen table, letting her mind wander back in time. She'd been such a lost soul at that age. Margaret had helped her find her place in the world, discover something she enjoyed. It wasn't until Elizabeth had been tasked with assisting in accounts payable that her love for numbers had emerged, and later, working directly with Margaret on payroll solidified it.

"They still are," Brooke said, startling her as she breezed past. "I boxed many of Margaret's personal items, clothing and the like, and put them in the basement. If you want the rest of her belongings put in storage or gotten rid of, just say so. I wasn't sure what you'd want to keep. Housekeeping did a deep cleaning of the place. Sheets and towels are all fresh." She opened a door beside the refrigerator. "The washer and dryer are in here, or if you don't want to bother with that, just put whatever you need laundered in this and drop it down the chute in the hallway." She replaced the tagged bag and gave Elizabeth a beaming smile. "I think you'll enjoy staying here. You have a lovely view of the grapevines and the sunset."

Elizabeth's dad had been a viticulturist for the third largest winery. No, she wasn't traveling down *that* memory lane. Not now. "I'm not here for pleasure. This is purely a business trip." She wheeled her suitcase to a stop just outside what had been Margaret's bedroom. Elizabeth had never been in there, and she wasn't sure she wanted to enter now. At least not with Brooke watching.

"Would you like another coffee?" Brooke rested her hand on a Keurig.

Maybe it would help the dull ache behind her forehead. "I think I might." Elizabeth moved toward it, but Brooke waved her off.

"I got it. Why don't you relax? You must've been in the car for hours, and going against the commute, too."

"Only until Emeryville." Elizabeth eyed the couch, the same one she used to sleep on occasionally, and opted for the straight-back chair at the small island. She didn't want to get too comfortable. Business. This was business. Though watching Brooke as she confidently moved about the space had her quite captivated.

"What kind of coffee do you like?" She opened a drawer filled with pods.

"Dark roast. Black, no sugar."

Brooke looked at her with that damned smile again. "You don't find it too bitter?" She chose one and fitted it into the machine.

"It suits me."

Brooke laughed. "That's not quite the word I would choose to describe you."

Oh, if Brooke only knew just how bitter Elizabeth was. But she found herself intrigued. "No? And your choice would be?"

Brooke squinted slightly as the coffeemaker began to gurgle. "Hmm. Reserved?" She leaned forward and rested her arms on the countertop, meeting Elizabeth's gaze.

Elizabeth wanted to scoot her chair back, but the deep blue of Brooke's eyes held her in place.

"No. Complicated." The last word escaped Brooke as a whisper.

This time, Elizabeth found her faculties. She stood and retrieved the steaming mug.

"Sorry." Brooke laughed softly. "Too close to home?" she asked, her smile ever-present.

"I never said that." Elizabeth blew across the top of the hot liquid. "Shouldn't we be getting to work? I'd like to review the financials."

She'd had enough of Miss Bubbly for now. She *was* quite pretty, though. Beautiful even. Being around her gave Elizabeth those rare, unsettling sensations that sometimes led to a one-nighter. But as attractive as Brooke was, Elizabeth was here for a reason, and she wasn't about to be sidetracked. She wanted Miss Bubbly in her rearview mirror, along with the rest of Calistoga.

CHAPTER FOUR

B rooke waited for whatever was sure to follow Elizabeth's long sigh as they worked on their computers, Brooke on hers, Elizabeth on Margaret's. They'd been sharing the office for the past two hours, and while Elizabeth might ostensibly be impassive, Brooke was already learning some of her little tells. The subtle yet audible exhalations. The tapping of her index finger on the desk. The rubbing of her forehead. Brooke had better be ready to explain something when those occurred.

"Why is the resort paying Kat Moses when you said she works for the spa? I thought they were separate."

Brooke wheeled her chair closer. "They are. Kat's a special case. Marcel only had a part-time position for her, so she works in housekeeping for the rest of her hours."

"Hmm." Elizabeth ran her finger down the screen. "And why are so many entry-level employees making quite a bit higher than minimum wage? Even new hires. These positions don't require any education."

"When you think about it, after taxes, it's not *that* much money." Brooke retreated to her own desk. She wasn't particularly liking this side of Elizabeth. "Margaret believed in taking care of her employees."

Elizabeth huffed. "From what I've seen, her lack of financial acuity would soon run the resort into the ground."

Startled, Brooke moved to Elizabeth's workstation again. "What?" She scanned the information on the monitor but didn't understand much of it. "She mentioned nothing about that."

"I've reviewed the tax returns for the last three years. She could've been making much higher profits." Elizabeth pinned Brooke with a cool stare.

Brooke heated under the scrutiny. Was she accusing her of something? "Look, I managed the resort, and Margaret took care of the financials. She didn't share money matters with me. But I'm sure it appears worse than it is. After all, Harvest Springs has been successful for decades. Plus, if things were that bad, I would've had an inkling."

"You must've been aware of the rates she paid the staff. Why do housekeeping, servers, and bartenders need that much when they earn tips?"

Brooke frowned. "They *should*, but I've found that wealthy guests at luxury resorts don't tend to leave great gratuities, and for the room staff, sometimes none at all." Perhaps an attempt at humor would be better. She smiled. "Maybe that's why they're rich. They hold onto their money so tightly."

Elizabeth remained unreadable, her attention on the numbers before her.

It left Brooke a little in awe. Elizabeth was so stoic, so…regal, so composed, her spine straight and her hair tucked behind her ears. She was all business. It fascinated Brooke. But why? She had the potential to upset Brooke's life in a major way.

Brooke had to flip this around. She needed Elizabeth to look at her, to see *her*. Elizabeth had to witness how the resort thrived, had become a destination spot, successful because of *her*. Once Elizabeth saw its value, acclimated, and fell in love with it, she'd want to keep it. Right? *If* that happened though, it'd mean Brooke would work for an owner who was…well, not exactly a bitch, but certainly bitchy.

"Those extra wages add up to an atrocious amount over a year. No wonder the profits aren't higher." Elizabeth tapped the desk.

Brooke considered her. "Wouldn't that be Margaret's call? She cared about each one of those people and wanted the best for them." She tried for her most buoyant tone. "That should count for something."

Elizabeth made a snorting sound. "Altruism is the quickest way to shutter a business."

What a cold and heartless outlook. Brooke couldn't imagine living life with that attitude. No more nuggets of wisdom seemed forthcoming, so she returned to her tasks, at least until the next issue arose. The schedule for the front desk needed to be redone with Nik's need for bereavement leave factored in, so she opened the software and focused, but before she got too far, another long sigh broke the silence.

Brooke bit her bottom lip and waited.

"This suite or apartment where you reside, I didn't see any rental payments during my review of the last few months." Elizabeth shifted in her chair to face Brooke.

There it was. Brooke turned to her with yet another smile. Her cheeks were getting sore. "It's a special arrangement."

Elizabeth's forehead creased. "Explain."

Brooke cleared her throat, feeling like a defendant on the witness stand. "I needed a place for my daughter and me to stay when my ex-husband and I separated." Her face warmed. "The house was his. Margaret offered the apartment across from hers."

"You have no family here?" Elizabeth crossed her elegant legs, as though settling in for an interrogation.

Damn those calves. Focus. "I do. I grew up here, but my parents are going through some stuff. I couldn't burden them." She wanted to squirm under Elizabeth's scrutiny, but she didn't. Instead, she offered a small smile. "Margaret asked my company to amend my contract to include the residence."

"Did it include lowering your pay to compensate for it?"

Brooke's face flamed. "No."

"So, you're staying here for free." Elizabeth folded her arms across her chest, her eyes narrowing as she studied Brooke. "In what is essentially one of the larger suites. Correct?"

Sweat pooled at the small of Brooke's back. She'd hoped to avoid this conversation. How foolish. "Yes."

"And are you aware of how much a suite like that costs per night?" Elizabeth shuffled some papers. "Because I am." She tapped the page.

Brooke winced at the sound she'd so quickly come to dread. Everything was about the bottom line to Elizabeth. Brooke lowered her head, unable to maintain eye contact. "Margaret was a kindhearted soul. I didn't ask for anything. She offered. I don't know what I would've done otherwise. I couldn't afford to live in this area, which would've meant losing my job."

"Hmm." Elizabeth watched her. "So, your living arrangement is secure as long as you don't breach your contract."

Her demeanor changed, but Brooke still couldn't get a read on her.

"Do you think Margaret did that because she knew she didn't have long to live, even if it wasn't the best decision for the business? To protect you?"

The thought of that amount of kindness overwhelmed Brooke. She reached for a tissue, then wiped her eyes and blew her nose, all while Elizabeth waited silently for an answer. What a grand first impression she was making. "I'm not sure." She looked up. "I needed to provide a safe and stable home for Rory, and Margaret made that happen."

"Rory is your daughter?"

Brooke nodded. "She's seven."

Elizabeth paled, then blinked a few times.

What an odd reaction. Brooke had to consciously keep her eyebrow from lifting. "The divorce was hard on her." Brooke *should* explain the apartment situation further, but discussing the details of her failed marriage and her family's troubles with someone she'd just met felt too personal. Besides, what good would it do? Elizabeth hardly came off as the most compassionate person on the planet. Suddenly, the tension between them became too much. She wanted to run, but leaving would only make her look like she'd done something wrong.

Then, to Brooke's astonishment, Elizabeth was the one to retreat. With grace Brooke had never possessed, Elizabeth rose and walked to the window overlooking the vineyards covering the field and climbing the hill behind the resort. "Am I correct in assuming that the sale of Harvest Springs would nullify your contract?" she asked, her tone tight and her back to Brooke.

Her trim figure made for a striking silhouette against the cloudless sky. "You are," Brooke said, a shiver of apprehension running through her.

Elizabeth faced her. "You have quite the reason to hope I don't sell."

"Yes," Brooke whispered, feeling inches tall. She was one step away from falling to her knees and groveling. *No.* Absolutely not. That wasn't her. She squared her shoulders and gave Elizabeth her best smile yet. "But I believe once you meet everyone and see what a wonderful place this is, you won't want to part with it."

"Hmm." Elizabeth's demeanor remained frosty and her features impassive. She returned to Margaret's desk. "Does anyone believe in lunch around here?"

Thrown by the sharp change in subject, Brooke glanced at her smartwatch. Nearly one thirty? "Oh! I didn't realize the time." She'd given up any plans of *her* eating today because of the after-school program being shut down and Rory needing to be picked up early, but she should've thought of Elizabeth. God, how many ways could she mess up this first day? "I'm so sorry. I'd treat you, except that I have an errand to run soon. But the food in both the restaurant and the bar is great, although the latter has a smaller menu. Either way, I recommend the niçoise salad."

Elizabeth retrieved her purse. "I'll take it into consideration. I want a full tour of the property this afternoon." She left the office, her head high and without a second look at Brooke.

It was Brooke's turn to sigh, but she didn't. She was a professional. Yes, she had a selfish reason for the resort to remain in Elizabeth's hands, but also, she didn't want to see it sold and completely overhauled to look like one of the bland properties owned by the big hotel chains. Not after all the love Margaret had poured into it. No, she wasn't about to let the beautiful and unique Harvest Springs be gobbled up.

But how could she stop it?

She and Elizabeth hadn't gotten off on the right foot. It was up to her to help Elizabeth re-familiarize herself with the place, and hopefully rekindle some fondness. After all, Elizabeth had worked here for several formative years in her adolescence and grown close enough to Margaret for Margaret to leave the whole property to her. Surely, she had *some* good memories, and for Brooke to have any chance of achieving her goal, she had to root them out.

The two of them would need to work together closely, and it was clear that Brooke's upbeat disposition annoyed the uptight Elizabeth. While Brooke couldn't change her personality, she supposed she could tone it down. It was in her own best interest. Besides, she wouldn't mind getting to know Elizabeth a little better. Her formal manner and invisible armor intrigued Brooke. What was she like beneath all that? What a fun egg she'd be to crack.

Beyond that, though, Brooke needed Elizabeth. Rory had been making strides, opening up bit by bit. Brooke refused to uproot her again. Time to get creative.

To avoid a delay of Elizabeth's request, Brooke arranged for Dashiell to give her a tour of the resort. He was an outstanding assistant general manager, and she was sure to lose him to a property that needed someone like her to run the place, but she'd appreciate every minute she had with him until then. Everyone loved him, and she hoped that would include Elizabeth by the time they'd completed their circuit of the estate and grounds. He was outgoing and genial, impeccably dressed, and well-spoken. Maybe he could make up for all the mistakes *she* had made.

The drive to the school was a nice break from the stress of the morning, and by the time she and Rory were on their way back, Brooke had shaken off any remaining tension. She eyed Rory in the back seat.

Soft brown tendrils had escaped her braid and framed her face, reminding Brooke of when Rory had been a toddler with a head full of curls. She'd gotten her daddy's hair color, and Brooke often saw Sean in Rory's expressions and mannerisms, too, but Rory had inherited Brooke's eyes. The blend of the two of them in their beautiful girl always made her smile.

"Do you have homework?"

Rory didn't turn from the window. "Yes."

"How much?"

No response.

"Do you think you can finish it in half an hour?" Brooke switched to a question that only required a one-word answer, finding greater success with those.

"Yes."

Brooke pulled her car up to the valet podium and killed the engine. "All right, then why don't you go to my office and get started on it?" Elizabeth wouldn't be back from the tour yet. Dashiell loved to talk, and if Brooke had any criticism regarding him, it was that he did nothing quickly. "I need to see if they've gotten that pesky escalator fixed."

Rory climbed from her booster seat. "Okay."

She pulled her backpack out with her while Brooke handed her keys to Hilary, then came around to meet her. They parted ways in the lobby as they'd done many times before, but Brooke watched until Rory reached the front desk and Francine greeted her.

Rory knew her way around the resort, but Brooke didn't allow her to wander by herself. The most she'd concede was letting her take their private elevator upstairs to grab something. Margaret had walled their apartments off from the rest of the floor, and she'd installed the personal elevator when she started having trouble walking up the three flights. It only ran from their office to their residences, and no other employees' key cards could access it. An intercom system allowed them to buzz up room service and housekeeping if they needed something or if friends and family visited.

Which reminded her. She needed to give Elizabeth a master key.

Rory hugged Francine, then went into Brooke's office.

She'd be fine there, especially with Francine and Nik monitoring who came behind the counter. Brooke headed for the conference wing.

After she'd met with engineering and discussed the issue and how much repairs would cost, she passed the front desk. Nik assisted a guest checking in, and Francine had the phone tucked between her ear and shoulder. She gave Brooke a little wave as she went by.

Just outside her doorway, Brooke stopped short at the sound of talking. *Lots* of talking. And not just anyone. *Rory.*

"Auntie M colored with me sometimes. 'Specially after she got sick. But sometimes she'd fall asleep, and I'd finish the page for her." A sniffle. "Did you know she used to have a parakeet when she was seven?"

Brooke hadn't heard Rory speak this much in almost a year. But had she been crying? Brooke hurried inside and the scene froze her in place. Elizabeth and Rory sat on the floor, the waste basket between them and the tape dispenser to the side.

While Elizabeth sorted through the trash, pulling out crayons, Rory focused on mending a mint-green one, wrapping it enough to double its width. "Did you know they can live to be twenty years-old?" When she looked up, her tear-stained cheeks and red eyes confirmed Brooke's suspicions.

"I di—" Elizabeth stopped and lifted her gaze, too.

The mama bear in Brooke snapped to full attention. "What's happening?" Had Elizabeth been rude to Rory? She might be the current boss around here, but Brooke would stand up to *anyone* for her daughter.

Elizabeth turned to Rory. "No. I didn't know."

The largest Crayola box, the one with the sharpener Rory loved, stood open near Elizabeth's thigh, and she arranged the sticks within by color, unlike the jumbled mix when Rory replaced them.

Elizabeth looked at Brooke, panic in her eyes. "I cleaned out Margaret's desk and threw these away, not putting two-and-two together. She noticed them in the trash and..." Elizabeth covertly trailed a finger down her cheek. Her shoulders rose and fell with heavy breaths.

This was the least icy Brooke had seen her, although she questioned just how hard Elizabeth would've had to have thrown the box to have broken so many crayons. But this moment was about Rory. Brooke stepped around them to set her wallet and phone on her desk. "You didn't know. Broken ones color just as nicely. Don't they, Rory?"

She didn't answer, but Brooke hadn't expected her to. Many people on the spectrum found change hard, and Rory had already struggled with all that'd come with Brooke and Sean's separation. But things had started to settle down, and Rory had begun to speak again, even if only in short answers to direct questions. Like her counselor had said, *the more stability Brooke and Sean could give her, the better*. Rory's foundation had been rocked, and a psychological and emotional response like reactive mutism wasn't uncommon as she adjusted. This though? Full sentences amid a potentially triggering incident? If Brooke treated it nonchalantly, maybe both Rory *and* Elizabeth could move past it, because Elizabeth seemed strangely affected by the encounter, too.

"There. Counting those three you're taping, that's all of them. Again, I'm so sorry." Elizabeth stood, smoothing her skirt and retreating until her back almost touched the wall.

Brooke averted her gaze to hide her irritation. Was Elizabeth one of those people afraid of all the germs kids carried, and now that Brooke had taken charge of the situation, she could finally escape?

"Thank you." Rory forced a crooked sapphire-colored one into place with the rest of the blues.

Wow. Not only a verbal response, but manners, too. Brooke needed to keep her hopes up, even though that was often difficult, and she'd been labeled an eternal optimist more than once. Healing took time. "Margaret let her use half of her desk. She said she didn't need more room than that for her laptop. Me, I spread my stuff out." Brooke motioned toward hers. "It also allowed me to focus on what I was doing while they were busy."

"I didn't discard a coloring book." Elizabeth pointed to the garbage can, as if for proof, then wrapped her arms around her torso.

"It's in my backpack," Rory said, more chipper now. "I take it to class so I can work on it during free time when we're done with our stations. Or after school on days we don't have special clubs."

Who was this child? And what about Elizabeth made her want to talk? Brooke closed her slack jaw.

Rory frowned at Elizabeth. "Why are you using Auntie M's desk?"

"Honey, this is Elizabeth." Brooke jumped in, hoping to alleviate the alarm in Elizabeth's expression. "She's the new owner of the resort." She faced her. "I guess I never asked you if that's how you prefer to be addressed. Or is it Beth, or Liz, or Lizzie perhaps?"

At Brooke's mention of the last option, Elizabeth visibly blanched. "Just Elizabeth. No one's called me Lizzie since…" She flicked her index finger with her thumbnail. "Well, for a long time."

"Are you staying in her apartment, too?" Rory looked up at her. "She has a washer and dryer. We go over there every Wednesday night to do laundry and watch movies. We used to go to the laundromat, but it smells funny, and the table's sticky."

Good Lord. What a time for her daughter to turn into a chatterbox. Elizabeth certainly didn't need to know the unpleasant details. "Elizabeth lives there now, Rory. We'll find a new place, okay? Now, let me clean off a corner of my desk for you."

Elizabeth went rigid. "She's staying?"

Of course, the day Elizabeth arrived, Brooke had to drag her daughter to work. So unprofessional. It'd been different with Margaret. "She's usually at her after-school program until Sean or I pick her up. They had to cancel today, and I didn't have another option."

Elizabeth didn't respond for a moment, creases appearing on her forehead. "Perhaps you could move the printer to the top of the filing cabinet." She pointed to a table in the corner, just big enough to hold the machine. "Rory could sit there, so you can concentrate on work." She took a few steps toward Margaret's desk, appearing more like the cooly composed woman Brooke had become accustomed to, and with the touch of a finger, woke the laptop. "As long as business comes first."

As long as business comes first. The immature singsong voice in Brooke's head was unnecessary, but she couldn't help it. Of course, that was Brooke's priority, especially with the owner's eyes on her. Come to think of it, she'd noticed Elizabeth looking at her *a lot.* Or was she imagining it? Even so, Elizabeth's suggestion of a solution for Rory was actually…well…considerate.

Brooke's phone vibrated. Good God. Her mother. *Not now.* Could this day bring any more issues? She declined the call. The screen showed her mother immediately calling again. What if something had happened to her dad? Brooke couldn't have this conversation here. "Rory, come with me. Now." She strode into the hallway and answered, praying Rory would follow. "Mom, what's wrong?"

"Hello to you, too."

She didn't need her mother's quiet reprimand. Not today. She headed for a corner of the lobby, grateful to see Rory right behind her. "Things are sort of hectic here. What do you need?" She sat on a sofa, and Rory dropped beside her with a thump.

"Can I buy a cookie?" Rory pointed to the small store near the front desk.

Brooke nodded, knowing whoever was working the register would put it on Brooke's account, and Rory jumped up and skipped off.

"It's not what *I* need. I'm calling to see if you need us to take Rory for you. Or is she with Sean? Michelle's daughter just dropped off her grandson for her to watch. Something about a broken water line."

"No, she's here and settled in with me." It would've been nice if Brooke could've taken Rory to her parents. But her mother had enough on her plate. "But thanks, Mom. I appreciate the offer."

"What about tomorrow?"

Brooke hadn't even thought that far ahead. "Let's hope they're open. If not, I'll figure something out. Maybe Sean can get off early."

"Okay, well, we're here if you need us."

Brooke wished that were true. Her mother had good intentions, but caring for her father sometimes overwhelmed her, and the hopelessness of the situation often left her spirits low. Brooke tried to help as much as possible. Meanwhile, her brother Brian seemed intent on doing the opposite. Since her father's decline, they'd barely seen him.

Rory returned with her treat, and Brooke welcomed her with an open arm as she settled against her. "Thanks. It's kind of you to offer. She has some homework, and she'll probably draw or color when she's done."

"Or practice chess," Rory said around a mouthful.

Chess. Did Elizabeth play? Could that be a way for Brooke to break the ice with her? And again, the talking. She studied Rory. Were the months of silence and one-word answers over? "Mom, I need to go. I love you. Give Dad a hug for me."

"Okay, dear. And kiss Rory for me."

They said their good-byes, and Brooke took a moment to catch her breath.

"Do you want a bite?" Rory held out the half-eaten cookie.

Brooke smiled. "No, thanks. I should've picked up a healthier snack for you. I guess you're having your dessert early." She kissed her on the cheek. "That's from Grandma."

Rory squirmed, trying to take another bite.

Brooke let her go and stood. "Let's head back."

"It was an accident." Rory said, getting to her feet.

"What?"

"That lady in there. She didn't throw away my crayons to be mean."

Stupefied, Brooke stared. She wasn't sure if she should address the sudden verbosity or not. She opted for the latter, not wanting to draw attention to it. If she did, and that made Rory clam up again, she'd be kicking herself. "I know. Come on." She rested her hand on Rory's shoulder as they headed to the office.

What was it about Elizabeth that made Rory talk? If anything, Brooke would've thought Elizabeth's frosty facade would've intimidated her. But Rory seemed to have connected with her somehow. Brooke couldn't blame her. She had to admit feeling some sort of pull toward Elizabeth, too, despite them being at odds most of the day. She *was* certainly quite attractive. There was no doubt there. But it was more than that. Something truly appealing, perhaps even warm, seemed to dwell beneath the icy surface.

At least when she wasn't picking apart the resort's finances.

CHAPTER FIVE

Five o'clock. Finally. Elizabeth closed the programs and tabs on the two computers she'd been using and quietly began tidying her workspace at Margaret's desk. The last thing she wanted was to draw the attention of either Brooke or her daughter and invite any unwelcome conversation.

The two had been surprisingly quiet throughout the afternoon, engaging in no chitchat. Even when Rory had finished her homework and switched to coloring, there'd been only some rustling of her backpack and a brief bout of whispering when she retrieved the crayons now being kept in Brooke's desk.

Those fucking crayons. A hard lump formed in Elizabeth's throat as her first interaction with the child rushed back in on her. The look on Rory's face. The crying. For an instant, it'd been Carly standing in front of her, a reminder of the promise Elizabeth had made but hadn't kept. It was the reason she adamantly avoided children. And yet, there she'd been, stuck with one in the middle of a meltdown.

For a moment, Elizabeth hadn't known what to do. Then muscle memory from times when Carly's tears had fallen when her block tower toppled or Elizabeth forgot to cut the crust off her PB&J had kicked in, and Elizabeth had dropped to her knees and begun digging in the trash, all the while talking to Rory and trying to quiet her.

Looking back, it probably hadn't been the most soothing voice, but Elizabeth wasn't sure she possessed one of those anymore. But

ALAINA ERDELL

her words had worked, and Rory had calmed. Too bad Rory's wet cheeks hadn't dried by the time her mother walked into the room. The expression on Brooke's face had turned feral.

Elizabeth had presumed the box of crayons must've been long forgotten in Margaret's drawer, maybe a remnant from some ridiculous staff team-building exercise. The mere thought made her skin crawl. What concerned her most, though, wasn't that she'd hurt Rory's feelings, but rather, she'd disappointed Brooke. And that made no sense at all. Brooke worked for *her*, not the other way around.

She closed her laptop and stuffed it into her bag.

Brooke and Rory looked up in evident surprise.

"Good evening, then." She stood and strode toward the door.

"Wait." Brooke rose and took a single step. "Do you have plans right now?"

Elizabeth halted. Her feet ached. Normally, heels didn't bother her, but *normally,* she spent most days sitting at a desk, not trudging around a six-acre property. All afternoon, she'd been looking forward to nothing more than flopping onto the couch in Margaret's apartment and kicking off her shoes. The handsome young man— Dashiell—had been considerate when he'd noticed her struggling near the vineyards and had taken pity on her, radioing for a golf cart. Too bad she hadn't hit it off as nicely with Brooke on their first meeting.

Perhaps she should make an effort. Besides, Brooke's question piqued her curiosity. "I do not. Other than going upstairs."

"Can we borrow an hour of your time?"

God, another sixty minutes? Her feet screamed, but Elizabeth wasn't about to admit they were killing her or ask to have ten minutes to go change. This had better be good. "What for?"

"A bit of relaxation." Brooke flashed that gigantic smile of hers.

Granted, it annoyed Elizabeth, but Brooke's lips were full and appeared soft and glossy. Sort of peachy. No, closer to a coral color. Holy hell. Elizabeth didn't need to be going down that road. "No more details are forthcoming, I take it?" Right before her eyes, Brooke's trademark smile transformed into a grin.

"Nope." Brooke turned. "Pack it up, my little one. We're going you-know-where. You can bring your drawing."

Rory lit up, shoving things into her backpack.

Brooke locked her wallet in a drawer but left her desk covered in papers, folders, and sticky notes. She didn't shut down her computer or even close the lid.

Elizabeth shuddered at the mess, barely able to refrain from straightening it herself.

But Brooke moved first, stopping beside her, almost touching her, and watched Rory finish.

The warmth radiating from Brooke's body so near hers threatened the control she customarily relied on in such circumstances. Although, usually when she was attracted to a woman, she simply took charge and got what she wanted. But she couldn't do that with Brooke. They had to work together. Elizabeth took a step away, regaining her personal space.

"Okay, let's go." Brooke's excitement was palpable as she gave Elizabeth's arm a firm but brief squeeze.

It took the entire walk across the lobby for Elizabeth to shake the sensation of Brooke's touch.

Brooke led the way to the bar, which was empty except for a couple sitting at a corner table. "Most of our patrons partake in tastings at the local wineries this time of day," she said, tossing a glance over her shoulder at Elizabeth.

Elizabeth nodded. Was Brooke worried she'd think they had no guests? Maybe she would have without the clarification.

The bartender, a young woman likely in her twenties with neon pink nails that matched the streaks in her long dark hair, greeted them.

"Hi, J'Nae. This is Elizabeth, the new owner." Brooke turned to her. "Do you drink wine?"

That damned smile again. But this one was worse—fucking *dimples*. Elizabeth bit the inside of her lip to keep her practiced indifference in place. "Occasionally." She supposed it was sacrilege to say otherwise while in Napa Valley. It wasn't necessarily her go-to, but she enjoyed it.

"Any preferences?"

"Nothing too sweet." Elizabeth shifted her gaze to take in the decor, trying not to think about what made Brooke's cheeks dimple. She failed. Was that her genuine smile? Had the others been fake, a professional facade? They certainly hadn't stoked the heat inside Elizabeth that this one did.

"A couple of my favorite, please," Brooke said to J'Nae, "and a Shirley Temple." She looked at Rory. "Extra?"

Rory nodded so hard Elizabeth half expected her head to detach.

"Two cherries, please. She's feeling frisky today." Brooke tucked an errant strand into Rory's braid, her expression soft and loving.

J'Nae flashed Rory a grin. "I know what my girl likes." She made Rory's drink, but instead of reaching for Maraschinos, she added a couple of Luxardos. "She's got good taste."

Elizabeth silently agreed. She enjoyed the same in her old-fashioneds. Rory beamed as she accepted the Shirly Temple, and J'Nae began to open a bottle of wine. Elizabeth tried to read the label.

"It's my favorite. A five-year." Brooke leaned closer as J'Nae poured. "Don't worry. It's a cabernet. I find it better aged." She picked up both glasses. "Thanks, J. Have a good night."

Elizabeth followed not Brooke, but Rory, and not to a table but to the elevator where Rory selected the second floor. The gym? The business center? The library? None of those places shouted relaxation. At least not to Elizabeth. The mezzanine overlooking the lobby? Maybe…if one were people watching…and only if she were alone. What had she gotten herself into?

Rory turned left when the doors slid open, then continued to the library.

Elizabeth had only given the room, and most others, a passing glance on her earlier tour with Dashiell. The entire resort remained ingrained in her mind from her youth, so she'd only wanted a general overview on that first pass. She'd do a comprehensive examination of the property soon. But since she was here, she took in her surroundings.

No guests, not even a lone couple tucked into a corner as in the bar. The familiar built-in walnut shelving filled with books lined the walls, and the same chandeliers hung from the ceiling. The room seemed untouched by time, other than the furniture and carpet having been updated and a sliding ladder that looked to be a recent addition based on how little wear the rungs showed. Where had that been when she'd had to dust in here? She'd hated having to climb up the stepstool to reach the higher shelves, back down to drag it a few feet, then rinse and repeat all the way around the large room. She'd been grateful to Margaret for giving her the job and continued to be to this day, but the library had been her least favorite part of it.

"Over here." Brooke set the wine glasses beside a chessboard poised for play on a small square table. Two cinnamon-colored accent chairs faced one another from opposite sides. "You can spread out beside us," she told Rory, pointing to a spot with a larger surface.

Rory dropped into a seat and began to unload her backpack.

Elizabeth sat closest to the fireplace and reached for her cabernet. "Should we move the game so we have more room?"

"Oh, no. We're going to play. You know how, right?" Brooke scooted her chair in closer across from her, offering her yet another smile.

No dimples this time, thank God. But was that a challenge peeking through? "Of course, I do." Elizabeth hadn't played in ages, but she assumed she recalled how. What was the point of this?

"Black or white?"

"White, since those are the pieces in front of me," Elizabeth said, also remembering it allowed her to go first. She pushed a pawn forward two spaces with her fingertip, then took a sip of her wine, the stress in her body immediately lessening. The strain of scouring so many programs and files had left a pulsing ache behind her eyes, and the confrontations she'd had with Brooke regarding the staff and finances hadn't helped either.

Brooke matched her move. "I thought this might be a good way to decompress after a long day," she said, as if reading Elizabeth's mind.

Elizabeth took another turn, then Brooke. Without hesitation, Elizabeth used her knight to capture Brooke's pawn. Indeed. She was feeling better already.

Brooke retaliated, taking hers.

Beside them, Rory colored, using the crayons Elizabeth had dug out of the trash. Frequently, though, Elizabeth caught her side-eyeing the game. She seemed curious. Elizabeth wondered if Rory understood any of it at her age, but it wasn't her place to explain.

An hour later, accumulated pieces lined the edge of the board, and all three glasses stood empty. She'd enjoyed the wine more than she'd expected. While playing, Brooke never rushed her, and she appreciated that. She'd been rusty at first, but some techniques and strategies had come back to her, and now, only a few pieces remained. In addition to the kings they were protecting and their queens standing tall, Elizabeth retained a rook and a bishop, while Brooke was down to a knight and a pawn.

"Isn't it interesting," Brooke asked, "how the object of the game is to capture the other player's king? But when you think about it, he's rather impotent, isn't he?"

Elizabeth looked up, startled at the unexpected question after playing mostly in silence.

"He hides behind a row of pawns," Brooke continued, "who basically have as little ability as he does. It's the queen who's all-powerful, the one who really matters." She rested her finger on hers before sliding it diagonally across the board. "No one wants to lose the most-coveted piece." She met Elizabeth's gaze.

"Agreed." Elizabeth moved hers between Brooke's royal pair, protecting it with her bishop. "Checkmate." Brooke's impassioned speech had obviously commanded her attention, and Elizabeth had trapped her king.

Brooke studied the board for a few seconds. "So, it is." She extended her hand across the table. "Good game."

Elizabeth clasped it, noting the warmth and softness she remembered from that morning. She let go and stood. "I should be going."

"Do you have dinner plans?" Brooke began to reset the board, most likely to ready it for the next players.

"I'll grab something."

"Just remember, if you order room service, you'll have to buzz them up. They don't have a key card. It's to ensure privacy for the residences." Brooke sat back, crossing her legs. "Or you could join us for pizza."

"I'd like to unpack." All Elizabeth really wanted was a hot bath and to burn her shoes.

Brooke nodded. "Understandable. If you change your mind, just walk across the hall and knock. The two of us can't finish one by ourselves."

Elizabeth needed quiet and a respite from the constant smiles and chattering. "I'll see you tomorrow." She picked up her bag and left.

It occurred to her in the elevator that protocol probably dictated she should've addressed Rory before leaving, especially after the crayon ordeal, but Elizabeth didn't have a template for how to act around children. How could she, when for most of her life, she'd done her best to avoid them? She'd try to do better with the girl next time.

With a sigh, she reached her door and breathed easier. At least *this* day was over.

CHAPTER SIX

B rooke hurried toward her office, on time but not as early as she'd wanted. The chess game last night had seemed to ease things between her and Elizabeth after the numerous confrontations and disagreements they'd had throughout the day, and Brooke had hoped for a fresh start this morning. But Rory had needed to be at school twenty minutes early for her field trip to the dairy farm, so taking the bus hadn't been an option. At least Sean planned to pick her up and keep her for the afternoon since he worked close by.

She strode past the busy front desk. Would Elizabeth already be there? A little thrill shot through her at the thought. Odd.

As she approached, the door stood open. Nothing greeted her but the sight of the clean surface of Margaret's old desk and her cluttered one. As she moved around it to put her things away, she stopped. On her chair sat a new, unopened box of Crayola crayons. The big one with the sharpener.

Brooke cracked the lid and inhaled. There was nothing like the scent. It transported her back to her childhood, to the days when Brian would walk her to school and watch out for her at recess. She closed the box, shutting away the memories. Nowadays, he knew very little of what happened in her life. They only spoke or texted if she made the effort, and rarely connected for long.

"Because I broke so many."

Brooke jumped at Elizabeth's voice. "I didn't hear you come in." She faced her and held up the gift. "You didn't have to do this.

As you saw, she was fine after a few minutes. Like I told her, even short, they still make pretty colors."

Elizabeth shifted in place, transferring a steaming mug from one hand to the other. "Yes, well, I made an error." She looked at the floor. "It's fixed now."

If only everything in life were as simple. "Thank you. She'll be very excited." Brooke set them aside, wondering where Elizabeth must've gone to buy them and when. As far as Brooke knew, she'd retired to her room after the chess game. It wasn't the first time Rory had taped crayons together, and she'd gotten over the issue quickly, but the kind gesture warmed Brooke. Nothing in the world came before her daughter, so an adult—a stranger—trying to make amends over something so insignificant meant a great deal. Perhaps more than it should.

Silence stretched between them. "If you need more coffee pods upstairs," she said, trying to shake off the discomfort, "you can ask the restaurant's wait staff to get them for you."

Elizabeth stilled. "Why would I do that?"

Brooke swallowed. "Because they know where they're kept." Something crossed Elizabeth's features, and Brooke tensed. She'd done it again, stepped in some invisible pile of something, and she dreaded whatever was coming next.

"Do all employees take resort supplies?" Elizabeth tapped her nails against the ceramic cup.

"No. I mean, I'm sure we have loss within normal limits, but…" Brooke mentally stumbled, trying to regain control of the situation. "That's just what Margaret did. You're the owner now, so I thought…"

"Hmm." Elizabeth sat, demurely crossing her legs, today's light gray skirt suit making her hair appear even more striking. "That complicates finances. I've purchased what I'll need. You can take the rest of the items upstairs back to the restaurant."

She waved her hand, as though assigning Brooke the task. Brooke clenched her teeth. She was the general manager. Since no one else had access to Elizabeth's temporary residence though, she either needed to swallow her pride and do it or tell Elizabeth to…Well, she'd put it more nicely than what was currently running through her mind. "I wouldn't want to invade your space. Why don't you bring them to the office, and I'll make sure they get put away."

Elizabeth paused mid-sip, then opened her laptop. "I plan to review spending, down to each line item. I'll also be scheduling an inventory soon. When did the last one occur?"

It'd been eons since anyone had interrogated her like this. Margaret had been so respectful, so compassionate, even if perhaps a tad too laid-back. As the owner, if Margaret had wanted the restaurant to order her K-cups, who was Brooke to say otherwise? She wasn't about to mention that Margaret had the staff wash and press her clothing. Elizabeth didn't seem to mind housekeeping cleaning the apartment or laundering her towels and bedding while she stayed here, though. Wasn't that the same? The two women approached things so differently. How was Brooke supposed to keep up?

Brooke smiled so sweetly her teeth ached. "Not since I've been here, so I'll have to check on that for you."

Elizabeth's forehead creased. "It's not done annually?"

Brooke gave a single shrug and woke her laptop. "Margaret wasn't insistent on it. She had her finger on the pulse of the resort's happenings. And she installed cameras everywhere, including in the bar. If large amounts of something went missing, either she or I would've noticed."

"Small amounts add up, too," Elizabeth said under her breath.

Brooke turned, unable to hold back. "And so do all the hours it takes to have every employee stop their normal jobs and count every sugar packet and box of tissue. Do you plan to pay them overtime for that, or should I start getting bids to *hire* an outside agency who specializes in this?"

Their intense stare down might've gone on for hours had Dashiell not entered.

"Good morning." He stopped just inside the door, his attire impeccable down to the sweater vest he wore beneath his navy jacket. He cleared his throat, then adjusted his tie, unnecessarily. "Brooke, may I see you a moment?"

She followed him into the lobby.

"We're short a valet. Marco didn't show again. He's not answering either. Shall I see if I can call someone else in, or do you want to see if Grayson can handle it himself?" He held his phone in one hand, ready to do as she advised.

"No, he's too new. I've noticed he gets anxious when there's a line, and his customer service skills suffer. He needs additional training. What about Alberto?"

Dashiell shook his head. "He's on security tonight."

"Then see if Hilary can come in. She always wants hours." It wasn't ideal. They'd have to pay her overtime, but with the resort at capacity and guests granted in-and-out privileges, it had to be done. "Leave Marco a message that I'd like to meet with him tomorrow morning. If he doesn't show—" Well, normally, Brooke would suggest Margaret let him go. Now, she'd have to share the problem with Elizabeth and let her decide what action to take. "Just tell him I want to see him."

"Sure thing." He took off toward the office he shared with Francine and Ximena, the overnight assistant manager.

Out of the corner of her eye, Brooke caught sight of Elizabeth striding toward the restaurant, a box in her arms. Had she gone upstairs and retrieved the items herself? Her skirt and jacket moved seamlessly with her, and the heels she wore accentuated her already spectacular calves. With her shoulders back and head held high, she appeared formidable. And quite captivating.

Brooke rubbed the back of her neck as she walked to her desk. Elizabeth's time here would test her. It'd be easier if Brooke disliked her, but she didn't. Elizabeth showed just enough of herself through barely visible cracks to leave Brooke quite intrigued.

She dropped into her chair. Nope. No way. No can do. Her divorce had only been final for six months, even if they'd separated long before that. Dating the past year had been painful, and she hadn't slept with anyone except the woman from the cheese-tasting event. Getting Rory settled and thriving again had been her priority. Between work, IEP meetings, lacrosse practice, chess tournaments, her parents, juggling custody, and all the little inconveniences that cropped up in an adult's life—like her recent jury duty—left little room for a social schedule. Even the Fromage Fête had been work-related when she'd attended in Chef Sophie's place at the last minute.

Still, she wanted to know more about Elizabeth. Like why had she moved away from Calistoga? She must've had family here. Did any remain? And why had Margaret left everything to her? Brooke paused, fingers resting on the keyboard, not really seeing the screen. It surprised her that interest in a woman had her obsessing like this, even if said woman did wear a suit like the boss she was.

Brooke shook her head to clear the image as she opened the reservations app. She neither had time for this, nor the inclination. She was drawn to Elizabeth, but she'd lived long enough to recognize the superficial nature of attraction. Not knowing the difference between lust and love had landed a younger, pregnant version of herself in a marriage she never should've entered.

Older and wiser now, she wouldn't confuse the two again. She simply needed to ignore Elizabeth's allure and focus on the oft-irritating personality behind it. Except that would be easier said than done. At times, she caught glimpses of a complex, mystifying woman beneath the mask Elizabeth usually kept in place. One who bought crayons for a little girl who'd cried. One who that little girl had talked to more in one day than anyone else in a year. That had to mean something, didn't it?

Absolutely not. Brooke pinched her arm to wake herself from this silliness. Time to refocus. She had one goal: to win Elizabeth over so she kept the resort. If Brooke failed, she'd be homeless and unemployed. Unacceptable.

"I returned the items to the restaurant."

Brooke jumped at Elizabeth's voice for the second time that morning. As she did, she knocked over the remnants of yesterday's coffee, spilling it over a pile of documents. "Shit." She grabbed what she could save, shoving the papers to the side. At least Rory couldn't overhear and make her put a dollar in the swear jar. She'd have enough for her much-coveted trip to Dave & Buster's soon enough as is.

"I'll get some napkins." Elizabeth left.

Shit. Shit. Shit. Brooke was never this jumpy, this scattered, only when she…

Oh, no. Brooke watched the caramel-colored liquid spread. She was a mess. With a large inhalation, she closed her eyes. Under no circumstance could she let her attraction for Elizabeth continue. Too much was at stake.

CHAPTER SEVEN

After returning the stolen—borrowed?—goods to the kitchen, Elizabeth had examined files on Margaret's computer for the remainder of the morning. For the past thirty minutes, though, as the workday neared its end, she'd only been pretending to appraise old invoices. Her vision swam from studying so many numbers. A few feet away, Brooke typed, her keys click-clacking softly.

Elizabeth rubbed her temples, wishing she felt as serene as Brooke appeared. This entire mess confounded her. She hadn't asked for this, or even expected it. She enjoyed her job and liked her life.

Click-click-clack.

Sigh. Brooke, again. Elizabeth resisted even a glance in case Brooke *smiled* while she worked. She pulled her attention from any of *those* thoughts. She missed Geoff. He was no distraction at all.

Elizabeth could simply sell the resort as-is and go back to the successful career she'd built. Or she could start her own payroll company. With her name and reputation, she'd have no problem attracting clients, but did she want all that pressure and responsibility? Hell, she could retire. But then what would she do? Would she become a daytime television addict? No, she'd never find satisfaction there. Travel? Not by herself.

Clickity-clack, clickity-clack.

Elizabeth stiffened. *Christ.* Whatever had possessed Margaret to share her office with a subordinate? Surely, there was other workspace *somewhere* on the premises where Brooke wouldn't be so close all the time. Maybe she could ask Dashiell. No, she wouldn't be here long enough to bother. She'd be selling. She was sure. Then Brooke would be no problem for her at all.

But *did* she want to get rid of Harvest Springs? Being back here conjured some rather pleasant memories she never would've recalled otherwise. She smiled at how she and Justin, a busser, would hide in the dark of the vineyard after their shifts, sharing funny stories of their interactions with guests while he smoked a joint and drank a beer he'd swiped. He'd had a thing for her. She'd known it but did nothing to encourage it, and he must have sensed her lack of interest, because he never made a move on her. He was a good friend who didn't ask too many questions and accepted what little she had to give. He'd frequently offer her a lift into Napa after work, but she'd only ride with him when he hadn't been drinking. She'd take the bus those nights.

Clickity, clickity, clackity, clackity, click-clack-click.

Enough! "*Why* are we using a company to wash the floor mats?" The question came out far harsher than she'd intended, but seriously...*enough.*

Brooke's fingers stilled, and she looked up. "If the staff steam clean them in place, they create a slipping hazard until they've dried, and they smell like a wet dog until then. We simply don't have the room on the premises to wash and hang them somewhere, and we'd need double the amount in rotation. The Cintas employees come in, roll them up, throw down clean ones, and cart away the dirty ones in record time. It's a minimal inconvenience to our guests. And we're not paying for the hours it would take our people to do the labor."

She had a point. Okay, several. Elizabeth drew in a breath and relaxed her shoulders. "Have you looked at competitors' rates to see if we can bring down the cost?" She assumed the answer was no, otherwise they would've already switched. Or had these kinds of things even been on Margaret's radar?

"I'd be happy to do another comparison. August was the last time I asked for quotes." Brooke had pinned some of her hair back today, and the remaining blond curls fell to her shoulders, giving her an angelic air. But when she ended her offer with a smile, neither her eyes lit up, nor did her dimples appear.

Elizabeth looked away, the tension between them growing the more questions she asked. How would she survive two weeks of this push and pull between them and—she could admit it—being drawn to Brooke? The only time they'd existed in a modicum of friendliness had been over chess.

It didn't matter. They weren't friends, and they could never have a fling. This was business, and the quicker Elizabeth learned about the property, the faster she could put it on the market. God, how she missed the quiet solitude of her home in the South Bay.

At least she didn't have to contend with tiptoeing around a child today. Rory hadn't shown, and it was already half-past four. Brooke hadn't mentioned her, so Elizabeth hadn't either. She didn't need that kind of stress two days in a row. There was something about the young girl that reminded her too much of herself—and Carly at the same time.

Maybe it'd been Rory's braid. Elizabeth's mother had used the same kind on their hair, and Elizabeth had always urged her to make hers tighter so it didn't come undone on the playground. Her mom finished by scraping her nails up the sides of Elizabeth's head, her favorite part, aligning the stray strands she'd then secure with barrettes. Elizabeth could almost feel the sharp snap of them against her scalp all these years later.

She shook herself from the daydream before it could fully transform and touch down as one of the many ways she'd failed Carly by not learning the technique herself until much later in life. Trips down memory lane never ended well.

She looked around for a distraction. Something to drink would be nice. She should move the Keurig down here. This is where she needed it. Perhaps she'd do that tomorrow. Then Brooke could use it, too—if she stopped giving her those saccharine smiles.

"I've been meaning to ask you," Elizabeth said, turning in her chair, "when was the last time the porte cochere has been painted? I noticed it's flaking."

Brooke flipped through a notebook. "It's scheduled to be redone in May. Would you like me to move that up?"

"Yes. It's the first thing guests see. And whatever number of months are usually between coats, shorten it."

"Of course."

Another damned smile. Who beamed like that so often? Elizabeth couldn't recall doing so hardly ever. But when it came to putting up with Brooke's cheerfulness, she'd have to grin and bear it, pun intended, because she needed her. No one knew more about the resort's operations, and if Elizabeth strived to get the maximum amount when selling, she had to rely on Brooke's knowledge and guidance. So, they needed to stay on good terms. Besides, Brooke had proven adept at managing issues, especially with the staff, who seemed to like and respect her. Elizabeth wanted no part of that.

She returned her attention to her screen and studied the QuickBooks page open before her. "Tell me more about the contract with the spa. From what I can see, they've paid the same amount for the space for the past decade, yet the resort's electricity bills have increased every year during that period."

Brooke rose and stood behind her, leaning down to look over her shoulder. "I knew their rent didn't go up this past year, but I wasn't aware it'd been that way for so long. Boy, Marcel's been fortunate. He's the owner."

Brooke's voice, so soft and close to her ear, sent shivers down Elizabeth's back, and damn, she smelled incredible. Was the scent from the resort's toiletries Elizabeth had seen in Margaret's bathroom but hadn't used? A specialty brand with scents of eucalyptus and bergamot, if she recalled correctly. If that's what *this* tantalizing fragrance was, she'd have to try them. Although, a part of her liked smelling it only on Brooke.

A light brush across Elizabeth's shoulder blade must've been Brooke's hand on the back of her chair. Elizabeth cleared her throat, eager to move the conversation along, and with it, Brooke out of her personal space because she couldn't think with her this close. Had the desk not been in front of her, she might've fled the enticing discomfort Brooke's proximity caused. "And the resort launders their linens and towels? Can that be right?"

"It is." Brooke straightened, her thigh lightly pressing against Elizabeth's arm. "It's included in the contract."

"I'd like to assess it." Elizabeth shifted, turning her chair slightly so they no longer touched. She tried to take a breath despite the tightness in her chest. "I'll draft an updated one before this one expires in two months."

Brooke returned to her desk. "You're not worried that Marcel will object and take his business elsewhere? You'd be pressured to find another company willing to take over on short notice."

"No, I'm not." How many spas would jump at the chance to relocate or open a branch on premises with hot springs and volcanic ash for mud baths already on site? She'd have potential lessees lined up from here to San Francisco.

Brooke began stuffing things into her tote. "Well, it's five, so I'm going to grab a glass of wine and head to the library. Would you like to join me?"

What else did Elizabeth have to look forward to? She could use some relaxation after a day of untangling numbers. "Yes, but the drinks are on me tonight." The offer wasn't to be nice. She'd always hated the feeling of being in debt, even if self-assigned.

"Fair enough. As long as you don't choose the house rosé," Brooke said, lowering her voice and grinning.

"What we had yesterday will suffice." It'd been decent. Luxurious. Was that an apt descriptor? Elizabeth packed her own bag. If she kept the resort, she'd have to study up on wine-country parlance so she sounded competent.

She straightened and froze. What was she thinking? She'd be gone soon, back home with a sizable nest egg and a job she enjoyed. What more could she want? It was a fine life. Comfortable. Predictable. There might not be anyone at home waiting for her or missing her. Well, maybe Geoff on occasion, but he had a busy life of his own. Whatever. She slung the strap over her shoulder.

"You look pensive," Brooke said from where she'd paused near the door. "Is everything all right?"

"Perfectly." Elizabeth shoved those thoughts away as they exited the office and crossed the lobby to the bar.

J'Nae was working again, and she held up one finger as she finished serving a young man a tumbler of scotch. Once she'd poured their wine, they carried their glasses to the elevator and rode in a slightly awkward silence to the second floor. Low voices greeted them as they entered the library, and Elizabeth spotted an older couple she recognized from earlier in the day when she'd gotten her salad from the restaurant. They, too, had drinks and sat in front of the window overlooking the vineyards, deep in conversation.

She followed Brooke to the same table, even though two other seating areas also had chessboards. Elizabeth didn't mind. Routine was her friend.

They'd been playing for a while, Elizabeth contemplating her next move, when Brooke sat back, cradling her glass. "Do you still have family here?"

Elizabeth startled, knocking over a few pieces, then quickly righted them. *Shit.* She hadn't seen that coming. "No, not anymore." Her thoughts raced. She had to shut this down. "What about you?"

"Oh, sure. My mom and dad still live in the house where I grew up. Sean, Rory's dad, is in St. Helena. We share joint custody. And there used to be my brother, but he's in San Diego where he works at an advertising agency." She turned and stared out the window.

Elizabeth followed her gaze to the verdant, vine-covered hills that popped against the cerulean backdrop of the sky. The sheer beauty of the area stunned her. She'd forgotten over the years just how striking it could be.

"We don't see much of him now," Brooke continued, wistfulness filling her voice, and her usually upbeat, glowing persona having faded. With a quiet sigh, she returned her attention to the game.

Was there more to that story? Elizabeth debated inquiring or minding her own business. While she considered it, she took her turn, freeing her rook from the corner in a sacrificial move.

Brooke slid her bishop diagonally and captured it.

Just as Elizabeth had hoped. With a sip of the cabernet, she studied her options. "Had you been close?" She couldn't quite let go of the topic.

"Hm? Oh, my brother and me?" Brooke tilted her head, and a tiny smile lifted the corners of her mouth. "Yeah, we used to be. He just…well, he doesn't adapt to change easily, and my family's going through some stuff and *will be* going through stuff for a while." She set down her glass. "His way of dealing with difficulty is to stick his head in the sand and pretend it doesn't exist."

"I'm sorry. That must be hard." Elizabeth couldn't imagine having a sister and choosing not to be a part of their life. An emptiness spread in her like hunger she couldn't assuage. It wasn't new, but she'd tamped it down for so long, it hadn't visited in some time.

"Mom!"

Elizabeth looked up to find Rory throwing herself into Brooke's lap.

"You're supposed to text Daddy, so he knows I'm with you," Rory said, letting go and landing on her feet.

Brooke picked up her phone. "He knows he needs to walk you in."

Rory flung her backpack atop a nearby table and began emptying it. "He said he was running late and don't be mad."

Today, Brooke had done Rory's hair with the plait sitting on top Dutch-style instead of twisted inside, the same way Carly used to want hers. Elizabeth's skin went clammy.

Brooke sighed as she typed something. "Did you have fun on your field trip?"

"Yep." Rory turned to Elizabeth. "Did you know that most dairy cows weigh about one-thousand-four-hundred pounds and that all of their teeth are on the bottom?"

Elizabeth froze. "What? Uh, no." Jesus. Children always transformed her into a fumbling fool, especially this one. "What's on the top of their mouths?" she asked, attempting to sound like the intelligent person she was. Besides, she was curious now, and it might distract her from her anxiety and thoughts of Carly.

Rory shrugged. "I don't remember. But they can also smell something six miles away."

"Hmm," Elizabeth said, still stuck on what the hell took up the space of the top row of teeth. Maybe, she'd look it up later.

Brooke finished texting and dug in the tote she'd set by her feet. She pulled out the new crayons and held them out to Elizabeth. "Here. Go ahead."

Elizabeth's apprehension flared. She shook her head and shoved her hands under her thighs so Brooke wouldn't see them trembling. "No. You do it," she whispered.

Brooke's eyebrows shot up, her expression serious. "Okay," she said quietly, watching her for a moment. "Hey, Rory, look what Elizabeth bought for you."

Rory gasped and grabbed the box. She opened the top and sniffed them. "Thank you."

Before Elizabeth could react, Rory flung herself at her, wrapping her small arms around her neck.

Elizabeth couldn't breathe. Rory was so tiny, so warm against her. She didn't know what to do or say. It didn't matter. Before she'd been able to respond, the little bird flew back to her gift.

When Elizabeth turned her attention to Brooke, what she found surprised her. The happiness and gratitude from when Brooke had found the crayons in the office was nowhere in sight. Instead, her eyes were slightly narrowed, and she'd drawn her lower lip between her teeth.

"Are you all right?" Brooke quietly asked with evident concern. "I'm sorry if you don't like being touched or…" She waved her hand as though she didn't know to end the sentence.

"It's fine." Elizabeth downed the rest of her wine. "I'm fine. It's fine. Let's just finish the game. I should be going."

She needed to retire to her apartment, find a place to have dinner, schedule a massage, or go for a walk. Anything that didn't involve children who brought back so many memories. If she had to stay here a few weeks, she needed to do her best to avoid situations like this. That might not be easy, working with Brooke and living across the hall from her and Rory, but it was the only way Elizabeth would get through this in one piece.

She held herself together for ten more minutes during which she banked another win shockingly quickly, then hurried upstairs where she could breathe easier. But neither the victory nor the solitude helped block the image of the confusion on Brooke's face.

Chapter Eight

After a quick dinner following her and Elizabeth's second chess game, Brooke had shuffled Rory into the car. Now, as she turned onto her parents' street, she smiled as Rory belted "Let It Go" from the back seat. Oddly, Rory's reticence with speaking since the divorce hadn't carried over into singing, and it'd been a rare bright spot in these long months.

Today with Elizabeth had been somewhat like yesterday, with many tense moments of Brooke having to explain every little detail Elizabeth found in the resort's records that she didn't like. Once they'd gotten to the library though, Brooke had enjoyed the comfortable silence they'd settled into as they played. Until Rory had gotten there, that is. What had *that* been about?

Panic. Full-blown panic.

That's what Brooke had seen when she'd offered the box of crayons to Elizabeth to give to Rory. But why? Sure, Brooke had put her on the spot, but she'd already met Rory the day before and had been thrown headfirst into having to deal with Rory's meltdown. That should've been more stressful than handing her a gift. Had Elizabeth been embarrassed giving them to her? No, it was way more than that. It'd looked like fear or anxiety. Or both.

For the life of her, Brooke couldn't figure out why Elizabeth had reacted that way. On the surface, she appeared composed and self-assured, if a bit cold and demanding. Educated, well-spoken, impeccably dressed—oh, wow, those skirts—a consummate professional. So, why did even the possibility of interacting with a child affect her so much?

Disliking children wasn't uncommon among adults. In her short dating life since she and Sean had separated, she'd experienced it more than once. Laughing, chatting, small touches over drinks until she brought up her daughter. Then, *bam*!

Suddenly, she was on a speed date. A few more superficial questions. Forgotten commitments. Emergency texts. Then the check, and it was over.

Okay, so some folks didn't like kids. Fine. Those weren't people she was interested in having a relationship with, anyway. Rory was her everything, her little beam of sunshine, and she didn't need someone in her life who didn't understand that.

Maybe Elizabeth was the type of woman who booked vacations at adult-only resorts and glared at loud little kids who couldn't sit still in restaurants. That's just how some people were. Yet, that shouldn't have caused her to tremble in her seat when Brooke pulled out the crayons.

Mystified, she parked in her parents' driveway. "We're only staying a little while," she said, opening her door. With the sun this low in the sky, she'd need to rush the visit to get Rory to bed at a decent hour.

Rory's little feet hit the pavement. "Okay."

"Don't slam your—" Too late.

"Sorry!"

"And remember, only one cookie if Grandma offers," Brooke said, as Rory bounded up the front steps.

"Yeah." She waited for Brooke to unlock the door.

"And say hi to Grandpa before you go play," Brooke whispered.

"I know." Rory sighed, sounding so much like Elizabeth that Brooke actually laughed.

"Hello," Brooke called as they entered the house.

"In the kitchen," her mom called.

The excitement in her mother's voice whenever her granddaughter arrived never got old. Not quite sixty-five, her hair that had been streaked with silver when Rory had been a toddler had gone completely gray in the last few years, and she'd lost at least fifteen pounds.

"Jack, the girls are here." Brooke's mom wiped her hands on a towel and hugged Rory. "How are you, my cherub?" She kissed the top of Rory's head.

"Good."

"Grandpa's looking at his garden." Her mom gestured to him at the back window. "We just finished dinner." She one-arm hugged Brooke. "Hi, hon."

Rory approached Brooke's father and awkwardly put her arms around him. "Hi, Grandpa."

He looked at her but didn't move. "Do I know you?"

Brooke's eyes stung.

Rory giggled. "I'm Rory."

Neither Brooke nor her mother joined in. No humor could be found in the situation, and barely any remained in the house Brooke once called home. Her mom looked tired, her skin wan and dark semi-circles under her eyes. Caring for an ailing loved one was never easy. Doing so for someone who didn't remember who you were was even harder. Brooke worried about the toll this was taking on her mom.

Brooke approached her dad and knelt on one knee to be eye level with him. She cautiously put a hand on his leg and spoke softly. "Hi, Daddy. I'm Brooke, your daughter. Are you enjoying looking at your flowers?" He'd once spent hours each week taking care of his prized blooms. Now, her mother paid the brother of one of the resort's landscapers to maintain the yard each week.

He looked again to Rory, who'd opened the cabinet where her mom kept cards and games from Brooke and Brian's childhood. Playing with the old things was one of Rory's favorite parts of visiting her grandparents. She began a solo game of Yahtzee, the rattle of the dice in the plastic cup filling the space.

How there were still scorecards left after all these years, Brooke didn't know. And how did her angel of a mother find time to sharpen those little pencils?

"Christine, you always cheat at that game. You never play fair," Brooke's dad said, his voice trembling.

Rory froze, looking first at him and then Brooke with wide eyes.

"It's okay." Brooke gave Rory a smile and squeezed her father's knee. "That's Rory, Daddy, my daughter. Christine's all grown now. She married Elliot, and they're at home." Knowing her aunt, she was probably still at her office working, but her dad didn't need that level of detail.

"Oh." His thick eyebrows drew together. "Of course."

Brooke patted his shoulder. She frequently wondered how often he used that phrase even when nothing made sense. Her heart broke for him as she rose and went to her mom.

"At least he's happy watching out the window for now." Her mom leaned against the counter, her glasses nestled in her hair. "He's been following me around all day. I've had a terrible time getting anything done. Every time I turn, I bump into him."

Brooke encircled her waist with one arm.

"I haven't even asked you how work's been." Her mom tucked a curl behind Brooke's ear.

It was something she'd done since Brooke was young, a lifetime trying to fix all the little things. Brooke leaned into the touch.

"What do you think of the new owner?"

Brooke paused, her thoughts suddenly filled with Elizabeth. "Oh, Mom. I don't even know." She exhaled a deep breath, fighting off discouragement. "I have to make her like—no, *love*—the resort. For her." She motioned to Rory. "But she—Elizabeth— is so…" Brooke searched for the appropriate word. "Frustrating, cold, condescending, opinionated. She thinks we've mismanaged the place financially. Well, not me. More Margaret." Even though Brooke had to agree with some of Elizabeth's numerical nitpicking, she'd never been one to speak ill of the dead. And certainly not after all Margaret had done for her and Rory. "Everything is about the bottom line to her."

"If you've been taking care of it like I know you have been from the start, it's in fine hands." Her mom gave Brooke's wrist a soft squeeze, then turned. "I'm sure she's just trying to get her bearings. Give her some time to come around." She retrieved a container from the back counter. "I've always thought Elizabeth was such a pretty name."

"She's really pretty," Rory said, and dumped the barrel of dice onto the tile floor.

Brooke hadn't realized she'd been listening.

"Do you want a snickerdoodle, honey?" Her mom popped the lid, and the warm smell of cinnamon wafted toward Brooke.

Rory jumped up and took one. "Thanks," she said on her way back to her game.

"Napkin," Brooke said, holding one out as Rory skidded to a stop and backpedaled to retrieve it.

"Pretty, huh?" Her mom set the cookies down after Brooke declined one.

It took a moment for Brooke to snap to. "Oh. Yes, she's beautiful."

"Single?" A raised eyebrow accompanied the question.

It hadn't occurred to Brooke. "I don't know. She hasn't mentioned anyone, and I haven't noticed a ring." But now that she considered it specifically, she'd studied Elizabeth's hands quite a bit—her *bare* hands—while they'd played chess, and the only jewelry she wore was a small pair of gold hoop earrings.

Why couldn't more of the time they spent together be like the hours they'd enjoyed in the library the last two evenings? It'd been comfortable and uncontentious, lacking all the confrontation and frustration that filled their days. Maybe her mom was right, and things would get easier once Elizabeth acclimated to how they managed and maintained the place. Brooke had been excited to show how many positive changes she'd made the last year, but no, they'd had to focus on how many Keurig cups and sugar packets were accounted for and if they could clean the mats more cheaply.

"Brooke." Her mom nudged her. "Where'd you go?"

"Sorry." Brooke gave her a smile. Her mother didn't need another person who didn't listen or respond to her. She had plenty of that.

"If she's pretty and single, maybe you should ask her out." Her mom gave her a wry smile. "Living in a town with a population of five thousand, and so many of us old folks, doesn't give you many opportunities to meet someone. Sean is happy, and I want you to find that, too. He got lucky, I suppose." She paused, then stroked Brooke's arm. "I'm sorry. I didn't mean it that way, hon."

"No, you're right. He was fortunate to find his soulmate. I'm glad for him." And it was true, even if she was a bit envious. "But I'm not asking Elizabeth out, Mom." Brooke had switched to a whisper in case Rory was eavesdropping. "She's only here for a few weeks, and we have to work together."

Her dad shakily rose, and her mom went on high alert, rushing toward him with outstretched arms.

"Easy, Jack. Go slow." When he'd made it to the chair closer to the window without falling, she returned and slid onto one of the stools. "His balance has been off today," she said, then brightened. "You know, there are ways to enjoy yourself, even if for a few weeks—not that *I've* ever done it, but I know some people do." She threw in a wink, as if Brooke hadn't clued in to her allusion.

"Geez, Mom. We're not having this conversation." But the mention of it planted ideas in Brooke's mind that shouldn't be blossoming there. Like unzipping one of those pencil skirts and watching it slide over those calves to the floor. Or the lingerie she'd find beneath. Or the scent she'd breathe in when she buried her face in Elizabeth's neck. Would Elizabeth want breakfast in bed the next morning or just her usual black coffee?

Brooke blew out a breath. Oh, heck no. She needed to shove this attraction in the bottom drawer of her mental filing cabinet and lock it up until Elizabeth left. What was a few weeks? Nothing a little self-control and her vibrator couldn't handle.

"I thought I'd make spaghetti and meatballs tomorrow night if you and Rory want to come for dinner."

Thankfully, her mom appeared to have abandoned Operation: Date Elizabeth. "We can't, Mom. It's Wednesday. We're going to the laundromat. I think Rory's dirty clothes are multiplying in the hamper at night."

"I forgot what day it was." Her mom leaned her head on her hand as Brooke took a seat beside her. "You know, now that Margaret's gone, you can do laundry another night. Why don't you do it here?"

"You only have one machine. I can do multiple loads at once at Bubbles." Brooke hated the thought of sitting in the shabby room with its dirty glass storefront, stained linoleum, and the TV that loudly and exclusively played soccer games, but it meant accomplishing the task in less time. Doing consecutive loads hadn't been an issue when they'd had movie nights at Margaret's and Brooke could fold the items as they finished and run across the hall to put them away. Besides, they'd made those evenings fun, something Brooke wasn't sure she could accomplish on a regular basis at her parents' house, watching her father's decline.

She looked at him, the man who'd once helped run a successful company, but now spent most of his days in a chair, unable to recognize the loved ones around him. He was alive, flesh and blood, right before her eyes, but he'd been gone for some time now. The days when he'd pace behind the backstop at her softball games, jingling the keys in his pocket so she'd know he was there supporting her, or dancing with her at her wedding and laughing together when he'd mess up the steps, or when he'd casually change the oil in her car as she sat on the sidewalk chatting with him about "this resort" or "that inn" were over.

The fresh sting of tears startled her. You weren't supposed to mourn someone who was still alive. It was so confusing.

"Hey," her mom said softly, wrapping her in a hug. "Everything's all right."

She'd always been so cognizant of her kids, so attuned to their emotions. And here she was even now, the one carrying the heaviest load with Brooke's dad every single day, and consoling Brooke, too. "I'm sorry."

"It's okay. We all have our moments." She rubbed Brooke's back.

Brooke sniffed and straightened. "Heard from Brian recently?"

"Hmm, not for a bit," her mom said vaguely.

Which meant months. The last time they'd seen him had been at Christmas two years ago. He'd told Brooke he couldn't take it, couldn't watch their father's mind deteriorate. He and their dad had always biked the back roads, hiked at Robert Louis Stevenson State Park, attended Giants and Warriors games in matching jerseys, and never missed their long-standing poker night. Brooke didn't understand how he could just move away like he'd done. He had to still be hurting, though. This was an illness from which you could run but not hide.

"It's not the end." Her mom patted her leg.

Brooke swiveled. Was she talking about her dad? "What do you mean?"

"I know you loved and miss Margaret, and everything is changing. And that's hard. But don't think of it as the end, but rather as the beginning of something new." She brushed her thumb across Brooke's cheek, wiping away a residual tear.

If there'd ever been a question where Brooke got her optimism, she'd answered it. "You're right." Brooke summoned a reassuring smile for her mom. It was the least she could do.

CHAPTER NINE

Elizabeth paced the length of her apartment as Wednesday evening settled in. With Brooke unavailable to go to the library after work due to her laundry, Elizabeth had changed into yoga pants, an oversized sweatshirt, and her Adidas. Why, she wasn't sure. It's not like she had anywhere to be. She could've easily put on pajamas.

On her next pass, she picked up her dinner plate from the table and scraped the remnants of a delicious Cornish game hen with a celeriac mash, white asparagus, and jus into the trash. Chef Sophie had tucked a small coconut tart for dessert in the bag. She'd refused to put it on the bill, saying her pastry chef was trying out a new recipe, and she'd appreciate her notes on it tomorrow.

It'd been decadent.

Good thing Elizabeth wouldn't be here long, because she couldn't get used to eating this way. It was a far cry from her take-out salads and Buddha bowls she subsisted on at home. The only thing her dinner had been missing was a glass of sauvignon blanc or pinot noir.

Or Brooke's favorite cabernet.

When Brooke told her she wouldn't be able to play chess, Elizabeth had faltered, not knowing what to do with her evening. It wasn't like it'd become routine. They'd only played two days, but even in that short time, she'd become fond of that hour in the library, that tenuous connection they'd found within those four walls that allowed the tension of the workday to subside. Nothing was stopping her from visiting the bar and heading up there by herself, but strangely, that option didn't hold as much allure without Brooke's presence.

She rinsed her plate and cutlery and put them in the dishwasher, then resumed her meandering. As she came to the window overlooking the vineyards, the low sun casting long shadows, she knew what she wanted. A walk. What better way to breathe some fresh air and reacquaint herself with the area? She grabbed her phone and her key card and headed to the elevator. The town's center couldn't be more than a mile or two away.

Outside, the slight chill of the breeze pleased her. Once she'd set a strong stride, she'd be comfortable in just her sweatshirt. When she reached the junction where the resort's driveway met the road, she inhaled deeply. Earthy, grassy, clean. So different from the smells of the city. She turned and headed toward town.

Unfortunately, she hadn't considered the scarcity of sidewalks on the outskirts of Calistoga—or their nonexistence, to be more specific. Conscious of the locale and intimate with the choices drivers made to get behind the wheel after a drink or more, she walked as she always had from the resort to the bus stop, facing oncoming traffic to give herself the benefit of seeing trouble coming. A split second might matter. At least her beige top made her visible.

After working up a mild sweat, she reached the main thoroughfare. Days ago, on her way to Harvest Springs, she'd passed through, but she'd been so anxious about arriving that she'd noticed little.

The false facades and brick masonry seemed to transport her back to the Gold Rush days, and she half expected to see a horse tied up in front of the gift shop. A boba cafe, the tourism office, and a gallery selling wine country originals replaced establishments like a mercantile, livery, blacksmith, or saloon. Not that there weren't spots to purchase necessities or alcohol if she wanted. They just came in the form of a grocery store and a brewery, with no lack of places to sample or buy the famous product of the region.

She walked on, from one end of downtown to the Napa River, enjoying the tantalizing scent of garlic outside an Italian restaurant and the happy hum of diners and drinkers emanating from every doorway and patio she passed. When she decided to head back, she chose a different route and turned into a residential area. The homes, mostly single-story ranches, weren't much to look at and packed close together. One barely stood out from another.

Until she reached a white picket fence and froze.

Memories rushed back. Could it be the same? Had she been drawn here subconsciously?

Surely not. She'd only stayed here once for a short time. And she'd *never* found her own way.

A car honked a few feet behind her, and she jumped from where she stood in the middle of the street. She stepped onto the curb to look at the place more closely. Someone had changed the cornflower blue paint to a golden yellow, but the tree in the front yard confirmed her initial impression. Half of its gnarled limbs reached out over the pavement as if to beckon her closer, and a large branch on the side closest to the roof had been cut off near the trunk, just as it'd been decades before.

The scene grayed and twisted. Impossibly, she heard the crying of her name. She squeezed her eyes shut and clenched her fingers around the pointed top of a fence post to steady herself. Years of paint touch-ups had rounded and smoothed its edges. When the dizziness subsided, she looked down the street in the direction in which they'd disappeared the last time she'd seen them. Her chest constricted, and she struggled to breathe. Her own screams from all those years ago echoed in her head.

She had to get off this street where her life had changed forever. With a dash back the way she'd come, she then wandered without purpose until her nerves settled. Finally, over an hour later, the front doors of the resort slid open, and she hurried inside, grateful to be somewhere safe again.

Questions dominated her thoughts, ones she'd asked a million times, then pushed from her mind so she could live with some semblance of peace, a necessity in order to exist, day-to-day.

A flash of blond hair caught her eye across the lobby. Brooke sat at a high-top just inside the bar. With a woman. They'd ordered drinks, and based on the four glasses on the table—two of them empty—they'd been there a while. Was she on a date? Did it matter?

Then Brooke noticed her and waved.

One of those damned smiles. Elizabeth raised her hand in acknowledgment but kept walking.

Whoever was with Brooke turned, and they exchanged a few words. The woman grinned and exuberantly motioned Elizabeth over.

After what'd happened on her walk, talking to people ranked among the last things Elizabeth wanted to do. She needed time to decompress and process. But she'd have to face Brooke in the morning and avoiding her now might make their interaction even more awkward than usual. The only time they seemed halfway comfortable with each other was while playing chess. She veered toward them.

Brooke pushed a stool out with her foot. "Hey. Join us? This is my friend Tiffany."

Tiffany flipped her chin-length brown hair and signaled J'Nae with a nod. "What do you want?" she asked Elizabeth. "We're having martinis. Extra dirty." Her glasses magnified her brown eyes.

Elizabeth leaned more than sat on the seat. "Nothing for me. I can't really stay."

"No?"

At Brooke's crestfallen look, Elizabeth caved. "Okay. Just one." She scooted back and crossed her legs, conscious of her sweatshirt sticking to the perspiration on her back. She wished she could've showered before Brooke had spotted her.

J'Nae appeared beside her.

"What they're having, please."

"You got it, boss." J'Nae slapped a coaster in front of her. "You two still okay?" At their affirmative, she retreated.

"I'm so excited I got to meet you. Brooke was telling me all about you. I'm currently doing payroll, too. Well, HR and payroll for a store in Napa and a farm and winery upvalley, but it's a temporary position. I'm looking for something full-time, but I also want to start my own business. Or maybe it'll be a side hustle at first. I haven't decided yet. Do you use ADP?" Tiffany finally took a breath.

Elizabeth blinked, a dandelion gone to seed in a tornado. "Um…yes. I do." She looked to Brooke for help.

Brooke smiled knowingly.

"I *love* their software. It's the best." Tiffany started up again. "We used to use Paychex, but we switched two years ago. Were you at the conference in Vegas last year?" She pulled an olive off the cocktail pick with her teeth. At Elizabeth's nod, she squealed. "Oh, my God. I can't believe we were both there and didn't meet! My room was in the Bellagio tower but not on the side where I could see the fountains. Where was yours?"

"Uh, I don't recall." Elizabeth took a gulp from her newly arrived drink. It certainly couldn't make her head spin any more than trying to keep up with Tiffany.

Brooke touched Elizabeth's arm but directed her attention toward Tiffany. "You were just about to tell me about your brilliant idea before Elizabeth walked in." Brooke picked up her glass, but didn't remove her other hand from where it rested.

That small touch grounded Elizabeth, providing an anchor and sense of security for the first time since she'd stumbled upon her past. She breathed a little easier and took a sip, this time enjoying the taste. But she'd missed the first part of Tiffany's TED Talk. "I'm sorry. It's what?"

"It'll be an option for visitors to travel to and from the wineries and resorts in the area. There are too many drunk driving accidents on Highway 29 and Silverado Trail, not to mention the ones that happen on smaller roads. People are killed and injured every year, and with so few ways to get through the valley, it causes huge traffic jams." She lifted her glass and smiled. "Instead, visitors can choose to take a pedicab or a horse-pulled carriage."

"Horses though, Tiff?" Brooke shook her head. "You'll have to have a plan for the cleanup and their boarding."

Tiffany shrugged. "They make it work in Central Park. Why not here?"

Intrigued, Elizabeth leaned forward. Intoxicated people getting behind the wheel in the valley created an *enormous* problem and had heartbreaking effects. She'd know. "Are you thinking the pedicabs and carriages will be independently owned?"

"I'd purchase the cab, carriages, and horses. The staff would work for me. I'd be the one hiring and training them. It wouldn't be like some cities where you get in a pedicab and pay an independent driver using their Venmo. They'd be vetted."

Elizabeth tapped the side of her glass, considering. "Would you be interested in an investor?" She had plenty in savings. It's not like she spent it going on exorbitant vacations to gorgeous and exotic destinations with a partner every year. And if she sold the resort, she'd have additional funds with which to play.

Tiffany's eyes widened, and her mouth opened. "Oh, my God. Yes! Are you serious?"

Solving this problem of drunk drivers on these roads was something close to Elizabeth's heart. Personal. She wanted to help. "I might very well be." She flipped over her phone. "Why don't you give me your number? Let's talk more."

Brooke gave her arm a few excited pats, then let go.

Tiffany dug in her purse until she found a business card and slid it across the table to Elizabeth. She clenched her fists and grinned. "I haven't even told you the best part. I've thought of the perfect name." She raised her hands, fingers spread. "Cabernet!"

"Cabernet?" Brooke frowned. "Yes, it's wine-related, but marketing-wise, I don't think it'll give people an idea of what service you're providing."

"No. Cab-OR-*nay*."

Elizabeth looked at Brooke, who had a little crease between her eyebrows. It was admittedly…cute.

"Every employee would wear a polo with the name and logo." Tiffany sighed, likely at their still mystified expressions. "Listen to me. Cab or N-e-i-g-h." She made three little boxes with her fingers in the air and spelled out the last word. "Get it? Cab…the pedicabs. Neigh…horse-drawn carriages."

Brooke let out a small groan.

Elizabeth laughed. "I'm sold. It's unique, and it'll give visitors scenic views of the valley they obviously want. They pay money to rent bikes for the same thing."

"Isn't it adorable? I've already come up with some possible logo ideas. My sketch pad's filled with them. I can't decide if I want it to be realistic or cartoon-like. I'm not a graphic artist, though, so I'd have to hire one. And of course, I need to research county codes and everything. My neighbor's an attorney, so I can ask her for help. Lyndsey Bartoletti."

Bartoletti?

Elizabeth couldn't swallow. Her hands began to shake, and she broke out in a sweat. She wanted to rip off her top to lower her skyrocketing temperature, but she only wore a sports bra beneath.

Tiffany hadn't let up. "...and recently opened a firm in St. Helena. The place is endearing. It's in an old Victorian on the north end of town that she painted a light lavender and has tons of daffodils out front. The combination is absolutely gorgeous. I forgot to ask her what she plans to plant in the fall. If she can't answer my code questions, I'll see if she can ask her dad." She nudged Brooke. "You've probably heard of him. Judge Bartoletti?"

Elizabeth had.

He hadn't been a judge back then, only a lawyer with high aspirations. Apparently, he'd reached them. A daughter though? It was a punch to Elizabeth's gut.

"I've heard his name," Brooke said, studying Elizabeth. "Lyndsey was a few years behind me in school, but I don't know her."

Tiffany stirred her drink. "She's hilarious. Totally different than what I'd expect from someone in her profession. Her little dog is the most precious thing I've ever seen. His name is Nugget. Or maybe Nougat. Which would make sense because he's super sweet. He's some kind of Pomeranian mix. He has the cutest little fluffy bed, but he insists on sleeping on her bathmat instead." She finished her martini. "Oh, boy. Excuse me. I need the ladies' room." She slid from her stool, leaving them in the quieter buzz of the bar.

"You look pale." Brooke touched Elizabeth's arm again. "I'm going to get you a water." She came back with three, pushing one toward Elizabeth.

Elizabeth still reeled from the name dropped so casually in conversation and the uncanniness of her past rising up and hitting her twice in one evening, both times with enough force to topple a utility pole.

"Please?" Brooke inched the glass closer.

Elizabeth drank, the chill of the ice-cold liquid cutting through her much like the mention of Bartoletti. There couldn't be more than one, not with an unusual surname like that.

He and Elizabeth's dad had met in college at UC Davis. He'd grown up in Boston and been a fervent Celtics fan, even placing a bright green sticker on the back of his truck.

"What's wrong, Elizabeth?" Brooke leaned closer.

Had Brooke addressed her by her given name before? It sounded pleasant on her lips, intimate. It soothed Elizabeth, made her wish they were alone. But they weren't. "I…I'm tired. I should go." She liked Tiffany, but she couldn't tolerate any more of her exuberant prattle. Not tonight.

"Okay," Brooke said slowly. "I'm glad you joined us. And thanks for supporting Tiff, even if you were just saying it to be nice."

Elizabeth stood and picked up her phone. "I meant it. I have personal reasons for investing in her idea." She met Brooke's gaze. "A drunk driver killed my parents near Rutherford when I was seven." She'd only uttered that sentence a handful of times in her life. Why she'd told Brooke wasn't clear, but the events of the night and the alcohol made her brain foggy. Hopefully, a good night's sleep would dull the pain that'd resurfaced.

Brooke's eyes widened. "Elizabeth," she whispered.

Before either of them could say more, Tiffany appeared. "You're leaving? What'd I miss?"

"She's calling it a night." Brooke jumped in without a word about what Elizabeth had shared. She stood and wrapped her in a warm, tight embrace that seemed to go on longer than necessary.

Not being much of a hugger, Elizabeth wasn't sure about the last part.

"Thanks for stopping," Brooke said, releasing her.

"Nice to meet you, Tiffany," Elizabeth said as she glanced at Brooke, suddenly a bit embarrassed. "I'll see you in the morning."

Brooke didn't answer, and Elizabeth thought she could feel her eyes on her all the way to the office to take the private elevator.

Would Brooke share with Tiffany what she'd just told her? Elizabeth didn't think so based on the way Brooke had responded when Tiffany returned. But did it matter? Nothing would change the fact the tragedy had occurred. Nor the one that followed.

❖

Elizabeth raced down the street, but he caught her, his tight grasp pinning her arms to her sides as he lifted her. She screamed and twisted, but it didn't loosen his hold.

In the distance, the taillights receded.

She kicked, connecting with his knees and thighs. It only made her shoes fly off, leaving her bare feet flailing.

He carried her inside despite her crying and begging. She screamed louder.

"Elizabeth. Elizabeth." He grabbed her shoulder.

She jerked away and screamed again, her voice hoarse.

"Elizabeth. Wake up. It's just a nightmare. You're safe."

She opened her eyes but couldn't see. The room was dark. Her breaths came fast, her arms still pinned. She struggled against the restraint.

The touch on her shoulder returned, gentler than before, or had that been part of the dream? A shift on the mattress, then the soft glow of the bedside lamp.

"Here, let's get you untangled."

Brooke.

She pulled at the sheet that'd wrapped around Elizabeth's upper body.

Elizabeth flinched.

"It's okay. It's just me."

With Brooke's help, Elizabeth freed her arms, moving them a bit to reassure herself she wasn't trapped. The cool air grazed her skin from the hem of her shorts down. Who knew where the comforter had ended up. "My slippers. I need something on my feet." She had to rid herself of the feeling of kicking into nothingness.

"Sure." Brooke bent and retrieved them, then helped Elizabeth sit up.

Elizabeth's T-shirt, wet from sweat, clung to her back.

"I'm sorry I barged in on you," Brooke said, "but I heard you screaming. I knocked and knocked, but you didn't respond. I thought something bad was happening to you, so I used my master key."

As Elizabeth's breathing slowed, she noticed something beside Brooke on the bed. "What's that?"

Brooke picked it up. "Rory's lacrosse stick."

"Were you going to fend off an attacker with it?" Despite her still-racing heart, Elizabeth's chest warmed at the thought of Brooke protecting her.

Brooke raised her chin. "I was." She smiled.

The one with the dimples. Elizabeth's reaction went from warm to hot. But then she realized just how soaked her top was from the nightmare. She plucked at it, pulling it away from her skin.

"Do you want a shower?" Brooke asked, her gaze dropping to the wet fabric. "I could start it for you."

"That'd probably be good," Elizabeth said, as the bad dream faded with each passing minute. "I can do it myself, though. You should get back to Rory."

Brooke rose, flipping on the bathroom light. "She's at her dad's." She moved aside so Elizabeth could enter. "Jump in there, and I'll change your sheets. Did you move the spare set, or are they still in the hall closet?"

"I haven't touched them." Elizabeth hadn't even known they existed. It unsettled her how well Brooke knew the apartment and where things were kept. Brooke must've been quite close to Margaret.

"All right. Off you go." Brooke waved her away.

Elizabeth grabbed a fresh pair of pajamas and quickly showered. She didn't know whether to expect Brooke to be there when she emerged or not. A part of her hoped she would be. Another remained mortified at what'd transpired. It shouldn't have come as a surprise, though. Her past had come knocking twice the night before. No wonder it showed up in her subconscious.

She wished her parents' faces would. They'd faded over time in her mind as much as they had in the one family portrait she had of all of them in Christmas attire in front of a photographer's fake backdrop of a roaring fireplace. Elizabeth stood beside her mother, who snuggled one-year-old Annie on her lap. Her father held Carly in one arm behind them with his other hand on Elizabeth's shoulder. The photograph had yellowed with age, just as her memories of them had degraded over time.

As she toweled off, she debated whether to leave things as they were with Brooke just thinking she'd had a nightmare or explain what'd happened earlier as well. After all, Brooke already knew Elizabeth's parents had died. She decided to keep it vague unless Brooke asked.

When she entered the living area, Brooke turned from an electric kettle that hadn't been there before. "Chamomile?" she asked, holding up two mugs.

"That would be nice."

She carried them to the small table. "Sugar?"

"No, thanks." Elizabeth joined her, wrapping her fingers around the warm ceramic.

"Feeling better now?"

Brooke wore a swishy pair of shorts and a thin hoodie partially open to reveal a tank top beneath. For the first time since she'd awoken, Elizabeth noticed the braid Brooke wore. While it looked innocent on Rory, it provided a lovely view of the smooth lines of Brooke's slender neck, somehow making her look stylish in the middle of the night. Seeing Brooke like this, with her hair up and in comfy clothes, made this encounter even more intimate.

Elizabeth cringed at the thought of what *she* looked like. She ruffled the wet hair clinging to her neck. "Yes." She took a tentative sip and burned her tongue. "Thank you. I'm sorry I woke you."

"You didn't. I was having trouble sleeping." She sat in silence for a moment, blowing on her cup, as Elizabeth did the same. "So, you were adopted?" she asked finally.

Elizabeth closed her eyes briefly. They were going there. "Not exactly." Naturally, Brooke assumed the nightmare had been related to trauma stemming from the accident. The questions her parents' death generated were one of the reasons Elizabeth rarely spoke of it.

"You don't have to talk about it if you don't want to." Brooke lifted her tea. "I know we've only just met."

It was thoughtful of her to give Elizabeth an out, but Brooke had gotten up in the middle of the night, whether she'd been asleep or not, to save Elizabeth from an unknown threat. Repaying her with an explanation seemed the least she could do. "I grew up in a foster home. Two, actually. The first one was temporary." She looked up.

Brooke blinked a few times. "Here?"

"In Napa." If it'd been Calistoga, she wouldn't have had to take the bus or bum a ride all those times for her job at the resort. "A kind couple. I know some children have horrible experiences, but mine wasn't like that. There were four of us kids. Three foster and their biological daughter. I wasn't near any of their ages." She paused, but Brooke didn't interject questions or commentary, so Elizabeth continued, if only to fill the lull. "They did the best they could. It was a busy household, so there wasn't really time for emotional bonding. I'm sure they loved us, and I had most things I needed, but they never felt like my parents. Don't get me wrong. I'm grateful they took me in." She didn't know how better to describe her relationship with them. "My foster dad, Ben, died of a heart attack six years ago, and Lily, his wife, moved to Phoenix to be near her daughter."

Brooke simply reached across the table and took her hand. "I enjoy knowing more about you."

Elizabeth had expected sympathy, pity, more questions, the usual things that accompanied this revelation—and the reason she rarely offered it. Instead, the quiet of the night enveloped then, the calming effects of the tea settled in, and Elizabeth did something she hardly ever did. She allowed someone to just *be* with her. When she finally withdrew from Brooke's grasp, she first gave Brooke's fingers a small squeeze. "I should probably try to sleep. I have my meeting with the accountant in the morning."

"That's right." Brooke took their mugs to the sink, then turned and leaned against the counter. "Do you want me to stay with you?"

"What?" Like in her bed? "No. I'll be fine." Elizabeth ran a hand through her drying hair. "Again, sorry I woke you, or whatever." She walked Brooke to the door.

Brooke stopped and turned, closer than Elizabeth had realized.

Elizabeth froze. There was that fragrance again, so intoxicating. And Brooke's blue eyes, bright and inviting. And her lips, parted ever so slightly.

Brooke's gaze fell to Elizabeth's mouth, then she cleared her throat and stepped away. "I left the lacrosse stick for you in case you need to fight off any more demons." She winked.

Amazing how such a small thing could lighten a moment so much. "Thank you." Elizabeth debated how much good a piece of children's sporting equipment would do against any threat, but the gesture softened her.

Brooke tilted her head, her expression thoughtful. "What a beautiful smile. I don't think I've seen it before." She put her hand on the doorknob. "Sleep well."

No one had ever complimented Elizabeth's smile besides her mom, and back then, it'd been half-filled with baby teeth and gaps. The door clicked shut, and Elizabeth's exhaustion rushed in, as if Brooke's presence had been keeping it at bay. The emotions of the previous evening and the nightmare had wrung her out.

Elizabeth glanced at the clock. Only three thirty. A few more hours would've allowed her to stay up and avoid encountering who-knows-what in her subconscious state. Maybe some—what had her therapist called it?—affirmative thinking would help. She'd have to try, even if it meant having another embarrassing episode. Tomorrow would go terribly if she attempted to operate on this little rest.

After turning off the lights, she retreated to the bedroom and crawled under the covers of the freshly made bed. Images of Brooke smoothing out the sheets and pulling down the comforter, thoughts of her hands, soft and warm as the one holding hers had been, delectably overtook her, the effects beginning to move through her body. All right, as *affirmative* as those imaginings were, they certainly weren't going to help her sleep.

Instead, she closed her eyes and envisioned a chessboard, all the pieces standing tall in their starting positions. In her mind, she made the first move.

Then she waited to see what Brooke would do.

CHAPTER TEN

As Elizabeth peered intently at her laptop, Brooke pressed the button on the coffeemaker, and the small appliance filled their office with a gentle hum. *Theirs.* That's how she thought of it now, rather than as Margaret's. She'd arrived last week to find Elizabeth had brought the machine downstairs, along with all the accoutrements she'd purchased. Brooke had to admit its convenience, as opposed to brewing a pot in the morning while trying to get Rory on the bus on time. Still, it posed environmental concerns, so she'd look for reusable pods and buy freshly ground beans when she went to the store.

At her desk, Elizabeth shuffled some papers and sighed. "Why does Miranda Rodriguez start her shift two hours before the other housekeepers?"

Brooke had been waiting for the day's questions to begin. "Margaret made an exception for her because she has four kids, and leaving two hours earlier helps her and her husband avoid childcare costs." When possible, Margaret had always tried to be flexible with her employees.

"Making allowances for one means you have to do the same for everyone." Elizabeth tsked. "It sets a poor precedent."

Brooke waited. A few moments of silence signaled she wouldn't have to discuss Margaret's apparent transgressions further, at least right now.

Almost a week had gone by without either of them bringing up Elizabeth's childhood. Brooke figured if Elizabeth wanted her to know more, she would've volunteered. Prying, especially into the life of someone she hardly knew, seemed intrusive and unprofessional. Elizabeth was the owner. The resort's contract might be with J & C Hospitality Specialists, so Elizabeth couldn't outright fire her, but Brooke worked for her, all the same. Which had made it feel even stranger keying into Elizabeth's apartment when she'd heard her crying out.

Brooke's heart raced again, just thinking about it. She normally reserved that level of worry only for Rory. Thank goodness, it'd only been a nightmare, but whatever Elizabeth had been dreaming about had clearly disturbed her.

"Do you want another cup?" She looked at Elizabeth, who'd appeared on Monday with reading glasses. Had she not wanted to wear them last week, or were they new? Brooke approved of the look.

Elizabeth peered at her over the frames. "I shouldn't." She leaned back in her chair and rubbed her forehead as Brooke returned to her desk. "I'm working on a headache."

Brooke pulled a bottle of medicine from her drawer and rolled her chair over to set it on Elizabeth's desk. "We can skip our game tonight if you'd rather lie down."

"No." Elizabeth's answer came quickly. "I mean, unless you're tired of losing."

Brooke had yet to take home a win. Their sessions had become a bright spot in her day, a time to set aside their frequent confrontations and focus on something other than the resort. She grinned. "I'm up for it if you are. Just to warn you, though, Rory will be there in the beginning."

Elizabeth flinched, ever so perceptibly.

"Kali's picking her up to go with her and Sean to sample wedding cakes. They wanted to include her."

"Your ex is remarrying?" Elizabeth swiveled toward her. "How do you feel about that?"

Brooke had become adept at answering this question. It was a small town, after all, where everyone loved to talk about one another's business. She smiled. "I'm happy for him." Normally, she tried to stick to professional topics at work and reserve personal matters for other times, but Elizabeth had asked, so she elaborated. "He suggested the divorce, but we both knew it was the right thing to do." She twirled a pen between her fingers. "We were still in that glorious first phase of dating when everything was all sunshine and rainbows when I became pregnant. He was handsome and funny and smart, and we were totally into one another. When he proposed, I said yes without hesitation. It seemed the obvious solution, not because of optics or avoiding having a child out of wedlock, but in terms of providing our baby with a family."

"Were you in love?" Elizabeth set her glasses aside.

"Looking back now, it was infatuation and attraction." Brooke gave a feeble laugh. "We figured that out soon into our marriage, but we kept going for Rory. Then, he met Kali, and he realized what true love looked like, and it wasn't what we had. We talked, were open and honest with one another, and decided to end things. Even I could see what existed between them." She picked at her fingernail, unable to meet Elizabeth's gaze when she admitted the truth. "I've never experienced what they have." The silence stretched on so long, Brooke finally looked up.

"I see," Elizabeth said, after blinking a few times.

Nothing followed, and Brooke balked. That's it? She'd opened her heart and shared something vulnerable, and that was Elizabeth's only response? Sometimes she didn't know what to do with Elizabeth's closed demeanor. Enough about her own life. "What about you?"

"I've neither been married nor divorced."

Brooke softly laughed, only making Elizabeth frown. "Are you seeing anyone?"

"No." Elizabeth shook her head. "My last girlfriend got a job offer across the country and took it."

Girlfriend. Noted. Brooke schooled her features.

Elizabeth tucked her hair behind her ears. "I've gone on dates, but I haven't been involved seriously with anyone since."

Brooke wondered how long ago that'd been. She'd learned that treading carefully was the best way to approach Elizabeth. One wrong word, and she'd snap shut like a clam. Best not to ask for too many details and stick to the overarching picture. "You've never wanted to be married, never wanted kids?" Brooke sipped her coffee, hoping it'd be the perfect temperature and was pleased to find it was.

Elizabeth faltered, her mouth slightly open, like she'd been asked to explain the mechanics of flight. She softly cleared her throat before speaking. "Marriage, yes. I suppose I'd like that, someday. I've never been much of a kid person." She slid on her readers and turned to her laptop.

Snap. Any progress Brooke had made hacking her way inside had been resealed behind a seemingly impregnable wall right before her eyes. She wanted to give Elizabeth one of her own patented sighs.

Well, it was good to know where Elizabeth stood. Brooke didn't understand people like that. She avoided dating them, too. It remained one of her few non-negotiables. "Let's skip going to the library today, then."

"No." Elizabeth unscrewed the bottle top and popped two pills, dry swallowing them. "I mean, you already have a plan in place. There's no need to change it."

So, she minded being around Rory, or she didn't? Brooke's head spun. It'd be nice if she made up her mind.

"Oh, by the way," Elizabeth said, typing as she spoke, "I can't have an employee traipsing through the lobby with their laundry each week. Use my machines tomorrow evening instead." She waved her hand, as if it'd been decided and she'd already become bored by the topic. "The television, too. Do your movie night thing. You have a key."

Brooke gripped the edges of her chair, unable to keep up with the whiplash. Sure, she'd hauled multiple loads from her car last week because Rory couldn't carry a basket by herself. Francine had been at the front desk, and Brooke didn't recall any guests being present, so it's unlikely one had lodged a complaint. Elizabeth had just gone from saying she didn't like children to inviting Brooke and Rory to share her space. What was happening? Did she plan to be there? This woman was beyond confusing. "Um...okay. Thanks." It'd certainly be easier than going to the laundromat.

Brooke wished she knew more about what made Elizabeth tick. Had what she'd experienced as a child made her the way she was? Brooke tapped her lip with the pen. Elizabeth had lived in Calistoga before her parents died. Could Brooke learn more?

Curiosity piqued, she angled her laptop slightly away and opened a new browser tab. Then closed it. No, how wrong. Heat crept up her cheeks. It was a grievous invasion of Elizabeth's privacy. She had no right.

Then again, perhaps interacting with Elizabeth would be easier if Brooke knew more about her. She needed all the help she could get if she were to win Elizabeth over and convince her to keep the resort. It was in Brooke's best interest. And Rory's. She opened another tab and clicked into the search bar.

Brooke paused. What was she doing? It was beyond intrusive. She tucked her hands between her knees and stared at the blinking cursor. How would she feel if Elizabeth researched *her*? Brooke hadn't shared the issues with her dad. Would she feel betrayed if Elizabeth found out by sleuthing? She chewed her lower lip as she debated what to do.

Then there'd been the terrifying dream. What had made Elizabeth so upset she'd screamed? She was obviously hurting, and Brooke wasn't sure how to help her if she didn't know what was going on. If Elizabeth woke her by having another nightmare, Brooke might be able to better calm her if she understood what'd happened. Deciding it was best to be informed, though remorse already made her neck itch, she scooted her chair closer and typed her query.

Even though the accident had happened decades ago, it didn't take her long to find a newspaper mention and Elizabeth's parents' obituaries. Brooke leaned closer. She garnered few details from the article, except that the other driver, who also perished, had been a man from Solano County who'd been driving under the influence. Elizabeth's father had been pronounced dead at the scene, as had Elizabeth's grandmother, and her mother died en route to the hospital.

Then, she bit back a gasp. The obituary held the breath-stealing revelation. *"Surviving are their three daughters, Elizabeth, Caroline, and Annaliese."*

Elizabeth has sisters?

Brooke thought back, trying to recall Elizabeth's exact words when she'd told her about the foster home. She said there'd been multiple children, and it'd been a busy place. Funny she hadn't mentioned siblings, though. Or her grandmother also being in the car. Had she been Elizabeth's only grandparent? Why hadn't any family stepped in to raise the three orphans?

With a guilty glance Elizabeth's way, Brooke closed the tab and switched back to her inbox. A heavy mass lodged in the center of her chest. Learning more hadn't given her the satisfaction she'd hoped, and she certainly couldn't bring it up. It'd been a grave invasion of Elizabeth's privacy, so unlike her. Her desire to know Elizabeth better had gotten the best of her for a moment. Now that she'd committed the abhorrent act, she wished she could go back and reverse her decision.

"Why hasn't the resort switched to drought-tolerant or drought-resistant landscaping?"

Brooke jumped like a tween with a stolen candy bar stashed in her pocket.

Elizabeth pointed at her screen. "A xeriscape would save money on both irrigation and maintenance. Do you know how much it costs to water premises this size?"

Brooke put on her best smile. "Not offhand, but I could find out for you." She double-checked she'd closed the evidence of her meddling and stole another peek at Elizabeth. With her glasses and signature suit, she looked every bit the owner, the woman in command. The aura of power and the immaculate attire stirred something inside Brooke, something worth noting, but that wasn't what captivated her. She had a feeling the woman beneath the surface wasn't as put together as she appeared.

That's who interested her.

CHAPTER ELEVEN

Elizabeth sipped her cabernet in the library and skimmed the *San Francisco Chronicle* she'd found on a coffee table as she waited for Brooke to arrive after picking up Rory from her after-school program. Aside from her, the room remained empty, and she preferred it that way.

She'd wavered earlier when Brooke told her Rory would be joining them, and she'd considered making an excuse why she couldn't attend. Being around Rory, who was the same age Elizabeth had been when the accident happened, clawed at her. Every time she glanced up, it was like looking into a mirror and seeing the past. Her heart simply couldn't take it.

Yet, if she canceled, she'd miss her time—*game*, her game—with Brooke, and she'd come to enjoy it, even look forward to that hour of decompression. Plus, being around Brooke always seemed to put her in a lighter mood.

"Here we are. Sorry, we're late." Brooke rushed in, Rory behind her. "Oh, you already got wine. Bless you." She sat, letting her bag fall to her feet, and took a drink.

"Here." Rory held out a paper cup filled with wildflowers, some worse for the wear and hanging over the lip. "I picked these for you at school. I had to reach through the fence."

Elizabeth stared at them.

"So much talking," Brooke murmured, before using her normal voice. "I told her you didn't care for them, but she doesn't believe me."

Rory pushed them into Elizabeth's hands. "But they're so pretty."

Elizabeth tensed, taking the cup before water spilled on her, but it only contained the yellow and purple blooms. "It's not that I don't like them. Sometimes they smell strongly, and I don't care for that."

"Why don't you leave them in the library for other people to enjoy?" Brooke glanced between them, seemingly trying to please them both.

Elizabeth raised them to her nose. "These seem fine." She set them beside her glass. What had made Rory think of her? Should she have ordered Rory something to drink, too?

Rory beamed and skipped the short distance to her table.

"Okay, finish your math. Kali will be here soon."

"I know."

Brooke turned to Elizabeth. "Ready?"

Elizabeth nodded and moved her pawn. They'd only gotten in half a game before Brooke's phone vibrated.

Brooke glanced at it. "It's Ximena. Oh, no." She looked at Elizabeth and lowered her voice. "There's been a possible incident of sexual harassment involving one of the housekeeping staff. I need to deal with this."

"Shouldn't I come with you?" Elizabeth started to rise.

"No, that's what you pay me for. There are protocols in place you aren't aware of to handle this type of thing." Then, the weight of what she had to do hit her. "I hate to ask you…" She glanced at Rory. "Is there any way you could stay with her until Kali gets here? It should only be five to ten minutes. I'm sorry, I know—"

"It's fine." It wouldn't have been her first choice, but what other option was there? Rory couldn't very well go with Brooke and overhear whatever conversation she was about to have. Besides, Brooke's passing squeeze of her shoulder almost made it worth it. Elizabeth only hoped Brooke was as good at her job as she seemed to be. A lawsuit certainly wouldn't help entice potential buyers.

Brooke kissed Rory on the top of her head, then hugged her from behind. "I'll see you when you get back, baby." She hurried from the room.

While she waited, Elizabeth watched Rory. Instead of homework, she seemed more concerned with her braid that'd come undone.

"Shouldn't you finish those two problems before you go?" Elizabeth asked, glancing at the worksheet on the table.

"I have to fix this." Rory tried to secure it, but only succeeded in making more hair escape.

"You could just take it out," Elizabeth suggested.

Rory clenched her hands into fists at her sides. "I don't like it tickling my neck. I need my mom to fix it."

"She can't right now. Ask Kali to do it for you."

"She doesn't know how. Only Daddy does, and he'll already be there." Tears formed in Rory's eyes, but they didn't fall. Yet.

Oh, no. Elizabeth wasn't dealing with more crying. And so far, Rory had only shown frustration, but what would happen when it transpired into a full-blown meltdown? What story would Kali later tell Brooke about the state she'd found Rory in when she arrived? This wouldn't do. Elizabeth didn't need Brooke raising up like a mama bear on her hind legs again. "Bring your chair here."

Rory carried it over.

"Sit sideways. I'll fix it."

"Do you even know how?"

When Rory raised an eyebrow, she looked so much like Brooke that Elizabeth almost laughed. Instead, she sighed. "I used to. When I was younger."

"How do you know you'll still remember?" Rory craned her neck to look at her.

Elizabeth wondered the same. "I don't. Cross your fingers." She carefully turned Rory's head so she faced forward and finger combed up to where the plait remained intact.

"I can braid my friend Shayla's hair, but I can't do mine because I can't see what I'm doing. I used to do my friend Jaxon's, too, when his parents thought he was a girl. But when he got old enough, he told them they were wrong. His name used to be Jacqueline, and they asked him what he wanted to be called, so he picked Jaxon. And cut his hair really short."

Huh. Was it really that simple for kids? Adults could learn a thing or two. "Good for him." Elizabeth tried to concentrate on what she was doing amid Rory's chatter. Oddly enough, the motions came back to her, muscle memory moving her hands in ways she believed she'd forgotten. Rory's hair, so thin and fine, reminded her of Carly's. Where Elizabeth's had always been straight, Carly's had a tiny bit of natural curl like their mom's had. Was Carly's hair still like that? Elizabeth shook away the thought. This was not the time for pointless wondering.

She reached the end. "Do you have a hair tie?" She almost laughed when she caught sight of the royal blue band dangling off Rory's thumb, her index and middle fingers crossed. Ah, children, so literal.

Rory tentatively felt the back of her head. "It feels good. Wrap it around a bunch of times, so it doesn't come off."

Bossy, just like Brooke could be. Elizabeth caught herself smiling. "Yes, ma'am." She raked her nails up the sides just like her mom used to. "There you go."

With a spin on her bum, Rory looked at her. "Do you know how to do math, too?"

With a sigh and a nod, Elizabeth followed her to the other table. Brooke owed her big-time.

CHAPTER TWELVE

With Rory and Elizabeth occupied, Brooke had time to think as she folded the last of Rory's school uniform polo shirts and set the pile in the basket at her feet. On Elizabeth's television, Elsa and Anna surveyed the shipwreck scene in their search to find out what happened to their parents. At Margaret's old dining table, Elizabeth sat at her laptop, but her hands hovered above the keys, and she stared at the TV. Did watching a movie like *Frozen II* stir up emotions for someone whose parents had died? How old had Elizabeth said she'd been? Seven? No older than Rory, who sat on the floor between them.

What would Rory's life be like if an unfortunate tragedy happened to Brooke and Sean? Well, her parents—or at least her mom—could step in, not that it would be easy for her. Soon, legal rights would extend to Kali in such an event, too. Brooke had no doubt Sean's parents would also make sure Rory had a loving home. What about Brian? Would he raise his niece despite his own issues? Brooke liked to think so.

How had Elizabeth ended up in foster care? The thought made Brooke's heart ache. She looked at her again. "You wouldn't have to turn your neck if you sat on the couch." She moved the clean clothes she still needed to fold closer. "Why don't you come over here? Bring your work if you want."

Elizabeth hesitated. "I just finished. Let me close my tabs first." A minute later, she tentatively sat on the other end of the sofa and crossed her legs.

Brooke had worried about invading Elizabeth's space after her comment about kids, but Elizabeth had offered up her interim home. Brooke had been doubly surprised when she knocked, her master key card at the ready, and Elizabeth had been there. Brooke had been certain she'd find some excuse to leave her apartment tonight. Drinks in the bar, dinner out, errands to run. But no. And here she was, in the same room with them.

Elizabeth stared at Brooke's pile of unmatched socks.

"The last load is in the dryer. Thank you again." When Elizabeth didn't respond, she continued. "This is so much more comfortable. It's familiar here, you know?"

"Mom." Rory slumped and pointed at the film.

"Sorry." Brooke picked up the remote and turned on closed captions. "She doesn't like if I talk while it's playing. Afraid she'll miss something in a movie she's seen thirty-seven times. This allows both of us to enjoy it."

Elizabeth watched for a bit. "They're actually helpful. It allows me to catch things I'd probably miss."

Brooke watched her. It surprised her none. She'd noticed similarities in Elizabeth and Rory, their need for things to be a certain way. "Good." She ran her hand from Elizabeth's shoulder to her elbow, the briefest of touches, and this time, Elizabeth didn't tense or flinch.

Brooke enjoyed touching her. She even looked for excuses to do so. Not going out of her way, but in instances where bolstering support or giving encouragement seemed natural.

Rory turned, facing Elizabeth. "Are you coming to my game?"

"Game?" Elizabeth looked to Brooke.

"Lacrosse. You don't have to," Brooke hastily said, catching Rory's immediate frown out of the corner of her eye.

"When is it?"

Rory perked up. "Saturday at nine."

"You have a bye this week. Remember? It's a week from Saturday," Brooke said.

"Oh, yeah."

Elizabeth straightened. "I suppose I could use a dose of vitamin D. I've been spending too much time indoors."

"Oh." Did this mean she planned to stay longer than a few weeks? Or did she not want to decline in front of Rory? Brooke tried to imagine Elizabeth sitting in the stands at a children's sporting event. Brooke couldn't picture her clapping or cheering. She barely smiled. "All right. Would you like to ride with us?"

"That'd be fine." Elizabeth turned back to the show.

Brooke returned to the never-ending pile of Rory's clothing. How did one child wear so much in a week?

If Elizabeth legitimately planned to attend the game, it meant Brooke had that many more days to convince her to keep the resort. Additional days she desperately needed. When she glanced at Elizabeth again, Elizabeth watched her. "What?"

Elizabeth re-crossed her legs, still clad in the skirt suit she'd worn all day. "Do you mind talking work for a moment?"

"Not at all." Brooke tossed Rory's balled-up unicorn socks into the basket.

"I was reviewing last years' books today and noticed construction costs. What was that for?"

Brooke wracked her brain, switching quickly from mom-mode into general manager. "That was part of The Improvement Plan, or TIP, as Margaret and I nicknamed it."

Elizabeth slowly nodded. "Yes, I've seen that a few times. What is it?"

"When I came on, I analyzed how the resort was being run, what was working and what wasn't, and what was needed. I devised a list of things we could do to expand, market, or revitalize in some way." She finished folding a pair of shorts and turned her body toward Elizabeth. "Margaret approved most of them, and I've been implementing them this past year. The construction was for the new outdoor bar that serves the hot springs area. It's more convenient, and it limits guests trekking through the resort barefoot in swimwear to get a drink. That posed a slipping hazard, and generally didn't provide a good look for the rest of the guests." She leaned an arm on the back cushion. "Hiring an outdoor bartender wasn't much of a cost difference than a server would've been to take and run orders outside. The plans didn't need to be very involved, so I sketched what I had in mind, and we had it built to code."

"You did all that?" Elizabeth's eyebrows rose.

"Mm-hmm." Brooke watched her process it. "I've worked with the contractor before. She understood exactly what we wanted."

"Tell me more." Elizabeth leaned back and folded her hands in her lap, looking ready to conduct a job interview.

It might as well have been. Brooke tempered her nerves. "Well, I increased marketing efforts to book the conference center. Funds needed to be redirected at groups, organizations, and events that would thrive in a small-to-medium-sized space. Now it's scheduled ninety percent or more of the time." She tapped her finger against her lip. "The small room off the gym used to be used for storage. Now we partner with a studio in St. Helena and offer yoga classes every morning that are well-attended."

Elizabeth spun her watch in an absentminded manner. "I had no idea."

"Oh, there's more." Brooke smiled. "If you've ever been up early, sixty to seventy visitors pour off buses every morning and fill the restaurant. I worked with three different hot air balloon companies to incorporate a buffet breakfast into their pricing." She wanted to puff out her chest at its success. "Their clients love it. They rise before dawn and work up an appetite, so the meal is extremely popular. It gives them time to reminisce after the excursion and come down from their adrenaline rush."

Elizabeth's mouth had fallen slightly open.

Brooke stared at Rory and tried to recall additional upgrades. "What else?" She jerked her thumb toward the window. "Oh, I contracted with the Freshelli Family, the nearest winery, to lease the acres of vineyards behind the property in exchange for supplying the resort with a certain number of cases each year. Plus, Freshelli now offers tastings on weekend afternoons in the otherwise-vacant space off the lobby that really serves no purpose. It's proved to be a hit with visitors *and* the locals, which I hadn't anticipated." She smiled. "Those are the big ones."

"I can't believe you made all those improvements, and in that short of time." Elizabeth's eyes widened, and she shifted in her seat. "I thought you managed the staff."

Brooke shrugged and gave her a bright smile. "I do a bit of everything. It's what's needed in a position like mine. A little over a year ago, Margaret reached a point in her age and health where she could no longer do it on her own. I was happy to step in and help." The dryer buzzed. "Be right back." She left Elizabeth with a mystified look on her face.

When she returned with the warm load of fresh towels, her space on the couch had shrunk. Had Elizabeth moved closer? Maybe she'd just readjusted. Wearing her work clothing was probably uncomfortable. "You're not a fan of loungewear?" She motioned to her own jogger sweats and long-sleeved T-shirt.

"I am." Elizabeth looked down at her own outfit.

Was that a blush? "Don't be formal on our account. Rory's already in her pajamas."

Rory twisted around and popped up, showing off her bubble gum pink set covered in butterflies. "Look, they have pockets." As proof, she pinched the fabric at her hips and held it out. "And a big one here." She slid her hands into the material over her tummy.

So many words. A month ago, Brooke would've been thrilled to get that many from her in a week.

Elizabeth frowned. "Why do you need pockets at night?

Rory mirrored her expression. "I don't know. Snacks?"

Elizabeth laughed, a low, pleasing rumble that left Brooke wishing Rory would say something to make her do it again. Leave it to the two of them to have a discussion over something so strange.

Apparently done with the conversation, Rory flopped on the floor again.

"You have until these are folded, then it's bedtime." Brooke had learned to give her fair warning.

"But the movie won't be over." As anticipated, Rory's lower lip jutted out.

"We'll finish tomorrow. I'm sure Elizabeth has things to do."

"Actually," Elizabeth said, "I wouldn't mind seeing how it ends, if it won't keep her up too long."

Brooke looked between the two of them, their pleading eyes too much to deny. "I…Fine."

Elizabeth stood. "Would it be possible to pause it for two minutes while I change?"

Rory jumped up. "I'll do it." She retrieved the remote as Elizabeth disappeared into her bedroom.

True to her word, Elizabeth returned quickly, and Rory resumed the film. Brooke glanced at Elizabeth's matching black yoga pants and hoodie as she folded washcloths. She'd also added slippers to the ensemble.

"Better?"

Elizabeth turned. "Much."

"You know, as the owner, if you want to dress less formally, you can." Brooke reached for a hand towel, enjoying the warmth on her lap as she folded it. "I basically wear the same uniform as our front desk personnel most days. Margaret preferred jogger suits. Unless you're more comfortable, mentally, I mean, in your skirt suits."

Elizabeth smoothed her hand over the fabric on her thigh. "I didn't bring much else."

"I can take you to St. Helena or give you recommendations where to go. There are wonderful shops downtown." Brooke didn't want to presume Elizabeth wanted to spend more time with her outside of work.

"Perhaps after the game? If you're free."

Well, Brooke hadn't been expecting that. "Of course. Rory will be going to her dad's afterward."

Elizabeth nodded. "It's a da—let's plan on it then." She tucked her hair behind her ear, then rested her hand on Brooke's elbow, the first time Brooke could remember her initiating the touch. "Your changes…they'll be helpful when I put the property up for sale."

Brooke pulled away. Damnit. Instead of Elizabeth seeing the improvements and wanting to keep the resort, Brooke had given her ammunition for when she put it on the market. Which was exactly what it sounded like she planned to do. How soon would Brooke be looking for a place for Rory and her to live? Within the month? How far away would she end up to afford it? Vallejo? Fairfield? The commute would be atrocious. Highway 29 was a nightmare. And they'd be that much farther away from Sean and Kali and Rory's grandparents. Would what Brooke saved on housing be spent on fuel? She finished folding the last towel, laying it atop the pile.

"Did I upset you?" Elizabeth studied her.

Lying about her thoughts was Brooke's first inclination, but why not tell the truth? Maybe she could appeal to Elizabeth's heart—not that Brooke was sure she had one—with her predicament. "It got me thinking about how Rory and I will need to move when that happens. I went down the rabbit hole concerning where and what it'll mean in terms of work and her family."

"I see."

Elizabeth grew quiet, staring at the TV, but Brooke wondered how much she absorbed based on the far-away look in her eyes.

After a few minutes, Elizabeth turned. "It's not like I want that to happen." She raised her hands, then let them fall. "I don't mean to sound ungrateful, but this place fell into my lap, and I need to make a decision." She shifted toward her. "I considered retirement, but I don't know what I'd do. I love my job, and I'm good at it. And I can't see myself being an absentee owner, not with my personality and so much at stake. My home and life are in San Jose, not here." She rubbed her arms. "And, as you witnessed by the nightmare, this area stirs up memories I'd rather not revisit."

"Of the accident?" Brooke asked, before her mouth caught up with her brain. It wasn't her business.

Elizabeth glanced at Rory. "Perhaps we can talk about it after she goes to bed."

"Sure." Bedtime didn't take as long as it used to when Rory was younger, but Brooke still read to her every night. "I'll need fifteen or twenty minutes."

"That'll give me time to get us wine from downstairs, if you'd like some."

Brooke nodded. "That'd be nice. We'll need to move to my apartment." She made a back-and-forth motion. "I'm not comfortable leaving her over there when I'm here."

"Obviously." Elizabeth returned her attention to the show.

Oh, God. Brooke's heart raced. Elizabeth would be coming to her apartment. Breakfast dishes sat in the sink, and Rory's dirty lacrosse gear was probably still by the door where she always shed it after practice. The science fair project Rory had been working on was spread out on one end of the table and her art caddy sat on the other. Gabby's Dollhouse playset and all its accoutrements covered most of the living room floor.

If Brooke made an excuse to take the laundry over early, she'd have time to clean up, but leaving Elizabeth to watch Rory didn't feel right. She'd done it once, and while it seemed to go fine based on how she heard Elizabeth had fixed Rory's braid and helped her with math, Brooke didn't want a repeat. She needed to respect Elizabeth's attitude toward children. The messy apartment would have to remain as is. But how was she supposed to present herself as a competent, capable general manager of a thriving resort if her home life was a disaster? She crossed her fingers it'd give a homey, lived-in look.

Chapter Thirteen

In the resort's bar, Elizabeth added a bottle of Brooke's favorite wine—and hers now, too—to her account. When she arrived at Brooke's apartment, propped open by a shoe as Brooke said it'd be, she took a step inside and came to an abrupt halt. Something covered every surface. A paper mâché volcano, coloring books, art supplies, dishes, clothing, a half-eaten granola bar, toys, and more. The hairs at the base of her neck stood on end.

With a deep breath, she picked her way through the debris toward the kitchen. Then, she let her shoulders relax. Brooke, a single mom, appeared to be juggling all of Rory's activities, joint custody, and work, among probable other things that she hadn't shared with Elizabeth. Perhaps Elizabeth should cut her some slack.

By the time she'd poured two glasses to let them breathe, Brooke emerged from Rory's room, gently closing the door behind her.

Rory. What had inspired Elizabeth to volunteer to go to her lacrosse game where there'd be not one child, but *children* present? She couldn't even blame alcohol. It was like she'd become possessed by her ESPN-watching alter ego. Even the WNBA didn't interest her, and it must've been pure luck she hadn't had her lesbian card revoked for that offense. While adroit in many subjects, her knowledge of athletics rivaled that of people who used the term *sportsball*. What did one even wear to such a function? She drew the line at wearing faux team costumes—or whatever they were called—like many fans.

"Oh, that looks delightful," Brooke said, spotting their drinks. "Shall we sit?" She plucked a jacket from the couch and hung it on a hook by the door. "Sorry. Life gets hectic." With her foot, she moved aside the toys on the rug. "I've found making Rory put away her dollhouse after she's worked to get it the way she wants upsets her more than it's worth." She sat beside Elizabeth. "When you have a child with ASD, you pick your battles."

"ASD?" Elizabeth handed Brooke a glass.

Brooke tucked her legs beneath her. "Autism Spectrum Disorder. She was diagnosed in kindergarten. Her teacher noticed some signs, and at his suggestion, we got her tested. She's high-functioning, so we—Sean and I—had simply thought her meltdowns were due to her age, or her need to have everything just so part of her personality. Although, I suppose in a way, it is."

"So, Asperger's then." Elizabeth couldn't look away as Brooke ran her fingers through her hair, untangling it at the ends.

"They don't call it that anymore, but essentially, yes."

"It's quite prevalent in Silicon Valley." Elizabeth took her first sip. Delightful.

"I've heard that." Brooke rested her head against the cushions. "I'd been a stay-at-home mom, but when we filed for divorce, I had to go back to work. I'd done this before, prior to having Rory, so that was fine. But suddenly Sean and I were running back-and-forth to meet with school personnel about her Individualized Education Plan or with a mediator to resolve our mess. I was frazzled and needed a place for us to live. My aunt assigned me this position, and Margaret offered me the apartment soon after. I'm not sure what I would've done otherwise."

"You're employed by your aunt?" This was news.

Something crossed Brooke's features. "My aunt and my dad. They formed the company decades ago. Both my brother and I worked there, at least until I had Rory and Brian moved away." She stared at the far wall, her glass midway to her lips.

Elizabeth cleared her throat, and Brooke appeared to shake whatever'd had a hold on her.

"Sorry. My dad…"

Brooke trailed off and seemed to compose herself before she resumed.

"He was diagnosed with dementia a few years ago. It's progressed rather quickly, so my aunt has been running the business by herself."

Elizabeth wasn't sure how to respond. It obviously troubled Brooke. "Will you or your brother have to take over for him?"

Brooke turned to her. "I'd rather be out in the field, like this"—she motioned with her hand—"not locked up in an office all day." She stiffened. "And Brian couldn't handle seeing my dad's condition, so he left."

"Leaving you and your mom to deal with everything." A spark of anger flared despite Elizabeth having no horse in the race.

"I don't mind." Brooke's voice climbed a bit too high to be believable. "They're my family. But I couldn't ask more of my parents, not at that time. My aunt had already given me a job. I don't know what I would've done had Margaret not stepped in."

"Your dad's memory issues…how bad are they?"

"Poor enough that he hasn't recognized me in over a year." Her eyes grew shiny, and she quickly picked up her drink.

Elizabeth had never been good in situations like this. She awkwardly reached over and rubbed Brooke's leg.

Brooke caught her hand and held it.

Elizabeth couldn't breathe. Her pulse skyrocketed. Was she having a panic attack? She wanted to pull away, and yet, she didn't. The softness of Brooke's skin, the warmth of her, kept her from doing so.

"Thanks," Brooke said quietly. After a bit, she looked up from where she'd been studying their clasped hands. "You said you wanted to wait until Rory went to bed before talking about your nightmare."

Oh, that. Elizabeth didn't know if she was ready for it even now. She took a deep breath. "You asked if it'd been about the accident." Her dream came rushing back, dragging all the emotions along with it. "And no, it wasn't, but tangentially related, I guess."

"Do you want to talk about it?"

She didn't, at least, not ordinarily. Yet, here she was, about to open her mouth and divulge something she'd never spoken about outside of therapy. "It was about my sisters."

Brooke nodded, not appearing surprised. "Before you go any further, please don't be angry. I admit I googled you after you mentioned you were from here and your parents died in an accident. Their obituaries mentioned the three of you." Her cheeks pinked. "I just wanted to get to know you better."

"You…you looked me up on the internet?" Elizabeth pulled her hand away, her muscles tensing. "You had no right." Had Brooke's digging been a penchant for drama or like she'd said? Either way, it left Elizabeth feeling vulnerable in a way she hadn't experienced in some time. "Why would you do something like that?" She set her drink on the coffee table and stood.

Brooke rose and caught her sleeve. "I wanted to help you, especially if you had another bad dream, and didn't know how. Being back has obviously upset you, and I thought if I had more information, I might be able to—I don't know—do something. I shouldn't have. I'm so sorry. I don't know what came over me."

"That doesn't make it right." Elizabeth didn't pull away even though she wanted to walk out the door. She needed to know exactly what Brooke had learned first.

"No, it doesn't. I'm so sorry. Please don't leave."

Brooke's eyes held regret, and her apology appeared heartfelt. She hadn't been obliged to tell Elizabeth, but she had. That counted for something. Elizabeth sighed and sat, and Brooke followed. "You didn't find out anything else?"

"Just their names."

Elizabeth nodded, suddenly feeling the shakiness in her confidence. Maybe she couldn't do this after all. "It's a long story." Something in Brooke's gaze made her relax, and the way Brooke gave her time and didn't fill the silence with talk, also helped. Elizabeth stared at a spot on the rug. "When they died, my grandmother was in the car, too." When she glanced up, Brooke gave a small nod. "They'd gone to pick up my grandfather's ashes. He'd passed away from a heart attack the week before. My mom never knew her dad, and her mother refused to talk about him or tell her who he was. And she, my maternal grandmother, died from breast cancer right before my mom finished high school." Elizabeth paused a moment, preparing herself. "My parents had no siblings. I had a great-uncle who lived in Germany, but he was older and had no interest in taking on three children he'd never met. So, when the accident happened, there was no one left."

Brooke rested her hand on Elizabeth's leg.

"We temporarily stayed with my father's best friend Nicholas, an attorney, until the court decided what to do with us. The three of us cried ourselves to sleep in his small guest room, all in one bed, for…I don't know…too many nights in a row." She gave a feeble-sounding laugh. "I begged him to keep us, to be our new dad. He explained how he couldn't because he wanted to be a judge and worked too much to have kids. I wept for days trying to convince him. I insisted I'd do everything—take care of my sisters, feed them, get them dressed, play with them. He refused."

"Oh, love, you were only seven." Brooke covered her heart with her hand. "You poor darling."

The understanding in Brooke's eyes bolstered Elizabeth's confidence enough to continue. "One day, a car pulled up and a couple emerged. Apparently, they were adopting Carly and Annie and taking my sisters to live with them. The adults decided not to tell us beforehand." Elizabeth couldn't help it. Hot tears streaked down her face, and she dashed them away.

"You don't have to continue if it's too difficult." Brooke rubbed Elizabeth's knuckles with her thumb.

"Just give me a…" With a deep breath, Elizabeth wiped her face. "Nicholas later told me the couple couldn't have kids of their own and wanted the experience of raising young children. They must've been in their early twenties, and apparently, the husband insisted they couldn't afford more than two kids. As the oldest, I was out." Her vision went hazy as the memories transported her back to that day. How she'd watched her sisters dragged away from her. Forever.

A strangled sound escaped.

"Come here." Brooke wrapped her arms around her. "How awful, how absolutely awful." She held Elizabeth tightly.

For the first time in her life since her parents died, Elizabeth allowed someone to comfort her. And when she began to cry, it came out not as a meager trickling of tears, but as great heaving sobs, and Brooke's soft voice cracked the wall of stone that had been holding everything back.

"That's it. You're safe here." With a gentle rocking motion, she murmured more tender words, and Elizabeth couldn't seem to stop, to find the off switch.

After a few minutes, and when her hiccupping subsided, she tried to pull away. "I'm getting your shirt wet."

"It's okay." Brooke didn't let go. "It's okay." She trailed her fingers through Elizabeth's hair.

So, Elizabeth allowed herself to relax, to let the teary episode resolve itself. Against Brooke, with her warmth and compassion, it came easily. Accepting her comfort didn't bring the horror and humiliation Elizabeth had expected it would. Instead, the emotions she'd bottled up for so long flew free. A weight lifted. Sharing the story with Brooke seemed to take her pain and break the enormous chunk that had choked her for so long into manageable pieces, something even therapy hadn't accomplished. With that realization, she closed her eyes and didn't rush the moment.

Bruises would mark Elizabeth's skin where his fingers dug into her flesh. He lifted her off the ground, his arms wrapped around her chest. All she could move were her legs, so she kicked as hard as she could, though it did little good.

In the distance, the car grew smaller. She thrashed and screamed, but she couldn't draw in enough air, couldn't breathe.

"Elizabeth. Elizabeth, wake up." Brooke shook her.

The feeling of being restrained faded with Brooke's soothing caresses up and down her back. After a moment of clearing her mind and realizing where she was, Elizabeth opened her eyes. At some point, they'd reclined on the couch, and she'd rested her head on Brooke's chest. She couldn't have been dreaming long. At least she hadn't grown sweaty.

Brooke squeezed the arm lightly wrapped around Elizabeth's shoulders. "Another nightmare?" Her eyes held empathy and perhaps something else, but Elizabeth was too tense to analyze it right now.

Elizabeth sat up and rubbed her face. "The same one." She glanced at where their legs had been entwined moments ago. "Did I kick you?"

"No." Brooke also moved into a sitting position. "It was more like violent twitching." She patted the cushion beside her. "Come closer and tell me about it. Maybe talking will dispel some of its terror."

After a beat, Elizabeth scooted beside her. Discussing emotions and the past meant treading into unfamiliar, rarely visited territory. "It's always the same."

"What is?" Brooke leaned her elbow on the back of the sofa, seeming to settle in.

"The dream. I'm on a street—an actual one here in Calistoga. I happened upon it on my walk the other evening. I think that's what's triggered these episodes again." She tucked her hair behind her ear as she sorted her thoughts. "It's where his house used to be. Judge Bartoletti."

"The one Tiffany mentioned?"

Elizabeth nodded. "He wasn't one back then, just an attorney with his eyes on the bench. We were there. Me and my sisters. That's where Carly and Annie's adopted parents picked them up. The adults barely gave us time to say good-bye." She bit her tongue to hold back her tears. "They quickly packed them into the back seat and drove away, not even bothering to take all their belongings. I ran after them, screaming and crying. Nicholas caught me and held me back. He lifted me off the ground, and all I could do was thrash my legs. I fought until I couldn't see the taillights anymore."

Brooke caressed Elizabeth's cheek. "When I think of that happening to Rory…I wouldn't be able to sleep soundly either." Her eyes shone with unshed tears. "What can I do for you?"

"This." Elizabeth covered Brooke's hand with hers and momentarily closed her eyes. "It's comforting. It helps."

After a bit, Brooke shifted. "Come. It's late, and my bed is more comfortable than this couch."

Elizabeth followed her, too wrung out to decline. Once inside Brooke's room, she glanced around. The small lamp illuminated an unmade bed, but a space less messy than the rest of the house. It sported the same bland shade of paint that covered the walls of both apartments, but Brooke had brightened it with colorful throw pillows and vibrant photos of hot air balloons in flight over lush green vineyards. "These are beautiful." Elizabeth paused before each one, studying it.

"I snapped those right after we moved in using Francine's camera. I took an elective class in college and really enjoyed it." She tossed a T-shirt and shorts to Elizabeth, then turned away and pulled her top over her head.

Elizabeth spun, facing the photographs again. Was she supposed to strip right here, too?

"I haven't had any time since then to get out again." The lamp switched off. "You can change in the bathroom if you want." The mattress made a sound as it accepted Brooke's weight.

More confident now she wasn't in a spotlight, Elizabeth undressed and pulled on the clothing Brooke had given her. She moved to the side with the unrumpled cover and climbed in. As her eyes adjusted to the dark, she realized Brooke faced her. Had she watched her disrobe? Had she been able to see anything? Elizabeth's skin tingled. Did she mind if Brooke had?

Brooke looked almost angelic the way her curls cascaded over the pillow. She'd allowed Elizabeth to cry, to grieve, and she'd graciously offered empathy and kindness in the process.

They stayed like that, looking at one another, for a long while. Elizabeth tried to recall if she'd ever allowed herself to be vulnerable with someone in such a manner, not necessarily regarding her childhood, but anything meaningful. Certainly not her foster parents. And in hindsight, her romantic relationships had been rather superficial.

Elizabeth shifted closer and rested her hand on Brooke's cheek. Thoughts she'd so far left unacknowledged danced between them, weighted yet ephemeral, and before they could dissolve into the ether, she whispered, "I've never met anyone like you."

Brooke's expression changed into one of pleasant surprise. If anything could've shoved old memories back into the past for Elizabeth, that would do it.

She traced Brooke's lower lip with her thumb, and Brooke shivered. "I'd very much like to kiss you right now."

Brooke's slow but brilliant smile gave her the go ahead.

Perhaps exhaustion from the nightmare led to her disregard for the consequences. Elizabeth closed her eyes and bridged the distance between them without allowing time for second-guessing.

Bliss.

That's the only way she could think to describe what Brooke's mouth felt like against hers. The warmth, the silkiness, the way they fit together so perfectly. They started slow and tentative, feeling out one another, finding a pace.

And then Brooke took it up a notch when she slipped her tongue past Elizabeth's lips.

Where Elizabeth usually would've been the one leading a situation like this, she didn't mind letting Brooke control what happened next. Was her desire to seek comfort this way a result of her terrible dream?

Without pulling away, Brooke pushed up, rolling Elizabeth onto her back. Their kiss only grew hungrier and more intense as Brooke settled some of her weight onto her.

Elizabeth pulled her closer, eager to feel more of her. Brooke was softer than Elizabeth, curvy compared to her own lean form. She'd first admired Brooke's attractive shape the day she'd arrived.

Arrived.

My God. She was kissing the resort's general manager.

Elizabeth broke away, gasping for air. Not only that, but Brooke had a child who reminded her far too much of herself. And Elizabeth had a home in the South Bay she'd be leaving for as soon as she sold. She had no business doing this and never should've allowed it to happen. With a heavy heart, she slid from under Brooke and climbed out of bed.

"What is it?" Even in the darkness, Brooke's concern marked her beautiful features. "Did I do something wrong?"

"No." Elizabeth grabbed her clothing. "It was a mistake. *I* made a mistake." She headed for the door. "I'm sorry."

"Me, too," Brooke said quietly as Elizabeth left.

When Elizabeth let herself into her apartment, she shook away the chill despite it not being cold. It was Brooke's warmth she missed, Brooke's body atop hers. The way she kissed Elizabeth like she'd been wanting to for weeks. Had she? A warmth blossomed in Elizabeth's chest. She hadn't let herself imagine Brooke might return the interest she held in *her*.

Elizabeth slid beneath her covers. Tearing herself away from their embrace had been one of the more challenging things she'd done in life, and that said a lot. It'd been wonderful having Brooke reciprocate. Too bad it wasn't meant to be.

That didn't mean she couldn't relive that short moment of pure exhilaration, remember the softness of Brooke's lips and the way her own body had responded. She'd savor it now while she could, because it would likely be awkward in the morning when she had to face Brooke again.

CHAPTER FOURTEEN

Despite the early hour, Brooke rode the elevator down to the restaurant to see if she could purchase a pastry or muffin. Insomnia had tormented her again, so even though dawn had yet to break, she'd already showered, dressed, and now headed to the ground floor. Rory would be excited to wake to a sweet treat.

After their disastrous kiss two nights ago, she and Elizabeth had tiptoed around one another most of yesterday. Brooke had grasped for a way to break the tension between them, but her efforts proved futile. Stilted conversation and weak excuses to leave the office on both their parts hadn't helped. Elizabeth had claimed a headache and forgone their chess hour, and whether it was true or an excuse, Brooke had no idea. Neither had brought up *that* night, and Brooke wasn't sure what she would've said if the subject had been broached. Sure, she was her usual buoyant and confident self, but even an empowered women could feel the sting of another bolting from her bed.

Ordinarily, she tended to be quite astute when it came to understanding those close to her. Interpersonal skills were important, especially in her job. Yet, she hadn't seen Elizabeth's abrupt departure coming, though in hindsight, it shouldn't have surprised her. She hadn't known Elizabeth long enough to read her accurately.

Brooke entered the restaurant kitchen, and the warm scent of cinnamon greeted her.

Jade, one of the two pastry chefs, slid a tray of cookies into an oven. "Perfect timing. The turnovers came out a few minutes ago." She pointed to the speed rack. "Is that what you're here for?"

"It is." Brooke pulled out a room charge slip from where Chef Sophie kept them near the expediting window. "I'll take two." Her pen hovered above the paper. "No, make it three." She scribbled her room number and signature.

When she looked up, Jade handed her the box of pastries with a smile. "Enjoy. Tell Rory to have fun at school today."

"Thanks. I will." Brooke returned to the elevator. Normally, she didn't leave Rory alone unsupervised, but now that she could read, Brooke left her a note in case she woke in the less than five minutes it'd taken to complete her mission. There were perks to living here, including an occasional delicious breakfast she didn't have to make that smelled like warm apples. She'd let Rory sleep a bit longer, then she'd need to get her up and on the bus.

When the doors opened on her floor, Brooke jumped. Elizabeth stood before her.

"Oh." Elizabeth took a step back.

She wore her usual skirt suit, a dark green one Brooke hadn't seen before. Brooke would've remembered. The color, the cut, the length—it looked amazing on her, and Brooke remembered they had plans to go clothes shopping. Or had. Would Elizabeth still want to now? She stepped out with a smile. "Good morning. You're up early."

Elizabeth nodded. "I couldn't sleep." She motioned to her apartment. "I saw the hot air balloons for the first time. They're incredible. I figured I'd find something to eat and watch them before I began my day."

Brooke lifted the box she held. "I brought a turnover for you. Care to join us for breakfast? We have a great view. They try to put down in the field to the east, though sometimes they miss." She had a hundred stories of random places chase crews had to pick up balloonists when the wind didn't cooperate, but now wasn't the time.

"Are you sure I'm not intruding?"

Brooke keyed into her apartment. "Rory will be thrilled." So was she, but she kept that to herself. The tension in her shoulders eased upon knowing Elizabeth seemed open to spending time together. "Would you mind starting a pot of coffee while I wake her? Everything's on the counter."

While Elizabeth did that, Brooke pushed open Rory's door and sat on the side of her bed. A heavy sleeper, Rory looked like she hadn't budged since Brooke had tucked her in. Brooke smoothed back the hairs on her forehead. "Rise and shine, sleepyhead. I have a surprise for you."

Rory opened her eyes but didn't move. "What kind?"

"Two, actually." Brooke rubbed her arm, hoping it'd help her awaken. "One to eat, and someone to eat it with."

With a squeak, Rory popped up, eyes bright. "Who?"

Brooke rose, allowing Rory to slide out. "Go see, but brush your teeth first."

Grumbling followed Rory to the bathroom as Brooke went to the kitchenette. A wonderful aroma and gurgling indicated Elizabeth had found what she needed. After two sleepless nights, *Brooke* certainly needed the caffeine a cup or two provided.

Elizabeth stood looking out the picture window. Two balloons had landed with another seven in the process of descending.

"If you watch them from outside some morning, you can hear the whoosh of the burners and the people talking." She stopped beside Elizabeth. Vans drove into the grassy field and began loading passengers.

"I've never been up in one." Elizabeth cleared her throat. "I have an unfortunate fear of heights."

"I'm sorry." Brooke turned. "I haven't either but not because of that. I've just never found the time." She plated the pastries.

Elizabeth joined her. "Those riders will go to the restaurant now?"

"Mm-hmm. It's a great buffet. If you want to try it sometime, just tell Chef Sophie the evening before so she has accurate numbers."

Rory emerged from the bathroom, and she'd taken her hair from the braid she'd slept in. The kinky strands added volume, making her look like a musician in the Muppets' band. Her eyes lit up when she saw Elizabeth. "Hi."

"Hello."

Rory slid into her seat at the table. "You sit here." She pointed to the chair beside her. "I didn't know you were my surprise."

Elizabeth's gaze darted to Brooke.

"I told her she had two—one to eat and someone to eat it with." Brooke handed them each a turnover.

Rory quieted as she peeled apart the flaky layers to get to the filling, and Brooke set a steaming mug in front of Elizabeth.

"Thank you."

She ate daintily, as if getting a crumb on her suit might necessitate a wardrobe change. Knowing what Brooke knew of her, it might. Brooke's gaze dropped to her lips as Elizabeth blew across the top of her beverage. Their softness had been gently pressed against hers. And then not-so-gently. Warmth flooded her, and she tried to ignore it. It obviously wasn't meant to be, and she needed to forget it.

"I've been wondering." Elizabeth wiped her fingers on her napkin. "What do the hot air ballooners do after they eat?"

Brooke stirred more creamer into her mug. "When everyone's finished, they're taken by van back to their pickup spots, normally a parking lot or the company's office."

"With so many people to feed and some eating faster than others, there must be a lot of waiting around."

"I suppose there is. You know how it is with all-you-can-eat food. Some people never want to leave. The drivers hurry them along if there are dawdlers." The conversation seemed headed somewhere, and she wasn't sure of the direction. "Those who've finished chat at their tables or wait in the lobby. A few wander outside for a cigarette."

Elizabeth looked toward the window where the rising sun created a dappled effect on the rows of vines. "What if we offered coffee and muffins or something like this early in the mornings"— she pointed to what was left of the baked good on her plate—"at the time they normally meet their groups? Five thirty or whatever. The ballooners could park here. The resort has the space, and then those ready wouldn't feel trapped afterward. Without as many people hanging around waiting, it'd give the restaurant more time to clean and transition to lunch, too."

Brooke considered it. "So, the riders leave their cars here, quickly enjoy a pastry and coffee to tide them over, then they're taken to their launch sites, go on their excursion, and return for a real breakfast at nine." She smiled, picturing it. "That's not a bad idea. Let me come up with a cost analysis. If it's feasible, I can offer the service to the balloon companies. They'll be saving fuel since they'll be transporting their riders shorter distances. Even if they all don't agree to it at first, seeing it in action may change their minds."

"One of the pastry chefs is always here that early," Elizabeth said as Rory fussed with her hair that'd only seemed to grow wilder. "It wouldn't take much additional staffing to make seventy muffins. They could even be prepped the night before. Tray the pastries and brew a few large urns of coffee. I'm thinking something like a fifteen-minute window. Riders can grab a cup and a bite to eat, and once a van's occupants have all arrived, off they go."

Rory huffed, trying to push her hair from her face without using her greasy, sugar-coated hands. "I need help."

With a smile, Brooke rose. "One braid or two today?"

"One, but can Elizabeth do it? She's the bestest braider." Rory looked between them. "Don't tell Daddy."

Brooke laughed. "The *best*. Don't worry about offending your poor mom, though." She retrieved a hair tie and a comb from her purse. "Let's let Elizabeth eat. Turn around, love." She wanted to save Elizabeth from having to decline.

"Actually, I'm finished."

Their gazes met. "You sure?" Brooke tried to read her expression.

Elizabeth simply plucked the rubber band from Brooke's hand. "Scoot your chair over here."

Rory sat sideways on it in front of her, and Brooke wondered if that's how Elizabeth had asked her to sit in the library. It certainly made it easier.

"And do the scratchy thing."

"Of course."

Brooke wanted to ask what that meant, but she kept quiet. Watching them gave her an odd sensation, one she couldn't quite put her finger on.

Elizabeth worked quickly. When she reached the end, she secured it, then raked her fingernails up the sides, making Rory hum.

"That's the best part."

Elizabeth softly smiled, but it appeared bittersweet. "I used to think so, too."

Brooke's heart gave a small twinge at her tender tone. "Did your mom used to do that for you?"

"Long ago," Elizabeth said quietly, as she took her dishes to the sink. "I should get to work."

It didn't surprise Brooke that she'd want to make a quick exit when things turned personal. But it gave Brooke little hope for discussing the kiss they'd shared. "And someone needs to get dressed if she's going to make the school bus," she said, giving Rory a gentle push toward her room.

"That was…enjoyable." Elizabeth motioned toward the table. "Breakfast."

"It was." Brooke walked her to the door. "I'll follow up on your idea when I get downstairs." Conversation between them might still be stilted, but at least Elizabeth was leaving in a manner that didn't include bolting from Brooke's bed.

As pleasant as the morning had been, by midafternoon, Brooke wanted to rest her head on her desk. She'd been running around all day, attending to the usual things that cropped up, tasks she'd planned to tick off her list, and had spoken with Chef Sophie and both pastry chefs about having ballooners meet at the resort for a muffin and coffee before their excursions. They'd brought up good points, like how some people would prefer decaf and others tea, so hot water would also need to be available. Muffin batter could be prepped the prior evening and simply scooped and baked. Sophie suggested finding a gluten-free, nut-free, vegan recipe to accommodate as many people's allergies as possible. All in all, it wasn't a complex setup, and everyone seemed to find it a good idea.

Including Brooke. Elizabeth had impressed her with the way she'd analyzed a situation she'd only barely witnessed and suggested a sound improvement. Brooke was slightly annoyed she hadn't thought of it first. She excelled at such things, one of the reasons she'd been successful in this position. Elizabeth tended to be against anything that might cost money, but Brooke believed they could pass the expense along to the balloon companies after she explained how they'd save on fuel and wages since they could start later.

She snuck a look at Elizabeth, who sat primly in her chair, legs crossed. The heels she'd removed lay sideways beneath her desk. Did her feet hurt? Even more reason for Brooke to take her shopping for more casual attire.

"Since you don't seem to be concentrating on whatever you're doing," Elizabeth glanced at her, "I want to talk about another idea."

Busted. Brooke cleared her throat. "Okay. What is it?"

"Regardless of whether I keep or sell the property, I want to install a water feature across from the entry in memory of Margaret."

Brooke hadn't been expecting that. She smiled. "That's a lovely idea. Like a fountain?"

Elizabeth nodded, spinning in her chair to face her. "Yes, with a plaque memorializing her."

At this angle, Brooke couldn't help but admire Elizabeth's legs. Maybe buying new clothing was a poor idea if it meant they'd be hidden. She knew Elizabeth took long walks, and it showed. She snapped out of her inopportune daydreaming when her gaze reached the hem of Elizabeth's skirt. "I'll look into it, get some bids."

With a wave of her hand, Elizabeth shook her head. "I wasn't tasking you with it, simply informing you of my plan." She fiddled with her thumb as she seemed to struggle with whatever she had to say. "You're an integral part of this operation, and I value your input and opinion."

Brooke leaned back, not expecting the compliment. "That means a lot, but I'm happy to help." She smiled. "That's what I'm here for. I know you're trying to sort out the finances and learn everything."

Elizabeth turned to her laptop. "Which reminds me. I'm staying longer. As you know, I only planned to be here a few weeks, but I'm nowhere near comfortable deciding the future of this place. I informed my boss first thing this morning."

Like after they'd had breakfast? Had the fact they'd been able to interact in a semi-normal manner played a part in Elizabeth's decision? "I'm glad to hear that. Do you have a timeframe in mind?"

Elizabeth scowled. "Why? Do you need Margaret's apartment for something?"

"Of course not." Brooke rose and leaned on the edge of Elizabeth's desk. "You're the owner. You can do whatever you want."

"I'll be here through the summer to witness the resort operating during its busiest season. My meeting with the accountant brought things to my attention I was unaware of. I need more time to get a better understanding of what's going on before I make my decision."

"Oh." Brooke hadn't been expecting that. She wanted to jump for joy. It'd give her that many more months to convince Elizabeth to keep the place. "Your employer didn't mind?"

"I've taken a sabbatical."

"Mom, look."

Brooke spun to find Rory and Sean in the doorway. Rory held a cup of dandelions. "Hi, baby. What're you doing here?"

Sean pulled off his cap and ran his fingers through his hair, just slightly darker than Rory's and curling over his ears. He needed a cut, but it was no longer Brooke's place to remind him.

"We discussed this last week. The after-school program is zip-lining today, and you didn't want her to go. But I have an appointment in Sonoma and can't watch her."

She'd forgotten. Would there ever be at time when she wouldn't be juggling a hundred different things at once? "It's not that I didn't want her to go. I want to be present the first time to make sure it's safe, and it's not ideal for me to be absent from work right now." She caught Elizabeth watching her. "Sorry. Elizabeth, this is Rory's dad, Sean. Sean, this is Elizabeth. She owns the resort."

"Pleased to put a face to the name." He extended his hand. "I've heard so much about you."

Elizabeth looked at Brooke.

Brooke held up her hands. "Not from me."

Sean squeezed Rory's shoulder and mimed a talking mouth with his hand. "Is this happening around you, too?"

Rory rolled her eyes and moved from under his touch. "I'm not little. I know you're talking about me." She held out the paper cup of yellow flowers to Elizabeth. "I picked these for you."

Oh, no. More weeds. Brooke rapidly sought a way to rectify a situation that could turn sour any second. But before she could open her mouth, Elizabeth took them, albeit cautiously, like they might be harboring a murder hornet.

"Oh." Elizabeth blushed. "Okay." She set them on the very edge of her desk.

Rory beamed and did a happy little dance.

That had gone better than Brooke would've expected.

"I'm sorry, but I gotta go." Sean said. "You'll figure something out?"

Brooke had no idea. "Sure. Yes. I'm sorry it slipped my mind."

"Third time this month." He shook his head. "Nice meeting you." He looked from Elizabeth to Rory. "Can I have a hug?"

Rory wrapped her arms around his waist, and he leaned to kiss the top of her head. "If you have questions on math, just save 'em. I'll help you tonight when your mom drops you off."

"I can ask Elizabeth. She knows how."

Sean looked between Elizabeth and Brooke. "Okay, well, yeah. Okay. See you later, little bug." He left with a wave.

Brooke helped Rory shrug out of her backpack. "Let me send this email, and then I'll take the rest of the afternoon off." She turned to Elizabeth. "I'm sorry I forgot to put this on my calendar. Normally, I'd never leave on such short notice unless it was an emergency."

Elizabeth stood and addressed Rory. "Do you have worksheets or something?"

Rory looked up at her. "Only spelling and math."

"What about coloring books?"

Rory smiled. "Yep. Two. They're in my backpack. Did you know they have stickers in them?"

"I…did not." Elizabeth glanced at her watch, then turned to Brooke. "I suggest that you finish up whatever you need to do while Rory does her homework. And yes, I can help with math if she needs it." She pulled out the small table that Rory had used before. "When we're all finished, perhaps we can have a game of chess. And if you don't have dinner plans, there's a place I've been told to try." She looked at Brooke. "If you're interested."

Brooke smiled, unsure at the turn the afternoon had taken, but not displeased with the result. "We happen to be free." She laughed. "Actually, let me check my calendar. The way things have been going lately…" After pulling up the screen, she turned to Elizabeth with a smile. "No commitments."

Elizabeth returned to her desk. "Good. I've heard positive things about the place."

As Rory settled into her homework routine, Brooke leaned toward Elizabeth. "I really am sorry. It's just," she said quietly, "it's not an irrational fear, but she's my baby, and I didn't want her flying through the forest if I wasn't there the first time to assess whether the staff pay attention to safety matters." She looked down. "I know having my child at work like this isn't professional."

"Stop." Elizabeth's sharp word had Rory glancing back at them.

Brooke froze, too. Was this the beginning of a reprimand? Would apartment hunting be in her near future?

Elizabeth leaned in. "I wouldn't condone this across the board, but she's proven to be well-behaved, and her presence doesn't appear to affect your ability to work. She's welcome here whenever you need." She stared at a spot somewhere behind Brooke. "The mention of my mom this morning had me thinking. I'd give anything to go back and steal a few moments with her." She straightened and rolled her chair back a few inches. "Don't take time with your daughter for granted. We never know what's around the corner."

Brooke nodded and looked at Rory, hoping no tragedy would befall herself or Sean, at least until Rory was grown. She couldn't imagine that scenario.

"What are these for?" Elizabeth whispered.

Brooke turned to find her pointing at the primitive butter-yellow bouquet. She smiled and said quietly, "That's her way of saying she likes you."

Elizabeth's eyebrows rose, and she paled. "Oh."

Unfortunately, Brooke couldn't decipher what the single word signified, but she didn't spend too much time dwelling on it. She hit send on her email and began to search for landscaping firms and artists specializing in water features. Her daughter was happy, she was pleased, and Elizabeth seemed to be—well, content. At least for the time being. Brooke would take it. It was almost enough to allow her to stop fixating on that mind-blowing kiss.

CHAPTER FIFTEEN

In the library, Elizabeth admired how the late afternoon sun shined through the grape leaves outside while Brooke studied the chessboard. Across from them, Rory colored while humming a song that sounded vaguely familiar. Maybe it'd been in that movie they'd watched.

Finally, Brooke took her turn, exactly the move Elizabeth had hoped she'd make. "Checkmate. Again." Elizabeth couldn't help but gloat a little. The game had come back to her easily, and she found it odd Brooke continued to play with her when she never won. Maybe Elizabeth should throw her a game. Although, that'd be easier said than done with the competitive streak she'd always had.

"One more?" Brooke reset the pieces.

"If you're up for it." Elizabeth reached for her nonexistent wine glass, then stopped herself. She'd opted to forego it since she'd be driving them to dinner soon.

Brooke's phone vibrated, and she picked it up. "Not again." She typed a quick response but didn't put it down.

Elizabeth finished setting up the game.

"I need to assist Francine. There's an issue with a reservation, and Ximena is busy."

"Do you want me to go? Technically, you're off the clock." Elizabeth admired how Brooke gave the resort her all, but she didn't want to take advantage of her either.

"It's easier if I handle it." Brooke glanced between her and Rory. "Would you like me to take her with me?"

"That's probably not advisable if you need to deal with a guest. She can stay." It wouldn't have been her first choice, but Elizabeth appreciated being asked.

Brooke touched Rory's back. "Be good. I won't be long."

Elizabeth took out her phone. She'd catch up on emails until Brooke returned. After reading a few, she glanced over to find Rory watching her. Or rather, staring at the chessboard. Since she'd already finished her homework and moved on to leisure activities, Brooke wouldn't mind if Elizabeth taught her a bit about the game, right? She'd learned at Rory's age, if not earlier. "Do you want to play? I'll show you how."

With a dimpled smile so much like Brooke's genuine one, Rory slid from her seat and into the one Brooke had vacated. "I know how everything moves."

"Oh." Elizabeth should've figured. She seemed like a smart girl and quickly applied the tips Elizabeth had given her in math. "All right, then. What color would you like to be?"

"White."

Elizabeth spun the board.

Rory moved her king pawn up two spaces.

Elizabeth stopped it with hers.

Then Rory moved again, and Elizabeth countered. Rory took her turn, and so did she, with Elizabeth now using both her knights to combat Rory's last moves. They'd worked quickly, with her mimicking Rory's fast pace. She usually spent more time considering her strategies.

Rory moved her queen. "Checkmate."

"What?" Elizabeth leaned forward and surveyed the board. They'd each only moved—what? Four times? How could it be possible?

"It's okay," Rory said, flopping back in the chair. "It happens to a lot of people I play. Well, not a lot. The person you're playing has to make certain moves for it to happen. Did you know you can beat someone at chess with two moves? It's called Fools Mate because you're a fool if you fall for it."

Elizabeth wasn't feeling far off. She had yet to drag her eyes from the game. Clearly, there was a way out of this she wasn't seeing.

"Don't feel bad." Rory rested her arms on the table and her chin atop them, her eyes barely visible above her still-upright king. "I've been playing for years. I'm in the after-school chess club."

That didn't make Elizabeth feel any better. She'd just been drubbed by a seven-year-old. Her cheeks heated.

"Oh, no." Brooke stood over them with a huge smile. "Rory. You didn't."

Rory shrugged. "It just happened."

Elizabeth glared at Brooke. "When did you plan to tell me your daughter was a chess prodigy?"

Brooke laughed and tugged Rory from her chair. She sat and pulled her onto her lap. "I figured you'd find out eventually."

Calistoga had excellent schools, but giving kids this kind of instruction, in extracurriculars no less, seemed above and beyond. "Do all the kids they teach become this good?" Elizabeth hoped Brooke wouldn't want to play another game. She needed time to lick her wounds.

"They didn't teach me. Mom did." Rory leaned her head against Brooke's shoulder.

Elizabeth eyed the two of them with narrowed eyes. Something was fishy. "Your mom, who has never beaten me, taught you how to play like that?"

Rory's face pinched. "She says she's not losing on purpose, but I don't believe her."

"No," Elizabeth said, holding eye contact with Brooke. "I don't either." She rose. "I think she owes us for being dishonest. Don't you?"

Small creases formed at the corners of Brooke's eyes.

"I think she should have to buy dessert."

That had Rory off Brooke's lap, jumping in place. "Yes."

At that moment, with the way Brooke was studying her, the only treat Elizabeth wanted was to be back in bed with Brooke's mouth on hers. But she wasn't going down that road again. "I'm going to change." Elizabeth picked up her phone. "Shall we meet in the lobby in ten minutes? We need to take your car because…" She motioned to Rory.

"Yes, her booster seat." Brooke stood. "Gather your things, love."

Rory began to pack her belongings.

"What should we wear?" Brooke asked, turning.

Elizabeth, who had moved to leave, almost ran into her. Off-balance, she wrapped her arms around Brooke to keep from falling.

In her embrace, Brooke's cheeks pinked, and her gaze dropped to Elizabeth's lips, only inches from hers.

Was Brooke thinking the same thing she was? About the last time they'd been this close, and how she wished she hadn't cut their kiss short? Elizabeth pulled away. "Sorry. Um, casual. Jeans or something." She allowed herself a quick peek at Brooke's mouth, tinted the faintest coral from lipstick she'd applied earlier in the day. "Is ten minutes enough time to undress and…you know, dress?" For crying out loud. Elizabeth rarely had trouble speaking, yet fumbled for words. Now all she could think about was Brooke in a clothing-less state, and try as she might, she couldn't shake it.

"I thought we were going." Rory looked up at them, gripping the straps of her backpack she now wore.

Brooke took a step back, looking a bit dazed. "Six fifteen. Lobby. We'll be there."

Elizabeth watched them leave. Would *she* be able to pull herself together in that short amount of time? She wasn't sure. Elizabeth didn't know what had inspired her to suggest dinner. Dessert though? That'd be on Brooke. Elizabeth shook her head. What'd she been so preoccupied with that she hadn't considered that Brooke might've been letting her win? An uneasy inkling of the answer grew inside her, but she wasn't going there.

Assess. Sell. Go home. The plan remained the same.

Upstairs in her bedroom, Elizabeth tucked her cell between her chin and her shoulder to better ransack her closet and drawers, looking for something to wear.

"You did what?"

Elizabeth put the phone on speaker to protect her eardrum from Geoff's high-pitched screech. "Take it easy."

"My boss and best friend decides to disappear for the entire summer, and I find out from Leo? You owe me the time to vent, Elizabeth."

"If you're worried about your Labor Day trip, I'll return before then."

Geoff sighed. "I don't know if we're going this year. Lawrence and Isaac are having troubles. It's you I'm concerned about. I thought you'd be itching to get back by now."

"I should've told you first. I'm sorry." Elizabeth pulled on her least-dressy pair of pants. "I needed to let him know right away, and I didn't want to call you in the middle of your workday."

He was quiet a moment. "Something else is going on. What aren't you telling me?"

"Nothing. I need to go. I don't want to keep Brooke wait—" She held her breath, not intending to let that slip.

"You don't want to keep a woman waiting." His tone held amusement. "Is she hot?"

"No. Yes. I mean, her daughter's coming, too."

Geoff chuckled. "You're taking out an attractive woman *and* her child? Who are you, and what aren't you telling me, Bettancourt?"

"Nothing." Had her voice squeaked? "She's the general manager of the resort."

"Oh, it gets even better. A forbidden romance. No wonder you're acting strangely. You've got an acute case of *the feelings*." He couldn't disguise his glee. "Do you need me to overnight a cure? I know a fantastic compound pharmacy."

"Hush, you. She's not actually my employee," Elizabeth said, slipping on her shoes. "And it's just dinner."

"Yeah, sure. Because you frantically rush around worried about what you're going to wear to ordinary meals with others."

She double checked she hadn't been video chatting while she'd gotten half naked. Did he have a hidden camera?

"Maybe you *should* be receptive to a little something-something with her."

His suggestion froze her in place. Should she? She liked Brooke, obviously enough for Geoff to pick up on it, but there were a dozen reasons she couldn't. "No. No, there's no future with her."

He didn't respond right away. "You know best, but I wouldn't mind seeing you happy."

She scoffed. Who was he to judge her emotional state? She was doing just fine in that department. "I'm perfectly content with my life as it is." Wasn't she?

"If you say so." He paused a moment. "I miss you around here, you know."

Elizabeth let her shoulders relax, pleased he'd let her *feelings* or whatever for Brooke go, at least for now. "Well, I don't *not* miss you." He remained the only person she could truly call a friend.

The sound of his laughter rang in her ears even after the call ended.

Fifteen minutes later, outside the St. Helena roadside food stand both Dashiell and Francine had insisted she absolutely had to try, Elizabeth followed Rory and Brooke to a picnic table. Brooke carried their food while she followed with their drinks.

"One falafel salad," Brooke said, setting it in front of Elizabeth. "And chicken tenders for you." She pushed the tray toward Rory, who sat beside Elizabeth. Brooke settled across from them, inspecting her kimchi burger. "I haven't had one of these in ages."

Elizabeth plucked a sweet potato fry from where Brooke had placed them for the three of them to share. She looked around. The sun dipped behind the Mayacamas Mountains separating Napa Valley from Sonoma, but its warmth remained, and a slight breeze made for a lovely evening to eat outdoors, as evidenced by the crowd. They'd been lucky to get a table and ate the fantastic food without speaking for several minutes.

"I already know what I want for dessert." Rory dipped a bite into barbecue sauce. "I'm getting an Oreo shake."

"Let's see how much room you have when you've finished your dinner." Brooke reached for a fry at the same time as Elizabeth, and when they touched, they both yanked their hands back as though they'd been burned.

"You promised." Rory wasn't about to be dissuaded. "For not telling the truth."

Brooke leaned forward. "I need you to understand there's a difference between me wanting Elizabeth to feel good about herself so she'd want to keep playing chess with me and outright lying."

"But you didn't say so when I asked you." Rory said.

Brooke rolled her eyes, with Rory's attention on her food again. "You're right. I should have. But just because I messed up doesn't mean I don't expect honesty from you."

"I know. Did you know there's a thing called lying by a mission?"

"Omission. And yes." With a sigh, Brooke opened her wallet and handed Rory some cash. "Can you order by yourself?"

Rory spun out of her seat and dashed toward the order window, a "yeah" trailing behind her.

"Kids." Brooke shook her head as she watched Rory go, then turned her attention to Elizabeth. "So, I've been wondering. Have you've ever tried to find your sisters?"

Elizabeth hadn't been expecting the topic, and she choked on the bite she was swallowing. When she'd recovered, she shook her head. "The State of California seals adoptions, and I don't know their surname."

"Have you ever considered a DNA test? There are a few genealogical sites that help connect relatives."

Elizabeth appreciated Brooke hadn't mentioned her sisters with Rory around. For some reason, she didn't want Rory to know the story. "No. Definitely not." She swirled her cup of iced tea. "They're grown and surely have families of their own. They've probably forgotten about me. I don't think showing up after all this time would be the best idea, even if a match were found."

"How can you say that? You're their flesh and blood."

"I could just as easily be an unwanted intrusion into their busy lives they didn't ask for." Elizabeth took a now-tasteless bite, hoping Brooke would drop the line of questioning. She pushed her food away, her appetite having fled.

"What if they have children?" Brooke leaned closer. "Aren't you curious whether they might look like you or your parents?"

Would they? Dizziness threatened. It was too much. "Let it go." Elizabeth didn't want to think about it, any of it. "Please."

Brooke had the decency to look sheepish. "Sorry. Not my place."

Elizabeth's thoughts ran rampant as Brooke finished her burger. A change of subject was in order. "Why *did* you let me win all those games?"

"You know." Brooke smiled, then winked at her.

Elizabeth shifted on the bench. "No, not really." She craned her neck to see the front of the line, looking for Rory.

"Don't worry. I can see her." Brooke stood, gathering their garbage. "I told the truth," she said, stopping beside Elizabeth. "I wanted to spend time with you."

With a shake of her head, Elizabeth looked up at her. "We share an office every day."

"Not like that." Brooke swept her hair over her shoulder, looking simply stunning in her short-sleeved sweater and cropped jeans. "Socially. Time when you relax and let your guard down a bit. I enjoyed our sessions and knew you're competitive, so I let you win knowing you might not want to continue if you lost. Unlike my daughter, who goes for the jugular"—she picked up the tray and leaned close to Elizabeth's ear and whispered—"I prefer to play the long game, Ms. Bettancourt."

Goose bumps sprang up on her arms, and Elizabeth sat transfixed as Brooke walked toward the waste receptacles. Either the falafels had been a poor choice, or something else was happening inside her. The unfamiliar sensation puzzled her, but it wasn't entirely unwelcome. Worrisome more than anything.

CHAPTER SIXTEEN

A few days later, Brooke stood in the port cochere's shade and watched the crew dig up the earth in front of the resort. She'd sacrificed a row of hydrangeas for Margaret's monument, but Margaret had never liked them anyway, always complaining about their toxicity.

"Make sure there's none of that fake blue-green water in this fountain. Tell them to spare no expense. UV light, chemicals, whatever it takes."

Interesting. Brooke hadn't heard Elizabeth come up beside her and certainly hadn't been expecting that. "Of course. Have you thought about what you want the plaque to say?"

Elizabeth watched the workers for a moment. "A general idea, but perhaps you could help me refine it. You have a way with words."

What made her say that? "I don't have Rory tonight. Would that work?"

"Oh."

Elizabeth turned to face her, the wind lightly blowing her hair back and making her look like a model mid-photoshoot. Brooke refrained from pulling out her phone and taking a picture.

"I didn't mean you had to spend time outside of work doing it."

"I don't mind," Brooke said, with a nudge to Elizabeth's shoulder. "Perhaps after I beat you at chess."

"You never know. I might win." Elizabeth crossed her arms. "Even if you've stopped toying with me." She narrowed her eyes. "Or you better have. I want my victories to be honest ones."

"Cross my heart," Brooke said. "I swear on Rory's well-being." She didn't like talking about such things, but she needed Elizabeth to know the truth. And honestly, Elizabeth was a talented player in her own right. She'd be a force if she learned to show more vulnerability and sacrifice more pieces. However, that seemed neither her strategy nor her personality. Maintain, retreat, barricade. That seemed to describe Elizabeth's philosophy in general.

Elizabeth turned toward the building.

"Oh, no. Wait." Brooke pressed her hand to her forehead. "I can't tonight. I'm staying with my dad for a few hours so my mom can attend her support group."

"How do you manage it all?" Elizabeth slid her hands into her pockets.

"All what?"

"Raising Rory, getting her to and from school and her afternoon program, taking her to practices and games, all those meetings with teachers and stuff, doctor's appointments, helping your parents out. When do you ever get time for you?" Elizabeth leaned closer. "You're a great mom. I've seen you in action, but you never prioritize yourself."

Brooke laughed. "It's not like that with a child." In the light, Elizabeth's eyes glinted like silver. "They're helpless, at least at first. Dependent upon you." Something crossed Elizabeth's expression, fleeting, then gone before Brooke could decipher it. "I'm her mom, and these things need to happen. It's not a much different strategy than during a chess game. Many moving parts but one goal. I want her to have a vibrant childhood, a decent education, and try activities that will give her social interaction with her peers and help her find hobbies or even a profession she likes. My needs are secondary."

"Are there professional female lacrosse players?" Elizabeth raised an eyebrow.

Brooke shrugged. "Maybe in ten years, there will be."

"What time are you going?"

"My mom needs to be there by seven thirty, so by six forty-five."

Elizabeth blinked rapidly, tucking her blowing hair behind her ears. "How's this? I'll ask Sophie if she'll make us sandwiches, or

I'll order something from the menu to go. And I'll come with you to keep you company." She grimaced. "Unless you think that'd upset your dad."

"Not at all." Brooke touched her arm. "It'd be nice to have you there. Visitors brighten his days, at least after the initial frustration in determining whether he should recognize them passes. But be prepared for anything."

"I survived the thrown-away crayons, so..." A small smile flickered across Elizabeth's lips.

Had she made a joke? "Yes, you did quite well, in fact." They began walking toward the entrance, stopping to let one of the valets pass with a BMW.

"Does your dad play chess?"

"He used to," Brooke said, as they made their way inside. "That's how I learned. We stopped when we both became busy, him with work, and me with Rory and then the resort. And honestly, since his initial decline, we've played memory games with him almost entirely."

"Maybe you should try."

Brooke considered the possibility. "I could see how it goes, and if he's frustrated or can't remember the rules, we can transition to something else." She laughed. "If you ever do play him, though, be prepared to lose." Her dad was cutthroat. Brooke hadn't bested him until she'd turned fourteen. Within seconds, her good mood slipped away like the sun behind a cloud. It seemed a lifetime ago.

In the lobby, a loud voice drew her attention to the reception desk. A man slapped the counter, and Francine tried to calm him. Brooke picked up her pace, crossing the space between them in a handful of strides. "What seems to be the problem?" she asked, slipping beside Francine.

Francine shot her a grateful look.

"I come here every year, and all I want is an early check-in, but she refuses to give it to me." Redness had crept up his face and neck, and sweat stains peeked from his underarm area.

"Sir, check in time is two o'clock. We don't have a room for you yet, but we'll be happy to hold your bags for you while you visit a winery or see some of the valley's sights. Our concierge would be happy to help you find something." She motioned to Nik at the far end.

"I don't want my luggage sitting somewhere unattended. I have valuable things in there. I want to unpack and change."

Brooke inhaled. "I'm sorry. Until housekeeping has a chance to clean, that's not possible. We can text you when your room is ready, though."

"You imbeciles. This is fucking ridiculous." He slapped the surface again, the noise reverberating throughout the lobby. "Do you know who I am? Do you women know how much money—"

"That'll be all."

Brooke had felt—or was it sensed?—Elizabeth behind her before she spoke.

"I'm afraid we don't have a room for you. Period." Elizabeth came shoulder to shoulder with Brooke, and Francine slid from her stool, took her cane, and went to stand by Nik. "I won't have anyone talking to my staff like that. I wish you luck finding a reservation at another establishment, especially this weekend."

Tingles ran up Brooke's spine. This unexpected side of Elizabeth thrilled and excited her.

"Hey, this bitch—"

"No." The sharpness of Elizabeth's response stopped him mid-sentence. "If that was the start of an apology, your attempt is severely lacking. You're no longer welcome here, now or in the future."

Brooke glanced at the windows for signs of frost. Elizabeth's tone had taken on an icy quality.

"Hey, lady, I didn't mean—"

"Will you need help getting your bags to your car?" Elizabeth stepped out and reached for one, as though she'd personally do it. "My security staff would be—"

The man grabbed the handle, yanking it closer. "You just wait. I'll be leaving you a nasty review on TripAdvisor." He shot angry looks at all of them before striding out, luggage in tow.

Brooke moved to stand beside Elizabeth, who seemed intent on watching him until he drove away. "That was impressive."

"Hm?" Elizabeth looked at her. "He was rude."

"It happens though. It's not the first or last time." Brooke could tell stories. "Although, he was particularly nasty."

"Hitting things is one step away from landing blows on a person. Even without that threat, you didn't deserve his verbal abuse. Neither did Francine." Elizabeth laid a hand on the small of Brooke's back. "I know you can handle yourself, but I'd like to be the type of owner who cares for her employees, like Margaret did." Elizabeth got a faraway look in her eyes and dropped her hand. "Even if it's temporary."

Brooke didn't know how to respond to that, and the wind left her sails. The unknown, or rather the high probability she'd be out of a job and home come end of summer, was beginning to exhaust her.

"Thank you, Elizabeth," Francine said, settling on her stool once again. "Do you still want to shadow me tomorrow morning?"

"Yes. Six sharp." Elizabeth turned and went into their office.

"She wants to learn the front desk?" Brooke raised her eyebrows.

Francine shrugged. "I guess so. She said she used to do it years ago and should be able to pick it up again quickly."

"But why?"

"Told me she wants to play a larger role in the day-to-day running of the place." Francine smiled. "But don't worry. She likes you, based on what just occurred. Your job is probably safe."

For now. "She was standing up for you, too."

"Uh-uh. I didn't get no lower back massage." Francine winked at her.

There had been that. Brooke had wanted to lean into Elizabeth's touch, her warmth, even despite the arctic tone Elizabeth had adopted when speaking to that man. Granted, her usual voice wasn't dripping with honey, but Lord, it could've turned Francine's latte covertly tucked under the counter into a frozen treat. Brooke fanned herself as she went to her office. Why did she find that so hot?

When Brooke reached the lobby that evening, Elizabeth waited for her with an enormous brown bag featuring the restaurant's logo.

"Dinner?"

Elizabeth held it up. "Chef Sophie's special grilled chicken sandwiches, chips, and side salads. I got enough for your mom and dad, too."

They'd finished eating around five thirty. "That was kind of you to think about them. My mom said she fed him already, but they can enjoy it tomorrow. Ready?"

When they arrived at her parents' not long after, her mom waited for them, her purse and keys in hand. They were early, so it likely meant she'd had a difficult day and needed the break more than usual.

"Mom, this is Elizabeth. Elizabeth, my mother, Marion Staley. That's my dad, Jack, over there."

"Pleasure to meet you, dear. I'm so glad you came." After hugs for both her and Elizabeth, her mom ushered them into the living room. "Jack, the girls are here. I'm going now." She turned to Brooke. "I left some cookies on the counter. He might want one or two later. And help yourselves. Thank you both for keeping him company." With a flurry of blown kisses, she hurried to the garage.

Elizabeth looked at Brooke. "I'll put this in the kitchen and join you in a second."

"Sounds good." Brooke deposited her purse on a chair and went to say hello to her dad. He lounged in his recliner, legs up, watching an underwater nature show. A school of sardines swirled on the screen. "Hi, Daddy. It's Brooke." She gave him a one-armed hug and kneeled beside him. "How are you doing today?"

He stared at her. "You're taking care of me while Marion is gone?" His bushy eyebrows pinched together.

"I am." She rubbed his arm. "We'll spend time together like we do every week." She motioned toward Elizabeth, who'd come into the room. "I brought my friend Elizabeth with me. I thought we might play a game of chess, if you're up for it when your program finishes."

Elizabeth bent, making eye contact with him. "Hello, Mr. Staley."

"Jack," he said.

"Okay. Jack." She gave him a nod, then stood. "Nice to meet you."

"Do you play?"

Elizabeth hesitated a moment. "I do."

When he said no more, Brooke stood. "Are you hungry, Daddy?"

"I ate dinner."

"Okay. We'll be right over here." She took Elizabeth's arm. "Come, let's eat."

With their meal spread on the table between them, Brooke circled back to their earlier conversation. "So, Margaret's plaque. What are you thinking?"

Elizabeth finished her bite of sandwich. "Something about how she had a big heart. Maybe a line describing how she saw things in people, potential, and encouraged them."

Brooke took out her phone and typed a few notes. "That's a good start. What about a quick history of her role within the valley, what year she started the resort, and how many decades she ran it?"

"That'd be good." Elizabeth opened a bag of salt-and-pepper-flavored chips, Brooke's absolute favorite, and set it between them.

Had she known? Brooke had munched on them in the office once or twice when she hadn't had time for a proper lunch. Was Elizabeth that observant? Regardless, it was a blessing how she'd made sure Brooke had a decent dinner tonight. Without her, she'd be snacking on the cookies her mother had baked. Beyond that, though, Elizabeth had come along to keep her company. Well, there was this business of Margaret's memorial, but they really could've done that at any point. Tonight seemed more about spending time together, and Brooke buzzed a little at the thought.

Elizabeth stopped eating. "I'm not sure if you know the extent of what Margaret did for me. She helped me study for standardized tests and apply for scholarships and to college. When I finished high school, she made me a deal. If I maintained at least a 3.25 grade point average, she'd pay for any remaining tuition and expenses that weren't covered."

"How generous. And did you?" Brooke wasn't surprised Margaret would've made Elizabeth an offer like that.

Elizabeth nodded. "I graduated magna cum laude and paid her back within three years."

"I can see that," Brooke said, suddenly proud of both her and Margaret. "Was repayment part of the deal?"

"No, but of course, I did." Elizabeth straightened. "I was also thinking about interring her ashes behind the plaque. Nothing involving any fanfare. I know she wouldn't want that. Maybe just you and me. But I think she'd like to remain in the place she loved so much."

Brooke smiled, thinking of Margaret and how much joy the resort had brought her. "That's a wonderful idea." She took a few more notes, then turned her attention back to her food after glancing over to make sure her dad was fine.

He looked content, his gaze following an octopus across the screen.

As she chewed, her thoughts strayed to her mom. She wished she could give her more help. But her mother insisted on doing everything, including helping her father dress and use the bathroom. How long could this go on? It was only going to get worse. Tears threatened out of nowhere, and she quickly tried to blink them away.

Elizabeth reached over and held her hand without speaking.

Brooke savored the soft, warm comfort of Elizabeth's fingers around hers as they finished eating in silence. It was more than that, though. Elizabeth's presence tonight also gave her a sense of solace. Elizabeth didn't have to enter this turbulent situation that made even Brooke's own brother uncomfortable, yet she'd volunteered. Similarly, she didn't need to learn the reception desk, but she was trying there, too. Was she, little by little, seeing more of the world around her and showing that through her caring? Brooke hoped so. And she hoped that she'd perhaps played a small part in it.

CHAPTER SEVENTEEN

Elizabeth crossed her legs on the resort's poolside chaise lounge and adjusted her wide-brimmed hat to block the afternoon sun. Beside her, Brooke contemplated a move on the plastic chess set they'd brought down, while in the water, Rory dove for brightly colored weighted rings.

Out of nowhere, a thought hit her, raising goose bumps on her skin. "When does summer vacation start?" Elizabeth hadn't considered Rory would be out of school for three months when she'd told Brooke she didn't mind her being in the office.

"Not for a few weeks." Brooke glanced up. "And then, she attends a day camp over the break until three, when Sean picks her up. He either takes her home with him, or he drops her off to hang out until I get off work. That is, unless she has swimming lessons or gymnastics." Brooke grinned. "Don't panic. She won't be hounding you all day."

"I wasn't—I mean..." Elizabeth sighed. Brooke had her number. "Okay."

How Brooke kept track of everything bewildered her. Although, she didn't always. Elizabeth lost count of the instances when Sean had to make a trip over with Rory's favorite shirt or jeans for the next day or Brooke needed to take Rory's homework folder to his house because it'd been forgotten. That, and opting for relaxation were the main reasons she and Brooke hadn't made it to St. Helena yet. Which was fine. Elizabeth wasn't a fan of shopping and was used to her suits. An excursion alone with Brooke would be nice, though. But life with a child seemed hectic. Sometimes, Brooke would schedule a game of chess with Elizabeth and forget she had Rory that evening. It never ended up being a big deal. Rory contented herself with coloring or playing the occasional match with Elizabeth if Brooke got called away for an issue, and when they took the board outside, she'd splash and swim near them in the shallow end of the pool.

The last was the most stressful, like today. Elizabeth was sure Brooke kept an eye on her, but Elizabeth still scanned the water for Rory's bright blue swimsuit and fluorescent green goggles at least once every twenty seconds. The worry exhausted her. She planned to investigate the cost of hiring a lifeguard.

"I can see her," Brooke said, taking her turn.

Elizabeth glared at the rook she'd just lost. "Aren't you afraid you'll forget for a few minutes, and something will happen?" She made her own move.

"I'm paying attention." Brooke captured her knight.

So much for this game going well. Elizabeth sighed and glanced at Rory, again, then studied the board.

Brooke pushed Elizabeth's plastic wineglass toward her with a finger on its base. "Take a drink and relax."

She did the former, but the latter was easier said than done. How did people manage with children? Kids came with no hard shells, spikes, or magical force fields. They existed as soft underbellies susceptible to all kinds of unmentionable dangers. How did parents ever think they could protect them?

An image of her sisters flashed in her mind, the last visual she'd had of them in the back seat of the car, Carly sobbing, her arms tight around Annie. Elizabeth grew dizzy and broke out in a sweat just thinking about it. She gave herself a shake and took her turn, a dumb move that cost her another pawn. Oh well, this game hadn't been destined to be a win in her column, anyway. She found Rory again. Were her shoulders pink? "Is she wearing sunscreen?"

"SPF seventy." Brooke grinned. "Waterproof. Good for an hour. Satisfied?"

Elizabeth made a noncommittal grunt so she wouldn't have to share her real thoughts on the subject.

Even now, with Brooke surely annoyed by Elizabeth's constant worries, she managed to be cheerful. The optimism Elizabeth had once found irritating didn't bother her as much anymore. It intrigued her how Brooke had a different way of looking at things, and to Elizabeth's consternation, she was often right. And Elizabeth had begun to look forward to Brooke's bright greeting each day and her smile that lit up the room.

While Brooke studied the chessboard, Elizabeth checked on Rory, then surveyed the outdoor area. She'd miss it when she went home. Laps in the pool had become her favorite early-morning pastime, and she enjoyed soaking in the hot springs under the stars. She warmed, remembering the swimsuit Brooke had worn a few days ago, a teal two-piece. Maybe she'd suggest they revisit the thermal pools tonight in hopes of viewing it again.

Oh, wait. They couldn't. Brooke had Rory. Children weren't allowed, and Brooke would want to spend the evening with her daughter. It mildly frustrated Elizabeth that she had to take Rory into consideration when planning her time with Brooke, but she supposed parents had to deal with those sorts of scheduling issues all the time. Besides, she had no rights to Brooke. They were simply— what were they? Boss and quasi-employee? Neighbors? Associates? Friends? No. There'd been that kiss.

Damn it. That changed everything, including her ability to pretend *nothing* had changed. Even Geoff had picked up on something going on between them with his insistence Elizabeth was developing *feelings*.

Oddly enough, she'd grown to like living at the resort. She missed her house and life in San Jose and wanted to go back, but she had to admit living above where she worked and a restaurant with an amazing chef and delicious offerings at every meal was quite convenient, the scenery beautiful, and she enjoyed all the time she spent with Brooke.

And there she was again, always jumping to the forefront of Elizabeth's thoughts.

"Are you going to take your turn?" Brooke eyed her.

Elizabeth snapped out of her reverie and sat up, frantically scanning the water for Rory.

Brooke pointed. "She's right there, playing with the boy on the float."

With a grateful breath, Elizabeth turned back to the game, one she'd lost interest in finishing. "See, that's why I could never be a parent. I'd daydream for a few minutes and a disaster would happen." She wanted to kick herself. All her vigilance, and it'd only taken the thought of Brooke in a bikini to start her down the path to la-la land. Pathetic.

Brooke looked at her, an obvious question in her eyes, but she didn't ask it.

Thank God. Elizabeth moved her bishop. What would it feel like when she went home? When she didn't have these games to occupy her time, or movie and laundry nights, or Saturdays soaking up the sun while cheering on Rory? What was she going to do without them in her life? Somehow, she didn't think her typical escape to Santa Cruz when she needed a breath of fresh air and a change in scenery would fill the vast void she already knew would settle inside her.

Elizabeth admired Brooke. She was a good mom—no—a great one. It came naturally to her. Elizabeth didn't know how she did it. Sure, she made mistakes, but she had a ton to manage and no one to depend on. Yes, Sean carried his half of the load, but he had Kali to help him while Brooke had nobody. And while Elizabeth was no expert on children, or child development and rearing, raising one with special needs had to increase the degree of difficulty.

She took her turn and blew out a breath. It didn't matter. Summer would end, and she'd be headed back to the South Bay. She didn't have room in her life for a long-distance relationship, let alone with someone who had a kid. It was too hard watching a little girl with her precociousness and quirks that reminded Elizabeth so much of herself. And then there was what it dredged up for her around Carly. Someone innocent. Vulnerable. At the mercy of others. No, it wouldn't work. Couldn't work. Besides, Brooke would hate her when she sold the resort and left her unemployed and homeless.

Elizabeth swallowed the rising swell of nausea.

Brooke would despise her and never speak to her again. Is that what Elizabeth wanted? No, she wanted to see Brooke every day, share breakfast, make her coffee the way she liked, talk to her about anything and everything, watch movies snuggled on the couch, and wander through vineyards together. She'd never experienced this kind of desire to do rather mundane things with her prior girlfriends. Fear gripped her.

Holy hell. They weren't even dating. When *had* Elizabeth developed feelings? "I have to go." She leapt up, knocking over the wine.

"What's wrong?" Brooke righted the plastic glass.

One of the pool guys rushed over with a towel. Robert, Elizabeth recalled. She'd been trying to learn everyone's names without needing to look at their tags. "I'm sorry. I need to go." She grabbed her towel and phone off the table and almost sprinted for the doors.

With Rory in the water, Brooke wouldn't be able to rush after her, and hopefully, Elizabeth could get a handle on whatever was happening by the time she'd have to face her again.

CHAPTER EIGHTEEN

The morning sun beat down on Brooke's scalp as she walked the outdoor path of pavers from the spa to the lobby's rear entrance. She'd dealt with Marcel's complaints about his employees having to refold the towels the housekeeping staff delivered daily. The sheer ridiculousness of it made her want to roll her eyes again. Sure, transporting them over the cobblestones jarred them enough to knock a few of them over, but it appeared to be a case of needing to straighten rather than refold. Still, she'd ask Jesse, who was usually in charge of delivering them, to be extra careful and neaten them on arrival. She'd worked with Marcel long enough to know he always needed something to complain about. Playing mediator consumed much of her role.

As she neared the building, sunlight sparkled on the pool's surface, and she recalled how Elizabeth had bolted from it the night before. She hadn't answered her door when Brooke knocked later, but she'd responded she was fine to her text, just feeling unwell. Elizabeth had declined Brooke's offer to get anything for her, so Brooke had let her be. Obviously, Elizabeth wanted space. When Brooke arrived at work this morning, their office had already been opened and the smell of coffee hung in the air, but Elizabeth was nowhere to be found.

Just like now. Brooke settled at her desk to review their new brochure that'd be featured at the Napa tourism office and at the farmers' markets promoting the fall crush season. It needed to be approved before going to the printer.

Fall. Elizabeth would be leaving then. Brooke almost hesitated to commit to this marketing expenditure, not knowing what the status of Harvest Springs Resort would be then. With a sigh, she straightened. It didn't matter. Her job was to ensure the success of the resort, and she couldn't focus on what-ifs.

Elizabeth walked in, a stack of folders tucked under one arm.

"Good morning." Brooke gave her a smile that landed in the vicinity of a small-town homecoming queen greeting her family and friends from her parade float. "How are you feeling?"

"Fine." Elizabeth dropped the pile on her desk and began to brew another cup.

"No lingering effects?"

Elizabeth froze, her finger above the start button. "Nothing I can do anything about."

Strange answer.

Elizabeth started the machine, and within seconds, the caramel-colored liquid spouted downward, splashing off the drip tray and onto her pants and the carpet. "Shit." She shoved a mug beneath it and began cleaning up the mess.

Brooke watched her, debating whether to offer to help, but Elizabeth still seemed a bit prickly. Best to let her be. She could handle a small spill. Brooke went back to proofreading the spread.

About ten minutes later, after Elizabeth returned to her desk and seemed more at ease, Brooke softly cleared her throat. "We're going over to my parents' later for birthday cake. Would you like to come?"

Elizabeth's eyebrows dove together. "Whose birthday?"

"Mine." She smiled. "The big three-seven."

"Today." Elizabeth stood and paced, her face ashen. "Why didn't you tell me?"

Brooke shrugged. "It's not a big deal. I've had many of them."

Elizabeth stopped. "You should allow the same things for yourself you want for others." She put her hands on her hips. "You take care of everyone around you but take nothing for yourself."

Why was Elizabeth upset? "It's just a day like any other for me," Brooke said. "Rory has her swim lesson, and we'll probably order pizza. Although, tonight, there'll be dessert, so I hope you'll join us. For pizza, too." It's really the only thing she would've asked for had she been the type to make celebratory requests. More time with Elizabeth.

"Um…" Elizabeth spun her watch around her wrist. "Sure." With that, she walked past Brooke toward the elevator. "I'll be upstairs. I won't be long."

With a small shake of her head, Brooke tried to return to what she'd been doing. She wasn't sure what'd just happened. The last thing she'd expected was Elizabeth getting upset.

Less than five minutes later, a mechanical whir announced the elevator's arrival. Brooke looked up to see Elizabeth step out with—what? She couldn't tell, but it appeared soft and bulky.

"I didn't have any wrapping paper," Elizabeth said, handing it to her.

Upon closer inspection, it appeared to be one of the hotel's robes wrapped around a box, the belt holding it together and tied in a bow on top. "What's this?"

"Open it and see." Elizabeth perched on the edge of Brooke's desk.

Brooke pulled, letting the robe fall away. She lifted the lid and gasped. A digital Canon camera awaited her. "Elizabeth, you didn't have to do this." She picked it up, taking off the lens cap and powering it on. "It's beautiful."

"It's not new," Elizabeth said. "I saw it in a store window downtown. The woman said she knows the prior owner, and it's in great condition."

Brooke set it back in the box and stood. She wrapped Elizabeth in a hug, and after a moment, felt Elizabeth's arms go around her. "It's perfect." Elizabeth felt wonderful, solid yet soft, and her scent reminded Brooke of kissing her. She wanted to, but she settled for pressing her lips to Elizabeth's cheek before pulling away. "Thank you."

Elizabeth colored. "You're welcome. I bought it a while ago thinking, eventually, I'd have some excuse to give it to you."

Brooke picked it up again. "I adore it."

"That's not all." Elizabeth pointed to the box.

Brooke pulled a folded piece of paper from the bottom. "You want to take Rory? By yourself?"

"Just for an afternoon." Elizabeth eased away, leaning against her desk. "So you can go out and take photos."

"I know how you feel about kid—"

"A few hours." Elizabeth straightened her shoulders. "I can manage."

Okay, then. Brooke couldn't restrain her grin as she inspected her gift again. "And you'll come for cake?"

"On one condition." Elizabeth raised an eyebrow. "I made a reservation for three when I was upstairs. Tonight calls for more than pizza."

"Oh." When was the last time anyone had done anything to celebrate her, really done something? Sean used to bring her coffee in bed and help Rory buy her a small gift, but nothing that made him go out of his way. If her mom hadn't always invited them for dessert, she probably wouldn't be blowing out candles tonight. "Really?"

"Yes," Elizabeth stood and gathered the robe. "Wear anything but jeans. I made it early, five forty-five, because I wasn't sure how late you wanted Rory out."

Considerate. Intelligent. Attractive. Why did she and Elizabeth seem destined to want vastly different things? Even if that were the case, she wouldn't let that destroy her mood today.

At five, Brooke excused herself to meet Sean as he dropped off Rory after swim practice, then went upstairs to change. She chose a dress, but nothing fancy. A vertically striped, above-the-knee number that she completed with a pair of wedges and a sweater to be brought along in case of over-aggressive air conditioning.

"How's this?" Rory appeared in her doorway wearing her favorite skirt and her purple tennis shoes. Her braid needed to be redone.

"Very nice. Do you like how you look?"

Rory grinned and nodded.

"I do, too. Come here." As she fixed Rory's hair, she considered what to do with hers. "There you go. Elizabeth should be here soon."

"What's fusion?" Rory flopped on the end of her bed.

How should she explain? "It's when they take two types of food and combine them." Brooke had mentioned she loved that type of cuisine weeks ago in passing. Had Elizabeth remembered? "Think about how you enjoy pancakes but also really like street corn."

Rory nodded.

"Imagine that a chef decided to make a pancake with street corn in the batter and drizzled that sauce you love on top."

Rory's eyes lit up. "They'll have that?"

"No, but that's the kind of thing they do. And they serve small plates, so they'll send out little things for us to share, and then another dish will arrive shortly after that." Brooke had wanted to go to this restaurant since it'd opened last year, but either never had the time or hadn't been able to get a reservation. How had Elizabeth managed? "Be polite and try a little of everything. You don't have to like it."

"Okay."

Including Rory in tonight's dinner plans had been sweet of Elizabeth. She probably knew that Brooke would want to spend it with her daughter. She and Sean always adjusted the custody schedule so that parent could share their special day with Rory.

Brooke had barely finished applying makeup and pinning back a portion of her hair when a knock sounded. "Let's go."

When she opened the door, she found Elizabeth staring at her much the same way she was likely doing in return. Elizabeth wore the same pants she'd had on earlier, but she'd paired them with a silky cream blouse whose fabric cascaded over her chest, drawing Brooke's attention to her cleavage. Elizabeth wore no jewelry but a pair of gold hoops. A necklace would've been an unneeded distraction. "You look lovely."

"As do you. And you," Elizabeth said, turning to Rory. "Ready?"

Elizabeth offered to drive Brooke's car, so they'd have Rory's booster seat. They arrived a few minutes early and soon found themselves situated at a corner table.

"Do you know what I saw advertised on my social media this morning?" Brooke asked after trying her wine.

"What?"

"Ten percent off one of those DNA tests you do at home. I still think you should consider it." Brooke unfolded her napkin and took in the eclectic decor. Beside her, Rory colored a vineyard and hot air balloon scene the server had given her.

Elizabeth bit her lower lip. "Let's leave that talk for later." She picked up the menu and perused it.

Did Elizabeth not want to discuss it in front of Rory or simply want to avoid the conversation completely? With a positive little shrug, Brooke decided the only way to know for sure would be to bring it up again another time. The potential it had to change Elizabeth's life hung in the limbo between knowing and not knowing. Certainly, Elizabeth would want to find her sisters at some point.

By the time their food began to arrive, they'd moved on, and no discomfort seemed to linger. "Here." Brooke placed a fried ball on Rory's plate. "Remember those risotto balls you like at the Italian restaurant? These are like those, but they have fish instead of cheese inside, and this is a barbecue sauce." Rory didn't need to know eel was the protein contained within, but she'd always been an enthusiastic fish-stick girl, so Brooke crossed her fingers. When the first nibble seemed to go fine, she turned her attention to Elizabeth, who'd been watching her.

"What?"

Elizabeth shook her head, her cheeks pinking. "Nothing."

"What?" Brooke tapped Elizabeth's arm with a finger. "Tell me."

"You're a good mom," Elizabeth said quietly. "That's all."

Brooke cut into her arancini. "Thank you." She took a bite and savored the flavors. "And thank you for the camera. And this delicious dinner."

Elizabeth met her gaze, which seemed more intense in the romantic, candlelit ambiance of the restaurant. "Happy birthday."

With a smile, Brooke reached over and squeezed her hand, longer than necessary, but trying to convey how she felt. Not only her gratitude for the evening out or the thoughtful present, but how Elizabeth made her feel without those bonuses included. Seen, cared for, understood. She let go, returning to her food, but not before she caught the smallest of smiles from Elizabeth. That, itself, would've made her birthday.

Over an hour later, they gathered their things. Brooke had loved the food, Rory had done better than expected, and even Elizabeth had seemed to enjoy it. "I'm so happy to say I've finally been there," Brooke said as they settled in for the short ride to her parents' house. "I've wanted to go for so long."

"Good," Elizabeth said, seeming to sit taller in the driver's seat. "She's secured, right?"

"You buckled?" It'd been ages since Brooke had to check. Rory would make captain if they had a special seat belt police force.

"Yep. Did you know Grandpa said they didn't have booster seats when he was a kid?"

"They didn't have many things you enjoy now." As they made their way north on Highway 29, Brooke noticed the gap between them and the next car seemed to be getting wider. She glanced behind them. A line of vehicles followed them as far back as she could see. "You can go a little faster," she said, noting the digital thirty-one on the dash.

Elizabeth's knuckles had gone white. "After-dinner drivers worry me. The drinking, the all-day wine tasting."

Ah, yes. Elizabeth's tragic brush with that had derailed her life. Why wouldn't she be cautious? She'd gone with Perrier at dinner, too. Brooke rested her hand on Elizabeth's thigh for support. Okay, she couldn't kid herself. She liked touching her. But also, for support.

Gradually, Elizabeth increased her speed, and they soon reached Brooke's parents' place. When they stopped, Rory bounded out, halfway to the door before Brooke had gathered her phone and purse. "That was amazing," she said, briefly taking Elizabeth's arm on the short walk to the porch. "This is the best birthday I've had in ages." She cupped Elizabeth's cheek. "Because of you."

Elizabeth nodded, her eyes growing wide.

Was she trembling? Brooke dropped her hand. "Shall we?" She motioned toward the house.

Inside, Brooke headed toward the kitchen, and Elizabeth followed. There, she found her mom with her arms around Rory, who was describing their meal in detail.

"And they used this little thing to scoop the crumbs on the table."

Her mother smiled. "I need one of those for me and Grandpa." She looked up. "Hello, girls."

Her dad turned from the television where a western played, looking at each of them in turn.

Brooke knelt before him and took his hand in hers. "Hi, Daddy. I'm Brooke, your daughter, and your granddaughter Rory, and my friend Elizabeth.

"Hi, Grandpa." Rory skipped past them.

Elizabeth sat on the edge of the ottoman in front of the chair her mother liked to use. "Hi, Jack. Are you enjoying your show?"

"Hmmph. Nice horses but too much shooting."

"Do you ride?" Elizabeth asked, leaning forward.

He stared at her, then his lower lip trembled. He started to speak, and his hand shook as he lifted it to gesture at something. His eyes grew wet.

Brooke squeezed his knee. "It's okay, Dad. I remember you telling me how you and Chris used to ride horses at your uncle's place in the foothills when you were a kid. You rode them into the Sierras and camped during the summer."

He blinked a few times, and his breathing seemed to slow. "Sonora. Uncle Bob's place was in Sonora."

"That's right." Brooke patted his hand.

"Chris and Elliot were going to try to come over," her mom said, standing in the doorway. "But Elliot's flight is at seven in the morning, and she has to drive him to Oakland."

"That's okay." Brooke stood. It'd already been a great birthday. Anything now was icing, as they said.

Her mom threw an arm around her. "I'm sorry, but we're having a store-bought angel food cake. Normally, I'd make it, but it was kind of a stressful day around here, and I just didn't get to it. I'll make sure it tastes good though." She squeezed her.

"That's great, Mom." Brooke hugged her. "You do enough as it is. Do you want help?"

"I'll do it." Elizabeth rose. "It's your day."

"You can whip the cream. I already cut the strawberries."

Brooke watched them step into the kitchen before sitting down beside her dad. Rory had pulled out the old games and now fiddled with them on the floor. "Do you want to play chess, Dad?" It could go one of two ways. Well, or possibly upset him, but the desire to connect with him on some level won out.

"You have to set it up."

Brooke retrieved the box and cleared the side table between them. Like Rory, he always liked white. "You go first."

He studied the pieces, his hand hovering and shaking above the board.

Would he remember how to play? Would he be annoyed or angry if he didn't? Brooke walked a tightrope, desperately trying to keep her balance.

He moved a pawn.

A good sign. Brooke took a turn.

"It's your birthday?" he asked, studying her.

She smiled. "Yes."

He nodded. "And you're Brooke?"

"Yes."

"Happy birthday, Brooke."

He might've already forgotten she was his daughter, but the gesture touched her. She fought to take a breath, her chest tight with emotion. "Thanks, Daddy."

"Remind me if I'm taking too long. I probably don't remember it's my turn."

She hadn't heard him say so much, so clearly, in a long time. "Okay. You're doing great." He was. So far, his moves had been competitive, each piece doing the correct thing. Why did this part of his brain seem to be intact while others weren't? The unfairness of it stung her eyes, but she wouldn't let him see her tears. And she wouldn't cry on her birthday.

When they'd each captured four or five pieces, his turn seemed to go on too long, and when she glanced at him, the side of his head rested against the backrest of his recliner, his mouth open, and his chest rose with long, heavy breaths. She quietly began to put away the game.

"You played?" Elizabeth came to stand beside her.

"A bit." Brooke gave what she hoped appeared a positive smile. "He did well."

Elizabeth rubbed Brooke's back as she finished packing away the pieces in their molded-velvet spots. Brooke wanted to close her eyes and savor Elizabeth's touch, bask in it, hope for it never to end, but she finished her task and closed the wooden lid.

Elizabeth pulled Brooke's head against her and kissed the top of it. She released her and returned to the kitchen without a word.

If someone had told seven-year-old Brooke that this is what a birthday would look like at thirty-seven, she might've balked. Overall, though, she had everything she needed and then some. She rested a hand on her father's knee. A new camera to play with, a wonderful dinner, her loved ones, a kind woman—

No. Absolutely not. Brooke had to stop indulging in this attraction or whatever it was she had for Elizabeth, because Elizabeth clearly didn't feel the same. As wonderful as Elizabeth had made her birthday, the way she'd sprinted away after their shared kiss had made that clear.

CHAPTER NINETEEN

Brooke shifted her car into park in a spot on the north end of St. Helena's picturesque downtown and turned to Elizabeth. "You have two options." She killed the engine. "There's a boutique that specializes in women's wear, and there's a high-end consignment store a few blocks away."

Outside, the temperature hovered around eighty, which had made for a perfect morning to watch Rory's game. Elizabeth had done well, even if she'd appeared rather uncomfortable at first. By the end, though, she clapped louder than anyone when Rory's team made a goal, and Rory hadn't even been on the field when it happened.

Elizabeth opened the passenger door and climbed out. "Let's start with the traditional one."

Brooke met her on the sidewalk. "Do you want a coffee or something first?"

"I'm fine."

Elizabeth walked stiffly, the rigidity in her gait perhaps mirroring her feelings toward the shopping endeavor. Brooke tucked her hand into Elizabeth's elbow. "I know trying on clothing can be a hassle, but think about how much more comfortable you'll be at work. I can have Francine make you a name tag if you're concerned you won't appear to be management."

"I'm not."

Elizabeth's terse reply left Brooke uneasy. Was this still a holdover from the-kiss-that-shall-not-be-discussed? Maybe they needed to get it out in the open and talk about it. This tension between them had to go. She pulled Elizabeth into the shade of the bank. "Okay. So, we kissed. And you obviously realized it wasn't what you wanted, and that's fine. No hard feelings. We all make mistakes."

"It's not that." Elizabeth pressed her lips together and looked down the street. "I've thought about it a lot." She met Brooke's gaze. "*A lot.* And I enjoyed it, probably a bit too much, but you practically work for me."

The bustle of the surrounding people went silent, Brooke's full attention on Elizabeth's words. A lot? *Too* much? Her day just got sunnier. "Technically," she said, smiling and taking pleasure in the slight darkening of Elizabeth's eyes, "I work for J & C Hospitality Specialists. And trust me, I'd have to do something egregious to get fired. You know, embezzlement, harassment, tax evasion."

Elizabeth's eyebrows rose. "You've thought a lot about this, too."

Brooke laughed, already lighter knowing Elizabeth had enjoyed the moment as much as she had.

Elizabeth slipped her arm from Brooke's loose grasp. "I'll be going home at the end of the summer."

What was she saying? Brooke leaned against the building, studying her. With anyone else, she wouldn't consider doing what she was about to do, especially being the busy mother of a child with special needs, but Elizabeth was different. And it wasn't like Brooke would miss out on dating someone else if she ignored them in favor of Elizabeth. No line of suitors existed.

Brooke shot her a grin. "Maybe you'll fall in love with the resort and won't be able to leave." Or fall for something else.

"You have a fathomless well of optimism, don't you?" Elizabeth crossed her arms. "I want to be candid with you. I have every intention of going back to the South Bay, my house, and my job at the end of August."

It was akin to having a bucket of cold water thrown on her, but Brooke hoped she hid her disappointment. "Then we have a few lovely months ahead of us where we can explore one another." With more kissing or…other things. Tingles shot up her spine.

Elizabeth's breathing had grown shallow, her focus on Brooke's lips.

Brooke pushed herself off the wall and stepped closer. They might as well get this out of the way, or she'd be thinking about it all afternoon.

As she neared, Elizabeth unfolded her arms.

Brooke's cell blared. She groaned until she recognized the special ringtone she and her mom had chosen for her father's phone, not that he used it anymore. A call from that line meant only one thing: her mom needed her urgently.

"Mom, what's going on?" She stepped away from Elizabeth.

"Honey, I need help. I can't calm him down. He thinks he's in a war zone. He's digging a trench—*a trench*!—in the backyard. He's going to hurt himself."

Brooke pressed her fingers to her temple and made eye contact with Elizabeth, whose forehead wrinkled. Had she overheard? "I'm in St. Helena, but I'll be there as soon as I can. If you bring him a chair, maybe he'll sit." Her father had never served in the military, as much as he'd wanted to, a heart deformity disqualifying him. Apparently, he was living out that fantasy now.

Elizabeth took her hand and pulled her toward where they'd parked.

"Do you think I should call the police?" Her mom sounded near tears.

"No. That'll only alarm him, and the last thing we want is for him to end up in a psych ward. He wouldn't understand." Brooke quickened her pace. "We're on our way."

"I thought Rory was with Sean?"

"Elizabeth is with me. I'm going to hang up now, but we'll be there in a few minutes, okay?" She got in and started the engine as Elizabeth opened the passenger side door and dropped into the seat.

"Drive safely. I don't need to worry about you, too."

"Yes. See you soon." Brooke hung up and pulled onto the main street. "How much did you catch?"

"Most of it." Elizabeth gently touched her leg, then left her hand there. "This must be difficult, seeing him like this."

Brooke bit the inside of her cheek to quell the threat of tears, uncertain whether it was the pain of losing her dad to such an insidious illness or Elizabeth's compassion that made her emotional. She made a U-turn at the intersection and headed north. "Every time I think I've reached a level of acceptance and have a handle on it, it catches me unaware. It's unfair, you know?" Her vision momentarily blurred. "His body shouldn't outlast his mind. He's there, but he's not, and none of us really know what to do. It's not like I can stop loving him."

Elizabeth squeezed her leg. "Of course not. It's a different kind of loss. Where some of us lose our parents in the blink of an eye, yours is prolonged." She was silent a moment. "I'm not sure which is worse."

Brooke covered Elizabeth's hand with hers, and Elizabeth intertwined their fingers. They drove like that until they pulled into her parents' driveway. Instead of going to the front door, Brooke ran to the gate leading to the backyard and unlatched it. "Can you make sure it's closed?" she called over her shoulder.

Behind the house, long strips of lawn lay uprooted near a shovel, and a painter's tarp covered what appeared to be a body. "Jesus." She stopped short, and Elizabeth collided with her, only keeping them both from falling by grabbing Brooke's waist.

Her mother came out the back door, a water bottle in her hand. "Oh, Lord. You got here fast." She motioned to the stained canvas. "I convinced him to camouflage himself from the enemy. It's worked for a few minutes, so I ran inside to get him something to drink. He's been exerting so much energy in the scorching sun."

Brooke knelt beside her father and lifted an edge.

"Go away." He yanked it back into place. "You'll give up my position." His sharp whisper lacked any resemblance to make-believe.

She rose, going to her mom. "Give him a minute." Dejected, she led her mother to one of the patio chairs and took the water.

Elizabeth followed and perched on the edge of her seat, looking like she'd rather be anywhere but in this mess. Brooke didn't blame her.

"It was kind of you to come along," her mom said to Elizabeth. "I'm sorry you got dragged into this."

To Brooke's surprise, Elizabeth gave her a beautiful smile. "I'm happy to be here. Your call saved me from clothes shopping."

Brooke's mom laughed.

Elizabeth looked between the two of them. "She gets her smile from you," she said to Brooke's mother.

Elizabeth seemed somewhat awed, and Brooke had to turn away, the intensity in her gaze too much.

"We resemble each other physically, but her sharp mind she got from her daddy."

A tight knot formed in Brooke's stomach. If she'd inherited that, would she be bequeathed the same mental fate as him, too? She swallowed the surge of nausea and picked up the water, needing a moment of escape. "I'll be right back."

Next to her father, she lifted the edge of the tarp enough to shove one end of the bottle beneath. "Use your rations, soldier."

He swiftly pulled it under.

Brooke stood and walked back. She hated what was coming. Reluctantly, she returned and sat beside her mother. "Mom." She took her hand. "I think it might be time to revisit the discussion about an assisted-living arrangement."

Tears welled in her mother's eyes, and she swallowed hard. "But how am I supposed to live without him? That wasn't the agreement. We exchanged vows, made promises."

"I know." Brooke's heart broke for both her parents. She squeezed her mother's fingers.

Elizabeth cleared her throat and rose. "I should give you some privacy."

Brooke's mom caught her sleeve. "Stay. Please stay, dear. I mean, unless we're making you uncomfortable, of course."

Elizabeth's only response was to settle into her chair again, this time leaning against the backrest rather than remaining poised to dart from the yard at any moment. She met Brooke's eyes with a steadying gaze.

A rush of emotion filled Brooke. When was the last time she'd had support for one of these conversations? She sent Elizabeth an appreciative smile, grateful to have her strength to lean on. Emboldened, she turned to her mother. "It's for his safety. And you could still see him every day. He'd have round-the-clock care, and it'd be good for you, too." She softened her tone. "I know you haven't slept through the night in years."

Brooke's mom shook her head. "I don't know…"

"You don't have to decide right now," Brooke said. "Just think about it, okay?" She stood. "I'm going to see if I can get him to come out now." As she passed Elizabeth, she touched her shoulder and mouthed, *thank you.*

Brooke's mom sniffled. "I'm sorry, dear," she said, clearly to Elizabeth. "Would you two like some lemonade?"

Brooke left them, letting the question fall to Elizabeth, and sat beside her father. "Hi, Dad. It's your daughter, Brooke. The enemy's retreated for the day. You did well. Permission to pull back your cover?"

Before she could, he crawled out, droplets of sweat covering his brow. "I thought they'd never leave."

She helped him up and glanced at the shovel, wishing she'd had the foresight to put it away before she'd approached him.

He didn't notice it, his attention focused on Elizabeth. "Do I know her?"

"You met her once," Brooke eased him into a chair. "That's Elizabeth, a friend of mine."

"Are you the one who likes boys *and* girls?" he asked Brooke as he cleaned his glasses on his shirttail.

Brooke laughed. "I am."

"Is she your girlfriend?" He slid them back on, his eyes wide as he surveyed the two of them.

Elizabeth blushed as Brooke's mom returned with drinks.

"Daddy, ask me again next time you see me." To her delight, Elizabeth deepened a shade.

There was zero hope he'd remember, but at least it shut down that avenue of conversation. They stayed until they'd finished their lemonade, and Brooke even managed to secure all the garden tools without her dad noticing. When they left, he slept in his favorite chair, and her mom had calmed considerably. Whether she'd take Brooke's advice on getting the help they needed remained to be seen.

In the car, Brooke leaned close to Elizabeth for the kiss that'd been forestalled earlier by her mother's incoming call. If it'd happened then, it would've been seductive and maybe a bit urgent. But she made this one soft. "Thank you for being there with me," she whispered.

Elizabeth only gave a short nod, but her eyes held so much more.

Two hours later, they exited the boutique, each carrying bags. Almost all of it belonged to Elizabeth, who'd clearly liked the store's style, something Brooke had been betting on. They tended toward conservative dress casual. Elizabeth had even found two pairs of low-heeled shoes she'd purchased.

Brooke's wallet hadn't escaped damage, though. When she'd tried on the sunny, buttercup-yellow sundress and stepped out of the changing room for a spin in front of the triple mirrors, one look from Elizabeth told her she'd be buying it. If the store hadn't been so small and the staff so attentive, she would've pulled Elizabeth into the dressing room with her for a memorable five minutes.

"I like your purchase," Elizabeth said, setting her bags in the back of the car. "It suits you."

Ah. So, Brooke wasn't the only one pondering it. "Thank you. I think I'll wear it to the gala."

Elizabeth paused. "What gala?"

"The annual Every Child, Every Meal fundraising event. Did they not do that when you were here?" She closed the door.

"I don't remember." Elizabeth shielded her eyes with her hand to block the sun. "When is it?"

"Next weekend. Margaret's been hosting it at the resort forever. Francine could tell you how long. It raises money to ensure that every child in Napa Valley gets three healthy meals a day."

Elizabeth frowned. "That seems like a strange organization to need in such an affluent area."

Brooke moved onto the sidewalk so that Elizabeth wouldn't have to squint to see her. "There's a lot of poverty in the valley. Because of the tourism, many of the jobs are entry-level and pay little. I always respected Margaret for trying to do the best for her employees." Brooke opted for a lighter subject. "Lunch? There's a great little place right down the street."

Elizabeth nodded. "Sounds good." She fell into step beside her. "I'll treat since you orchestrated my shopping spree."

"Hmm. I should've chosen a more expensive place," Brooke said, her tone teasing.

"You can change your mind."

Brooke took a chance and slipped her hand into Elizabeth's, pleasantly surprised when Elizabeth didn't pull away. She swung their arms between them. "Next time. You'll love the sandwiches here. It's so unpretentious, most people don't realize the owner has a couple of Michelin-star restaurants because you order at the counter and bus your own table."

As they passed the town's pharmacy, the door opened and Miranda, one of the resort's housekeeping staff, ushered her four kids out. One boy lingered. "Mikey, let's go." She looked up, noticing Brooke. "Oh, hi." She herded the children, waving the white prescription bag she carried.

Elizabeth freed her fingers from Brooke's grasp.

"Hello." Brooke looked at the kids. "You've all grown so much since I've seen you."

"Yes, too fast," Miranda said. "Will Rory be at the next game? Her team is playing Daniela's."

"She will, although I won't be. Her dad is taking her." Sean and Kali were bringing Kali's relatives, so Brooke decided to give them the day for themselves. "Have you met Elizabeth Bettancourt, the new owner of the resort?"

"I've seen you before," Miranda said, pulling her youngest boy away from the store's window where he'd been making a fish face on the glass. "I'm the one who empties your garbage and vacuums your office."

"Oh, yes. Right." Elizabeth shifted from one foot to the other. "Nice to see you again."

Something was off, but Brooke wasn't sure what. "Well, we'll let you go. Enjoy the nice day."

They walked around the small family toward the restaurant. Brooke let the silence linger to see if Elizabeth might volunteer whatever she was thinking.

A block later, Elizabeth glanced behind them, then looked forward again. "Even with the inflated salaries Margaret paid the housekeeping staff, they still don't earn much above minimum wage. Why would someone choose to have that many kids when they hardly make any money?"

Brooke stopped, anger sparking a blaze within. She could put up with a lot, but she had her limits, ones that precluded pretending to enjoy a meal together after *that* comment. So, it needed to be dealt with first, even if it ruined the rest of their day.

"I know everything is about the bottom line to you," the words flew from her mouth, "but there's more to life than money. Yes, she *chose* to have four kids. So did her husband, who's a police dispatcher. After Miranda's sister and brother-in-law were killed in a fire, Miranda and her husband *chose* to adopt their children because they knew if they went into the system, they'd be split up." She took a breath. "Maybe stop occasionally and remember that everyone has a complicated life you know nothing about."

Elizabeth turned a sickly pallor. "I didn't know."

"Obviously." Brooke stared at her as she tried to regain her composure.

"Me, of all people…" Elizabeth muttered. With a dip of her head, she reached out, palms up. "I'm sorry."

They studied one another.

When Brooke didn't speak, Elizabeth continued. "You're good for me. You make me see things I normally wouldn't." She gave her a wry smile. "Would writing a hefty check at the charity event help make up for my obtuseness?"

Brooke took a small step to bring them closer, then clasped Elizabeth's hands. "I know you've had a hard life, and you've experienced things others never will. But you don't have a monopoly on tragedy," she said quietly. "Life is hard for everyone. If we have the potential to make someone's life better, I think we should." She smiled. "And yes, a *sizeable* donation will go a long way. Now, let's get some lunch."

As they walked down the street, she threaded her fingers between Elizabeth's again, longing for the connection they'd had earlier. This, whatever they had between them, wasn't destined to last with Elizabeth's planned departure in a few months, but it certainly felt good in the moment. Brooke knew she needed to accept it for what it was, but somehow, her initial goal to make Elizabeth fall in love with the resort had morphed into something new. How nice would it be if Elizabeth fell in love with *her*, too? Because Brooke knew, this thing she was experiencing wasn't something she'd ever encountered, and she wasn't sure she could handle it ending. She'd only begun to see through the cracks in Elizabeth's fortress, and she liked what she'd found. What multitudes of wondrous things would she discover if given the time?

"So, you'll definitely wear the dress to the gala?"

Brooke spun in front of Elizabeth and, walking backward, smiled. "Do you want me to?"

Elizabeth tugged her into her arms. "Yes." She lowered her head and captured Brooke's lips between hers.

With a sigh, Brooke settled against her, encircling Elizabeth's neck. The unexpectedness of it caught her off guard, but here she was, on her tiptoes on the public sidewalk in St. Helena, bent like a crescent moon as Elizabeth made her tingle all over. Finally, she pulled away with a gasp. "Okay. Wow." She touched her lips. "So, the new outfit it is." She smiled.

Elizabeth returned it with a scintillating one.

Brooke cupped the back of her head and kissed her again. The end of summer seemed a long way off.

❖

Brooke surveyed the resort's largest ballroom where they held the charity gala each year. The nonprofit had chosen a Starry Night theme, and the new dress Brooke had bought a week earlier complemented the decor perfectly. They were only an hour into the evening, but guests filled the room. Known as one of *the* events at which to be seen in the valley if you were anyone of note, tickets sold out fast, and rumors circulated of scalpers making three or four times the set amount. Too bad people prone to such activity weren't likely to donate their gains.

With a glance around, she spotted the owner of the oldest winery in the valley, the representative for their district, and the retired talk show host known to fly her private jet into the Napa Airport multiple times a year. Wine flowed freely, with nary a hand empty.

"I chatted with a developer who's now a venture capitalist," Tiffany said, coming up beside her. "She might be interested in being an investor for Cab or Neigh."

"That's wonderful."

Tiffany pulled a card from her clutch. "I had a logo designed with the name so I wouldn't have to spell it out every time."

Brooke studied it. "Good idea. That makes it clearer." She handed it back. "As much as I enjoyed watching you pantomime it to Elizabeth and me."

"It's not my fault the two of you couldn't hear the clear distinction." She flipped her hair. "Speaking of Elizabeth, where is she?"

"I'm not sure." Brooke had hoped she would've arrived by now. She hadn't asked Elizabeth what she planned to wear. Brooke had her money on the charcoal skirt suit. It seemed like something Elizabeth would choose for this kind of event. She shifted her gaze to the far wall where patrons browsed the silent auction items, and the air left her lungs.

Elizabeth stood before a Methuselah from one of the valley's most popular cellars. She wore wide white pants and a matching vest that dipped low in front, her shoulders bare. Her hair, sleek and flawlessly styled, coiled into a knot at the nape of her neck. Red lipstick accentuated her lips.

As though summoned by Brooke's stare, Elizabeth looked her way, then started a slow—deliberately?—seductive walk in her direction. With her stilettos, she seemed to tower over Brooke as she drew near.

"Well..." Tiffany said, "I refuse to be the third wheel on whatever is happening here. I'm going to find more rich people and part them from some of their money." She darted away.

Brooke gave her a small wave, never taking her eyes from Elizabeth.

"If it isn't my favorite dress." Elizabeth's sultry voice resonated low.

Brooke had to give herself an inner shake to come up with a response. She spread her skirt with her hands. "This old thing?" Already familiar with Elizabeth's opinion of her planned attire, Brooke had hoped to wow her further by curling her hair into a sophisticated ponytail with lots of loose tendrils and ensuring her makeup popped. Based on the way Elizabeth couldn't tear her gaze away, she'd hit her mark.

In the corner, the band began playing an upbeat song, and attendees moved toward the dance floor.

"You look"—Elizabeth swallowed and motioned toward her—"fantastic."

Brooke smiled. "Thank you. As do you. I don't recall seeing this among your purchases." It'd been in the boutique window, although the store had paired it with a purple blazer, which Elizabeth had thankfully foregone.

Elizabeth's lips spread into a slow smile. "I acquired it later to surprise you."

"Well done." Brooke hadn't been prepared for her own voice to take on such a husky tone. "Do you want to dance?" She considered it a luxury to attend the function as a guest and not as the manager. Her event staff were professionals and had years of experience putting on the gala. She could relax and have fun, and she intended to do just that.

With a glance around, Elizabeth shook her head. "No. Sorry."

Elizabeth looked so ill at ease that Brooke's heart went out to her. Was it a lack of coordination? A fear of being watched? She'd kissed Brooke on a public sidewalk in broad daylight, so it couldn't be that she didn't want to dance with another woman. "It's all right."

Elizabeth rubbed her upper arms. "Can we step outside for some air?"

"Sure." Brooke took her hand and led her through the large open doors onto the grounds, meandering around the pools and along the edge of the vineyards. "Better?"

"Yes." Elizabeth stopped and pulled Brooke into an embrace, then began to sway to the music filtering outside.

Brooke pressed against her. "I thought you didn't want to dance."

"I didn't want to dance in *there*." Elizabeth leaned down and placed a kiss just below Brooke's ear. "Where there's no privacy," she whispered.

Brooke slid her fingers over Elizabeth's bare shoulders, then up the sides of her slender neck. "I see how you are, Ms. Bettancourt. Lure the woman outside into the dark of night where you can do whatever you want with her."

"It wouldn't be the first time I've gotten up to shenanigans out here."

Brooke leaned back, grinning. "I don't believe it."

Elizabeth dipped her head, her lips almost touching Brooke's. "You have no idea, Ms. Staley."

Breathe. Brooke blinked. She'd once known how to breathe.

Elizabeth looked around. "When I was young, a busser and I used to sneak back here on our break or after our shift. We'd hide out and talk, and he'd smoke an occasional joint."

An unexpected spindle of jealousy pricked Brooke square in her chest. "Kissing?"

"No." Elizabeth cupped Brooke's hand and touched her lips to the inside of Brooke's wrist. "I've always reserved that for the girls."

The heat of Elizabeth's mouth lingered on Brooke's skin. She barely held back a moan. "And did you bring any of them here?"

"Just one." The band transitioned into a slower song, and Elizabeth adjusted, expertly twirling Brooke into a spin, then pulling her back. "The first girl I kissed." She motioned with her chin. "Right there, up against the brick behind the restaurant. Where Sophie's herb garden is now."

Up against the wall? *Jesus.* Every bit of attraction, desire, and need Brooke had been feeling for Elizabeth since day one converged in a single point, then pulsed downward, low and deep. "And?" Brooke managed—barely.

"And what?"

Brooke rolled her eyes. "What happened to her? Did you date?"

"No." Elizabeth stared into the darkness for a moment. Then she straightened and moved her hands lower, holding Brooke by the hips. "I made my donation inside and placed what I consider an unbeatable bid on an enormous bottle of wine." She nuzzled Brooke's neck. "What do you think about listening to the rest of the setlist from upstairs?"

Brooke searched her face. Was she asking what Brooke thought she was? Her enlarged pupils and the flush on her chest said she was indeed. Brooke wanted to play it cool, just in case, but she was on fire. "I have a nice vintage I've been saving for a special occasion." Could Elizabeth detect her underlying urgency? Did she feel the same?

Elizabeth bent and kissed her sweetly and languidly. "It'd be a shame to open it and leave it to be forgotten," she said against Brooke's lips.

With Elizabeth's meaning clear, Brooke grabbed her hand and led her back through the ballroom. A fleeting thought of Tiffany peeked through all the salacious images in her mind of what she and Elizabeth were about to do but vanished quickly. Tiffany was networking tonight, and besides, she'd seen Elizabeth decked out and sexy as hell. She'd understand completely.

Upstairs, Brooke let them into her apartment. She'd cleaned up earlier just in case they ended up here for a drink, but when you had a child, there was no hiding all the clutter. Either Elizabeth accepted it, or she didn't.

As soon as the door closed, Elizabeth kissed Brooke deeply, first against the wall, then the small island.

So, clearly, she did.

"I hadn't planned to leave so early," Elizabeth said, her gaze dark with desire. "But then I saw you looking like this."

Elizabeth's sensual tone gave Brooke goose bumps. She trailed her fingertips around the buttons of Elizabeth's vest. "We've been leading up to this moment for a while, haven't we?"

With a twitch of her eyebrows, Elizabeth stopped the rhythmic movement of her thumbs on Brooke's hips. "I'm still not entirely convinced it's a good idea."

"What're you afraid of?" Brooke cupped Elizabeth's jaw and gently lifted her face so they were looking into each other's eyes.

Elizabeth swallowed. "A hundred different things." She moved closer. "But they're not going to stop me. Not tonight." She pressed her lips to Brooke's.

Brooke's own reservations should've been enough to reconsider whether this was wise, but standing before her was the most beautiful woman she'd ever seen. Complex, mysterious, wounded. She wasn't perfect by any means, but that didn't draw Brooke to her any less.

Their mouths met in heat and want and something more.

Elizabeth kissed like she'd studied it as a long-lost art form. She focused mostly on Brooke's lips and mouth but occasionally sprinkled soft presses to her chin, neck, and behind her ear. Her fervor seemed to escalate, pushing Brooke's sense of insatiability higher and higher.

Brooke pulled her closer, arching and tilting her head back to offer her throat.

A low, guttural sound escaped Elizabeth, and she grazed her teeth across the sensitive skin.

A low moan escaped Brooke.

Without looking, Elizabeth reached behind Brooke and swept the island clear of Rory's drawing of a rainbow over the Golden Gate Bridge and their family calendar. The papers fluttered to the floor. She lifted Brooke onto the counter.

When she moved between Brooke's legs, Brooke wrapped them around her, the position shoving Brooke's dress up around her thighs.

Elizabeth took immediate advantage of the skin on display, running her hands over every exposed inch and more. "You're so soft," she murmured.

The pulse between Brooke's legs from downstairs surged to a full-on ache with their bodies pressed together. Brooke leaned back, bracing herself on the tiled surface, and opened wider.

Elizabeth tugged her hips closer. She pushed the rest of Brooke's skirt to settle around her waist and traced the edges of her lace bikinis. "Pretty."

Brooke huffed. Fuck pretty. She tried to gain some friction against Elizabeth, but Elizabeth didn't allow it.

Elizabeth drew her thumb up the center panel with just enough pressure to bring Brooke closer to the edge.

Brooke closed her eyes and thrust upward, needing more. Just a little bit more. Then the touch was gone. "Please. Don't stop."

"Shhh. I'll take care of it," Elizabeth said soothingly. "Come here." She slipped her arm around Brooke's back and eased her up, then carefully undid Brooke's hair, letting it tumble free. She bent to kiss her collarbone as she slid the dress's straps from Brooke's shoulders, baring her breasts. She palmed one through another searing kiss, leaving Brooke gasping for air, then flicked the nipple into an even harder point. Almost immediately, she lowered her mouth to it and began to suck.

"Oh, my God, yes." Brooke was ready. She'd been ready for days. Weeks. Now that Elizabeth was actually touching her, kissing her—she was so close. She needed Elizabeth to make it happen. Now.

"Please," was all she said, and it was enough for Elizabeth to push past the thin fabric and into her folds, her heat, her wetness.

Elizabeth stopped at her entrance. "May I?"

"Oh, for God's sake. Yes!" Brooke almost screamed.

Elizabeth entered her.

It was everything and too much all at once. She wanted it, but she also wanted it to last, and she couldn't have both. Not the first time.

With Elizabeth supporting her, they moved together as Elizabeth accentuated her thrusts with her hips.

Brooke needed to touch her, to feel her skin. She slipped her fingers beneath Elizabeth's vest, finding her braless. The thrill of Elizabeth inside her combined with squeezing Elizabeth's soft breast, the perfect handful, was too much.

She buried her face in Elizabeth's neck, her arm tight around Elizabeth's strong shoulders. Their days of flirting, of stolen glances and tentative touches, of sharing their pasts and their messy presents, had come to a culmination. "Don't stop. Please, don't stop." She clenched her eyes shut. The room stilled. Elizabeth tipped her over the edge, the silence shattered by Brooke's cry of pure release.

As she basked in her pleasure and regained her senses in Elizabeth's comforting embrace, her mind drifted to what came next. Brooke wanted Elizabeth. Needed her. This couldn't be the only time. She had a list half a mile long of the things she'd like to do to her. But would Elizabeth, who was always-in-control and often so guarded, allow Brooke to make love to *her*?

CHAPTER TWENTY

Elizabeth stood beside Brooke's kitchenette island with Brooke's legs still wrapped around her. Her heart pounded, matching the throb of arousal between her thighs. Eyes closed, she held Brooke tightly against her, listening to her ragged breaths slow. She ached for her own orgasm, while simultaneously wanting to build Brooke's need for a second one.

She moaned when Brooke's hand, still holding Elizabeth's breast, moved slightly and Brooke thumbed her nipple.

"Mm." Brooke left a warm kiss at the base of Elizabeth's throat, then made her way upward with more. She stopped just long enough to unbutton Elizabeth's vest.

With Brooke's guidance, Elizabeth let it slide down her arms and drop to the floor with minimal thought about what it'd cost her. Whatever the price, she would've paid double if she'd known how Brooke would respond to seeing her in the outfit.

"This was fantastic," Brooke said, kissing between her breasts, "but let's move to the bedroom. I need space to do my thing."

Oh, my. Elizabeth's desire surged. She stepped out of her heels and scooped her up, Brooke's dress still hanging around her waist. This moment would stay with her, a snapshot she'd never forget. Recently, so many of them involved Brooke. She seemed to have become a constant, and every minute with her brought something new and exciting.

Elizabeth carried her down the hall, and within seconds, had her on the bed and crawled up to lie beside her.

Now what though? She yearned to go down on Brooke, but Brooke clearly wanted a turn. Not that Elizabeth minded. Being inside Brooke, feeling how ready she'd been and how beautifully she'd come for her, had Elizabeth longing for relief.

So, she did what she rarely did with her sexual partners. She allowed herself to be rolled onto her back and let Brooke divest her of her pants.

Brooke then stood and shed the rest of her clothing, gazing down at Elizabeth's naked body the whole time. Her eyes darkened and her neck and chest flushed deeper the longer she stared. "You're so damn gorgeous," she said breathlessly. Then she pounced, straddling Elizabeth and kissing her, claiming her.

Elizabeth had never been with someone who wanted her so fiercely. She wrapped her arms around her and pulled her in tightly, wanting to feel Brooke's full weight pressing her into the bed, desperate for her length all along hers. She couldn't keep from moving under her, thrusting against her. She ran her hands over her smooth, soft skin, cupped her breasts, rolling the nipples between her fingers, exploring as much of Brooke as she could until Brooke pinned her wrists above her head.

Brooke gazed down on her, need still in her eyes, but her manner softening. "Easy now." She kissed her tenderly. "Relax." She patted Elizabeth's forearms, then grazed her fingernails over the sensitive flesh of the inside of her elbows.

Elizabeth shuddered and sucked in a breath, either from the sensation or the nonverbal command to leave her hands there.

"Let me do this," Brooke whispered.

Having surrendered so much, the rest was an easy slide. Elizabeth nodded.

With the randomness and lightness of a feather caught in a slow breeze, Brooke trailed kisses down the column of Elizabeth's neck, around and across each breast, casually teasing the nipples with her tongue and teeth, and over her stomach. Up and down, back and forth, she left Elizabeth squirming and writhing beneath her.

Jesus. Had Elizabeth even let a few whimpers slip? She had to have more. She thrust upward, wrapped her legs around Brooke's waist, and pulled her against her wetness.

Brooke smiled and moved lower. She trailed a single finger between Elizabeth's open legs, tracing her wet folds.

Elizabeth moaned at the tender touch.

Brooke kissed Elizabeth's inner thigh.

Elizabeth shivered. How much more could she take? She wasn't used to this.

Finally, Brooke's mouth. Her tongue. Elizabeth groaned and arched her back. She wanted desperately to rock against her, needing more. She craved Brooke's silky hair between her fingers, to pull her harder against her. But she'd been told to remain as she was, so she'd submitted. She'd never experienced such exquisite torture.

"I know you need more," Brooke said, darting her tongue out for a swipe that had Elizabeth raising off the bed. "Don't worry." She took her into her mouth and soon had Elizabeth pressing her palms to the headboard.

The sound of Elizabeth's own ragged breathing filled the room. Usually, this would be the point she'd tell her partner she wanted her fingers, but she remained silent. Brooke was different. *She* was different *with* Brooke. She didn't want to tell her what to do. Something about the way Brooke took charge, inside the bedroom and out, had Elizabeth's head swirling. It was intoxicating. And based on the way her body responded, Brooke didn't need any coaching.

With a hand to the back of her knee, Brooke lifted Elizabeth's leg toward her chest. The position, along with the exquisite demand of Brooke's mouth, sent Elizabeth reeling. The heat low in her belly spread, and she arched up, heels slamming to the mattress.

Brooke somehow stayed with her, her skilled lips and tongue continuing their magic.

A cry caught in Elizabeth's throat, and she rode out the waves of pleasure, one hand fisted into the pillow behind her, the other having found its way into Brooke's hair.

After a bit, she lowered her hips to the bed. Brooke rested her head on Elizabeth's thigh, her arm still wrapped around the other, and Elizabeth stroked her temple.

When her mind cleared, she squeezed Brooke's shoulder. "Come up here."

She did, bringing the covers with her, and they kissed slowly and without the frantic haste of earlier. Then Brooke lay beside her and rested her head on Elizabeth's chest, her arm circling her waist.

Elizabeth buried her nose in Brooke's hair and breathed in her scent, one she'd grown to think of as only Brooke's. One that stirred things in her again, although she didn't want to move and break the spell of this shared moment.

They'd done it, it'd been spectacular, and it didn't feel like the world was crashing down around her. At least not yet. Could they continue this for another couple of months? And then what? A clean break, quickly rip off the bandage, and maybe she'd be able to forget about Brooke after a few weeks of being home. At least she wouldn't be in this damned town with unwanted memories lurking around every corner.

❖

Elizabeth jerked awake. Something was off. Where was she? She lifted her head and tried to see in the darkness. Brooke's bedroom. That's right. *Shit.* She'd fallen asleep. Brooke lay beside her, breathing evenly, her expression peaceful.

Carefully, Elizabeth slid out of bed and felt around for her pants, bumping the bed as she searched. There they were.

"What're you doing?" Brooke sat up, holding the sheet over her breasts. She touched a lamp, and it illuminated not only the room but the disappointment etched across her face.

Elizabeth glanced around surreptitiously for her underwear. "I was going back to my place."

Brooke studied her. "That's not going to work for me. Not if we're doing this." She motioned between them. "Can you sit and talk with me for a minute?" She got up and went to her dresser. "Here." She tossed some clothing at Elizabeth and pulled on a similar set.

Elizabeth held up the soft gray T-shirt with USF Dons across the front. She pulled it over her head, the fabric so worn and well-loved, she feared it might disintegrate if she breathed on it too hard. Shorts followed. Then she sat, a bit confused, beside Brooke.

"Do you usually leave after you have sex with a woman?" Brooke gathered her hair and pushed it over her shoulder.

Elizabeth thought about it. "Not always. If we're at my house, *she* goes home."

Brooke frowned. "Certainly, you've had girlfriends."

"Yes." She shrugged. "We had our own places."

"How long were you together?" Brooke tucked one leg under her, facing Elizabeth more.

"Well, Janice and I saw each other about..." she looked at the ceiling, thinking, "...seven months. Heather and I were together about ten."

Brooke leaned back. "And those were your longest relationships?" At Elizabeth's nod, she asked, "You never felt the need to spend the night? Cuddle with them? Make them breakfast?"

"I don't usually eat in the mornings."

Brooke shook her head and covered her face with her hands. When she looked at Elizabeth again, she exhaled loudly. "I'm going to tell you how I feel about this, then you can share your feelings. All right?"

"Sure." Elizabeth shifted a bit, not knowing where this was going.

"When you dash away after a kiss or sneak away in the night after we've had sex, I feel...used." She tilted her head. "Or, at least, unworthy of your time and attention."

Elizabeth flinched. "I never intended it to come across that way." She balled the hem of the T-shirt in her fist.

"It's just"—Brooke bit her lower lip—"I have abandonment issues of my own." She met her gaze. "Go easy on me."

"Sean?" Elizabeth had forgotten he'd left Brooke for another woman.

Brooke gave a sardonic laugh. "Him, Brian, my dad who's fading away before my eyes. Strange how it's all the men in my life."

Elizabeth threaded their fingers together. "I'm sorry I tried to leave. I shouldn't have. Not that it excuses it, but it was habit."

"Is it one you can break?" Brooke smiled, giving her hand a squeeze.

For those dimples? Elizabeth's entire being softened looking at Brooke, her hair down and curly and mussed from sleeping. "I think so."

Brooke tugged her back into bed and extinguished the light. She curled into Elizabeth, tucking her head just below Elizabeth's chin. "Can I ask you a personal question?"

That prompt usually made Elizabeth search for the nearest exit, but in the darkness, in the safety and comfort of Brooke's embrace, it didn't feel as daunting. "Sure."

"Have you been in a relationship where you've talked about things and shared your past? You know, where you've been vulnerable and told the person things you tell no one else?"

Elizabeth stiffened. That wasn't her. She liked women, and she enjoyed going to bed with them, but she rarely needed more than that. Sure, she found their company pleasant and appreciated having someone to go to restaurants and movies or plays with, but they didn't need to know all the traumatic events of her life to have a relationship with her. Or did they? What would Brooke think of her answer? Her heart raced. "I'm—I'm not sure."

"Hey." Brooke lifted her head and rubbed Elizabeth's arm. "I'm not judging you. I just want to know more about you, what makes you *you*."

When Brooke caressed Elizabeth's cheek, Elizabeth relaxed again.

"How many of your ex-girlfriends know about your sisters?" Brooke asked.

Right to the heart of the matter. So Brooke. "None of them." Elizabeth couldn't come up with a good reason and not because she was put on the spot. "Telling them would've meant…I don't know." She started to turn away.

Brooke stopped her and gripped her hand. "I understand." She kissed Elizabeth's knuckles. "I do. But I want it all with you, even if you're leaving in August."

"All what?" Elizabeth was going to need a road map for this excursion into foreign territory.

"For starters," Brooke said, "I want to spend the night with you in my arms, listening to your heartbeat, sharing your warmth."

Elizabeth could do that.

"I want to wake in the morning with your mouth between my legs and have breakfast—or coffee—outside under the hot air balloons."

Elizabeth squirmed. The first half of Brooke's statement fanned the embers of last night's desires. She hadn't gotten to do that. And had she ever *woken* a woman that way? She could definitely give Brooke that. And the second half? They'd already had coffee together in the office each morning. Now, it'd just be a different location, and the beauty of the balloons would certainly be a perk. So, no problem there. But what about the first half again? She imagined it, suddenly aching to taste Brooke. But she'd screwed up, trying to run away like she always did. She owed it to Brooke to follow her lead. It wasn't a terrible plan, after all.

"I want long walks, quiet talks, competitive chess matches, and stolen moments when Rory is asleep or with her dad." Brooke snuggled into her side.

Rory. There was Rory. Elizabeth didn't know how to be around her, but even so, Rory seemed to like her. Besides, Brooke wasn't asking her to co-parent or even spend time with her daughter. "Okay."

"Yeah?" Brooke smiled her dimpled smile.

Elizabeth pulled her closer and kissed the top of her head. "Yeah. I might need some reminders along the way, though." The lengths she'd go to for this woman.

"Mm." Brooke's breathing had grown shallow. "Don't worry. I excel at being bossy."

A warning bell rang in Elizabeth's head, but it was much fainter than any time in the past. Still, what the hell was she doing? Here she was, in a strange bed instead of retreating to her privacy. She'd avoided going back to work with the excuse she needed to learn more about the resort—which she did—but probably not enough to warrant staying over three months.

She hated to admit it, but she wanted *this*. This woman, in her arms, in her life, in her bed. And so, she'd remained here, because it'd meant being around Brooke longer.

Elizabeth didn't know what she was doing. It was a slippery slope she was on, and danger loomed at the end. What was the worst that could happen? She'd sell, essentially evicting Brooke and Rory, leave Brooke jobless, move home, and Brooke would hate her forever.

But that was in the future. Elizabeth would deal with it then. In the meantime, she had this. She turned them and spooned Brooke, and Brooke gave a contented sigh. Maybe Elizabeth would come up with some miraculous way to make things right between now and then that didn't involve keeping the resort. She had no desire to live in this haunted town.

Right now though, it seemed unimaginable to give up this strange life she currently led.

CHAPTER TWENTY-ONE

Brooke woke, not by Elizabeth going down on her, but clearly on her way to doing so. It wasn't Elizabeth's fault she was a light sleeper. She had been ever since she'd had Rory. Motherhood did that.

Brooke shifted, allowing Elizabeth to push her shorts down and settle between her legs. A bit of light filtered through the blinds, but the sun clearly hadn't risen yet. She lifted Elizabeth's hair, heavier than hers, but not as sleek as usual after sleeping on it. Did she blow it or straighten it? So many things for Brooke to learn about her.

Then Elizabeth's mouth was on her, and thoughts of styling methods disappeared. She closed her eyes, relaxing into the moment, still playing with Elizabeth's hair. "Oh." Her hips rose off the bed, but Elizabeth put an arm across to hold her in place. "Keep doing that, and it won't take long." Why hadn't they done this sooner?

After a few minutes of working her up, Elizabeth slipped a finger inside. She withdrew and added a second.

Brooke was breathing hard now, and the cool air and sheen of perspiration on her skin made her shiver. She was close. Elizabeth curled her fingers, and Brooke came with a small cry. After a few seconds, she loosened her hold on Elizabeth's hair and gasped. "Sorry. Hope I didn't hurt you."

Climbing up beside her, Elizabeth kissed her, her lips soft and warm. She finally pulled back. "You didn't. Good morning," she said quietly.

Brooke smiled. Yes, indeed. The light in the room had grown brighter. "Are you still interested in breakfast outside?"

Elizabeth pushed herself up on one elbow. "That was the plan, right? What's the dress code for this?" She glanced down at the clothing Brooke had loaned her.

"Go grab some yoga pants or sweats. Mine will be too short on you. And a jacket. It'll still be cool. I'll make a thermos of coffee."

"Shall I run downstairs and buy some pastries while you do that?" Elizabeth pushed herself into a sitting position and smoothed her hair.

"Sure."

She leaned over and kissed Brooke's bare stomach. "I need to find the willpower to leave this room first."

Brooke laughed and pushed her away, but the humor faded to seriousness. Elizabeth had had no trouble doing that when Brooke had caught her sneaking out in the middle of the night. Talking had helped, though, and she was proud of the way they'd come to an understanding. It's not like discussing abandonment didn't leave her vulnerable, too.

Elizabeth turned in the doorway. "I'll see you in about ten minutes." Then her expression changed. She came and sat on Brooke's side of the bed and leaned down and kissed her again. "Ten minutes too long," she murmured, before leaving.

It turned out to be closer to fifteen, but the bright hot air balloons still floated high in the sky when Brooke shook out a blanket on the grassy area behind the pool hedge. Because it involved stepping over a rock wall to access it, guests never ventured here, and she used it now and then when she needed a few minutes to herself.

Elizabeth settled beside her and opened a box containing two blueberry muffins. They pinched off bites and sipped coffee as they watched the show above them. The occasional whoosh of a burner had her trying to spot the ascending group.

"It's a busy morning. I count fifteen." Elizabeth lay back, one arm behind her head.

To the east of them, brightness crept over the hills, the sun about to make its entrance. Its rays already touched the colorful orbs floating above them. Brooke almost didn't want it to arrive. It'd been a wonderful night, and a very nice morning, and she didn't want it to end.

"When does Rory come home?"

Brooke turned to look at her. Elizabeth had a glimmer in her eyes Brooke had only seen once or twice. "Not until tomorrow evening. Sean always takes her the weekend of the gala."

Elizabeth rolled on top of her, letting her lips hover just above Brooke's. "I have ideas."

"Oh, do you?" Brooke held Elizabeth by her waist, letting her hands slide just beneath the material to trace the delicate skin at her sides.

"Do you think they can see us?" Elizabeth glanced above them.

"Well, we can see and hear them, so yes."

Elizabeth grinned. "Good." And she kissed her in a manner that left Brooke breathless and the blanket beneath them tangled around their legs.

Hooting and whistles from above had them laughing and gasping for air.

"Let's take this inside." Brooke scrambled to pick up the remains of their meal. It wasn't quite June, but she was already dreading the arrival of August.

❖

Brooke had asked Tiffany to meet her for a glass of wine downtown, not because she was avoiding Elizabeth, but she didn't want to look like she was kissing and telling, even if that was sort of what she was doing.

"Did you think I wouldn't notice the two of you had disappeared?" Tiffany leaned her forearms on the high top.

Brooke grinned. "Honestly, Tiff, I wasn't thinking much about you right then."

"I'm happy for you." Tiffany idly spun a coaster. "You needed to get back on the horse."

"You and your equine references. Are you going to be intolerable if Cab or Neigh becomes a thing?"

Tiffany flipped her hair. "You never know. Maybe it'll become so popular, I'll be mayor by the time I'm forty, date some Hollywood lesbian who jets up to use me for my body, and then get rich when my idea turns into a franchise."

Brooke held up her hand. "Rein it in, girl."

Tiffany took a sip and grinned. "Get off my high horse?"

With a groan, Brooke laid her forehead on the edge of the table. "You've always been a bad influence." She sat up.

"Let's get back to you," Tiffany said, a wicked gleam in her eye. "*I* had nothing to do with what happened after—or was it during—the gala?"

"Yeah, yeah." Brooke waved the taunt away.

"You have more moxie than I give you credit for." Tiffany studied her.

Brooke frowned. "What do you mean?"

"Sleeping with the enemy."

That stung a bit, maybe because it hit too close to the truth.

"What do you hope to get out of it? Other than sex, obviously."

Brooke studied the garnet liquid in her glass. "I'm not sure." She shrugged. "I mean, I wish she'd change her mind about selling the resort. Beyond that, it'd be nice if she liked me enough to stay, but I'm not a hopeless romantic, and I know how these things work." She downed a swig.

"Do you?" Tiffany touched her arm. "I'm worried that you're going to fall in love with her over the next few months and get your heart broken."

If Tiffany only knew how far down that path she'd already traveled. "I'm aware of what's at stake. I know that her decision might mean Rory and I are out on the street."

"And what is that going to do to your feelings for her if that happens?"

Brooke straightened. "If she sells, my feelings won't matter. She'll be in Silicon Valley doing her thing, and I'll be here doing mine."

Tiffany looked at her with sympathetic eyes. "Of course, they'll matter. Feelings don't like to be shoved in bottles and corked."

"Then I'll deal with them then," Brooke said.

"And if they get shaken up and blow their top before that?" Tiffany's eyebrows inched toward her hairline.

"I thought you were going to ask me if she's good in bed, not these nit-picky emotional questions," Brooke grumbled.

"Oh, we'll get to that." Tiffany leaned in. "I don't mean to beat a dead horse, but—"

Brooke poked her in the arm, hard. "One more pony pun, and I'm out of here."

"All right, all right." Tiffany laughed. "I had to get you out of your pathetic mopey state somehow. How's Rory?"

"She's good. Excited to be hanging out with Elizabeth tomorrow afternoon."

"Why?" Tiffany had heard about Elizabeth's take on kids. "Is that safe?"

"Yes, of course. Elizabeth gave me a camera for my birthday, and she offered to take Rory for a few hours so I can take photos."

"Wow." Tiffany raised her eyebrows. "That's a thoughtful present. I gave you a twenty-dollar gift card to Panera."

Brooke squeezed her hand. "I love their mac and cheese."

"What I mean was, that's not really the type of gift you give someone you don't care about, you know?"

Yes, Brooke knew. She'd known the moment she'd opened the box. "Yeah."

"You really think there's some way you two can find a solution to"—Tiffany waved her hands around—"whatever situation you have going on with the two of you and the resort?"

Brooke wrapped her fingers around the stem of her glass. "I'm not sure." No matter which angle she approached it from, it didn't look promising. That didn't mean she wasn't willing to try. Elizabeth was beginning to take hold of her heart, and Brooke wouldn't let her walk away. If she could help it.

CHAPTER TWENTY-TWO

In the resort's loading zone, Elizabeth started Brooke's Volvo and glanced at Rory in the rearview mirror. She looked so tiny and fragile that Elizabeth got out again, went around the car, and opened the back door. "Sorry," she said, tugging on Rory's belt. She gave the booster seat a push to test if it moved. It didn't, so she got back in. At least this make of vehicles was known for its safety rating. That provided some consolation.

"Did you know there are forty thousand muscles in an elephant's trunk?"

Elizabeth closed her eyes. She hadn't even pulled away from the resort. "Did you learn that in school?"

"No."

When Elizabeth had offered to take Rory for the afternoon so Brooke could play with her camera, she hadn't considered the specifics. Like how she'd have to carry on a conversation with a seven-year-old. Constantly.

"They also eat sixteen hours a day."

"You must like elephants."

"Uh-huh. And monkeys." Rory giggled. "I saw one poop at the zoo."

An idea struck Elizabeth. She'd walked by the brochure in the lobby every day since she'd arrived. It was only a matter of seeing if they had any openings left on such short notice. She pulled out her phone and did a quick search. "I have to make a short call."

"Then we'll do something fun?"

"Yes." Elizabeth had planned to take her to a bookstore in Napa and then pray for a bright idea to kill more time, but this would solve everything. "Hello, do you have any tickets left for this afternoon?"

The answer was no, at least for the group tours.

When the woman on the phone suggested a private one, relief washed over Elizabeth, though she winced at the cost. "Let's do it. Yes, we can be there. Thank you." After giving them her credit card number, she hung up and gave Rory a smile, not able to hold it back. "We're about to have an amazing afternoon."

Twenty minutes later, Elizabeth pulled into the parking lot.

"This is where we're going?" Rory peered out the window at the sign. "A safari?"

"What do you think?" Elizabeth watched to see her reaction.

Rory beamed. "I've never been on one." Her smile faded. "Is it safe?"

"Yes." Elizabeth fervently hoped so. She recalled how Brooke hadn't wanted Rory to zipline until she could assess the dangers. But Elizabeth was here, and she'd protect her. Rory was Brooke's daughter, and Elizabeth would lay her life on the line for her. "I'll be with you the entire time."

"I didn't know these kinds of animals lived around here." Rory unbuckled her belt.

"They usually don't. This is an enormous park. It's fenced in, but the animals feel like they're free because it's so big." She hoped. At the very least, it appeared light years better than a zoo.

Once they'd checked in, they met their guide outside, a bald young man named Juwan.

He led them to an open-air vehicle with bench seats, including a row up top. "Where would you like to sit?"

Rory shuffled beside Elizabeth and took her hand. "I don't want to go up there," she said quietly.

"Okay, how about here?"

They slid into the front row behind Juwan.

Within minutes, they'd entered a gate, and animals appeared everywhere as Juwan drove a meandering route. Elizabeth had never seen Rory's eyes so big, so she handed over her phone. "Take as many photos as you like."

And Rory did, pointing and laughing at the wildebeest's ungainly run, taking pictures of antelopes, gazelles, rhinoceros, zebras, cape buffaloes, and more. Juwan provided facts about the animals, told them stories, and even let Rory feed leaves to a giraffe, its black tongue curling to grasp the greens. Through more gates, they encountered carnivores like hyenas and cheetahs. Further on, they came upon the primates, where Rory might have stayed all day. At the end, they viewed egrets, flamingoes, and ostriches, among other birds. All the while, Elizabeth kept a protective arm around her, making sure Rory wasn't too close to the side or near any animals besides the hungry giraffe. She watched Rory more than the wildlife to ensure she was safe so Elizabeth could return her to Brooke in one unharmed, happy piece.

At the end of the three hours, Rory slumped against her, tendrils escaping her braid. Elizabeth undid her barrettes, scraped her nails up the sides and received a cheetah-like purr from her, then secured the loose strands again. She took her phone from Rory's grasp before it slid off the seat, wanting to curl up on the padded bench herself. At least she could finally breathe easily. Why had she chosen this, and how did parents do it? A safe bookstore would've been so much less strain on her heart.

"She's tired out," Juwan said, bringing the vehicle to a stop outside the main building. "The sun will do that."

"All the animals made me sleepy," Rory said as Elizabeth helped her down.

"We should probably skip the gift shop and go straight home then," Elizabeth said, waiting for a reaction.

Rory did an admirable job of perking up, a miniature impression of her mother. "I'm fine," she said with a smile.

Elizabeth laughed. "Let's find a souvenir then."

"Do you want a photo first?" Juwan pointed at the open-sided 4x4. "If you stand here, I'll take it."

Why not? It'd be something to show Brooke. Elizabeth stood by the front tire.

"Jump up on the step," Juwan told Rory.

She did, then threw her arms around Elizabeth.

Elizabeth tentatively held her, discomfort screaming from every pore. When had been the last time she'd hugged a child? She hoped she wouldn't appear stiff and unnatural.

"Smile." He took a few. "Nice."

After tipping Juwan and thanking him, they went inside. There, the fatigue hit, and she let Rory browse while she bought a coffee.

"Can I get this?" Rory held up a stuffed giraffe, brown and cream and about a foot tall.

"I think that's perfect."

Rory clutched it to her chest. "I love him. I'm going to name him Sparkles." She provided no further explanation.

Elizabeth hadn't been driving for five minutes when she checked her mirror and found Rory asleep, the animal in her arms. When she reached the resort, she pulled up to the valet podium where Hilary waited.

"Are you in for the night?" Hilary asked, taking Brooke's keys.

"Yes." Elizabeth went around the car. "Has Brooke returned? She was driving mine."

"Just a few minutes ago," Hilary said. "Grayson is parking it now. Do you need it?"

"No." Elizabeth scooped up Rory, who put her little arms around her neck, the giraffe trapped between them. "Thank you." She handed Hilary a few bills.

"Thanks. Have a good evening."

Elizabeth carried Rory toward the entrance, the girl so much smaller and lighter than Elizabeth had expected. Had Elizabeth picked her up earlier in the day, she would've rethought the safari, considering how fragile Rory seemed. Could she really be seven? Elizabeth recalled feeling so much older, more mature, and… robust…at that age.

When Elizabeth entered the lobby, Brooke leaned on the end of the front desk talking to Francine, her camera around her neck.

She straightened and beelined toward them. "What happened? Is she all right?" She put her hand on Rory's back.

"She's fine. Just tired."

"What's this?" Brooke tweaked the giraffe's head.

"A memento." Elizabeth motioned with her chin. "Let's go up."

Brooke leaned in. "I can take her."

Elizabeth turned slightly. She'd made it this far. "I've got her. You get the elevator."

Once inside Brooke's apartment, Elizabeth laid Rory on her bed, and Brooke slipped off her shoes. She tucked Sparkles in beside her, and they quietly left the room.

Brooke deposited her camera on the table. "Have a seat. Want something to drink?"

Elizabeth dropped onto the couch, the full effect of the afternoon's activity weighing her down. At least her heart rate had returned to normal. "Whatever you're having."

"Water it is then." She brought over two glasses and sat beside Elizabeth. "Hi." She leaned over and kissed her.

Elizabeth wove her fingers into Brooke's hair, kissing her back. "Hi."

Brooke pulled away and took a drink. "Are you going to tell me what you did?"

"You first." Elizabeth couldn't wait to hear if Brooke had enjoyed using her gift.

"I drove up to Robert Louis Stevenson Park and walked around and took photos. I hiked to an overlook and took more of the valley floor. I got some great shots of rock formations and mountains in the distance. A few wildflowers, too, and a raptor in flight." She stopped, breathless.

Elizabeth smiled. "That's wonderful."

Brooke leaned against the cushions. "It was. I haven't done that in so long." She gestured toward the kitchen. "The camera is amazing." She poked Elizabeth with a stockinged toe. "Your turn."

"I had a last-minute idea, and it panned out."

Brooke raised an eyebrow.

"We went on a safari."

Brooke sat up. "The one we advertise downstairs?"

Elizabeth nodded. "They gave us a private tour. I'd estimate Rory took eight hundred photos. Maybe she'll be a photographer like her mom."

"I can't believe you took her there. I never would've expected that." Brooke's mouth hung open.

Elizabeth stiffened, waiting for the admonishment about the danger, but it never came. "Yes."

"That's incredible." Brooke shook her head, as though in disbelief. "And so nice of you. She adores animals."

"I picked up on that." Elizabeth took a drink.

"May I see the photos?"

Elizabeth wavered, wanting to show her but knowing that Rory would get so much more out of it. "Only one." She pulled up the snapshot Juwan had taken.

Brooke studied it, smiling. She looked up. "This is officially my favorite picture ever." She studied it for a moment. "To cap off the most perfect birthday."

"Good. I'm glad." Elizabeth wanted to give Brooke everything, yet she had so little to offer. A hard knot of something formed in her chest, knowing she'd made Brooke happy but also realizing it wouldn't last long. A few months, at most.

"What made you think of going?" Brooke straddled Elizabeth's lap, pushing her fingers into her hair.

Elizabeth ran her hands up Brooke's legs to her waist. "She was spouting facts about elephants."

"Ah." Brooke nodded, kissing her lightly. "She watched a show on them recently. Did they have them there?"

"No." Elizabeth slid her hands under Brooke's shirt and lightly trailed her fingertips over her belly. "Lots of other ones, though." She leaned in, kissing her harder, and pulled Brooke closer.

Brooke sank into it, touching Elizabeth's face, her neck, her breasts through her shirt. But when Elizabeth slid her hand beneath Brooke's bra, she halted her progress. "If we're going to take this further, and I wouldn't mind if we did, we need to move to the bedroom."

Elizabeth adjusted Brooke's clothing. "She's probably not down for the night. I didn't feed her dinner."

Brooke gazed at her as she sorted wayward strands of Elizabeth's hair back into their proper places. "Can you wait?"

Of course she could. "Yes." She'd waited this long for an incredible woman like Brooke to walk into her life, not that she'd been conscious of it. She'd been satisfied, working, unaware someone so amazing existed. The worst part was, the longer she pretended their connection was real, the harder it was going to be to leave. She wouldn't miss freaking out about keeping Rory safe, though. At least the afternoon had been a success, and she'd been able to give Brooke a breather.

CHAPTER TWENTY-THREE

In front of the resort, Brooke stood beside Elizabeth as three men and a woman wearing her keys on a carabiner lifted the sculpture from the back of the truck and moved it to the center of the fountain. A somber mood hung over Brooke despite the quintessential summer afternoon. Did Elizabeth feel it, too?

"This way. A little more. Okay, set it down carefully. That's it. Good." The woman straightened and looked at Brooke. "It'll take us about thirty minutes to weld it in place, and tomorrow we'll hook up the water and test it. You'll need to keep the barricade up to keep people back until then." She hooked her thumbs in her pockets. "You'll have to get out of here, too. Looking at the flame is harmful."

Brooke eyed the temporary plywood walls they'd built. Unsightly didn't begin to cover it, but guest safety was paramount. "Got it." She turned to Elizabeth. They'd witnessed one of the crew encase Margaret's remains in concrete and place her plaque atop it. Elizabeth had held her hand the entire time. "Ready?"

Elizabeth nodded as they walked toward the entrance. "It really turned out beautifully."

"Didn't it?" Brooke had bought the fountain from a local artist who'd designed the ten-foot-tall copper piece. Water would soon flow over hundreds of grape leaves, dropping from one onto another. She imagined it would sound lovely.

"What do you think we should do with the coins people will inevitably throw into it?"

The basin surrounding the sculpture measured twenty feet across, and spouts of water would burst from the surface at the four marked positions of the compass. Lights would illuminate it at night.

Brooke shrugged. "Donate it?"

Elizabeth stopped in the lobby. "Perhaps to the nonprofit that does the gala." She motioned toward the bar. "It's been an emotional afternoon, and it's close enough to five. Do you want a drink?"

"Let's get one and go to the library." They hadn't played chess in over a week. Other things had kept them busy—in bed, and on other surfaces. Brooke's body gave a little stir just thinking about it.

Wine in hand, they headed upstairs, and thankfully, no one occupied their table and board. They took their usual chairs.

"Which color do you want?" Unlike her father, Brooke didn't have a preference. She'd learned to play strategically based on either start.

"White," Elizabeth said.

Midway through the game, Brooke remembered something. "I bought a kit for you. It's upstairs."

"A what?" Lines formed across Elizabeth's forehead.

"A DNA test kit. The one that'll link you to any family trees if you have the same genes."

Elizabeth paled. "I told you. I'm not interested in doing that."

Brooke held up her hands. "You don't have to use it, but you'll have it if you decide to."

Splotches formed on Elizabeth's exposed chest. "You shouldn't have bought it. That's not your decision."

"Maybe I'll do Rory's at some point. It's not a big deal." Brooke tried to play it off nonchalantly, but her pulse raced seeing Elizabeth's reaction.

"It *is* a big deal." Elizabeth threw back a large gulp of wine and set the glass down roughly. "I asked you to leave the topic alone, and you keep bringing it up. Just drop it."

"But your sisters—"

"Are *my* sisters, and I have no interest in contacting them." Frown lines bracketed her mouth. "Jesus. They're in their mid-to-late thirties. They probably have families."

"Exactly." They'd abandoned the game. "Wouldn't you like to meet them? What are you afraid of?"

Elizabeth stood. "Maybe you haven't noticed, but I don't possess your Pollyanna outlook. Some days, the sun doesn't shine, and try as you may, you can't make it. I'm forty-two years old. I've made it this long. I don't need a family." She strode out of the library, leaving her wine, the unfinished game, and Brooke behind.

Brooke didn't understand where she'd gone wrong. She'd gotten a great deal on it, twenty-five percent off. Her intention had only been to help. Was she projecting? Because she missed Brian and wished he was still in her life? She finished her drink and reached for Elizabeth's. So much for trying to be helpful.

Her gut told her to let Elizabeth stew, but after depositing the empty glasses at the bar, she went upstairs and knocked on her door.

Elizabeth answered it shortly.

"Hi." Brooke pushed her hands into her pockets, feeling a little woozy from downing the wine so quickly. "I came to apologize."

Elizabeth leaned on the doorframe, not inviting her in. "Okay."

Brooke gnawed on her lip. "It's not my place, and I shouldn't have interfered. I'm sorry."

With a nod, Elizabeth straightened to her full height. "Thanks." She looked down. "I think I need a little time alone this evening, if you don't mind."

"Oh, sure." Brooke took a step back. "I'll be at"—she jerked a thumb over her shoulder—"my place." She tried for a smile. "I'll see you in the morning?"

"Yes." Elizabeth broke eye contact. "Good night." She closed her door.

Brooke stood there a minute. Interring Margaret had been emotional. Maybe it'd contributed to Elizabeth's sour mood. Regardless, Brooke wouldn't bring up the DNA testing again, though it would've been incredible if Elizabeth could've found her sisters. Brooke let herself into her apartment, and a sense of loneliness washed over her. Even Rory's bright presence couldn't lift her spirits. Sean had her the next few nights.

Brooke's mood improved as she recalled Rory packing for her dad's and making sure Sparkles went with her. She'd loved spending time with Elizabeth and talked about their safari nonstop. In fact, she'd been verbally effusive ever since Elizabeth had arrived in Calistoga. Brooke didn't know why her daughter had connected with Elizabeth, but she had. Whether the opposite was true was still in question. Elizabeth appeared so uneasy around Rory, stiff and almost troubled, at times.

Brooke sank onto her couch and hugged an orange throw pillow. She knew she shouldn't go out with someone who didn't like kids, but she and Elizabeth weren't dating. Basically, they seemed to be having sex while Elizabeth was here, if Brooke hadn't wrecked things tonight. She hadn't even received a kiss good night. Elizabeth didn't know about Brooke's burgeoning feelings, and Brooke wouldn't open her heart when disaster likely descended in a few months. Elizabeth appeared to tolerate Rory, and that was enough—enough for this strange limbo Brooke found herself in.

CHAPTER TWENTY-FOUR

Elizabeth yanked open her refrigerator. She shouldn't have reacted so harshly, but she'd had enough of the constant reminders Calistoga held without Brooke urging her to find her sisters every time she turned around. They'd been taken from Elizabeth decades ago, and she'd come to terms with it. She'd had to in order to get through life. They weren't the same little girls she remembered, but adult strangers. She didn't need a setback. She didn't need to sift through the heartbreaking memories. And she certainly didn't need Brooke nagging her about it.

Her annoyance escalated as she assessed her choices. She'd been eating meals with Brooke and Rory so often lately she hadn't gone shopping, and her kitchen held few options, none of which looked appetizing. Seltzer water, wilted baby carrots, a brand of Greek yogurt she found too grainy, and condiments. Her rummage through the pantry fared no better. She supposed she could eat at the restaurant or order Chef Sophie's nightly special as room service. Which would she prefer? Hiding away or venturing out?

Sulking sounded the most tempting. Maybe she and Brooke needed a break from one another. They'd been spending almost all their time together when Rory was with Sean, whom Elizabeth had grown to like. He clearly adored Rory and had no problem playing dolls with her or letting her paint his fingernails. Add in handsome and funny, and if Elizabeth were into men, she could see what Brooke had found alluring. But she wasn't. So, her admiration and respect for Sean remained platonic.

With no dinner options sounding the least bit interesting, Elizabeth changed. A walk would do her good. If she came across something while out, so be it. If not, she didn't care. She simply wanted to get downstairs without Brooke trying to swab her cheek. Brooke's success at the resort might rely on her keen ability to problem-solve, but Elizabeth didn't fall into that category. She wasn't Brooke's issue to fix.

With luck gracing her, she made it to the lobby with no interception. There though, she heard her name, and a soft impact hit her thighs. She looked down to find Rory hugging her and tentatively laid her hand on Rory's back.

"Where're you going?" Rory gazed up at her.

"For a walk." Elizabeth looked up. "Hi, Kali."

"Hello. I've heard so much about the safari." She gave Rory a loving glance.

Elizabeth hoped Rory had been complimentary.

"She's trying to talk her dad and me into staying overnight there." Kali shivered. "I don't know. I'm not into camping, and the thought of all those creatures right outside terrifies me."

"If it makes you feel any better, they looked like well-built cabins." While there, Elizabeth had briefly flashed to an imagined scenario of her and Brooke staying there with Rory, nestled in sleeping bags, trying to discern the origin of a growl or shriek. If Sean and Kali took her, there wouldn't be much point. The thought didn't bring relief though, but a hollow sensation of missing out on something. "How is the wedding planning going?"

Kali laughed. "It's crazy. I never realized how much work it would be. I'm enjoying it, though. Sean less so, but he's been great humoring me when I ask for his opinion."

Rory tugged Kali's sleeve. "We need to hurry. I left Sparkles in the car."

"All right, kiddo." Kali put an arm around Rory's shoulders. "Let's get your swimsuit. Nice seeing you again."

"You, too."

"Bye, Elizabeth."

Rory hugged her again, and once more, Elizabeth wasn't sure what she was supposed to do. She settled for tucking a loose curl into Rory's braid. "Bye. I'll see you in a few days." When Rory would be back with them.

She froze mid-step.

No, back with *Brooke*. What the holy hell? Elizabeth needed to get outside and breathe in some of Mother Nature's elixir, fast. She passed Johnny the bellhop. "The lobby air is stale. Open the doors and air it out."

"Yes, ma'am." He flinched and hurried toward the entrance.

If her sharp tongue made people scurry away like rodents and keep their distance, good. The less she became attached to here, the better. She headed outside.

Right before her walk took her toward downtown, her phone rang. Geoff. She answered. "Hi, you. Everything okay?"

"It's great. I'm calling for pleasure, not business." Music filtered through the phone. "I happen to be in Napa. My buddy needed a last-minute date for a wedding, so I agreed to come. He's busy doing rehearsal dinner stuff tonight and said I could join him if I wanted, but I don't know anyone and wanted to see you if you're free. Any interest in meeting me?"

Elizabeth stopped. The evening was young, and she hadn't seen Geoff since she'd left. "I'd love to. I can be there in an hour."

"Fantastic." He sounded more excited than she'd thought he'd be. "There's a lovely restaurant on the riverfront with outdoor seating." He gave her the name. "I'll be sipping a drink, enjoying the view, and waiting for you. No hurry."

Elizabeth had already turned and headed back. "I look forward to it." She hadn't seen his crooked smile and slouchy clothing for too long. They hung up, and she increased her pace. After her argument with Brooke, a night out with a friend would lift her spirits.

Less than an hour later, the host, a short man wearing a vest and askew tie, escorted Elizabeth onto the cobblestone patio.

"That's him. Thank you." She approached Geoff, who stood and hugged her.

"You look fabulous." He held her at arm's length. "Wine country looks good on you."

"You look great, too." He'd dressed nicer than he did for work, and it made her wonder if he was trying to impress the guy he'd come with. "So, who's your date?" She sat beside him and picked up the drink menu, not that she planned to order anything alcoholic, but more and more places served tasty and inventive mocktails.

"He works in engineering. We met when he dropped by the office wanting to adjust his withholdings."

"You just met?"

Geoff rolled his eyes. "No. I've probably known him almost as long as you've been gone, which seems like forever."

It had, in some ways. She hadn't known Brooke all that long, mere months, yet Elizabeth had connected with her on a deeper level than with anyone, even Geoff.

"Ma'am?" Their server, a young woman with a long braid that reminded Elizabeth of Rory, stood waiting, a tablet at the ready to take her order.

"Oh, sorry." Elizabeth glanced at the menu, picking the first non-alcoholic cocktail that jumped out. "I'll have an Oxbow."

"One Oxbow and another Lagunitas. I'll give you some time to look at the menu." She darted off.

When their drinks arrived, they ordered an appetizer and settled back. Fairy lights above twinkled on, and the gentle lapping of the river and murmured conversation of the other guests created a welcome and relaxed environment.

Geoff cracked the knuckles of one hand with his thumb. "So, what's really keeping you here?"

"What do you mean?" What was he getting at? She wished he'd simply speak plainly.

He studied her. "You're one of the most brilliant people I've ever met. Either the resort's finances are so effed up you should've offloaded it in March, or there's more to the story. It wouldn't take the Elizabeth Bettancourt I know this long to understand whatever's going on." He gave her a grin. "What's her name?"

"What do you mean?" She looked away and took a sip.

"The woman you mentioned. Is that who has you acting strange?"

Elizabeth must've hesitated too long, because Geoff laughed loudly enough to make a few patrons glance their way. He waggled his eyebrows. "She *is*."

"She's…I mean, the resort…I needed to learn how the resort functioned, and she basically runs it." Elizabeth could give a TED Talk on global payroll, yet she couldn't seem to form a coherent sentence when it involved Brooke.

"What does she look like?"

"She…" Elizabeth faltered, not knowing how she'd gotten talked into discussing Brooke. "She's absolutely beautiful." Elizabeth might as well give up the ghost. Geoff knew her too well and would see right through her.

"But she's your employee." He smiled and crossed his legs.

Elizabeth relaxed, too, her secret out in the open. "The resort has a contract with the hospitality company she works for."

"She must know her stuff."

"She does. As general manager, she's fantastic." Elizabeth could tick off a few more things on her fingers Brooke excelled at but refrained.

Geoff thanked the server, who deposited the warm dip they'd ordered. "So, what's the problem?"

Elizabeth blinked. "Do you recall that empty house you're supposed to be checking once in a while?"

"I do." He scooped some chips onto his plate. "I go in, look around and make sure your housekeeper is doing her job and leave. You stopped your mail. It's not like you have any pets to care for or plants to water. Honestly, it's kind of dark and depressing in there with the blinds drawn, but I get that you're saving energy while you're gone."

"You can turn lights on while you're there."

"I do." He took a bite and chewed while she put a spoonful on her plate. "I just mean it's sort of dead. Nothing alive. It gives me the willies to be inside when you're not there."

Did he just call her house creepy?

"You know what I mean," he said, picking up his beer.

She wasn't sure she did. Should she be offended? "I can ask someone else to look in on it."

"Don't overreact, Elizabeth. I don't mind doing it. I'm just saying it might be nice to bring in a violet or two when you come back."

"How very lesbian."

He grinned.

She thought she'd be able to shake off her funk when she'd arrived at the restaurant, but mild irritation continued to simmer. Who was he to tell her how to decorate her home? First, she'd been upset with Brooke, and now with Geoff, arguably the two people in the world closest to her. This perimenopausal crap was getting tiresome. She took a drink, slightly annoyed it wouldn't take off any edge.

"So, you like this woman." He didn't state it as a question.

Elizabeth sighed. "It doesn't matter." She looked out over the water where a small boat tugged toward the dock. "I'm only here temporarily, so it's not going anywhere with her. Besides, she has a daughter."

"Oh, ouch for you." He, too, seemed to appreciate the scenery before them. "I don't know, though. If I had a means of staying here, I would, kid or not."

She pointed at his beer. "You don't even drink wine."

"I know, but look at this place." He gestured toward the river and vine-covered hills. "It's gorgeous."

Elizabeth couldn't disagree. She'd always loved the beauty of the valley, even as a child. Could she imagine a life here, with Brooke—Brooke *and* Rory? The resort had been her home-away-from-foster-home as a teen, and Margaret, her savior. The property would always have a special place in her heart. Could she one day drive around without recalling the store on the corner was where her mom used to buy her father's favorite aftershave? Or cross that one street without thinking of Bartoletti and her sisters? Could she, with a bit more time? Were Brooke and Rory worth it? Or was Elizabeth like she'd always thought, someone uncomfortable around children and content with her predictable life at home?

She didn't stay very late since Geoff had plans the next day, and this amount of introspection always tired her. It'd been nice to see him, to hear about how her department was doing, apparently just fine under his watch, as she'd suspected it'd be. At the pace he'd progressed, he'd be running his own soon. There wasn't anyone for her to ask about. She didn't consider any of the processors her friends, and with work being the focus of her life, no time to make any outside of it either.

So, Elizabeth drove back to Calistoga and, like a teenager coming home an hour past curfew, snuck up to her apartment. She didn't run into Brooke, and as she locked her door for the night, disappointment hit her like a train ramming into a car stalled on the tracks.

CHAPTER TWENTY-FIVE

At her desk, with the workday almost finished, Brooke thought back to yesterday's confrontation with Elizabeth. A quick glance found Elizabeth focused on her laptop screen, her glasses sliding down her nose, and a little crease between her eyebrows that often appeared when something perplexed her.

When she'd greeted Elizabeth that morning, she could've sworn she'd dreamed up the entire argument over the DNA test. Elizabeth acted like nothing had happened, so Brooke swallowed her reservations and did the same. Maybe a good night's sleep had changed Elizabeth's outlook, or perhaps she'd realized that Brooke had been well-intentioned and had forgiven her. Whichever the case, Brooke gratefully gave silent thanks she didn't have to tiptoe around Elizabeth and could focus on her job.

"I emailed you my suggested front desk schedule," Francine said from the doorway as she lifted her purse to her shoulder. "I'm done for the day." She tapped her cane once on the floor.

"Thanks, I'll look at it." Brooke smiled. "Enjoy your evening."

"What are your plans tonight?" Elizabeth asked after she'd gone.

Brooke looked up. "I don't have any. Last night, I had a craving for—" She glanced at her vibrating phone. "Hang on, please. It's Sean."

"Hi."

"Brooke, you need to come to the school right away."

Brooke stood, already opening her drawer to grab her wallet. "Is Rory all right? What's going on?" As she headed for the door, Elizabeth rose and followed.

"I got here to pick her up, and they don't seem to know where she is."

Sean's tone frightened her. Not much unnerved him, but Brooke didn't like the way his voice cracked. "Oh, my God. What do you mean they can't find her?"

"She's lost?" Elizabeth jogged beside her.

Elizabeth reached the valet station two steps ahead of Brooke. "Her car or mine, whichever one we can get out quickly," Elizabeth said, holding out her hand to Marco. "Hurry."

He sprung to life, opening the locked cupboard. "Here's yours. It's right over there." He pointed to where they'd backed it in. "Want me to get it?"

Elizabeth had already grabbed the keys and taken off running.

In Brooke's ear, Sean asked someone a string of rapid questions. His heavy breaths came across the line, and she wondered if he was running. "Sean." Brooke ran after Elizabeth, who pulled forward so she could get in. "When did they see her last?"

"I don't know. I'm trying to get answers. They're looking for her, but we're calling the authorities for help. Can you just get here? I can't talk to you and them at the same time. I just want to find my goddamned daughter."

"I'm already on my way. Call me with any updates." Brooke hit end and looked at Elizabeth. She white-knuckled the steering wheel as she sped toward Rory's school. "Be safe," Brooke said quietly, a cold sweat making her shirt stick to her back.

"They can't find her?"

Brooke turned, the sheer terror in Elizabeth's voice throwing her. "These day programs, they're run by young adults, sometimes teens. It's probably just confusion." She wouldn't voice the horrific, dark thoughts running through her mind that read like an arm-length rap sheet for a prisoner at San Quentin. She should've made Rory carry a tracker. She shouldn't have let her go to summer day camp.

She should be the one driving so she could go faster, faster and rescue her daughter from whomever or whatever had befallen her.

At the sharp pain, Brooke relaxed her fists, staring at the curved impressions her nails had carved into her palms. The clock said they'd only been in the car for a few minutes, but it felt like an eternity. Should she call Sean and check in? Brooke bit her lower lip and tried not to cry.

Elizabeth reached over and squeezed her knee. Soon, she made the turn into the school parking lot and screeched to a halt in the fire zone near a group of people.

Brooke had her seat belt off and the door open before they'd come to a full stop. She raced toward where Sean gestured wildly at a woman with corkscrew-curly hair. Without looking, Brooke knew Elizabeth would be right behind her. She grabbed Sean's arm.

He barely acknowledged her. "I want to talk to the last person who laid eyes on her and what time that was. Now."

"The kids have had a busy day," the woman said. "They've been doing activities inside and ou—"

"I don't care." Sean's face looked like it might pop like an over-inflated balloon. "Your entire job is to watch over them."

Brooke stepped in. "Where were you when you discovered Rory was missing?"

The woman's eyes filled with tears, and she pointed. "In there. We asked all the kids to get their backpacks ready to go home and go back to their tables. A boy in Rory's group noticed she wasn't there." She sniffed. "Staff are searching the rest of the rooms." People indeed milled about in a disorganized fashion with no one appearing to know what to do.

Sean had already taken off toward where she'd motioned, but Brooke didn't know his intentions. To open all the cupboards and closets? Surely, someone had already done that, right? Brooke's heart was about to beat through her chest wall. She stepped closer. "What's your name?"

"Beth."

"Beth, did you call the police?"

"Ryan did." She pointed. "He's talking to them now."

Unfortunate acne covered Ryan's cheeks and forehead, and he looked to be barely out of high school. Brooke turned, but Elizabeth wasn't behind her anymore. She looked toward the parking lot. The car was still there. Where had Elizabeth gone? Brooke spun, and movement caught her eye. Someone ran toward the wooden fence that separated the playing area from the field of golden mustard and wildflowers beyond.

Elizabeth.

When she reached the boundary, Elizabeth grabbed the post and hurled her body over the fence line, landing smoothly on the other side. She stopped and bent toward the ground, then burst into the dense thicket of tall overgrowth and disappeared.

Brooke slipped out of her low heels and took off at a sprint. "Elizabeth!" She ran, following the same direct path, rocks and sticks poking the soles of her feet until she reached the rough-hewn wooden beams. At her height, she wouldn't be able to clear them, so she squeezed herself between the top two. Her shirt snagged and ripped, but she pushed through and stood. "Elizabeth?" No rustling of greenery. "Rory?" No voices returning her shouts. She took a few steps toward the bright yellow and green plants and stopped. There on the ground, a few feet apart, lay Rory's purple shoes, one upside down. Had she taken them off? Had they fallen off when someone grabbed her? Brooke didn't want to touch them in case the authorities would need to gather evidence, and the thought squeezed her chest like a vice. She didn't have enough air, enough room for everything inside. The pain. The love she had for her daughter.

"Rory!" she screamed with all her might. This time, Brooke heard something.

CHAPTER TWENTY-SIX

Elizabeth sneezed. Crashing through the towering weeds in the field next to Rory's school had stirred up clouds of pollen. "Rory?" She pushed on, noticing some stalks near the ground looked trampled. Without any landmarks to guide her, she had to rely on her sense of direction. She estimated she'd gone thirty yards, but she hadn't reached the other side, though she could hear the passing cars on the road there.

She'd been standing near Brooke, feeling helpless when she'd looked around, hoping to spot someone or something that might give them answers. That's when she'd noticed the field, the one abloom with mustard and smaller purple weeds. Knowing Rory's penchant for picking flowers, Elizabeth had taken off.

There. Near her feet lay a broken stem, as if someone had snapped off the upper half. Nearby, something had crushed others. "Rory?" She parted the tall plants.

Then she heard it.

"Who are you?" The question held confusion rather than fear.

Elizabeth's heart skipped a beat. "It's me. Elizabeth."

"Why're you here?"

Elizabeth strained to determine the direction from which Rory's voice emanated. The sound bounced around the foliage, obscuring it. She needed to find Rory, but she also didn't want to alarm her. Elizabeth had an idea. "I'm here to talk elephants. Did you know their trunks have a-hundred-million-thousand muscles?"

A laugh.

Had it come from the left?

"No, they don't. Forty thousand."

"Are you sure?" Elizabeth pressed on, parting the greenery with her arms before stepping through. "I heard it was more."

"Uh-uh. That's not true."

Her heart rate began to slow, but behind her, Brooke and Sean had no idea she'd located Rory. When she reached in her pocket for her phone, she came up empty. In her haste to follow Brooke, she'd left it on her desk. "Who told you that? Are you with someone?" While she believed Rory to be alone, she needed to make sure.

"No. I saw it on my favorite show."

Elizabeth needed to keep her talking. Rory sounded closer now. "Did you know they eat twenty-four hours a day?"

Laughter. "No, they don't. When would they sleep?"

"Elephants sleep?" Almost there.

"Only an hour or two a day. Did you know they only lie down every few days? They can sleep while they're standing."

Elizabeth burst through, and Rory stood in her stockinged feet holding a handful of blooms. She scooped her up, examining her. "Are you all right?"

"My socks got muddy. But I took off my new shoes so they wouldn't get dirty."

The innocence of it all speared Elizabeth's heart. "Everyone is very worried about you. We need to get back." She shifted Rory to her hip so she could part the way with one arm.

"Is Ms. Wimple mad?"

"Just worried. We all were." Elizabeth wished she'd told Brooke where she'd gone. Now that she'd found Rory, the stress and the exertion seemed to be getting to her. She sucked in a deep breath.

"I can walk." Rory tightened her hold around Elizabeth's neck, her little bouquet tickling Elizabeth's ear.

"It's okay. I've got you." Elizabeth hoped she headed the right direction. She stopped, trying to gauge the sun's position so she could find her way back to the school. With no trampling sounds, she heard it.

"Elizabeth? Rory?"

Brooke.

"In here. We're coming out. Keep talking to me so I can head toward you."

"Rory?"

"Mom, I picked you some flowers. They're really pretty."

Jesus. Elizabeth shifted Rory to her other hip. She'd need an antihistamine after this. As much as she tried, she simply couldn't draw in enough air.

"You did? Elizabeth, I'm waiting at the edge for you by Rory's shoes. Is everything…" A pause. "Is everything okay?"

Brooke was clearly inquiring whether Rory was in harm's way at any point without explicitly asking. "We're great. All by herself playing florist. We're trying to find our way through the jungle now."

"Well, I'm right here waiting for you, and Daddy and Kali are almost here, too."

Of course, Sean would've called his fiancé, too. Elizabeth wiped her face. Had pollen gotten in her eyes? She tried to blink them clear. When was the last time she'd eaten anything? Dizziness seemed to be setting in. Low blood sugar? "Uh, Brooke."

"Right here. You sound closer now. Should I come in?"

"No, just keep talking." Elizabeth's chest ached, and she hugged Rory tighter. Why had the little thing run off? Hadn't she been taught the dangers?

"We're all right here, and I have your shoes, Rory. Kali has your backpack, and all the staff are waiting to see you, too."

Elizabeth pushed on toward Brooke's voice. In her arms, Rory barely weighed anything, so ephemeral and fragile, her fingers, no bigger around than crayons, grasping her prized collection. Why had she wandered off and caused them all such a fright? Whether because of negligence or more nefarious means, Elizabeth couldn't take the thought of losing her. She nearly tripped. When had that happened?

"Are you okay?" Rory wrapped her legs tightly around Elizabeth.

Was she afraid Elizabeth would drop her?

"I think we're almost there. Momma sounds close." Rory pointed, never letting go of whatever she'd picked. "That way."

Elizabeth's vision swam, and she concentrated on putting one foot in front of the other. How long had she been in here?

"Elizabeth? Are you okay?"

Brooke's voice pulled her back. *Get to Brooke.* "Almost there."

"Okay. Take your time. We think we know where you are based on the rustling. Do you want me or Sean to help you?"

Elizabeth tried to respond, but her mouth had become so dry, she couldn't. She gathered whatever she had left and moved toward Brooke's voice. *Get to Brooke. Get to Brooke.* She pushed through, and more light came through the less-dense weeds. A little more, and suddenly she broke through to the clearing where Rory had discarded her beloved purple sneakers.

"Oh, my God." Brooke grabbed Rory, crying and crushing her in a hug. "I'm so glad you're safe. You scared me to death."

Sean and Kali stood beside her.

"You can't wander off like that, little bug." He rubbed Rory's back. "We're going to have to have a talk about safety again."

Brooke kissed Rory's cheek again and again. "Never do that again, please."

By now, tears streamed down Rory's cheeks, too. "I just wanted to pick you some pretty flowers."

"I know," Brooke said, "but you scared us. No one knew where you were."

"Elizabeth knew," Rory said, sniffling.

The reunion took place as though on the other side of a glass wall. Voices had become muffled, and everything took on a surreal quality. Elizabeth's heart raced, the blood pounding in her ears.

Brooke turned to her, saying something, and her eyes went wide. She shoved Rory at Sean.

The last thing Elizabeth remembered was Brooke shouting her name as she grabbed a fistful of Elizabeth's shirt, and the ground came up to meet her.

❖

Elizabeth took a drink from the water bottle Brooke handed her. With Brooke's help, she'd raised herself to a seated position on the grass.

"Any better?" Brooke's eyebrows drew together in obvious concern.

Elizabeth nodded and instantly regretted it as her lightheadedness returned.

Sean stood nearby, hands in his back pockets, and Kali and Rory had disappeared. The day-camp staff seemed to be leaving, as did two police cruisers Elizabeth hadn't heard arrive. Their taillights reminded her of those receding ones long ago. Her head still buzzed, and someone's breathing sounded ragged. *Hers.*

"It's the adrenaline wearing off," Brooke said.

It was more than that. "Where's Rory?"

"Kali took her to the bathroom to wash up before they go home. Thank you for finding her." Brooke kissed Elizabeth on the forehead from where she knelt beside her.

Sean looked away.

"You're getting your pants dirty."

Brooke scrutinized her. "I don't care. Are you okay?"

"I think so." Elizabeth tried to stand and accepted Sean's help. "Thanks."

"We can't thank you enough." He shook his head. "Of course, she would've gone toward the pretty things."

"Yes." Elizabeth pressed two fingers to her temple. She couldn't deal with this. Not again. "I think it's time to go home."

"Let's get you back to the resort." Brooke hooked her arm through Elizabeth's.

That hadn't been what Elizabeth had meant, but she desperately wanted to get away from here, from what'd almost happened. "You should probably drive."

"Planned on it." Brooke clung to her more tightly as they said goodbye to Sean. Then she gently squeezed Elizabeth's hand. "Seriously, I can't thank you enough."

"It's fine." Elizabeth waved her off. Guilt slammed into her for telling Brooke such a blatant lie, but until she could carve some time out for herself to make sense of it all, she didn't know what else to say. This is what it all came down to. She'd tried for decades to fake being whole, to paste on a successful and psychologically well-adjusted facade, and it'd come crumbling down in the span of a summer afternoon. "I think I'll sleep for a bit."

"Sure. Whatever you need."

"Do you need to see Rory first?"

"I already told her goodbye. She doesn't need me crying over her again. Sean and Kali will address what happened tonight." Brooke led her to her car and helped her get in.

Everything had been such a blur earlier, so frantic and crazy. But not now. Elizabeth had found Rory. So, why did her heart pound like nothing had changed?

When they returned to the resort, Elizabeth retrieved her phone from their office, and she and Brooke took the elevator upstairs and paused outside their doors.

"Do you think you should be alone?"

Brooke's concern-filled eyes tugged at something in Elizabeth's chest, but she nodded. "I'll be fine." Someday.

"Okay." Brooke lingered. "Can I check on you later?"

"Sure. Text me." Elizabeth keyed in and rested her back against the closed door. She doubted she'd be able to sleep, but it gave her an excuse to be alone, and she needed the space. The afternoon's events, with no warning, had set things in motion.

There'd be no going back after this. Especially with Brooke.

CHAPTER TWENTY-SEVEN

As Brooke sat on her sofa and buckled the straps on her wedge sandals, her thoughts strayed to Elizabeth. When she'd checked on her last night, she'd only received a short text in return. At least she knew Elizabeth was feeling better and not unconscious. She would've like to have seen her, though. The stress of the day had zapped her, too, and she wished they could've relaxed together by watching a movie or simply talking.

She considered calling Elizabeth and suggesting they take a day off. Dashiell would be there, and surely the resort could survive eight hours without them. Maybe they could go wine tasting or ziplining, or take a walk along the Napa River.

Brooke rose upon hearing a knock at the door, knowing it could only be one person. When she opened it, Elizabeth stood before her in her charcoal skirt suit and heels. "Hi."

"Hi." Elizabeth didn't make eye contact. "May I come in?"

Brooke stepped aside. "Of course."

"Thank you." Elizabeth gestured toward the living room. "Can we sit?"

What was happening? "Yes." A premonition told Brooke to remain standing, not to give in to whatever this was, but she took a seat on the sofa anyway. To her surprise, Elizabeth chose a spot away from her on the overstuffed chair and perched on its edge. "How are you feeling?"

Elizabeth looked up but didn't answer right away. She folded her hands. "The adrenaline rush, or whatever that was, has passed."

"That's good." The slow start to this conversation made Brooke fidget. Even her neck itched.

"I wanted to talk to you."

There it was, that phrase that preceded nothing good. Sean had said the same thing the night he told her he'd met Kali, developed feelings for her, and thought he and Brooke should separate. "About?" The word barely got past the knot in her throat.

"I've decided to sell the resort." Elizabeth looked away.

A weight slammed into Brooke, not unlike when she'd heard Rory was lost. She tried not to show her deflating emotions. "What made you come to that decision early?"

"This town, it's not good for me. There are too many reminders here, too many painful memories I keep bumping into."

The chair looked like it might swallow Elizabeth whole. She looked small, frail, sitting there. This wasn't the strong, powerful woman Brooke had met a few months earlier. Maybe it wasn't too late. Perhaps she could still get through to her. They'd established a connection, a strong one, at that. "Is there any way I could change your mind?"

Elizabeth shook her head, meeting her gaze. "I called a real estate agent yesterday. She's put it on the market and said she already knew of two buyers who'd expressed interest in the past."

It was all happening so fast. Brooke glanced around. This apartment she and Rory had called home for over a year would be gone soon. How much time did she have? Would she find another place for them? The sale also meant she'd likely be looking for a new job. Most resorts hired management staff of their own. Brooke wanted to bury her face in her hands. It was all so much, and she already dealt with a shitload of things every day. How would she manage it all?

"I'm sorry," Elizabeth said quietly. "It's not personal."

Brooke laughed, wanting to disagree, and the sardonic sound startled her. "Yeah, well." She took a deep breath. "I suppose this means you'll be leaving soon." Elizabeth had to have known what this would do to them. Obviously, Brooke didn't factor in enough to have mattered.

"I packed last night. I didn't have much." Elizabeth shifted on the cushion.

She'd been right. Elizabeth *was* ready to bolt. Always running away. Even her connection with Brooke hadn't been enough to stop a habit that strong. "When do you leave?"

"When I'm done here." For just a moment, something flashed across Elizabeth's face, as though her leaving might be as hard on her as it'd be for Brooke, but it quickly vanished.

Brooke joined her hands to stop their shaking. "I'm sorry to hear that, for many reasons." She looked up. "Rory will be sad she didn't get to say good-bye." How would she explain this to a seven-year-old? That someone she cared about could up and disappear from her life without a word. How could she when she didn't fully comprehend it herself? "Did what happened yesterday have something to do with this?" Her chest ached and her mind whirred as she tried to understand.

"It made me realize I can't live here. I tried, and…" Elizabeth didn't finish.

After she clearly wasn't going to continue, Brooke shifted down the sofa closer to her, to possibly connect with her one last time. "Are you sure this is what you want?"

A beat passed, then Elizabeth nodded.

Darkness settled over Brooke. This woman who'd come to mean so much to her had decided to leave with hardly a backward glance. It was time to lay all her cards on the table. "I…I have feelings for you, you know."

Elizabeth's eyes welled with tears, and she nodded again. "I know." She swallowed. "I have them for you, too. But I can't keep reliving my past, so we can't have a relationship, no matter how much I care about you."

Brooke wanted to reach out and take her hand, but she didn't. It wouldn't change anything. That much was clear. "I hope, eventually, you can get yourself to a place where you can admit you were a child back then, one without options. I hope"—she choked back a sob—"I hope you find some peace." She swiped at an errant tear and stood, her back to Elizabeth.

Cold and dismal silence surrounded them. The only exceptions were the thudding of her pulse in her ears and one escaped sniffle. After a bit, a squeak of hinges and a click told her Elizabeth had left.

Brooke didn't know how long she stood there. What was she supposed to do now? Should she go to work like her heart hadn't just been broken and hold her breath until she received word the place had sold?

She'd never been one to sit back and wait for something to happen. Initiative might be the one thing to help her get through this. She'd take a few days off and search for a place for her and Rory to live. If she got lucky and found something, she'd pack and move. Maybe this was the universe's way of telling her it was time to give Rory a proper home.

CHAPTER TWENTY-EIGHT

In a sour mood and clearly avoiding her actual work, Elizabeth was arranging the pens and sticky notes in her desk drawer when Geoff barged into her office.

"You've been back for three months. This snapping at the processors every time they make a mistake has to stop." He folded his arms.

"Who complained?" Elizabeth wouldn't give him the satisfaction of making eye contact. Not if he was going to admonish her.

"Who hasn't?" He came around to sit facing her. "When they decide to go straight to Leo again, you're going to have a problem."

Would she? Elizabeth glanced out the window at the fountain with its unnaturally colored water. If he let her go, would she miss these monotonous days? And not just at work. When she'd returned home, oddly enough, she'd seen what Geoff saw in her house. She'd immediately bought two spider plants, but they hadn't filled whatever void seemed to exist. It depressed her to be there, and she couldn't figure out how she used to pass her time, so the last few weekends she'd driven over the mountains to Santa Cruz and wandered the beaches until darkness fell.

"Elizabeth?"

Had there been a question? She closed the drawer. "I'm fine." That should cover it.

Geoff leaned his arms on her desk. "You're clearly not. Have you talked to Brooke at all?"

Brooke? Wasn't this about her employees? "About?"

He shrugged. "Anything? Everything? Whatever happened between the two of you?"

"What happened is, I sold the resort, and she'll hate me forever." And why wouldn't she? Elizabeth detested herself, and Margaret probably condemned her from on high. It seemed her only option a few months ago. She'd been in San Jose less than seventy-two hours when she'd realized her mistake. Her frantic call to her real estate agent had been too late, despite her pleading. Furthermore, the woman had flat out refused to relay Elizabeth's wish to buy it back at a higher price. She'd insisted her reputation was worth more than her commission would be. Besides, she told Elizabeth it wouldn't do any good. Apparently, the buyer had wanted the property for years.

"Has Brooke said as much? Have you talked to her?" Geoff lifted his eyebrows.

A serious tone she'd rarely observed in him replaced his usually humorous disposition. "No. I requested the buyer keep any current employees for six months unless they committed a crime or had a serious infraction, but I don't know if they did. It was the best I could do."

He eyed her as if he didn't believe it for a second. "So, you never called."

Elizabeth shifted her gaze to the fountain again, so much uglier than the one Brooke had installed for Margaret. "I tried a few times the week it sold." She looked at him. "She didn't answer. I contacted the front desk, but they said she was in the process of moving and wasn't there. I guess the new ownership didn't keep her on after all."

"That's it then?" He leaned back, resting one dirty-soled skate shoe on his knee.

Some things never changed. Actually, Elizabeth took that back. She wore the burnt orange top and navy pants she'd bought in St. Helena with Brooke, after realizing how much more comfortable she could be at work while still looking professional. "It has to be."

That hollowness she'd almost learned to ignore raised its irritating head again.

"Let me get this straight. You're miserable, sitting on an ungodly amount of money you never spend"—he ticked off his fingers—"regret a decision you made in haste you knew was wrong, haven't apologized for it, and long for the woman I believe you fell in love with but aren't doing a damned thing about it. Did I miss anything?"

"I didn't know it was wrong when I sold," she grumbled.

"I notice you didn't correct the falling in love part." He laced his fingers behind his head. "You should take some time off and do some thinking, some soul searching. You're clearly unhappy, and I worry what'll happen if your depression and self-loathing become worse."

She might lead a wretched existence, but she had no interest in suicidal ideation. "I'm not going to do anything drastic, if that's what you're concerned about."

"It is." He leaned forward again. "Of course it is. You're my friend, and despite your recent gloom, I enjoy being around you. I want you in my life when I meet the man of my dreams. You're the only person I'd ask to stand up for me at my wedding."

She was? The sentiment momentarily choked her up. "Thanks, Geoff." Elizabeth hadn't known he considered her that good of a friend. All his other buddies, the ones he usually went on vacation with, they weren't closer with him than her? Had she taken his friendship for granted, just like she had her relationship with Brooke?

"Can we come up with a plan?" He tapped his finger on her desk.

"I can't take more time off. Leo put up with me gone for months already, but I don't think it'll fly again, so I'll have to do my soul searching on my weekends." She gave him what she hoped was a winning smile, and even that reminded her of Brooke.

"What about Brooke?"

"What about her?"

"Are you going to call her again?"

Elizabeth shook her head. "That ship sailed. I knew what I was doing when I sold the resort—the consequences—and I did it anyway. I don't want to get into the details, but I put myself first, not caring how it might affect others. Now I need to live with my transgressions."

He closed his eyes for a moment. "I don't think it's that simple. You need to do something, enact some kind of change. I'm not sure how much longer you can go on like this. Look at you." He gestured toward her. "Your clothing hangs off you. And, girl, those eye bags ain't working for ya."

"Fine." She resisted touching the puffiness she'd witnessed that morning in the mirror. "I'll think it over this weekend and come up with something."

"Make it good." He stood. "I'm serious. I like you, but I don't need you on my mind *this* much."

"All right, all right." She waved him off with a half-smile. "Get back to work."

As he left, she lost herself in thought. Was Brooke as unhappy as she was? Elizabeth wasn't sure she wanted to know the answer. If so, she'd feel terrible. If not, then Elizabeth probably never meant that much to her.

Elizabeth took a long, cleansing breath and woke her laptop. A promise made to Geoff was one she'd keep. But what should she do? Change had never been easy on her. Too tumultuous, too many unknowns. Would he accept a baby step, or would that look like she was avoiding keeping her end of the bargain? She'd have to think about it.

As Elizabeth approved some of the changes her processors had completed, an idea struck. What about...

She unzipped her purse and pulled out the box she'd been carrying around for weeks. An advertisement had appeared on her screen one evening, and the product had somehow ended up in her cart. When it'd arrived in the mail, she hadn't found the nerve, so she'd been lugging around the DNA test kit ever since.

She turned it over as she considered what to do. Just because she sent it in didn't mean she had to do anything after that. Technically, she wouldn't even need to view the results if she ultimately decided not to. And even if she did, she might not get a hit with an existing user or family tree. And if it linked her, she still wouldn't have to make contact if it terrified her as much as it did now.

Elizabeth read the directions. Simple. Swab her cheek, swirl, mail. Then wait. She could drop it in the box at work today if she did it now. How proud would Geoff be, especially once she shared with him that she had sisters? *That* would be a conversation. A flicker of electricity shot through her. What if she got a hit? Would she chicken out and walk away? No use fixating on it now. There'd be time enough for that when the email arrived.

Elizabeth tore open the package, knowing Brooke would've been proud of her. Too bad she'd never know.

CHAPTER TWENTY-NINE

B rooke dropped the bags of groceries and prescriptions she'd offered to pick up for her mom on the counter in her parents' kitchen.

"Chris called again looking for you." Her mom rose from where she'd been sitting beside Brooke's father in the living room. "You can't avoid her forever."

"I know." Brooke sighed. Her aunt had been hounding her for a week now. It was no secret she wanted Brooke to take her father's place in J & C, but that type of position had never appealed to her. Did she have a choice, though? Her father obviously couldn't work, and it wasn't fair her aunt had to carry the entire load. Chris could hire someone, but Brooke knew she'd prefer to keep the management of the business in the family. While Chris and her father had sometimes quibbled about business decisions, it would be even more difficult making compromises with a stranger. "I'll call her. I promise."

"I'd offer to help her out, but I've got my hands full here." Her mom motioned to where Brooke's dad looked out the window.

Her mom had worked for the company for about a decade, starting when Brian and Brooke were in their teens. As the company became more digital, they needed her less, and she transitioned to spending her time volunteering instead. Unfortunately, caring for Brooke's dad prohibited that now.

Brooke pulled out a stool, and her mom joined her in the kitchen. "As conflicted as I am, I have to tell her no. I love my job."

"That's your prerogative. As much as *she* might pressure you, your father and I are not. It'll work out, one way or another."

Brooke doubted her father had any clue there was an issue.

"Does Rory like her new teacher?" Her mom put the perishables in the refrigerator.

"Loves her. Apparently, she's hilarious during their spelling tests."

"That's good." Her mom pointed. "Rory left Mr. Sparkles here."

Brooke looked over to where the giraffe lay sprawled on the fireplace. "I'm pretty sure it was on purpose, and his name is just Sparkles. She told me the other night that looking at him makes her sad."

"Because of his condition?"

Between the death grip Rory had him in at night and traveling stuffed in a backpack between Brooke and Sean's, his spindly legs had given out weeks ago. "No, because of who he reminds her of." Brooke still couldn't bring herself to say Elizabeth's name. It'd been over three months, and she avoided talking about her or what'd happened.

"Have you heard from her?" Her mother peeked out from the pantry.

"No, not since around the time she left." Left, walked away, fled. Take your pick. Brooke had been mid-move and feeling betrayed, so she'd never returned Elizabeth's calls. Later, she'd decided against it. Whether Elizabeth's intent had been excuses or apologies, neither would've changed anything.

"Maybe she needed to look out for herself," her mom said.

"Clearly." Brooke helped herself to a Coke.

Her mom scowled when she drank from the can. "Don't you want a glass?"

"No."

Her mother poured two iced teas, and after taking one to her father, joined her. "Your nose shouldn't be so out of joint about something that happened months ago. You still have your job, and it was high time you moved out of that place, anyway. I always worried about Rory living among so many strangers. Someone could've pulled her into a room."

"That's why I never let her go anywhere by herself." It was Sean who'd taken a shortcut once or twice when running late until Brooke brought up how dangerous it was. "You're right. Moving was good for us. I just wish we could've found someplace a little bigger." Rory's attic room on the second floor of their new duplex rental fit a bunk bed, a night table, and not much else because of the sloped ceiling. Drawers in the closet and room to hang a few clothes rounded it out. Rory was ecstatic to have sleepovers to show off her new space though, and what they didn't get in square footage, they made up for with the yard. Brooke spent most of July building Rory a treehouse in the huge almond tree out back—thank you, YouTube. The older couple who shared the home hadn't cared, and she'd had to sign an addendum to her rental agreement that they'd leave it if they moved. Rory adored it and spent hours out there. As for Brooke, having their own place made her feel more adult, more independent, both of which were positive. As busy as she'd been, it'd been worth it.

"The bigger the home, the more to clean. Look how lucky you are."

There was that glass-half-full, positive outlook her mother had always possessed. Brooke's own sense of optimism had taken a minor hit, but she did her best not to let it show. Here with her mom, though, she could let her guard down a little.

"Have you thought about contacting her? It doesn't have to be a phone call." Her mom's eyebrows pinched together. "Don't people your age prefer texting, anyway?"

It didn't matter the means of communication. "There's no point, Mom. She doesn't want to be here, doesn't want to be a part of our lives." Except Elizabeth *had* tried to contact her the week after she left. Maybe Brooke should've returned her calls.

"I think Rory going missing that day affected her more than you realize."

Her mom had always been a good reader of people. Her extroverted, amiable ways and acute interpersonal skills made her a great volunteer. A fantastic caregiver, too. Heck, a phenomenal wife and mom. She hadn't spent a lot of time around Elizabeth, but she didn't need much to understand someone.

Brooke took a drink. "It triggered her. That's why she collapsed. At least that's my theory. She had two young sisters who were adopted after her parents died. She…Elizabeth"—Brooke managed to say her name—"was not. I don't think she ever got over it."

"Oh, no. How terrible. No wonder the idea of losing Rory made her so upset."

And Elizabeth had mentioned to Brooke how Rory reminded Elizabeth of herself at that age. She'd brought it up a few times, with comments like how she couldn't believe Rory was seven because Elizabeth had felt so much older back then. It didn't surprise Brooke she ran. "Any word from Brian?" Brooke segued onto another topic, although she supposed Brian and Elizabeth both had running in common.

"Just a text wishing me a happy birthday."

Her mom stared at her glass, but Brooke had a feeling she wasn't seeing it. Brooke had tried calling him, and the few times they'd connected, he'd always been too busy to talk. She wondered if she'd ever see him again. "Well, that's something." Brooke stood and gave her mom what she hoped was a comforting hug. "I'm going to spend a little time with Dad." She took her drink and wandered into the living room.

They played a round of Go Fish. Chess seemed to frustrate him lately, so she didn't suggest it. When she went to leave, her mom walked her out. The uniquely cloying scent of an entire valley crushing grapes filled the air.

"Don't forget to call Chris."

"I will. I will." Brooke needed to get it over with. "She won't be happy. At least she'll have time to cool down before Thanksgiving."

"And think about making that other call. Or text," her mother said as Brooke reached her car.

"Let it go, Mom. Elizabeth wants nothing to do with Calistoga. She's made that clear." Brooke opened the door and tossed her purse inside.

Her mother watched her, one hand on the porch post. "I still love you."

Brooke laughed. "Love you, too."

"Oh, do you want the giraffe?" Her mom gestured behind her.

"Let's leave him here for now." Frankly, Brooke didn't need the daily reminder of Elizabeth either. She had plenty. And each one made her miss Elizabeth more intensely.

CHAPTER THIRTY

Elizabeth had been researching a state tax law in her office just after lunch on Friday when the genealogical site's email landed in her inbox with the grace of a grand piano dropped from ten stories high. By five thirty, it remained the only unread message on her screen, its bold subject line mocking her inability to open it.

She hadn't expected to hear anything so soon after sending in her sample, and it'd slipped from her mind. Now that the DNA results had arrived, she hadn't focused on a single damned thing in the hours since. Geoff had long gone home, as had all her processors. Hell, she was probably the only employee left in the building who didn't work for security or facilities. She either opened it now, getting it over with and giving her the weekend to process whatever she found, or risk spending over two full days and nights perseverating over it.

Tough choice.

She drummed her fingers on the arm of her leather executive's chair, wondering if she should have said something to Geoff. But telling him would've transferred the findings into the realm of public knowledge. Not that he'd share it with anyone, but *he'd* know, and she wasn't ready for that yet. She needed to do this on her own. She had to. The only person whose presence she could've imagined opening it with wanted nothing to do with her.

Elizabeth shut her laptop without closing out tabs or exiting her browser. The email could wait. In fact, she found some consolation in *not* knowing what the message contained. Until she read it, until she confirmed science had found no matches, a chance of finding her sisters remained—a Schrödinger's cat, of sorts. Once she knew what it said, all hope might be lost.

That mentality lasted all of three minutes. Not knowing was going to ruin any chance of her sleeping a wink this weekend. She opened the lid. Besides, if a match had been found, then she had a new set of circumstances to obsess over. At least it provided something to occupy her mind other than thoughts of Brooke. Or Rory. Had school started yet? She hoped Rory's days of wandering off had passed. Her pulse quickened just remembering that dreadful experience.

Elizabeth hovered her cursor over the email. She wasn't sure she had the strength needed for this. Were three decades plus of being on her own insurmountable? Then, a new thought made her freeze. Could any of the website's members view the outcome of her genetic test? Might potential matches already know about *her*?

That forced her to click the link.

It opened. Blah, blah, blah…*mostly English and Irish descent.* She'd already known that. Where was the good stuff? She scrolled. Traits and immigration patterns. *Jesus.* More scrolling. A new section.

You have a DNA match.

They'd buried the lede. Elizabeth remained motionless, staring at the screen.

Her heart raced.

She clicked the button. A generic pink box. A female with the username cstrauthers. Beside it, one word: Sister.

Carly.

Her hands trembled. She focused on one breath at a time. Had she truly weighed the consequences of opening it? Until now, her sisters had existed in a kind of liminal state. This though? This changed everything. It took the possibility and planted it firmly in the earth with roots. Her sister was alive and out there somewhere. Only one though? Elizabeth went back to confirm. *A* match found. Singular.

Her stomach churned. What did that mean? If something had happened to Annie, how would she react? Annie had been two, almost three, the last time Elizabeth had seen her. If she'd met an untimely fate, would Elizabeth mourn? Could she possibly do so any more than she already had? Based on the sickly feeling in her stomach, the arrow tilted toward yes.

Elizabeth read on. The page also contained a link where she could ask for an invitation to the Strauthers family tree. She hesitated, leaning back in her chair as goose bumps erupted on her arms. It might give her an answer concerning Annie, but this, all of this, was a colossal amount for anyone to absorb. No, she didn't want to see branches of Carly's big, happy adoptive clan. Too soon. Way too soon.

She maintained her composure and her sanity by focusing on Carly. Strauthers might be Carly's adopted surname or her married name. It was enough for Elizabeth to consider an online search, but she didn't move. Witnessing her sister's potentially full and wonderful life was one step further than Elizabeth could take right now. Consider it a damned miracle she'd navigated this far.

Brooke would've helped her, would've known what to do and say. Even with her sunny, optimistic outlook, Brooke wouldn't have believed she'd sent in the test. Elizabeth considered texting her, but Brooke hadn't responded to her earlier attempts at communication. What was the point?

She strangely couldn't wait to tell Geoff, though. Baby step? This was a monumental leap. But now what?

After looking at her watch and determining she'd stayed long enough on a Friday night, she meticulously closed her tabs, exited her browser, and shut down her laptop. The information she'd learned wasn't going anywhere. She'd take the weekend to weigh her options.

Before she'd closed the page, she'd noticed a tiny envelope, a way to message cstrauthers. She hadn't yet decided whether she would, but knowing the option was available reassured her. If she decided to reach out, she could, and it didn't involve potential photos of joyous birthdays, celebratory graduations, beautiful weddings, or newborn babies. Elizabeth hadn't steeled herself for those yet.

As she packed her bag, dread washed over her just like it had every evening the past few months as she left work. Maybe she needed to get outside and do some nature bathing. Take a long walk on the Los Gatos Creek trail, or drive to Carmel or Monterey. Determining the cause of her uneasiness so far had been futile. Adjusting to being home hadn't happened, and it'd been months now. Had she grown used to the slower rural life in Napa Valley so much that the bustling urban sprawl of Silicon Valley seemed foreign to her?

It hadn't before. She'd been happy here—or at least content—doing a job she loved, or used to love. Even at work, an unsettled feeling niggled at her. Maybe it was the monotony of her tasks, so unlike working at the resort where something new cropped up every day. The time she'd spent shadowing Brooke had kept her not knowing what to expect when she arrived each morning. Oddly, that hadn't bothered her. It'd rather seemed adventurous.

Elizabeth slung her bag over her shoulder and shut off the lights. Maybe she'd pick up dinner from the Italian place near the Egyptian Museum. The sun still set late enough this time of year that she could walk around the Rose Garden and stop to smell the flowers, literally and figuratively. But as she took inventory of herself on her way to her car, her weariness, or perhaps the emotion involved with opening the email, caught up with her. No, she'd order in, maybe stare at the TV. She'd never watched the movie preceding the one she'd watched with Rory and Brooke. That sounded like an option. She didn't like not knowing things, and curiosity over what occurred in the first film poked at her. Silly, she realized at her age, to be looking forward to takeout and *Frozen*.

What she could learn by messaging cstrauthers intrigued her. By the time Elizabeth fought through traffic on 280 and parked in her garage, she knew she'd reach out. Hell, she might do it tonight, if she could figure out what to write. What should she say to a sister she hadn't seen in thirty-five years? She'd come up with something.

And she did. It might have taken hours, but she'd done it.

When Elizabeth rolled over and looked at her phone the next morning, the first thing that jumped out was a notification from the family tree app she'd downloaded. Someone had responded to her message. She hurriedly sat up, smoothing down her hair for some unknown reason. After slowly inhaling, she let out her breath and opened the response.

My dear Lizzie,

I thought I must be dreaming when I saw your message. When I first sent in my genetic test years ago, I did it for one reason: so you could find me. I've long thought the choice to be yours. And now here you are, reaching out after all this time apart. I'd almost given up hope. Like I said, it must be a dream. It's too good to be true.

I told Annie I'd heard from you. She's in Modesto, and I live in Sausalito. I'd love to meet you—the adult you. You probably have a million questions, as do I. I'm happy to tell you anything you'd like to know, but I'd love to do so in person. Please consider it.

I've missed you so much.

Carly

Elizabeth must've reread the note forty times. Her sister, *her* sister had written her. Carly sounded…nice. Elizabeth tried to picture her but came up blank. And Annie. She was alive and presumably well. Relief she hadn't been expecting coursed through her. She'd noticed something on her umpteenth time through, though. "*I'd* love to meet you." Carly had typed it twice, never using the word "we." Had it simply been an oversight? It'd been "I've missed you" at the end, too.

Whatever. Elizabeth flopped back on her bed, warmth enfolding her. She had sisters. They'd been out there, but not real, though she knew that made no sense. Now they'd become clearer, like invisible ink slowly coming to light. If she met them, would they like her? Would she like *them*? Carly hadn't sent her an invitation to the family tree, and whether intentional or not, she didn't know. She hadn't asked for one, either. Was it like Carly had said, she wanted to tell Elizabeth everything in person?

Excitement crackled through her like electricity. What now? She wanted, no needed, to tell someone. *Should* she text Brooke? In all likelihood, Brooke wanted nothing to do with her, and who could blame her? The truth of it hit Elizabeth like a blast of ice-cold water from a fire hose. No, she needed to do this on her own. With ease, she made a decision that took little vacillation.

Elizabeth rolled over and grabbed her phone. She had a message to respond to.

❖

As Elizabeth drove through the rainbow arches of the old Waldo Tunnel—the Robin Williams Tunnel, now—she experienced that same magic she often did on this small stretch of 101. The dense fog obscuring the Golden Gate Bridge behind her miraculously disappeared as she exited the northern end, with blinding sunlight and azure sky replacing it, like she'd been transported through a wormhole. The way the Marin Headlands suppressed the marine layer from this tiny hamlet never ceased to amaze her. Would the day hold more wondrous elements?

Carly's email instructed Elizabeth to park in the driveway in front of her garage, saying she'd never find space on the street. As Elizabeth pulled up, she found it strange Annie didn't seem to be there already. Or at least her car wasn't. Maybe there'd been traffic on her way from Modesto.

The wood and cream home before her didn't offer much from the street, but a glance behind her verified the attractive facades all faced the water, which she couldn't see from where she stood before Carly's front door camera. Was she ready to meet her sisters for the first time since they were children? The fluttering in her stomach could've leaned either way. She pressed the button to her right, and chimes sounded inside.

The door opened almost instantly, as though someone had been waiting on the other side.

Elizabeth took a step back. Carly—or she assumed it to be—looked like a slightly distorted version of their mother. She bore the same high cheekbones, delicate bone structure, and curly hair. Even looking in her rich, brown eyes sent Elizabeth back in time.

"Lizzie?" Carly's grip on the knob had turned her nail beds white.

"You look so much like Mom." Elizabeth didn't bother directly answering the question.

"I'm sorry." Carly stood aside. "Look at me. Making you stand out here while I gawk. Please come in."

A whiff of something as Elizabeth entered reminded her of cherry blossoms, and without knowing why, she took comfort in it. When she turned, Carly studied her.

Carly shook her head slightly. "Is it okay if I give you a hug? I don't think I'll be able to think straight until I do. I can't believe you're here."

Elizabeth could count the number of people who'd done so in the past twenty years on both hands, Brooke and Rory included, but she didn't feel the hesitancy with Carly she normally did. After all, they'd done so many times before, albeit years ago. Before her stood a woman with whom she'd shared a bathtub, a bed, a parent's lap. So, it didn't feel strange at all to open her arms and allow Carly to step into them.

Carly's height surprised her. Elizabeth hadn't been expecting her to be taller by an inch. She'd been so much smaller than Elizabeth back then.

Carly made a small noise and tightened her hold.

The scent Elizabeth had caught a moment ago came from Carly's hair, and she closed her eyes and breathed it in. Carly hugged like their mom had, her entire body into it. Like this, Elizabeth could almost imagine she was there, looking down on their reunion. Elizabeth bit her lip to quell the sting of tears.

With a sigh, Carly pulled away first, her eyes misty. "Thanks, I needed that."

Elizabeth busied herself brushing wrinkles from her shirt that didn't exist. "Yes. Me, too." And to her shock, it was true. She glanced around. "Annie's not here?"

"Not yet. Come." With a hand on her elbow, Carly directed her toward the open area. "I suggested I meet you first. She's a bit nervous, and I wasn't sure if you would be, too. This way, hopefully, we won't overwhelm you. I want you to have time to relax and be comfortable."

To her surprise, Elizabeth didn't feel the least bit of discomfort. Talking with Carly felt like falling into a rapport with someone she'd known for years, not been estranged from for decades.

Carly left her in the living room and stirred a pitcher on the waterfall kitchen island. "Do you drink iced tea?"

"I do." Elizabeth took in the open home's clean lines and modern style. That is, until she stepped closer to the bank of windows overlooking the bay. They wrapped around the length of the house and around the northern side. "Your view is spectacular." White sailboats dotted the sapphire water between them and Angel Island. "Is that Belvedere over there?"

"And Tiburon," Carly said, pointing. She handed Elizabeth a glass. "When the fog lifts, you can see Mt. Diablo in the distance."

"It must be an incredible view at night. Is the scenery why you ended up here?"

Carly motioned for Elizabeth to sit, and when Elizabeth chose the sofa, Carly sat beside her. "Partly. I worked for an architectural firm in San Rafael, and I wanted a home on the water. Eventually, I branched out on my own." She gestured vaguely at the house. "Now I work from here."

"So, you're an architect?" Elizabeth dragged her eyes from the vista to Carly. With her smart attire and stylish glasses, she looked the part.

"I am." She smiled. "Once my children were old enough to be in school, I renovated this place. It involved moving out for a year, but it was worth it."

"It's stunning. And your husband? What does he do?" Elizabeth realized she'd been too preoccupied listening and staring at her sister to have sampled her drink, so she took a sip. Maybe it was due to her elated mood, but the herbal, fruity concoction might've been the best she'd ever tasted.

"Mike works for the phone company. We met on a job." Carly smiled, as though remembering. "He kept showing up with the lamest of questions as an excuse to see me, tripping over his words and sporting his hard-hat hair. I was a goner."

Elizabeth laughed. To each their own. "Where is he?" She'd prepared herself to meet the family Carly had mentioned.

"I sent him and the kids on errands. A.J. runs for his middle school's cross-country team and needed new shoes, and Beth had an appointment at the Apple Store's Genius bar. Slater doesn't care where they go as long as he can hang with his dad. So, they're all at the mall." She grinned. "Better them than me."

Elizabeth agreed, although shopping with Brooke hadn't been half bad. Brooke had chosen small stores, and Elizabeth admittedly enjoyed herself, like she always had when they were together. Kissing Brooke for the first time that day hadn't hurt either. "Wait. Beth?" She snapped to when she realized what Carly had said. It'd taken her a moment, but Elizabeth had wrongly been called enough iterations in her lifetime to know all the nicknames.

A slow smile spread across Carly's face. "Yes, I named her Elizabeth." She leaned closer so their arms briefly touched. "I always tell her I'm glad I had a daughter early, or I would've had to keep trying until I did. She was upset I wouldn't let her stay and meet her namesake today, but sending her to get her iPad fixed mollified her." Carly squeezed Elizabeth's knee. "There'll be plenty of time for you to get to know everyone."

"Hello?"

Carly turned in her seat. "We're in here."

A woman entered, her thick brown hair as straight as Elizabeth's but longer, almost to her shoulder blades. She carried a bouquet of flowers and a reusable bag stuffed full. Her gaze fixed on Elizabeth and didn't wander, even as she deposited the nylon tote on a chair and stopped near Carly. "Hi."

"Hello." Elizabeth rose, transfixed by Annie's eyes, the same blue-gray shade as hers. She had been considering initiating a hug since Carly had wanted one, something completely out of character for her, but Annie appeared to be wielding the blooms as a shield. With her closed-off stance, the embrace that'd come so naturally with Carly vacated the building.

Annie straight-armed the tiger lilies toward Elizabeth. "These are for you."

With a smile, Elizabeth accepted the gift, lowering her face to take in their scent. "They're gorgeous. How thoughtful."

Annie gave a half shrug. "I stopped to get them to give you two more time." She backed away to sit in the stuffed chair beside Carly. "There are cookies and wine, too. I wasn't sure what to bring."

"You didn't have to buy anything." Elizabeth waited until Annie looked at her. "Meeting both of you was enough." Annie tucked her hair behind her ear in what appeared to be a nervous reflex that Elizabeth had done thousands of times.

"I wasn't sure."

"See? I told you it would be fine." Carly smiled, one that seemed a bit forced, and nudged Annie's thigh.

Had Carly needed to talk Annie into meeting her? Her reception hadn't been as warm as Carly's, but Elizabeth wasn't a gooey person either. "Are you married?"

Annie looked at Carly, and Carly nodded as though giving her the go-ahead.

"It's probably easier if you tell me what you know about me. I'll fill in the blanks," Annie said.

Okay. So, it was going to be weird and awkward. Hopefully, that'd dissipate once they got to know one another. How could Elizabeth alleviate some of it? "Well, I know that you share a birthday with Georgie Black because I was eating a Smurf-blue cupcake to celebrate him in my kindergarten class when Dad pulled me out of school and took us to the hospital to meet you. Mom was appalled by the color of my lips when we arrived."

That brought a smile to Annie's face.

"I know that when it came to baby food, you loved sweet potatoes and hated peas."

"Some things never change," Carly said, reaching over to poke Annie again. "They're her favorite kind of fries."

"You wouldn't nap without a pair of Mom's rolled up socks for the longest time."

"What?" Annie's voice squeaked, but she smiled. "Oh, my God. Gross."

Elizabeth laughed. "You liked to lie in the clean, warm laundry as she folded clothes. You stole her fuzziest ones and cuddled them like a stuffed animal."

Annie shook her head. "Why was I so weird?"

Carly had grown quiet, and her eyes had become hazy. "I remember…" She dashed her hand through the air. "You know what? Never mind."

"Just say it." Annie shook her head. "You know it bugs me when you do that. If the sentence was important enough to start, it's important enough to finish."

"When Mom and Dad—our mom and dad," Carly motioned between her and Annie and received an eye roll in return, "picked us up the first day we met them—you know what—I changed my mind. I don't want to bring down the mood."

"It's all right." Elizabeth touched Carly's arm. "I think of that day often, and even more lately. I found myself in front of that house while I was recently in Calistoga. It was surreal. Suddenly, I was standing there reliving everything all over again." Despite their shared past being difficult for her to discuss, Elizabeth needed Carly to know she had a willing listener if she needed to talk about it.

"What day?" Annie looked between them.

"The day we were separated." Elizabeth was about to withdraw her hand, but Carly took it in hers.

"We were at some house. I don't even know whose it was, but I remember being so scared." Carly looked at her. "I didn't understand yet that our biological parents weren't coming back. But Elizabeth was there, so I knew we were safe."

A fist slammed into Elizabeth's throat. They may not have been in grave danger, but she hadn't kept them together.

"Hey," Carly said, "don't get that look. I'm not blaming you for anything."

Elizabeth cringed at being so transparent. Or was it a sibling thing, being able to read one another like that?

"What I meant, is that you made me feel brave. I witnessed how you tried to calm and take care of us, and it gave me courage. I tried to show that same kind of strength for Annie later." She glanced at Annie, who'd clearly become entranced by the conversation. "When they loaded us in the car so quickly, they neglected to bring Annie's beloved rolled socks. I knew she wouldn't be able to sleep without them, so I begged to go back. For those," she looked at Elizabeth with tears in her eyes, "and for you."

Elizabeth let go and walked to the window, unable to control the flood of emotion and not quite ready to cry in front of two women she'd basically just met. After sniffing a few times as she watched a ferry chug across the bay, she felt a soft touch on her back, and a box of tissues appeared in her peripheral vision. "Thanks." She took a moment to compose herself, then returned to the sofa. "Sorry."

"Don't ever be sorry." This time, it was Annie, who spoke with a fervor that'd been missing before. "*We're* sorry. You should've grown up with us. Our mother carries a lot of guilt surrounding that decision to this day, and even if I don't remember what happened, Carly and I have never gotten over losing you, though I know that probably means little to you. But through it all, over all those years, Carly kept the memory of you alive. She'd tell me stories about you, even though she knew she wasn't supposed to. And I'm ninety-five percent certain she fictionalized more when she ran out." She gave Carly a loving smile that quickly faded. "For the longest time, we both held resentment toward our mom and dad for splitting the three of us up, though losing a parent and then becoming one makes you try to let some of that go." She got up and sat sideways on Carly's lap, wrapping her in a loose embrace. "For what it's worth, though, Carly did her best to make sure I knew I had two sisters. You're probably more myth than real to me at this point, but I hope that changes."

Carly's face disappeared into Annie's hair as she tightened her hold. "I couldn't have said it better myself," Carly said, pulling back with a soft smile.

With a wiggle of eyebrows, Annie addressed Elizabeth. "So, what else can you tell me?"

Annie appeared captivated, her eyes holding more interest than Elizabeth had thus far seen in her. Though she acted like this was an entertaining game, Elizabeth got the inkling these tidbits meant much more. Grateful to redirect them toward lighter subjects, Elizabeth sifted through her memories.

"Mom and Dad talked for weeks about how advanced your fine motor skills were because you learned to pick up Cheerios early."

Carly nodded. "And now she's a plastic surgeon."

"Really?"

"Yes, cranio-maxillofacial," Annie said.

"Impressive." Elizabeth paused a moment, in awe. "Let's see. What else do I know about you?" Another sip of tea bought herself some time. "You learned to walk late becau—"

"What?"

Elizabeth might as well have said the moon was made by Cowgirl Creamery. She laughed at Annie's reaction. "Yes, because this one," she jerked a thumb in Carly's direction, "insisted on carrying you around when Mom wasn't looking, though she probably only outweighed you by a few pounds. You rarely had the opportunity to practice."

Annie looked pointedly at Carly. "Some things never *do* change."

Did that mean Carly acted like an overbearing older sister, at least in Annie's eyes? Elizabeth hoped with time, she'd learn more about their dynamic.

After they'd shared a short laugh, Annie looked at Carly. "Why didn't you tell me these things?"

Carly held up her hands. "I didn't know all this stuff! I was young, too. At the time, I wasn't *that* much older than you."

"You were twice my age."

"I wasn't even five."

"Right. Like twice my age."

Elizabeth watched the sisterly repartee with glee. She'd missed out on all of this, but here it was, still waiting for her when she finally showed up. She smiled. Brooke had been right. Elizabeth shouldn't have been so stubborn and done the DNA test earlier. Why hadn't she? What would Brooke think of all of this? With a pang of regret, Elizabeth wished Brooke were sitting next to her witnessing it. Over the last few months, she'd wished Brooke were beside her for many things. Elizabeth missed her, plain and simple.

Annie and Carly's verbal sparring abated, and Annie eyed Elizabeth. "Originally, I was asking what you knew about me *now,* but I enjoyed hearing those stories." She gave Elizabeth a soft smile.

"I only told her about my family," Carly said. "You should be the one to tell her about yours."

Annie rose and returned to her seat with a carton of cookies she set on the coffee table. "Like I said, I'm a doctor in Modesto. I'm married to a man named Isaiah, and we have two daughters, Meghan and Nina. They're six and four. Are you involved with anyone? Is there a husband or a wife waiting for you at home?"

The way she'd asked, so casually, left Elizabeth not knowing if Annie had excellent gaydar or always phrased the question like that. Maybe medical professionals had been taught not to assume heterosexuality as the default. "I'm not married, but if I was, it'd be to a woman." An image of Brooke came to mind, her curls strewn across the pillowcase. What would it be like waking up beside her every day, intertwining their fingers and admiring the matching rings they wore as a symbol of the love they shared? Elizabeth shook away the fantasy. That's all it would ever be. A dream. Her hasty decision and swift exit had ruined all other possibilities.

"So, are you dating anyone?" Annie's questions continued without either of them blinking at the revelation of Elizabeth's queerness.

Not knowing how to approach the vast experience known as Brooke, Elizabeth hesitated.

"Ooh, you have to tell us everything." Carly's eyes alighted with interest.

Emptiness filled her. "There's really nothing to say. It's over."

Carly tapped Elizabeth's knee. "Your expression says otherwise. Humor us. Do you know how long it's been since we've dated anyone? Let us live vicariously. I'm opening the wine." She snagged the bag and took it to the kitchen. "What's her name?"

"Brooke." The word falling from Elizabeth's mouth startled her, but the sense of exhilaration it brought, to hear it aloud again, helped give her strength to continue. Besides, sharing something—*someone*—so important with Carly and Annie seemed a step in the right direction if they were to become close again.

The ease of telling her sisters about Brooke should've come as a surprise, but beyond the initial sweating of her palms, she experienced no discomfort or anxiety, only a sense of being nestled in the safe cocoon of their visit. They listened and asked questions, but didn't offer advice, seeming to understand the fledgling status of their newly formed relationship. And while Elizabeth hadn't been looking for counsel, opinions on what she should do or not do regarding Brooke wouldn't have been unwelcome.

But no, Brooke was her dilemma. Elizabeth would have to arrive at her decision regarding what to do, much like the one to submit her DNA test, on her own time.

CHAPTER THIRTY-ONE

Brooke walked out of her office, which seemed overly spacious and dreary with only her desk occupying it now. "Francine, can you ask Kiersten to see me when she gets in? I have an accounts payable question for her." She leafed through the papers she held.

"Sure." Francine turned toward someone approaching. "Good morning. How may I help you?"

"I was actually hoping to speak with her."

That voice. Brooke recognized it. She'd know it anywhere.

She spun around. "Brian?" He'd replaced his surfer look with a tan poplin button-down and khakis. Both appeared to have been ironed, something he never used to do. And more startling, his normally chin-length sandy hair sported a stylish, close haircut. He'd even used product.

He gave her a sheepish smile. "Yeah."

She took a step and launched herself at him. It'd been too long since she'd hugged him, smelled his cologne, or even had a real conversation with him, but in that moment, she forgave him for everything. He looked well, healthy, and he was here.

He gave her a squeeze as she let go. "Do you have a minute?"

She turned to Francine. "I'll be in the library, but text me if something important comes up."

Francine's gazed darted between the two of them. "Sure thing."

"This way." Brooke led him to the elevator bank, her hand on his arm, not yet wanting to let go, like if she did, he might evaporate right before her. "I didn't know you planned to visit."

He gave her a small smile and a shrug as they entered. "I'm not. I'm back permanently."

"You don't say." Brooke didn't know whether to be thrilled or annoyed he hadn't given her some forewarning. She led him to a set of chairs, not the ones she'd always shared with Elizabeth. Those memories needed to be kept separate. "So, what brought this about?"

He colored, something she'd also never seen on him. "I've met someone." He grinned, his dimples appearing and his entire face lighting up. "We've been dating for over a year. Her name is Sara. She finished getting her master's in education this spring. I asked her to marry me two weeks ago."

"Married? My brother?" Brooke reached for his hand. "I'm so happy for you."

"Yeah." He rubbed his chin. "The thing is, she told me she wouldn't be the wife of a man who'd abandoned his family." He looked up. "So, she only accepted my proposal on the grounds we moved back here, and I started acting my age."

Brooke grinned. "Oh, I like her already."

"Yeah, she's terrific, and she's right. It's time for me to stop acting like a child. Mom needs me, and I'm tired of seeing Rory growing so fast in your social media photos and missing out." He fidgeted with his smartwatch. "I might not be okay with what's happening to Dad, but I'm sorry. It wasn't fair to run away and leave you and Mom to deal with it."

Brooke wasn't about to correct him, but his apology went a long way. "What do you plan to do for work? Have you looked at marketing positions, or are you going to ask Aunt Chris for another placement?"

"No." He gave her a sly look. "I asked her for Dad's job since, apparently, you didn't want it. She's agreed to take me on."

"You're kidding." Brooke exhaled in relief. Tension had filled the lunch meeting with her aunt, but Brooke had stood her ground, adamant she couldn't step into her father's shoes. She told Chris she loved her job and couldn't take on one more stressor in her hectic life. It'd felt good to say no, even if her aunt had been displeased.

Brian smiled. "Nope. I start today." He gestured at his clothing. "You know I don't normally dress like this."

She smiled, then turned serious. "Does Mom know you're back?"

"Sara and I spent the evening there last night. I asked Mom and Aunt Chris not to say anything. I wanted to surprise you." He gave her a light slug on her arm. "Best for last."

It'd been a common phrase among them growing up when they'd gag their vegetables down first and leave the most delicious part of their dinner to savor—when one wasn't trying to steal it from the other.

The light in his eyes dimmed. "Dad's gotten a lot worse since I last saw him."

Brooke nodded but didn't know what else to say on the matter. The truth hurt.

"Mom said Rory is with Sean, but I might pop over there and say hello if you don't mind."

"Not at all. She'll be thrilled to see you." Brooke knew Sean would be, too. He and Brian had always hit it off. "I hope you'll bring Sara. You four can chat about wedding stuff. I'm sure you heard they're engaged."

"Yeah, Mom mentioned that." He smoothed his pants with what appeared to be uncharacteristic nervousness. "I'd like you to meet Sara, too, but I wanted to talk to you alone today. You know, make sure you don't hate me or anything first."

"I could never," she said quietly. "But I've missed you more than you probably realize."

"Yeah, same." He motioned to the chess board across from them. "You still play?"

She nodded. "Yes, but I haven't for a few months." Memories of all the nights she'd spent in this room with Elizabeth washed over her, leaving her numb.

"Mom said you dated someone recently." He said it carefully, as if wary of her reaction.

How much had he been told? "I'm not sure what we were, but we're not anymore." Brooke looked around. "She actually owned this place for a short time."

"And now?"

"Now she doesn't." It was a bit more complicated, but Brooke had neither time to go into that now, nor could she bear it.

"I'm sorry to hear things didn't work out."

Brooke gathered her papers and rose, attempting to ignore the painful ache in her chest. "I should get back."

He joined her, throwing an arm around her shoulders. "Hey, if you ever want to talk about it, I hear there are a few places around here to grab a glass of wine."

"Maybe." It still felt too fresh, too raw. She didn't want to tear open a wound that hadn't yet healed. "I'm not sure I'm ready yet. We can still hang out, though."

"Yeah, no pressure, and maybe I have no right to offer you advice after disappearing for so long, but don't avoid something you might regret later."

Did he mean by not wanting to talk about Elizabeth or Elizabeth herself? Brooke turned it over in her mind. Was she? Or was she simply trying to put that part of her life behind her?

He faced her when they reached the lobby, adjusting the tuck of his shirt. "Well, wish me luck."

Brooke smiled. "You won't need it. Aunt Chris must be thrilled. You've always been her favorite."

He pulled out a pair of aviators and slid them on. "I know. It's because I'm the best looking."

She swatted his arm, then grabbed him in an impromptu hug, probably squeezing him too tightly. "I'm glad you're back."

"Yeah. Me, too." He let go after she did. "See ya later, Brookie."

He knew she hated that nickname, but right now, with her brother back and no sign of him disappearing again, she'd allow it. God, she'd missed him. The gaping hole in her chest filled in the tiniest bit.

Chapter Thirty-two

Elizabeth squeezed past a group of inebriated women clearly in Vegas for someone's bachelorette party as she entered one of the bars in the Bellagio. Their flashing penis necklaces gave them away.

"And what can I get *you*?"

The bartender, with her faux hawk, rolled-up sleeves, and tie no other employees wore, gave her a once-over and a predatory smile. She'd apparently flagged her, or maybe she hit on everyone, but Elizabeth wasn't in the mood. Day three of her payroll conference had left her exhausted. She'd brushed up on a few regulations coming into effect next year and knew it was an excellent opportunity to network with professionals in her field, but her tolerance for these events typically expired after forty-eight hours. Her company insisted she attended, though, so here she was, year after year. "An old-fashioned and a water."

"For you? Absolutely." She stared at Elizabeth's breasts as she reached for the bourbon.

"Keep my tab open, please." Elizabeth laid her credit card on the bar and slid onto one of the few remaining empty stools, thinking too late that she should've chosen a table away from the blatant ogling. She simply wanted to enjoy a drink or two before she retired to her room. Maybe it'd help her sleep through the night. When was the last time that'd happened? Deep down, she remembered, but mixing *those* memories and alcohol wasn't a good idea, so Elizabeth pushed her from her mind.

"Are you here for the payroll conference?" a soft voice asked.

Elizabeth turned to find a brunette beside her with dark inquisitive eyes, one hand toying with the stem of her martini glass, the other holding her place in a book.

"Yes. You?" Elizabeth hadn't noticed her in any of the seminars, but that didn't mean anything. This event garnered monster attendance numbers.

"No," she said, stealing a coaster to mark her page. "Your people simply dress better than me and my colleagues. We're a little more casual, at least here." She smiled and gestured toward her jeans and white button-down that'd probably been crisper that morning.

Elizabeth got no indication of interest stemming from her, simply someone wanting to have a conversation, unlike the bartender who'd dropped off her drink without a word but with a glare aimed at her seatmate. Elizabeth glanced down at her skirt suit. "I've always operated under the belief I might run into my next boss at one of these things. It doesn't hurt to look the part."

"Smart of you." The woman tipped her glass toward Elizabeth before taking a sip. "And do you plan on leaving your current job soon?"

Elizabeth hadn't outright considered the question. "I'm not sure."

She softly chuckled. "That sounds like there's a story behind it."

"What are you, a psychologist?"

"As a matter of fact, yes." She held out her hand. "Pardon my manners. Rebecca Jenkins. I'm here for the Children's Mental Wellness conference."

Elizabeth introduced herself.

"I apologize. You can take the doctor out of the office, but…" Rebecca gave a small laugh.

"It's fine." Elizabeth savored the warm bite of her cocktail as it slid down her throat. The Luxardo cherry in the bottom brought Rory to mind. "It just made me think."

Rebecca turned toward her a bit. "Of leaving your position?"

"More of why I'm staying." Elizabeth didn't need to. With enough money in the bank to do almost anything she wanted, why was she allowing herself to feel pinned down?

"If you left, where would you go?"

The answer came to Elizabeth instantly. "Napa Valley. Not to transition to a new company, just…to be there."

"Now *that* sounds like there's a story behind it."

"How much time do you have?" Elizabeth gave her a half-smile.

Rebecca flipped her phone over and checked the screen. "My flight leaves at seven in the morning, and I like to be at the airport a full two hours early."

Elizabeth chuckled, again not feeling any sort of flirtation, just genuine conviviality. "Well, believe it or not, I inherited a resort there earlier this year."

"That's wonderful." Rebecca's eyebrows rose. "I'd probably move there, too."

"I didn't keep it—well, I did at first, but then something happened, and I sold it and left." And walked away from the most important person in her life, though she hadn't realized it then.

"So, you don't own it anymore?"

Elizabeth shook her head.

"Too bad. I was about to hit you up for a discounted room."

"I'm afraid I can't help you there. I blew it." Elizabeth cupped her glass between both hands.

Silence stretched between them, though not in the bar itself, which had only gotten busier. Loud music, raucous laughter, and half-yelled conversations ricocheted off the mirrored back bar and tiled columns.

Rebecca leaned closer. "With permission to tell me to mind my own business, do you mean with the property or with…someone?"

The way Rebecca phrased it didn't pressure her. In fact, talking about it with her felt safe. They didn't know one another and would likely never meet again. What was the harm? "Both, actually."

"Did this person work there?"

"She did." Elizabeth watched for a sign of surprise, but none came. "We became friends and then more." She lifted her hand as

she searched for words to explain what'd happened. "The town...
it holds a lot of history for me, some of it not good." She gave a
CliffsNotes explanation of what'd happened to her parents and
sisters and how Margaret had taken her under her wing.

"I see. Places can trigger deeply emotional memories for us,
even many years later."

Normally, Elizabeth would've allowed the assumption to pass.
"I agree, but it was more than that."

The bartender stopped before them. "Another one?" She
looked at Elizabeth, then finally to Rebecca, as if she'd been an
afterthought.

They both said yes.

"Let's see if I understand. You didn't want to own a business
there because you couldn't handle the constant reminders of your
family."

"Not just the memories of them." Elizabeth struggled to
explain. "This woman, Brooke, has a daughter. She's the same age
as I was when all that happened. It felt so strange, because back
then, in my mind, I felt like an adult." She laughed, but it came
out bitter sounding. "A small one, but a grown-up, nonetheless. I
tried to make a bargain with a friend of my father to keep us. I
promised I'd take care of my sisters. I truly believed I could." She
paused while the bartender delivered their orders. "But when I look
at Brooke's daughter, there's a disconnect. She's tiny, just this little
thing, and so young. I can't imagine her going through the same
thing. This summer, she wandered off, and the thought of losing her,
too...I couldn't handle it. When it came down to it, I was afraid to
be around her and deal with all my memories, so I left."

"Seven years old, you said?" Rebecca chewed an olive. "Likely,
you were somewhere between the preoperational and concrete
operational stages of development."

"I was what?"

"Sorry." Rebecca laughed. "Dr. Jenkins in the house. Piaget—
you might have heard of him—divided children's cognitive
development into four stages. In the preoperational stage, a child
thinks in extremely literal terms. In the concrete operational stage,

which we normally see develop around age seven, children are still thinking in concrete terms, but they begin to be more rational. Logical. And in this stage, we start to see them notice how others view situations or how others feel." She paused. "From what you've told me"—she patted Elizabeth's arm—"and I'm not saying you weren't developmentally normal, but you didn't seem to have reached that level of thinking yet, that ability to view how your dad's friend saw the situation, for instance."

Elizabeth blanched. "And you think I *should've* been able to by then." The perfectionist in her took a hit.

"That's not at all what I'm saying. That state roughly spans ages seven to eleven. You were barely on the lower end of the spectrum." Rebecca leaned closer. "What I'm saying, is that you were young. Very young. And while you obviously loved them and tried your best, under no circumstances can you fault seven-year-old you for what happened."

The alcohol in Elizabeth's stomach churned. All these years, the guilt of failing to keep them with her, neglecting to keep them all together and safe, had eaten at her insides. Yet, this woman beside her, obviously an expert on the subject, was telling her to cut herself some slack. Could she?

"I hope I didn't upset you." Rebecca studied her.

"No." Elizabeth took a drink. "I'm good. I was just thinking."

"It's difficult, isn't it, to grasp something we've known to be true for so long and accept it when it morphs into something else?" she asked softly, staring into her glass.

Pain clearly radiated from her, and Elizabeth's normally icy heart went out to her. "*That* sounds like there's a story behind it."

"Maybe." Rebecca smiled, but it didn't reach her eyes. "But before the conversation veers somewhere else"—she laid her hand on the bar between them—"I hope you'll grant yourself some grace. You were a very young child, and what you did, in all its innocence, was heroic." She laid a hand on her chest. "And extremely heartwarming."

"Thank you." As Elizabeth swirled her drink, she didn't feel like a heroine. "I recently found my sisters, after all this time." She glanced up. "I did a DNA test."

"That's wonderful." This time, Rebecca's smile appeared wholehearted.

Why Elizabeth was sharing her life story with a stranger, she had no idea. But Rebecca was a good listener and talking to her filled Elizabeth with a lightness. Could she manage to forgive herself for what happened thirty-five years ago? For something she never had any control over in the first place? She stared at the libations lined up opposite her. In the mirror behind the bottles, their eyes met.

"So, this woman—Brooke, you said?—how spectacularly did you blow it with her?"

Elizabeth huffed out a laugh. "Badly." Seriousness sank in. "To top it off, I told her I had feelings for her right before I ran away like a coward. She hasn't talked to me since. Well, I haven't contacted her for months, but I called her a few times right after I left."

"People need time to deal with things. It allows for reflection and growth and the distance to have hindsight to ask, 'Did I act or react rashly, or were my actions or reactions justified?'"

Elizabeth let that soak in. Did Brooke feel the same now as she did then? As for Elizabeth, her views seemed to be changing by the minute. Was there any chance Brooke might forgive her?

"You're thinking about her, aren't you?" Rebecca circled a finger in front of her face. "You got this dreamy look. She must've meant quite a lot to you."

Meant. Past tense. Yet, it wasn't like that at all. "She means quite a lot to me still." And probably always would. Elizabeth envisioned herself as an elderly woman sitting in her gloomy house dreaming of the woman she loved and let get away. In one motion, she downed the rest of her drink.

Rebecca eyed her keenly.

"You've given me a lot to consider." Elizabeth mimed a signing motion to the bartender, and she strode toward the register. "I appreciate the free therapy session." When her bill arrived, she signed and tossed an extra couple of twenties on top. "Put these toward hers," she said, tilting her head toward Rebecca.

"You didn't have to do that," Rebecca said, shaking her head.

"Believe me, I want to. You've been so kind and helpful." Elizabeth extended her hand. "I didn't even ask where you're from."

"San Francisco." Rebecca gave her a light squeeze.

"No kidding. San Jose." Elizabeth straightened her shoulders. "Perhaps we'll run into one another again, Dr. Jenkins."

"Please, it's Rebecca. Especially after…" She gestured between them.

"Thank you, Rebecca." Elizabeth offered a rare warm smile. Her chest filled with gratitude, and paying for Rebecca's drinks didn't begin to convey it. She hoped Rebecca, who'd been so perceptive about other things, would understand. "Good night."

As Elizabeth walked to her room, she shook her head at the absurdity of it all. She'd found a child psychologist in a bar in Las Vegas who'd confirmed what Brooke had said.

She'd been *extremely* young.

Questions remained, though. Hearing it was one thing. Could Elizabeth bring herself to *believe* it? And if she did, did she have the strength needed for forgiveness?

CHAPTER THIRTY-THREE

With the workweek almost over, Brooke watered the plants she'd added to her office to satisfy them until Monday. The greenery inside contrasted beautifully with the fall crimson and ochre foliage outside the window. She'd needed some changes to make the space hers, and to stave off missing Elizabeth after she'd left three months earlier, so she'd also splurged on a new desk. She settled into Margaret's chair that she'd kept for sentimental reasons and started a text to Kali. Since Brooke would need to stay tonight later than she'd planned and Sean was in Sacramento, she was left with no option but to ask Kali for help.

Could you pick Rory up tonight? Hate to ask but my meeting got moved.

She waited, enjoying the view. The evenings were getting cooler now. One of these days, she needed to take Rory to pick out a pumpkin.

Her phone vibrated.

No prob

Thank you! Give her a hug for me.

Brooke tacked on a few smiley faces and a heart for good measure, the dreadful feeling of having to ask for help clawing at her insides. But she'd done it, and it'd been fine. And Rory would be thrilled for extra time to talk all things flower girl. This salesman had done this to Brooke before, claiming he'd be there at a certain time, then calling with an excuse for needing to reschedule. If his prices weren't the most reasonable for decent quality, she'd wave good-bye to him. It was all part of the job though. Sometimes, being a working mom meant asking for assistance, and fortunately, she had a deep bench.

Just last week, her mom had stepped in with a day of emergency childcare when Rory had been sick with a cold and Brooke absolutely had to hold her monthly staff meeting. But this reliance on others had never sat well with Brooke. There'd been a time when she'd believed she could do everything herself, but those days seemed to be in the past. How had she ended up with so many spinning plates in the air? Maybe this was simply what adulting looked like.

She opened her mini fridge, careful to clean it out every Friday since the Unfortunate Forgotten Tuna Salad Incident. Her remaining half-sandwich went in the garbage, but the drinkable yogurts still had a few days before their expiration.

"Francine and Nik, can I interest you in these?" Brooke held them up as she came through the doorway.

"Let me see." Francine pushed her glasses up as Nik wandered over. "I'll take the strawberry banana unless you want it."

"Go ahead," Nik said, scrunching up his nose. "I prefer blueberry anyway. Thanks, Brooke." He headed back to his station, shaking the bottle as he went.

Francine looked past Brooke. "Why, hello there."

"Hello."

Brooke knew that voice—in *all* of its nuances. A shiver ran through her as she spun around.

Elizabeth.

"Hi." Elizabeth looked at Francine, then Nik. "It's nice to see everyone." She turned to Brooke. "Would you possibly have a few minutes to talk?"

Minutes? She showed up unannounced after all this time and the way things ended and wanted a few *minutes*? Brooke's mind reeled. Should she be excited, curious, or mad as hell? "Sure. How about over there?" At Elizabeth's arched eyebrow, she led her to a couch in the lobby.

"Thanks for seeing me." Elizabeth ran her fingers through her hair.

She wore it slightly shorter than the last time Brooke had seen her. And she sported one of the shirts she'd bought with Brooke, the memory of the shopping trip one of many from that day Brooke tried to push aside. "Why are you here?" Might as well get down to business.

"Honestly, I came to ask if anyone knew how to find you. I got lucky. I guess you still work here."

Brooke blinked. "Of course, I do. You didn't know that?"

"No, and I have lots of questions, and I'm sure you do, too, but I don't want to have that conversation here." She gestured around them. "Would you be willing to meet me early tomorrow morning to go somewhere and talk?"

"What time?" It was her day off, after all.

Elizabeth winced a little. "Six?"

"Six?" Brooke didn't even try to mask her incredulity, but she softened it with a small eyeroll. "I suppose." She'd likely be awake all night now, anyway, wondering what Elizabeth had to say.

"Thank you."

Elizabeth's face was almost expressionless, but was that just the slightest lift of one corner of her mouth?

Elizabeth stood. "I won't keep you now, but I'll pick you up here tomorrow."

"Okay." What had Brooke agreed to?

"Bring a jacket. Oh, and your camera," Elizabeth called over her shoulder as she left.

Of course, she'd bring a jacket. She was the one who lived here and actually knew that October mornings tended to be chilly. But why her camera? She pushed herself off the sofa and wandered toward the front desk where dual sets of wide eyeballs bored into her as she neared.

"What was that about?" Francine asked in a whisper, as though Elizabeth were still lurking. Her eyebrows threatened to climb into her hairline.

Brooke shrugged. "I have no idea. I'll find out tomorrow."

"Have you two been talking?"

"No." Brooke recalled the last conversation they'd had with a lump in her throat. "Not since she left."

Francine patted her arm. "Well, you'll know soon enough what she wants. Don't fret."

Ha, good luck with that. Brooke had already been thrown far enough off-course to be paddling her canoe through Death Valley. How was she supposed to be mentally present for her afternoon meeting with Mr. Chronically Late after that? "I'll be in my office if you need me." She retreated to her private space where her thoughts could spin out of control with abandon.

Elizabeth had looked good, a bit too thin, but still elegant and gorgeous. Brooke hadn't laid eyes on her for months, and she'd drunk in the sight of her like a half-dead, dehydrated hyena stumbling upon a water hole.

Why was she here? What did she want? How long did she plan to be in town? Why hadn't she wanted to talk today? The questions kept coming, with only conjectures to follow. Brooke would just have to wait.

By five fifty-seven the next morning, Brooke had only added to her inquisitorial list, with a grand total of zero marks in the answer column. Only Kinsey, who worked the front desk, shared the quiet lobby with her. Brooke glanced down, making sure she hadn't worn a track in the carpet with her anxious pacing. Where was Elizabeth, and why had she made Brooke rise so early?

Brooke spun around at the glide of the sliding doors.

Elizabeth stood at the entrance, more casual than Brooke had ever seen, wearing a Pizza My Heart T-shirt beneath a faded denim jacket. "Ready?"

How had she missed her pulling up? "For what, I'm not sure, so maybe?"

"You'll be fine." Elizabeth motioned toward her car out front.

Brooke felt anything but. They walked outside, and she zipped her jacket to ward off the chill, then waved to Marco at the valet stand.

"Hop in." Elizabeth went to the driver's side and started the engine.

Inside, so close to Elizabeth, Brooke's traitorous body reacted in ways contradictory to her mind. She should still be angry at Elizabeth for leaving, for selling the resort, for taking off without so much as a good-bye to Rory. But sitting beside her brought back a cascade of other feelings and responses. She'd forgotten Elizabeth's sweet, spicy scent. It summoned a warmth within, one she tried to ignore but couldn't. Memories of her nose buried in Elizabeth's neck, inhaling deeply as they curled up together, came crashing in. Her hands on the steering wheel reminded Brooke of how her strong fingers filled her with so much pleasure and gave her such exquisite release.

But there was more to all of this than that. Beyond the physical, her chest ached with all she'd wanted to share with Elizabeth the past few months they'd been apart but hadn't been able to. Now she wasn't sure she should. She didn't know what she meant to Elizabeth at this point or what Elizabeth meant to her. And what was with all this cloak-and-dagger nonsense? "Where are we going?"

"We'll be there soon."

Great. A non-answer. "Are you going to talk to me at all?" The silence made her skin crawl.

"In a bit."

Brooke sighed and stared out the window. A telltale reddish hue at the horizon marked where the sun would climb over the Vaca Mountains. Wherever they were going, they headed south. They'd already passed St. Helena, and soon continued through Rutherford, Oakville, and Yountville. Just north of Napa, Elizabeth turned, heading east, then pulled into a field and parked beside a gray truck. An enormous yellow and royal blue hot air balloon stood before them, immense and imposing, and four men in hoodies chatted nearby.

"Is that for us?" Brooke opened her door, not sure what she thought of the idea. Going on one had always intrigued her, but now faced with the possibility, she wasn't so sure.

"Yes." Elizabeth walked toward it with Brooke in her wake.

"Wait. Aren't you scared of heights?"

"Yes."

This made no sense. "Stop."

Elizabeth did, turning.

"Don't do something you're afraid of to impress me or"—she flailed her hands—"whatever you're doing."

A sad smile appeared on Elizabeth's face, then vanished just as quickly. "That's the point. That's been my intention for over a month." She stepped closer. "I got my balloonist's pilot's license specifically so I could take you for a ride."

"You what?" Brooke frowned. Elizabeth might as well have said she'd learned to charm snakes or become an astronaut. "Wait, so you've been up numerous times?"

"Yes."

Brooke tried to wrap her mind around what was happening. "And *you're* going to fly it?"

"Pilot it. Yes." Elizabeth's eyes sparkled. "Just you and me."

"What?" Brooke cocked her head toward the men. "Not one of them, too?"

"No. Like I said, I'm certified. I have my license."

Brooke studied her. "Where did you do this?"

"Right here." Elizabeth swept her arm in a semicircle.

"You've been in Napa for weeks?" The idea of Elizabeth being physically so close yet so utterly absent made her head spin.

"Yes, Brooke. Though technically, I'm staying in St. Helena."

Hearing Elizabeth say her name almost broke her. She'd been hanging on by a thread as it was. "Why are you doing this?"

Elizabeth took her hands. "I told you. I wanted to take you up. You said you'd never been, and I wanted to be the person who gave you that experience. It was worth getting over—or at least facing—my fear." She looked down, breaking eye contact. "I also wanted to talk to you up there, and I want privacy, which meant *I* needed to learn how to pilot it."

She met her gaze again, and something softened inside Brooke. Elizabeth's warm hands cradled hers so softly, yet their strength provided a sense of safety. "Okay."

Elizabeth's features smoothed. "Good. Let's go then." She pulled Brooke forward. "Hang on." She scooped her up and lifted her into the basket, then climbed over the edge herself.

Brooke couldn't attribute whether her sudden dizziness came from being in Elizabeth's arms again or the impending ascent.

Elizabeth touched a few things, as though checking them. "Okay."

One of the guys handed her a walkie-talkie, and she tossed him her car keys.

"Hands off," she called, and detached the cable securing them to the chase vehicle.

The men moved away, and a whoosh filled Brooke's ears as Elizabeth turned up the burner. Brooke grasped the edge of the basket, expecting a jerk, but she almost didn't notice they'd left the ground. They floated upward smoothly, with none of the bumps or turbulence she'd expected. "Oh."

"It's magical, isn't it?" Elizabeth smiled, and it might've been the widest one Brooke had ever witnessed on her.

They left the group below behind them as they drifted. North of them, more multi-colored balloons floated toward the sky. "How do you steer?" Brooke investigated the great orb for the first time, and the crisscross of ropes inside surprised her.

"You don't, really. Up and down mostly. We're at the mercy of the wind."

Okay, so Brooke might've been better off not knowing that. Maybe she'd keep her future questions to a minimum. She twisted around, noticing the guys had driven both the truck and Elizabeth's car out to the road and begun to follow them. The vehicles now resembled children's toys. Brooke hadn't realized how high they'd climbed. Below, she admired the patchwork of vineyards in their vibrant crimson and yellows before she remembered the camera around her neck. She snapped a few shots as the sun peeked over the hills.

When she turned, Elizabeth watched not the scenery, but her. Her cheeks heated.

Elizabeth must've killed the burner because silence stretched between them.

"It's so quiet." Brooke whispered.

"Peaceful, isn't it? Don't let me keep you from your photos."

Brooke let the Canon hang by its strap. "That's not why I'm here. Are we going to talk?"

Elizabeth shifted, leaning on the edge.

Brooke's heart lurched. "Can you please not fall over?" She motioned for Elizabeth to come closer.

Elizabeth stepped toward her. "I heard you moved." Elizabeth reached up, and a whoosh followed. "I thought the new owners let you go. How are you still working at Harvest Springs?"

Why would Elizabeth think she'd been laid off? She might disagree with her aunt at times, but not enough to cause a family feud. "I moved because you were selling. I thought I needed to. And it turned out to be the right thing to do, even if it required a new school and temporarily upsetting Rory's stability. She showed resilience I hadn't given her credit for, and we're renting a small home with a nice yard."

Elizabeth nodded. "I'm happy for you. I know that was a big concern."

"Now it's my turn," Brooke said, biting back a retort about whether or not Elizabeth cared. "Did you really think I wouldn't stay on when you sold to my family?"

Elizabeth's brow furrowed. "What are you talking about? I sold to the highest offer, Christine Jackson Holdings, LLC."

"Yeah, my aunt and my dad. Christine Williams and Jackson Crawford. The family entity that owns properties is separate from J & C Hospitality Specialists. It's a tax thing." At Elizabeth's stupefied look, she asked, "You really had no idea?"

"No." Elizabeth shook her head. "I thought I caused you to lose your job. Two offers came in right away, and theirs was higher, so I jumped on it."

"My aunt must've assumed you knew who you were selling to. We never discussed it. I was also avoiding her for a bit." Brooke gave her a sheepish look.

"We never met. I wasn't involved." Elizabeth mimed writing in the air. "I signed the papers, and that's it. My real estate agent dealt with everything."

"She wanted me to take over for my dad, but I stood up for myself and told her no." Brooke squared her shoulders with pride.

"So, what's she going to do?"

Brooke smiled. "My brother Brian is back. He's working with her."

"You're kidding. I know how much you missed him."

Elizabeth's fond look disarmed Brooke in ways few things could. "I did. He's engaged, and his adorable fiancée set some ground rules early on. Both he and I needed to do a bit of growing up."

"I wouldn't say that."

Brooke thought for a moment. "It was time for him to stop avoiding our family and face that our dad isn't getting better. As for me, I didn't necessarily act immaturely, but I needed to be more independent, and I am now. Though I'm learning that asking for a bit of help now and then isn't the worst thing either." She tried for a self-deprecating grin.

"You?" Elizabeth smiled. "No."

"It's true." She breathed a little easier at the bit of banter, the tension between them dissipating some. "What about you?"

"What do you want to know?"

Brooke shrugged. "How are you? Did you take a leave from work again? How did you have time for this?" She motioned to the burner, then up to the balloon itself.

"So…"

The way Elizabeth drew out the word told Brooke the answers weren't simple and probably weren't what she was expecting.

"I'm renting an in-law cottage. It's charming and quiet. I'm enjoying the slower pace of life. I discovered I missed it when I returned to the South Bay."

Was that all she missed? A ripple of sadness moved through Brooke. "I can't believe you've been living so close all these weeks."

"Yes, but I've been busy. I had to accelerate my pilot program to finish before the season for flying closed." Elizabeth fidgeted with some sort of valve. "And I've put my home on the market. I don't intend to go back to San Jose."

Brooke struggled not to let her shock take over her features. "What about your job?"

Elizabeth shook her head. "I turned in my resignation. They posted the position, interviewed candidates, and hired my friend Geoff. He's truly the best person for the job."

"You've never referred to him like that before, always as a coworker."

"Yes, and I've been more cognizant of that. He means a lot to me, and I don't intend to take our friendship for granted anymore, even if we're no longer working together."

Was she saying what Brooke thought she was saying? "So, you're here?"

"Yes."

Those damned one-word answers. Brooke needed more. "Why *are* you here? Would you just say it?" She slammed her fist down on the edge of the basket, shifting the balance and making it sway.

Elizabeth reached out and pulled her toward the center. And closer to her. "Let me finish," she said softly. "Okay?"

"How long will this last?" Brooke pointed to the fuel tanks.

"We have time." Elizabeth let go of her. "Hold onto the side, please." When Brooke complied, she continued. "I made other major changes in the last few months, too. I sent in a DNA test kit and got a match."

Brooke gasped, then slapped her hand over her mouth. Elizabeth's grin told her there was more. "And?" She made a get-on-with-it motion.

"I reached out, and my sister Carly sent me a message."

"Elizabeth." Brooke swallowed the colossal lump in her throat. Had she been on terra firma, she would've jumped up and down. Instead, she took a careful step forward and gently clasped Elizabeth's hand in both of hers. "I'm so proud of you. I want to know everything."

Elizabeth laughed, her eyes shiny. "Both my sisters live within driving distance, so we met at Carly's place in Sausalito. She's great, very excited. She was four, almost five, when we were separated, so she remembers more than Anne." As Elizabeth had discovered she preferred to be called. Some of her jubilation faded. "Anne wasn't even three. Her reception has been cooler."

"I'm sorry."

"It's all right. Everything has turned out better than I'd ever expected." Elizabeth looked around, apparently assessing their position.

"Is there more?" Brooke wanted to hear it all.

"Um, okay. Carly said their parents—adoptive parents—were young at the time. Her father died of cancer a few years ago and hadn't allowed talk of the girls' former life. When he passed, their mother expressed regret that they hadn't adopted me, too. She said it's always haunted her." Elizabeth's eyes darkened. "I've met my sisters' husbands and kids, but I haven't met their mom yet." She rubbed the back of her neck. "I'm not ready. There are still… emotions…I'm working through."

"Of course. Many of them, I'm sure." Brooke brushed her thumb over Elizabeth's knuckles.

Elizabeth straightened. "I had an epiphany, if you could call it that. In Vegas, no less. I met a woman in a bar."

Brooke's vision wavered, and she released Elizabeth's hand. She didn't want to know what came next, even though Elizabeth had been free to meet and do whatever with whomever. It'd hurt too much.

"Hey, sit on the floor for a moment. You're really pale. Did you look straight down?" Elizabeth moved closer.

"No." Brooke shook her head, inhaling, then attempting to exhale the image of Elizabeth with another woman. In Vegas. "I'm fine."

"Okay." Elizabeth returned to the controls. "Anyway, we had seats beside one another and ended up talking. She turned out to be a child psychologist. I don't know why I told her my life story." Elizabeth shrugged. "Bourbon probably. She listened and explained some things to me I hadn't been aware of. I know you said I was young when everything happened, but it'd never felt that way to me. I was the oldest. Then I met Rory, and seeing her at the same age…I couldn't reconcile it. She's this fragile little bird. I'd never expect her to have to figure out a way to care for two younger siblings."

"No. She's a child, as were you." Brooke wanted to wrap seven-year-old and grown Elizabeth in her arms and hold them close.

"I walked away from that conversation and took some time to do some serious reflection. It allowed me to accept some grace for my childhood self. I understand now that I wasn't at fault, and it was never my job to fix the mess my parents' deaths left behind." She looked right at Brooke. "Having met Rory really helped with that."

Brooke couldn't stop the tears that gathered in her eyes, nor the ones that escaped that she wiped away. "It sounds like you're doing well. You've made great strides." The jealous pictures in her mind faded.

The wind whipped Elizabeth's hair, and she tucked it behind her ears. "Meeting my sisters again has helped me heal part of my past. I've come to believe that what happened was necessary for Annie and Carly to have a family and stay together. And ultimately, it gave me what I needed to succeed in life, not the least of which was meeting Margaret. Although I still have some work to do emotionally on the painful parts, in hindsight, what I went through was worth it. I'd do it again if I had to."

"Oh, Elizabeth." It was heartbreaking to hear, no matter how sincere.

Elizabeth held out her hand to Brooke. "Will you come here?"

Brooke joined her in the middle, their fingers touching.

Elizabeth intertwined them. "Throughout all of it, do you know the one thought I couldn't get out of my mind?"

Brooke couldn't look away from the intensity in Elizabeth's eyes. She shook her head as goose bumps ran down her extremities. The tightness in her throat didn't allow her to answer.

"I kept thinking, over and over, 'I wish Brooke were here to share this with me.'"

"You did?" It came out broken and high-pitched.

"Yes. I've missed you and Rory something terrible."

Brooke cupped Elizabeth's cheek. "We've missed you, too." She'd longed for her, thought of her every single day—probably every hour—even when she didn't want to, and more than she'd ever let on. Brooke let out a wry laugh. "Sparkles has to stay at my parents' house because he reminds Rory of you, and that makes her sad."

A tear slid down Elizabeth's cheek, and Brooke caught it with her thumb.

"I'm so sorry." Elizabeth slowly shook her head. "All my life, I've wanted to be part of something, and I pushed that very thing away. When I returned home and had to live without you, I realized I was miserable. It occurred to me that I hadn't protected myself by building walls. I'd built a cage."

"Elizabeth." Brooke caressed her face, tracing the line of her jaw. "Look at you. You've come so far. Because of your courage and strength, you found your family."

Elizabeth tilted her head, leaning into Brooke's touch. "They've invited me to come to dinner next month. Perhaps you'd like to accompany me?"

"Oh." Brooke hesitated. She lowered her hand to Elizabeth's shoulder. "Yeah, maybe."

"You don't have to decide now. I want them to meet you, but that's not why I'm here today." She pulled Brooke closer, only a few inches remaining between them.

Brooke wasn't sure if it was the heat above or Elizabeth's that made her suddenly so warm. Or if the butterflies dancing in her belly were due to the height or the expression on Elizabeth's face.

"I'm here because I'm in love with you." Elizabeth slid her hand to the back of Brooke's neck.

A tingling sensation skittered down Brooke's spine. She'd dreamed of this moment, but now that it was happening, it seemed so surreal. The way they floated along like a cloud and the silence as they drifted only added to the feeling. Had she heard correctly? She had to be sure. "You are?"

"I am." Elizabeth's gaze fell to Brooke's lips, then she met her eyes again. "I'm here to tell you I love you and ask for your forgiveness. I made a huge mistake. Not in selling the resort, but by leaving you."

Brooke began to cry outright, and she didn't bother to wipe away her tears. Was this really happening? "Of course, I forgive you. I knew why you did what you did, even if it hurt." She pressed her palm to Elizabeth's chest. "But I still can't believe you walked away from your career."

"You're worth more to me than my job. I'm fortunate to work in a profession that allows me to work anywhere, and I needed to live here in order to date you properly."

"You want to date me?" Brooke asked, and Elizabeth gave her a bright smile, one Brooke let herself think was reserved only for her.

"More than anything I've ever wanted before. I want to feel the warmth of standing in your sunbeam. I want to know what it feels like to be loved by you."

"You already do," Brooke said softly. "You've known for some time now."

Elizabeth's eyes widened, and her lips parted.

Brooke put a little distance between them but didn't let go. "But I have a rule against dating people who don't like or want kids. And I'm talking about *really* dating, not what we were doing before."

"I know. That's justified. I've spent a lifetime avoiding them because being around them reminded me too much of what I'd lost." Elizabeth held her gaze. "But it's not that I don't like or want them, especially Rory. I do, but the thought has always terrified me." She swallowed. "Lately, I've been working to get past my fears. Annie and Carly both have children, one almost Rory's age. The time I've spent with them has gone well. Really well." She blinked back tears. "You don't think it's too late for a woman my age, do you?"

"No. No, I don't." Brooke brushed Elizabeth's windblown hair back. "And I say that because I've seen the evidence. You're great with Rory."

Elizabeth shook her head. "I wasn't. And that day, when I thought I'd lost her, I couldn't bear it. I kept her at arm's length because I was afraid of bonding with her, what that would mean. I knew that when I eventually left..." A choked sound came out.

"It was too late. She already loved you," Brooke said, threading her arms around Elizabeth's neck. "As do I." She shook her head. "Damn you for making me fall in love with you. I wasn't sure I'd ever feel like this." She studied Elizabeth, then peered upward into the underside of the balloon. "How much fuel do we have left?"

Elizabeth glanced at her phone. "About ten more minutes, then I need to set us down."

"Would you mind if your chase crew witnessed a public display of affection between us?" Brooke couldn't tear her gaze from Elizabeth's lips. She recalled their softness and the ways Elizabeth had pleasured Brooke with her mouth. A warm ache bloomed low in her abdomen.

"No."

"Then, come here." Brooke drew her closer. "Leave it to you to sweep me off my feet in such a manner," she murmured, and kissed her in a way that promised to make up for months lost.

A low moan escaped Elizabeth, and she broke away with a laugh when Brooke's hand ended up on her breast. "Okay, we *don't* have time for that. Nor do I want my chase crew as an audience for it. Why don't I find us a good place to land."

Brooke reluctantly gave her a little room and watched as Elizabeth piloted the balloon like she did most things, competently and with a confidence that emanated from her core. It was quite alluring, and Brooke found herself more turned on by each passing minute. Her love for Elizabeth burned within her, simultaneously stirring her arousal and purging some of the pain of their past.

"I don't simply want to date you," Elizabeth said, glancing over her shoulder at her. "I want it all. The package deal. You and Rory. I want both of you in my life." She turned, reaching for Brooke's hand. "You need to realize you're worthy of love and deserve to be put first now and then, and I want to be the one to make it happen. You shouldn't have to carry the entire load yourself. If you want to do this, I want to do it with you. I'm not here simply to take you out to dinner or a movie, though I'll do that, too. I want us to be a team."

Brooke averted her gaze to the scenic vista growing closer. "You can't hurt my daughter again by running away. She might even still be mad at you. You're going to need to put in some work to repair your relationship with her."

"I understand."

"Do you know what she said when you went back to San Jose?" Brooke's heart almost broke at Elizabeth's stricken expression, but

Elizabeth needed to hear this. "She asked me, 'Doesn't she know you're not supposed to leave without saying anything because you worry people? Doesn't she remember how worried she was when I left to pick flowers?'"

"She's got a point." Elizabeth blushed. "I'm all in, Brooke. I promise. I'm not going anywhere. I'm sorry it took me so long to recognize what this is. I'm simply not familiar with the feeling."

Brooke kissed her palm and wrapped an arm around Elizabeth's waist. "What would you have done if I'd said no? You'd sold your house and quit your job."

With a small chuckle, Elizabeth looked at her. "I had to operate on the hope you'd say yes. I think...I felt in here"—she laid her hand over her heart—"that you would."

Brooke tipped her head slightly and smiled. "Why, Ms. Bettancourt, is that optimism I spy?"

"Don't get used to it," Elizabeth murmured, the hard edges of her consonants melting away like ice cubes in a drink. She kissed Brooke once more, this time to the whoops and hollers of her crew waiting below.

Elizabeth pulled away and exhaled. "Let's do this. It should only be a slight bump. Hang on." She reached for a red cord, and a sharp tug opened the top of the balloon, and they began to descend.

They touched down lightly, and the men immediately took over dismantling the setup.

"How was it?" The burliest of the three held out Elizabeth's keys.

Elizabeth looked at Brooke and smiled. "Perfect." She took her hand. "Thanks, guys."

As they walked to Elizabeth's car, Brooke couldn't stop staring at her. "I can't believe you're here."

"I am." Elizabeth smiled.

"What now?"

"Well, I've heard breakfast is the thing to do after these rides. After that, perhaps you'd like to see my new place." Elizabeth paused, a blush creeping up her neck. "Or maybe I could see yours."

Brooke laughed. "Yes. Oh, yes to all that, but I was talking about the future."

"Hmm." Elizabeth pretended to think. "I don't know about you, but I plan to date this smoking hot woman and try to win her daughter over. Beyond that, I hear there's a new transportation investment opportunity featuring pedicabs and horse-drawn carriages, and I've promised to invest in it."

"Really?"

"Yes." They got in the car. "And I happen to have a chunk of change I've been thinking about using to purchase an establishment here in the valley." Elizabeth turned to her. "And if I did, I'd need a professional manager to help run it. Maybe you know someone."

"Is that so?" Brooke asked, intrigued.

Elizabeth shot her a smile and started the engine. "But that's down the road. Right now, dating you and getting back in Rory's good graces are my priorities."

Brooke tried to envision it all but couldn't, and it surprised her that didn't bother her. Nothing ever went quite to plan, but she had faith that together they'd figure it out. "You're going to have your hands full."

Elizabeth winked. "I can't wait."

And Brooke couldn't either. But the only decision that was a must today was in which of their new beds would they be spending the weekend.

EPILOGUE

R ory," Elizabeth called up the stairs. "It's time to go." She put the last present into the bag and turned to Brooke. "You're sure she's not too young to get her ears pierced?" she whispered.

Brooke put her arms around Elizabeth's waist and smiled. "No. How old were you?"

"Eighteen."

Brooke's eyes widened. "Oh. I guess that makes sense, considering your childhood."

Elizabeth had woken early this morning. She was always eager on days she saw her sisters. But now, with Brooke in her arms, a serenity overcame her. She cupped Brooke's face as they stood in the house they'd bought a year and a half ago. "I probably don't say it often enough, but I love our life." She glanced around. "You, Rory, our home, Treehouse 2.0 you built like a pro. All of it."

Brooke smiled, that wholesome lovely smile that had once annoyed Elizabeth. It'd been so long since she'd found Brooke's cheerfulness and optimism stifling that she recalled those times with difficulty.

"I do, too, my love." Brooke raised up to kiss her. "Even though my mom said she'd arrive early and greet everyone, let's get Rory in the car and to the lake before we're the last ones there."

"She's the birthday girl. The party can't start without her." Still, Elizabeth released her. "Rory! Let's go."

Thinking about the last time Rory had taken so long to find something allowed Elizabeth to bask in the pleasant memory. It'd been almost two years ago. With the school bus due in a few minutes, Elizabeth had found her crying, half under the bottom mattress of her bunk bed in Brooke's old house. Rory wouldn't tell her what she'd hidden and lost, and Brooke finally came upstairs and calmed them both by retrieving something that'd become caught in the bottom sheet. With tears still in her eyes, Rory had pressed a small box into Elizabeth's hands. Inside was a key to their house, and accompanying it, a handwritten invitation—and drawing—from Rory to move in with them.

Elizabeth had turned to Brooke, asking, "Are you sure?"

Brooke had laughed, that pure, genuine, glorious one, dimples and all, that made something bubble up in Elizabeth's chest. "Yes. It's been fourteen months, darling. You've proven yourself."

The framed note and crayon rendition of the three of them in a hot air balloon hung in Elizabeth's office.

By the end of the month, they lived together. Then she and Brooke bought this house, twice the size and three times the yard, and right beside the eighteen-room bed and breakfast they'd opened together—along the Cab or Neigh route, of course, which had turned out to be a good investment.

Brooke pulled her back to the moment and handed her a necklace, the gold and diamond one Elizabeth had given her for their second anniversary. When Elizabeth held it open, Brooke turned, holding her hair aloft. Elizabeth had received a hand-carved olive wood chess set from Brooke that day she still insisted was too beautiful to use.

"Did Tiffany say whether she'd make it on time?" Elizabeth clasped the piece of jewelry and dropped a kiss atop it.

"Yes, she's already on her way." Brooke let her hair fall, turned, and caressed Elizabeth's cheek. "And remember, if taking people up in the balloon is too stressful, you don't have to do it. Just have fun today."

Elizabeth smiled. "I want to. I promised Rory." And if she'd learned anything about raising a child on the spectrum—not that it shouldn't apply to all children—those pledges needed to be upheld.

"Okay. Oh, one thing before we go," Brooke said, looking pointedly at her. "When I was reviewing the expenditures for last month, I noticed a wage increase for Flor."

Their longest tenured employee had been with them from the start. If Elizabeth could clone Flor, she would. "Oh, that." Where was Rory? Elizabeth might need some help getting out of this one.

"Yes, that." Brooke leaned back, eyebrows raised.

Elizabeth shifted from foot to foot. "That was me."

"I would hope so. You and I are the only ones with access to the system." With a squeeze of Elizabeth's waist, Brooke lowered her voice. "My question, is why?"

Thanks for nothing, Rory. Elizabeth was going to have to get out of this on her own. "She asked if she could pick up extra hours because her twins need braces. Since we haven't given her a raise in over a year, I decided to go ahead and do it now. I'll enter her review in the system on Monday."

"I would hope so. You know the manager gets cranky when you don't." Brooke smiled. "Orthodontia, huh?"

Elizabeth might as well come clean. "I want to be more like Margaret," she said quietly. "She took pity on me, and I want to pay it forward."

Brooke shook her head. "I don't think Margaret's generosity stemmed from pity. I never once picked up on that when she mentioned you. Like I said before, she appeared impressed by your eagerness and ability to learn all the resort's roles, by your fortitude and intelligence. She spoke of you with nothing but pride. Clearly, she saw something special in you. You impressed her enough— while still quite young—for her to want to nurture your growth and care about your future." Brooke smiled. "And I won't go as far to say she was clairvoyant, but she was certainly right. Look at you now."

Elizabeth had never been a fan of self-reflection. Yet, seeing herself through Brooke's eyes made something swell within her. Brooke observing the same things that Margaret had noticed in her, her good qualities, meant everything. "Thank you. So, you're not angry?"

"Not in the least," Brooke said, kissing her quickly. "I think it's sweet. But let's talk about it next time, okay? I don't want you to feel you have to hide your good deeds."

Elizabeth nodded. Being in a partnership, both in work and life, was something she was learning on the fly. But she didn't mind the steep learning curve, not when she got to hold Brooke in her arms every night.

They jumped apart at a raucous noise. Neither of them had grown used to the commotion a ten-year-old made hurtling down a set of stairs. Rory bounded into the room. "I found them!" She handed Elizabeth two purple barrettes shaped like fairy wings and turned around.

On autopilot, Elizabeth scraped her nails up Rory's scalp, eliciting a small shiver from her. She secured the loose strands on each side of Rory's braid that Elizabeth had finished almost an hour ago. With a kiss to the top of her head, she gave Rory a light push toward the garage. "Into the car, birthday girl."

When they reached Lake Berryessa, Elizabeth killed the engine and stepped outside. The August temperature already climbed into the nineties, and the blast of heat after the cool of the car's interior came as a shock. She and Brooke unloaded the bags they'd brought, and by the time they had, Elizabeth needed to wipe her brow. It'd be the perfect day to spend at a lake, though.

In the shade, Brooke's dad lounged in a lawn chair at the end of a picnic table, with her mom nearby securing lavender streamers from the edges of the pavilion. Brooke's dad lived in an assisted living facility now, and Brooke's mom visited every day. Brian knelt by his father, talking and jiggling the stroller holding his sleeping newborn son. His wife Sara helped with the decorations. Near Jack, Kali and Sean sat together, their nine-month-old son asleep against Sean's chest.

Someone shouted Elizabeth's name, and she turned to find Carly waving from the edge of the grassy field, a few of her kids throwing a Frisbee with some of Annie's. Elizabeth raised her hand in greeting.

Rory touched Elizabeth's arm. "Can I go play with my cousins?"

When she'd started using the term, it'd set off a small explosion in the center of Elizabeth's chest that sometimes still occurred when caught off-guard. "Sure."

"Thanks." Like a shot, Rory took off. "Love you," she called.

"I love you, too." Elizabeth carried her load toward a table where Francine and Tiffany arranged gifts into an attractive pile. "Hello. I'm glad you could get out of work early, Tiff."

"Wouldn't miss it for the world," Tiffany said, grinning. "Your friend Geoff is checking out my horses over there. I gave him a couple of apples. They're probably his besties by now."

Elizabeth warmed knowing Geoff had made the effort and drive to be there and glanced over to where Tiffany had parked the trailer. Both animals chewed, and she laughed as she watched Geoff take a big bite of apple, too.

She turned and set down the first of her packages with a smile. "Hi, Francine. Here's a few more." Rory would have her work cut out for her today opening all of them.

"Thank you, dear." Francine continued to adjust the mountain of boxes and bags.

"I like your dress."

At the sound of Annie's voice, Elizabeth turned. "Thank you." She'd opted for a simple blue sundress but brought a shirt and shorts for ballooning. They rarely had a conversation when Carly wasn't there acting as facilitator. Elizabeth stiffened, not sure of her ability to interact with Annie on her own. "I like yours, too." The splashes of orange and teal contrasted with Anne's rather introverted demeanor.

Annie smoothed the fabric. "I wasn't sure what to wear. Carly suggested this. She said it brings out my eyes."

Elizabeth studied her. "It does. They remind me of Dad's—our biological dad," she corrected her, waving a finger between them.

"You can just say *our dad*. I'm not as fragile as you and Carly think." She gave her a little smile. "Even if I can't remember them, they were still our parents."

Something passed over her expression, fleeting, but Elizabeth couldn't decipher it.

"You know, I've always been glad you came into our lives. I just need more time to adjust to things than Carly does." Annie ran her fingers over the plastic tablecloth.

Elizabeth nodded, noticing Carly approach. "I imagine it isn't easy, but I'm so happy I've had a chance to get to know you."

"Hi." Carly wrapped Elizabeth in a hug and kissed her cheek. "I tried to greet the birthday girl, but she had other plans." She motioned to where the kids played.

"She was excited to see them. It's all she's talked about all week." Elizabeth continued to unload the gifts she'd brought, including ones Chef Sophie and Nik had sent along. They couldn't attend because they had to be at the resort, which seemed to be running well under J & C Hospitality Specialists, even without Brooke there. Brian's decision to hire Dashiell as general manager had been a wise one.

Elizabeth lifted the heaviest item from the bag and placed her present for Rory on the table carefully. She hoped Rory would like the small stone chess set she'd bought for her. She'd asked Barros Family Jewelers to inlay an amethyst in the crowns of both queens, the gem Rory's favorite, even if it wasn't her birthstone. Elizabeth posed the last item in the bag in front, a stuffed bear wearing a violet T-shirt that said Grrl PowR. She looked at Francine. "How's that?"

"Lovely, dear."

"You had a bear." It came out softly and slowly.

Elizabeth turned to find Annie staring at the animal, her eyes glassy.

"What?" Carly's gaze darted between them.

"Elizabeth had one. About that size. It played..." Annie hummed a tune.

Elizabeth's jaw dropped, and Carly looked stunned, too. "Brahm's Lullaby." She couldn't move, frozen in place by Annie's words. "Koala. It was a koala."

Annie turned, awe in her expression, but Elizabeth had a sense she also found the unbidden memory overwhelming. Elizabeth certainly did. After swallowing the growing lump in her throat,

Elizabeth said, "Grandma Bettancourt brought it back from Australia."

"I remember it." Annie said, her eyes filling with tears. "I used to fall asleep to the song."

Elizabeth took the smallest step closer. "Mom and Dad used to let us nap together in my room."

"All of us in Lizzie's bed, as long as we were quiet," Carly added.

Annie turned to the stuffed animal again, softly stroking its fur. "It's like..." She laughed. "That tiny memory I didn't even know existed in my brain makes me feel a part of this more." She motioned between Elizabeth and Carly. Then she covered her mouth as a soft sob escaped.

"Would you like a hug?" Elizabeth whispered, and Annie moved into her arms. Around them both, Carly wrapped hers, and Elizabeth's chest ached with the immense love she'd developed for her sisters. Her sisters. *Hers.* Here with her. And not the bittersweet love tinged with pain she'd harbored for them as children, but a new, developing love she had for these two wonderful adult women. She never imagined she'd see them again, not until Brooke had urged her to do the DNA test.

As they pulled apart, Elizabeth looked around, and there Brooke stood by one of the pavilion's posts, fingers pressed to her lips, eyes teary.

A cry erupted from the playing field, the kind that suggested an injury. Elizabeth glanced over, finding Rory off to the side picking stems of delicate violet verbena, and she smiled. Typical Rory. As Carly and Anne rushed to discover who was bleeding or broken, Elizabeth wandered toward Brooke.

Brooke looped her arms over Elizabeth's shoulders. "So... Annie." She gave Elizabeth one of her brightest smiles.

"Yeah." Elizabeth couldn't hold back her own.

"I'm glad," Brooke whispered.

Elizabeth kissed her, not caring that Brooke's parents were a dozen feet away, Geoff was ambling over from the horses, or that her sisters would return at any moment. These people were her family, and Elizabeth could express her love for Brooke in front of everyone here with confidence, knowing they offered nothing but acceptance.

"What was that for?" Brooke asked breathlessly as she tucked Elizabeth's hair behind her ear.

"For making me fall hopelessly in love with you. I can't imagine my life any other way."

"Well, in that case." Brooke leaned close, touching Elizabeth's nose with hers. "Checkmate."

"What?" Elizabeth shook her head, not following.

"Checkmate," Brooke repeated, pressing her lips to Elizabeth's, then winking. "I told you I played the long game, Ms. Bettancourt."

Elizabeth chuckled. She couldn't argue with that, so she kissed Brooke again, then took her hand. They had a birthday to celebrate.

About the Author

Alaina Erdell lives in Ohio with her partner and their crazy but adorable cats. Prior to writing, she worked as a chef. She enjoys painting, experimenting with molecular gastronomy, reading, traveling, and spending time with her beloved nephews.

Erdell's *All Things Beautiful* was a 2024 Foreword INDIES Finalist in Romance. A full list of her books' awards can be found at alainerdell.com

Books Available from Bold Strokes Books

Brooke Takes Queen by Alaina Erdell. Brooke Staley faces personal and professional upheaval when Elizabeth Bettancourt, the emotionally scarred new owner of the resort she works for, considers selling. (978-1-63679-886-8)

Coda by Anna Gram. Parker is intriguing, magnetic, impossible to ignore—and completely wrong for Hannah. But sometimes love's melody refuses to end. (978-1-63679-926-1)

Secrets Under the Junipers by Suzie Clarke. Who killed Hallie Lynn Peeples? Cecilia McConnel needs to know. Bitsy Hanover holds the key. Can love uncover secrets? (978-1-63679-845-5)

The Debutante Dilemma by Jane Walsh. Two debutantes are engaged to wealthy and titled brothers…but discover they only have eyes for each other. (978-1-63679-896-7)

The Love Book by Gun Brooke. When literary agent Rowan Cross receives an anonymous manuscript that deeply resonates with her, Verity realizes she has accidentally sent her own manuscript, complete with her very real feelings for her boss! (978-1-63679-850-9)

Traveling Toward Forever by Erin Dutton. When almost-strangers take a road trip through America's national parks, love may be the final destination. (978-1-63679-894-3)

Beautiful Things by Emma L. McGeown. A warmhearted romance of missed chances, undeniable chemistry, and a stubborn love that maybe, just maybe, can find its way back. (978-1-63679-934-6)

Love Takes a Village by Karis Walsh. As Lena Preiss struggles to manage a busy restaurant in the Bavarian Christmas village of Leavenworth, Washington, chocolatier Devin Meyer brings an unexpected richness into her life, along with her delicious desserts. (978-1-63679-902-5)

Secrets of the Heart by Jenny Frame. When a beautiful stranger starts asking questions about Nikki Sharkey, head of an infamous crime syndicate, Nikki will stop at nothing to protect her daughter Isla. (978-1-63679-653-6)

Talon and the Songbird by Julia Underwood. In a world where survival depends on strategic alliances, Makayla and Talon must navigate not only complex politics but also the dangerous territory of their hearts. (978-1-63679-970-4)

The Great Popcorn Romance by Georgia Beers. Opposites attract, and Riley Shaw stands no chance of resisting Hannah Kramer's magnetic pull. But opposites know just how to drive each other crazy… (978-1-63679-910-0)

Three Blissful Days by Dena Blake. Kendall Jackson attempts to make her ex regret dumping her by announcing she's dating beautiful park ranger Ivy Patterson. But there's nothing fake about how attracted Ivy is to Kendall. (978-1-63679-707-6)

Chasing Her Scent by MJ Williamz. When Sheridan Rousseau walks into Lisette Mouton's charming little bookstore in Quebec City, she unknowingly holds the key to a mysterious box hidden in a secret room. (978-1-63679-900-1)

Heart's Run by D. Jackson Leigh. Hoping to recover an escaped racing mare, stock transporter Tobie Mason locks horns with local wild horse advocate Maggie Wilkes. (978-1-63679-825-7)

Scandalous by Kris Bryant. When a Hollywood actress trades places with her twin sister, everyone's in an uproar about getting duped, but Lindsay's more concerned about finding out which twin she made out with. (978-1-63679-874-5)

The Art of Love by Ali Vali. When Mimi and Bianca both set their sights on Jolly, sparks fly, loyalties are tested, and hearts collide as they navigate the unpredictable nature of their hearts (978-1-63679-719-9)

The Other Side of Forever by Kel McCord. Will Kenzie and Rachel be able to make love work when Rachel's cozy suburban dream feels like Kenzie's worst nightmare? (978-1-63679-812-7)

The Secrets of Rhydian Hill by Ronica Black. A doctor in need of a new start. A woman running from a killer. A love story that could end in tragedy. (978-1-63679-880-6)

Feeling Lucky by Krystina Rivers. What happens when, despite suddenly having enough money to buy almost anything, Lucy and Tanner start to discover that maybe all they need is each other? (978-1-63679-876-9)

Iceberg by Gun Brooke. When Lady Arabella hires Zandra, she never expects to find love, especially not as a disaster looms on the horizon. (978-1-63679-908-7)

It Happened One Semester by Aurora Rey. After a Pride night hookup, can eager new Assistant Professor Hudson Greene and Dean of Advising Callie Shaw overcome the odds and ace falling in love? (978-1-63679-814-1)

It's Kind of a Bad Idea by Sarah G. Levine. What happens when an emotionally unavailable serial dater meets the one woman she can't help but fall for—who happens to be the one woman who told her not to? (978-1-63679-920-9)

Thankful for You by Tagan Shepard. Everyone deserves to find their person, maybe Karen has finally found hers? (978-1-63679-884-4)

What Happens on Location by Nan Campbell. How can Helen produce a successful movie when its director is the woman responsible for the demise of her marriage? (978-1-63679-904-9)

When Love Comes Around by Radclyffe and Ronica Black. Can Maya Sanchez and Nolan Wright trust each other enough to build something real, or will the past tear them apart? (978-1-63679-930-8)